YESTERDAY'S PORRIDGE

GORDON FINN

Matador
9 Priory Business Park,
Wistow Road,
Kibworth Beauchamp
Leicester LE8 0RX, UK
Tel: (+44) 116 279 2299
Fax: (+44) 116 279 2277
Email: books@troubador.co.uk
Web: www.troubador.co.uk/matador

ISBN 978 1848767 829

British Library Cataloguing in Publication Data.
A catalogue record for this book is available from the British Library.

Typeset in 10pt Galliard BT by Troubador Publishing Ltd, Leicester, UK

Matador is an imprint of Troubador Publishing Ltd

MIX
Paper from
responsible sources
FSC
www.fsc.org
FSC® C013056

Printed and bound in the UK by TJ International, Padstow, Cornwall

To my long suffering wife, Tessa, who has spent many long hours waiting for me to emerge from my office.

ACKNOWLEDGEMENT

To Fred Waite of Ireleth Cumbria, another evacuee who empathizes with me on the experience and has drawn up the basic design of the cover.

FOREWORD

The word 'porridge' has connotations which associate it with a term of imprisonment which is how I perceived my formative years. The mere thought of yesterday's uneaten porridge conjures up a picture of something cold wet and slimy with a possible dried crust on top. I've chosen the title 'Yesterday's Porridge' both as a descriptive term applicable to my imprisonment and to the actual cereal. The dictionary states it is a dish made from oatmeal or other cereal cooked in water or milk to a thick consistency. There can be but a handful of people for whom the victual conjures up such images and memories as it does for me. Amongst those I would include a long forgotten colleague in the navy whilst on a deep sea voyage to the Far East. He was always keen to extol the virtues of the meal and had been eating it for breakfast for some eight weeks or more when he happened to be collecting rubbish from the galley one day and came across the empty porridge sack. To his horror the bottom was full of live weevils looking very energetic. He was promptly sick.

Whenever I hear the word mentioned my ears prick up. I listened to a light hearted radio programme recently in which the comedian Marcus Brigstock was interviewing the foreign correspondent Kate Adie. Under the title of 'Ten things I've never done' Marcus posed the question to Kate and I was surprised to hear that one of her ten was that she had never eaten porridge. She went on to mention her nausea with other foodstuffs such as tapioca and sago. With these two, especially tapioca, which I associate with frog spawn, I found I could relate to Kate, but with porridge we were poles apart. Porridge, which appeared on the breakfast table every day for almost four years, was a staple part of my evacuee diet. But the way in which our foster parent cooked it meant that it resembled something akin to wallpaper paste than a cereal.

'Yesterday's Porridge' is a novel based on my experiences as an evacuee during WW2 but seen through the eyes of Francis Tenby who makes a discovery some thirty five years later which alters the course of his life.

CHAPTER 1

'Sit there you old fool. I knew you'd suffer after working all hours like you do, it's time you realised you're not twenty five any more.'

It was during a visit to the supermarket with my wife that I had one of those dizzy turns most elderly folk have from time to time. She half supported my left arm, pulled on my right to spin me around then nudged me into the first available chair at the entrance to the cafeteria. A busy waitress carrying a tray of food destined for some nearby table quickly discarded it to lend a hand.

'Is he alright? He looks very pale. Can I get him something?'

'Yes dear, you're very helpful. I think a cup of black coffee should do the trick.'

'Whoa! There missy, what about my all-day-breakfast?' a voice rang out from the table expecting the now discarded tray as the waitress headed off toward the coffee machine. 'I know I ordered an all-day-breakfast but I don't expect to wait all day for it,' he shouted after her.

'Steady on there mate,' another voice chipped in. 'Can't you see that old chap's not very well? The girl will serve you soon enough.'

The angry man looked his watch, grumbled something inaudible then snatched the tray himself, spilling the iced drink over his meal in the process. He was already half way through by the time the waitress turned her attention back to him. She fixed him with a stare before walking away rolling her eyes to the ceiling. To her satisfaction she heard him choke when he was about to make some remark or other, but on noting that the other man was still looking in his direction, decided to say nothing.

My wife raised her hand in appreciation to the second voice before returning her attention back to me.

'Now stay there and don't move. I won't be long. I can get around much quicker on my own.'

It was a Friday, the busiest day of the week. I was a reluctant customer, dragged away from my garage and sanctuary, the place where

1

I could shut the world out. It was full of all manner of machines, tools, breeze blocks, timber and paraphernalia, where I could escape into my world of DIY. There was always something to make, something to mend, something to do. Getting up in the morning, even when retired, was never a problem. In contrast, this other busy world of the supermarket was one which held no attraction for me at all. Retail therapy has never been top of my agenda. I have the over-riding notion that the shopkeeper is like a spider in its web waiting to pounce the moment I pass through the doors. The ordeal would all begin at the door even before visiting the cash machine which, if you were lucky enough to tap in the correct card details, didn't gobble it up never to be seen again. Then there was another hurdle; finding a trolley. Not a single one to be seen. On this particular day, we managed to procure one from a tired elderly gentleman on his way out glad to be rid of the thing.

As she disappears amongst the traffic of trolleys and baskets, some empty, some loaded with everything from flowers to large bags of toilet rolls and others with young reluctant children in tow, I marvel at the sheer volume of goods which appear so necessary to live in these modern times. Every commodity anyone could ever wish for, aisle upon aisle of it, stacked to heights which make it impossible for the short of leg to reach. I spare a thought for people in wheelchairs. Sales promotional notices, some gaudily highlighted by flashing strobe lighting endeavour to coax customers into buying far more than they ever intended instead of sticking to their shopping lists. Notices advertising 'Three for the price of two' and 'Price reduced' because of 'sale by date' compete silently with girls noisily enticing people to taste new lines of cheese, wine, savouries and all manner of other foodstuffs. And then there are the confusing notices, usually too low down to read and in such small print the elderly have no chance of reading anyway. Buy in bulk, it's cheaper a voice tells me, but is it? It's like as if there's no tomorrow with a sort of 'hell for leather' pressure salesmanship to sell, sell, sell. It never used to be like this.

I let my mind wander back to pre-war days when people didn't seem to eat so much and where gardens came into their own with fresh grown produce. The family weekly budget for nine of us got by mainly on my father's donation of a mere four pounds ten shillings, but as kids somehow we never went hungry. Looking back I come to the conclusion that my mother was a master tactician and financial wizard with far more skills to produce meals from very little compared to some of today's wives who rely on tins of this and that, packaged meals, processed or otherwise and fish and chips. The result of it all can be seen in the large wheelie bins overflowing with packaging and waste. My thoughts are interrupted by a voice from behind me.

'She's right you know, take five. Have a drink.'

As I spin around in my chair, I find the smiling face of someone who looks familiar but I'm not quite sure where I've seen him before. Then I realise he is the friendly stacker and bag filler, now without his green and yellow fluorescent striped jacket and white Hessian trilby. He is in his seventies with greying sideburns and not much on top, the man who is always ready with a kind word, particularly for elderly ladies. They are often unable to fill their bags quickly enough before the check out girl says, 'Thirty three pounds seventeen, please.' As they fumble with slippery cheque cards that refuse to budge from their plastic pouches and then have to think hard to remember their pin numbers, he appears like magic. 'It's OK love, plenty of time –.' I feel that he is more than adequately qualified for his job. He has a 'till-side' manner which could easily compete with the best bedside manner of any nurse. His voice is calming, assuring and firm.

With my own condition in mind, he looks annoyingly healthy with a ruddy glow and I wonder why he's sitting at the next table 'taking five' as he put it. He looks at peace with the world and then I notice the lottery ticket he has just bought from the machine at the bottom of the stairs.

'I've just finished my shift; I've been on since eight.'

'I wish you luck with that,' I said pointing to the ticket, but I feel it's a tall order.'

'Yes you're right,' he replied somewhat defensively. 'I just have a go now and then and you never know, perhaps this week 'Mystic Meg' will cast her spell in my direction. I don't choose the numbers myself. When I'm nearly at the end of my Saturday shift I ask the last seven people to give me a number and I rigidly stick to those numbers however ridiculous they may be. To be honest, I don't need the money and I certainly wouldn't know what to do with millions and millions of the stuff anyway. I regard buying a ticket as a sort of challenge and I fantasise with the idea of sitting on some street corner just doling out the odd twenty pound note like some rich philanthropist to anyone who looked down at heel. But you know what they say, 'You have to be in it to win it'.

Like opening the flood gates he went on to say he had an obsession for numbers ever since his early school days when he found that he was good at arithmetic. Furthermore, he constantly had dreams and fantasies of winning and even convinced himself that with a permutation programme he had concocted, he was sure to win one day. He said he often used the numbers as an aid for getting to sleep, a sort of exercise like counting sheep to wear himself out. After a while he found he could work out quite complicated permutations in his head and provide answers to how many winning lines there would be for any given set of numbers being successfully chosen. Factorial numbers and cubic tables flooded his mind like a virus as easily as any nine year old reciting his ten times table.

'Now I'm more realistic, you just have to be lucky, very lucky indeed. I know people who have spent thousands over the years with very poor returns and I try to tell them you should be prepared to lose only the money you can afford. The chances of winning are very remote; it's like scoring a bulls-eye on a dart board when blindfolded.'

He suddenly changed track and brought his attention back to me, sliding his chair closer as he did so.

'You seem to be having as much luck today as I've had with the lottery. So what's happened?'

'I don't know really, I suddenly had a dizzy turn, but what upset me more was the fact that two elderly ladies, who I'm sure could give me twenty years, tried to help. My wife thought I had met an amorous lady friend from the past when she reappeared from behind the cereal stand to find the woman with her arms around me.'

'I couldn't help overhearing, but it sounds as if you've been burning the candle at both ends.'

'Yes but I like to be active and hate to waste daylight. I certainly don't like wasting time either and I have a habit of setting myself too great a target to achieve before the end of the day. Jobs seem to expand to exceed the time available. I know at my age I should be slowing down. Funnily enough this reminds me of a chat I had only yesterday with my elderly lady neighbour who apart from solving all the world's problems in five minutes, talked about the very subject of age. Her pet hobby horse was one of criticising the social lives of young people and how her father would never have sanctioned it, but eventually we floated on to discussing ages. Age seemed to be of primary importance in her life, not only her own but also of everyone else in the street.'

'Just look at the Morleys,' she said to stress the point. 'Some people are born old. Iris is only sixty four with no children but she looks worn out already.'

I wondered if she had looked into a mirror lately and then finally on weeding out my age, she rendered me speechless with her parting words.

'Let's face it you don't have many more years left.'

'Well I have no intention of popping off just yet,' I retorted, 'but I rather like to think along the lines of not having as many years left as I've had already. That's why I try to make use of every hour that God sends and I'm amazed how some folk can waste time in bed not bothering to get up until late in the day. I suppose they lack incentive, but with me it's just the opposite. The trouble is I am a workaholic and find it hard to strike the happy medium between work and leisure.'

'So, how did you come to get this job here then? I asked. 'You seem to have found the answer. It's something I'd like to do, being paid to chat up all the rich old ladies and stack a few shelves.'

He smiled broadly and coughed a few times.

'It's not always like that you know, some old biddies can be quite cantankerous especially when I pack something in the wrong bag and you'd be surprised how many miles I walk a day servicing the shelves. After the first few days of working here my arms were killing me from lifting heavy boxes from stacks in the stores onto trolleys and then man handling them again onto the shelves. One good thing about the job is that it keeps me fit so I've no need to visit the local gymnasium. I start two hours before the store opens and you only see me when I'm doing the nice bit at the tills.'

'Well, if it's any consolation, my wife and I think you do a grand job. We see you as an ambassador for the Company, a friendly service. Sometimes when the checkout girl has probably just returned from her tea break, batteries all recharged, goods seem to fly through the till and soon we're snowed under. That's when it's good to see you about.'

'It's nice to be appreciated, but I don't see this as a real job. I've always had front line contact with the public and I think it would be difficult for me to be a sedentary office worker or on a production line. I would miss having someone to talk to and apart from that, everyday is different. Take yesterday for instance. You can see how busy the store gets and we packers have to be ultra careful how we load the shelves and where we erect the pyramids. Two children aged about eight and ten were racing around the store playing tag, unattended by an adult. They were causing havoc bumping into people and treating the whole place like a playground. I could see them coming and purposely barred their way with my truck.'

'Move!' the boy shouted. You're in my way.'

'I beg your pardon,' I said, daring him to repeat the demand, by which time the girl caught up too.

'This is not a playground, where are your parents?'

'Haven't got any,' the girl replied.

'Then I'm afraid I'll have to escort the pair of you off the premises.'

'No you won't,' the boy blurted out. 'You can't touch us and my dad will come and sort you out first.'

A crowd began to collect, until a voice caused a gap to appear as a burly farming type in overalls and Wellingtons came forward.

'What's up Jake, has he touched you?'

'Yeah, he has, he knocked me with his truck and clipped me round the ear.'

'Did he indeed?'

He stepped two paces forward, shaking his fist menacingly.

'Who the hell do you think you are? I'll show you whose boss around here. Grab him Jake. Come 'ere—.'

Fortunately, by this time I had moved out of range behind the truck. Customers tried to tell him that his son was lying. In desperation the man pushed his loaded trolley against the truck with such force that it glanced off narrowly missing the girl and crashed into a carousel of cheeses and a pyramid of baked beans spilling the whole lot along the passage way. Security guards viewing the whole incident on closed circuit television were quick to act. They detained the man and called the police.

'The kids know you can't touch them,' I confirmed. 'They play on that. We don't need any more of the softly, softly touch.'

'I couldn't agree more, parental control from an early age is so important.' He went on, 'I could tell those kids a thing or two about how things used to be which might make them think twice about how lucky they are.'

'What did you used to do then?'

'I used to be branch manager of an estate agency and when I retired at sixty five I decided to do something different. Instead of getting a job and then somewhere to live I reversed the idea and found a county I liked first and then the job. One or two other things happened which gave me the impetus to change and now I'm happy with my lot. All good things come to an end sometime and I don't regret any of it.'

He sat staring out the window for sometime, strumming his fingers on the window sill. I finished off my now cold coffee and waited for him to continue. I felt I could hear his brain ticking over.

'They say that 'the first twenty years of your life is the longest half' and 'life begins at forty' but I think I've had three or four. My third one began in my forties and now I can please myself. This job pays for my two holidays a year, I like walking on the fells and I do a little bit of painting.'

'Yes I do too and I'm not very good at it but it's a peaceful way of enjoying the countryside.'

'Only a few days ago I was thinking how my life has changed over the years. I went on a hike with the intention of losing some of this rubber tyre,' he said patting his stomach, 'and took my painting gear with me just in case I found a suitable spot. I wanted to be fairly high up so that I could look down over the lake. Eventually I found a view through some trees I liked and set up my easel and paint stand. After an hour or of peace and quiet with only the birds as company I was quite pleased with my painting and sat back to enjoy a cup of coffee. Being up high seems to present a bird's eye view of life in general and makes all past memories of being sent away from home at a young age, becoming an orphan and a thousand other painful thoughts more bearable. Then just as I began to feel positive about it all, my thoughts were suddenly shattered by a low flying jet which appeared over my head from behind the hill and thundered down the lake below me and was gone in a flash. I jumped, spilling the paint pots over my painting and ended up on my back in a ditch. I wondered if the pilot heard my futile abuse and blasphemy which I shouted at his fast disappearing tail as it excreted a trail of exhaust fumes.'

I can sense his annoyance at his leisure time being so violently disturbed by the screaming jet. 'I bet the pilots don't even give it a thought,' I suggested.

'Well, I was not a happy bunny as you can imagine. I saw too much of the planes during the War not to like them much,' he went on. 'In those days the noise the planes made were more insidious and threatening. Unlike today, you could hear and see them coming. First of all there was the sound of the air raid siren which was followed by a deadly silence. Then the drone of engines getting closer and closer until the sky was full of them. You see, I was a foster child for four years sent away from the blitz of Plymouth in 1941 to a farm in Cornwall. In a way I've a lot to thank Hitler for because I met my wife as a result, but that was a long time ago.'

'That's a coincidence,' I said, 'I was an evacuee too, but for only three months and I cried all the time so my parents took me back home. I was sent from Newcastle to some place in Wales with an unpronounceable name and they spoke a different language. The billeting officer foisted me on to a young couple who already had two children of their own and didn't really want me. My parents could see that I didn't fit in. Firstly, although the whole family could speak English, they chose to speak in Welsh especially in my company and secondly, it was a culture shock. Their traditions, customs and way of life were so foreign compared to my former city one.'

'I still think you were lucky then,' he said, 'at least you had parents. Mine were killed in the air raids so I had no home and was completely alone.'

With that thought he turned to gaze out the window once again and fell silent. After a few minutes he carried on as if he hadn't stopped.

'My first foster parents were an elderly couple who lived in an old ramshackle farmhouse with no mains services. It was the smell of the place that I remember most which came from the oil lamps and the privy outside the back door. The couple were not very good with young children which increasingly caused me to spend as much time away from their company as possible. As a result, I created a few problems for myself.'

He paused for effect.

'What hectic times they were! I was lucky not to kill myself more than once and perhaps, on reflection, I might have been better off taking my chances with my school pals back home with the air raids. I was accident prone at that age. To begin with, I broke two ribs falling off a cart horse and about a week later fell off one of those high country hedges into a ditch full of stinking sludge. It was the effluent run off from the midden and when I went back to the farmhouse the farmer's wife wouldn't let me in and then her sadistic husband saw the opportunity to amuse his family. He made me stand in the yard to 'grow a bit' before he hosed me down with cold water and I made up my mind to get even with him one day. Unfortunately I never got the chance and even to this day I've prayed that he got his comeuppance with some unpleasant end. After that he had to hose me down again when I fell into a bog only on that occasion the hosing down was a small penance compared to what might have been. I used to take one of the farmer's Labrador dogs with me on my walks and it saved my life by raising the alarm when I fell in. I remember losing both shoes and socks on that occasion. Then I managed to push my lower teeth through my upper lip by jumping off a haystack and eventually broke my arm falling out of a tree. I was surprised at the consternation of my foster parents who felt responsible for my accident whilst in their care and eventually a lady from the WVS arrived in her old ford car to take me to the local clinic. There I was patched up with a splint and sling as a temporary measure so that she could take me to the hospital where my arm was reset in plaster. That was the end of my stay with the couple and I didn't go back. They decided that they couldn't cope with a hyperactive eight year old and I was moved on to another billet for a month or so during which time the WVS lady ferried me to and from the hospital every two weeks until the plaster could be removed. I remember her old car had no trafficators and she used to get me to use my good arm to indicate left turns. Following motorists must have been amazed at the length of the diver's arms since I'm sure that I wouldn't have been seen from behind the back of the front seat.'

My wife returned at that point complete with loaded trolley and was surprised to see me sitting with the gentleman laughing at the chapter of accidents he had just described.

'Oh hello,' she said. 'Thanks for putting that rude chap in his place earlier.'

'It's OK. Think nothing of it,' he replied. 'You'd be surprised how many people there are like that, they have no patience.'

'It looks as if I've got to thank you again for cheering my husband up and by the look of him there's no need to ask how he's feeling now, the colour has come back into his face.'

'He's as good as new now I've been amusing him with some stories.'

My new found friend snapped out of his thoughts and stood up as if to go, but then hesitated as he waited to speak.

'I was thinking of having our meal out tonight,' she said. 'Shall we stay and have a bite? I see they've got a special offer of lamb shank with mint sauce.'

'OK, why not? Let's save on the cooking and washing up just for a change.'

'That's a good idea,' he said. 'Would you mind if I joined you?'

'It would be our pleasure.'

Curious to hear more of his exploits I instinctively replied without giving my wife the chance to answer but there was no need.

'Well, OK then as you seem to be getting on so well,' she replied.

'This is my wife, Molly and I'm Matt,' I said. 'Let's sit over there by the window, I like to watch the people walking by.'

'My name's Francis,' he said as he took over Molly's trolley and manoeuvred toward the window as naturally as if he was still on duty.

As we sat down he took us both by surprise.

'Since I feel I've muscled in on your meal, would you allow me to do the honours? I fancy a bottle of Cabernet Sauvignon would go down well and I can buy it cheaper than you.'

We both felt we couldn't accept, but before we had a chance to say anything he anticipated our refusal.

'It's OK,' he said. 'I can afford it and it would my pleasure. Don't move I'll be back in a jiffy.'

As he went out of the cafeteria with a spring in his step that belied his years, I briefly told Molly what I had learned about our chance benefactor.

'He must be about your age, I wonder where he went,' she queried. 'He seems to have cottoned on to you right away with you both being evacuated.'

Francis came back, full of smiles, sporting the one litre bottle of red wine and I got the distinct feeling that we were not about to be leaving for some time.

The waitress came to take our order, 'Three lamb shanks please.' She could only have been about sixteen but I've never been very good at guessing ages. It was a simple order which presented her with no problem but we noticed another waitress of a similar age struggling with a husband and wife with two children who were not sure what they wanted. They were chopping and changing the menu to suit their individual likes and dislikes which left me thinking that they would have been better off at a buffet. In such a situation I thought my patience would have been short lived and I thought back to a time when as a kid of a similar age I ate what I was given and didn't quibble. Francis noticed it too and I felt sure he felt the same way. He suggested we open the bottle and 'have a glass to go on with' while we waited for our order to arrive.

'Ah! That hit the spot,' he said and gave me the impression that he was more used to wine than we were.

'If you like,' he said, putting his glass up to the light to view the clarity, 'I'll tell you the story of my foster days, the ups and downs and how it affected my whole life. Perhaps we can compare notes?'

'I might have a problem with that,' I added. 'Mine was what you might call a short holiday but I know from mates of mine how their lives away from home varied from being good and bad to downright horrible. Some lived the life of Riley with landed gentry on country estates and even became beneficiaries in their wills whilst others were badly treated and sometimes abused. For some girls it was a difficult time especially as prospective foster parents were not vetted.'

'Exactly,' Francis said. 'Not everybody agreed with the Whitehall decision to send the kids away, in fact for a city like mine the full scale commitment was delayed until after the blitz. With a little more thought, it ought to have been obvious that a dockyard city would have been a prime target but someone in their misguided wisdom thought to apply their priority elsewhere. It was not until our first house was blown away and the next one took a severe hammering that my dad decided on my evacuation. Sounds crazy now but the raids became less and less after I left.'

'Here are our meals. That was quick,' said Molly who until then had remained silent, occasionally nodding in agreement with our stories, some of which I'm sure she had heard before.

'Go on Matt, top up the glasses, we can always get another.'

Francis was quickly getting into party mode, using first names and looking more and more settled as our meal progressed. I looked across to Molly and sensed she was thinking, 'Why don't we do this more often?'

Francis began his story, although having to eat at the same time was an obvious problem. He was keen to get it off his chest and told us that it was something which had remained hidden in the recesses of his mind for many years. The busy life of estate agent and the subsequent happenings in his life had left him with neither the opportunity nor the will. With our chance meeting, the time was right and I knew that any future meetings with our stacker packer would never be the same.

He continued, 'Where does a story begin? I was listening to a radio debate the other day and that was the question which was posed. The resulting discussion focused on the chain of events which led up to a road traffic accident. It seems that it all began with something as simple and mundane as a glass of beer being tipped over in a pub. At least that was what the presenter of the programme was suggesting. It was further suggested that from that moment on, the die was cast setting everything in motion on some pre-ordained route which would inevitably result in the accident. Apparently, a girl had accidentally tipped over the drinks at a table where a young man was sitting. Profuse apologies followed where firstly the man apologised for his chair being in the way and she in turn admitted not looking where she was going. It was love at first sight. From that moment on, there was an immediate chemistry which needed no catalyst. She, sitting at the corner of a nearby table displaying that extra inch of a shapely leg and he discretely viewing her slender profile over the top of his beer glass, all but completed the equation. The final ingredient was supplied by her girlfriend who noticed and nudged her shoulder. Smiles beamed and before long phone numbers were exchanged.'

At that point Francis took a long look out the window and seemed to be looking at the clouds.

'Do you think it's going to rain Francis?' Molly asked.

'No I don't think so,' he said. 'When you see cows resting in the centre of a field as they are today, the weather is going to be fine. On the other hand if you can see the horizon is sharp and clear you can be sure rain is near.'

'Do you believe in those portents then Francis?'

'Yes it's something I learnt from my school days prior to choosing a career. I fancied being a meteorologist and liked drawing the forecast maps and now I rarely listen but just look out the window instead. Wouldn't it be great if life were so ordained, that the Almighty had mapped out our lives not quite like a short term weather forecast but from beginning to end in some Big Book? I could imagine the clatter of many feet rushing to take a peek at that Book. But I'm sure there would have to be a condition for viewing which might stem the rush, such as it being decreed that no changes could be made and that what you saw was what you got.'

'Like you looking out the window you mean?'

'Well it's a thought I suppose, but all rather too philosophical for me,' I said. 'I'm happy not to know and I can't say that I'm all that religious anyway.'

With our meals finished and the plates cleared away, Francis tried to pour the rest of the bottle into our glasses but stopped when Molly put her hand across the top of hers. I could see her complexion had taken on a pinkish glow and she had decided that no more bottles would be opened on our part.

'Do you know,' Francis said. 'For me to tell you my story I find myself having to take deep breaths, much like I remember many years ago when entering an examination room. Sometimes it was such a relief to find that the questions staring out at me from the paper were the very ones which I had swotted up the night before. With my head bursting with facts, figures and formulae it was then only a question of how quickly the required information could be transferred to the paper. It was like having a virus in my head, bursting to get out and spreading itself over the pages before the bell rang.'

Molly laughed, 'I think the wine may have something to do with the deep breathing now,' she said, 'I feel quite warm.'

'Well, perhaps,' he said. 'After the broken arm incident, I was re-billeted with a family which had quite different ideas of what fostering was all about. To draw a parallel with the radio programme posing the question of where a story begins, I suppose you could say it all began with the family grandma born as far back as 1860, that the proverbial die was cast for my eventual foster home. Looking to support herself she moved to England from Ireland when her family fell on hard times and eventually solved all her problems in one astute move by marrying an English publican. She had four children three of whom died at an early age but in 1890 she gave birth to her daughter Lou, destined to be my foster mother. We always knew her as Auntie and it was odd that for ages we never knew her name or indeed anything about her at all. There never was any mention of a husband and later in 1920 Auntie had a daughter Cicely, who became our second auntie. Her second name was Florence so we were told to call her Auntie Floe. Like mother, like daughter, in 1940 when the public house business began to fail, Floe left to set up her own home having married Richard who was in the RAF and finally in 1942 Floe's daughter, Connie arrived to complete the family. Lou relinquished the franchise on the public house soon after and rejoined Floe to set up their brand of foster care. When the local authority advertised the need for foster carers they recognised the opportunity of a good business. At an average of ten shillings per child they accepted twenty one evacuees which together with Floe's job as an usherette in the local cinema and Richard's pay as an RAF sergeant, they were well off. I joined the household in 1941 and remained there for the duration of the war which lasted until 1945. Then aged eleven I was sent to an orphanage.'

* * *

CHAPTER 2

The last time I saw Connie she was just a toddler. She was crying. She was playing with the larder door in that dismal kitchen I remember so well. It was more of a wide corridor than a kitchen. All the paintwork was brown and the wallpaper dated back probably to Grandma's younger years. Even the ceiling was brown especially above the coal fire range where daily deposits from the fire had left its mark. The smell of kitchen pervaded throughout the whole house and is one of my most vivid memories. The range was used for all the cooking and the fire was always lit. There was a deep earthenware trough at the far end beneath the window with hot and cold brass taps, but you would never have known it from their colour. Beneath the window opposite the range was a large plank top wooden table enclosed on three sides by wooden bench seats. At one time the table sported a linoleum cover but the passage of time had taken its toll with knife cuts and pieces missing. There were no curtains other than the muslin net ones on wires which covered the lower half of the two windows. The only other vestige of decoration took the form of a four bar clothes dryer slung above the range loaded with clothing which partially covered the blackened pots and pans hanging on nails at each side. I refer to the clothing as 'decoration' which is exactly what they were in that they varied from Connie's tiny vests and pants, Floe's frilly bits and pieces to Auntie's voluminous bloomers and brassieres.

Connie had chosen to play, as most children seem to do, in the main thoroughfare obstructing the entrance to the kitchen. I moved her to a place of relative safety twice but inevitably, bit by bit, she managed to shift back. The danger as I saw it lay in the fact that with Auntie's sheer bulk, seeing objects on the floor beneath her waist line within six feet was something of a problem. As an only child, she had been spoilt with plenty of toys but that day she chose to bounce the door too and fro against a pair of Wellingtons parked behind it. She was squealing and giggling with delight as the wet boots squeaked against each other to propel the door closed again. She knew nothing about the laws of physics or for that matter, Newton's Third Law. She was only three. The game came to an abrupt end when the door rebounded onto those tiny fingers, making me feel guilty for not having realised that particular danger.

Her tears were very real as they dripped onto her bare legs to mix with the blood slowly oozing from her fingers. We all have reasons to cry; even grown men have been known to do so. I for one at the ripe old age of eleven knew all about that having spent many weeks doing just the same, but on reflection not entirely without good reason. But unlike Connie, in my case the room was often full of people, my tears were wasted, no-one took any notice and I was alone. But that was four years ago. By then, time had edged its way wearily forward, I had learned to fit in and felt there were few tears left to shed.

She was born March 20th 1942, during the darkest years of the War and into an unusual family. It had to be. There were twenty three of us in total and all crammed into a small terraced house, nineteen of whom were boys with ages ranging from seven to fifteen. Originally there were two girls aged twelve and fourteen but they were soon transferred to more appropriate accommodation; a decision received with howls of derision by the bigger boys. All of them except one slept in the two attic rooms mostly on camp beds, twelve in one and six in the other. The oldest boy who had a job at the local paper shop slept in the box room whilst our foster parents occupied the more conventional rooms on the first floor. Grandma being less agile had her furnished bed-sit on the ground floor at the front of the house, a room that I only visited twice during the whole of my four years.

At the time of the larder door incident, I was avidly reading a medical book, one loaned to me by the Superintendent of the St John's Ambulance Brigade where I had been a club member for two years. I had an affinity for the subject right from the start and enjoyed the practical sessions when we learned how to apply bandages and splints. The superintendent was not best pleased when we trussed up one boy from head to foot with a splint as an additional spine and left him to howl his head off in the toilets. I was not old enough for any form of promotion but in scouting terms I became a 'sixer' and a leading hand in my age group. The other lads nicknamed me the 'bookworm' although they used to spend just as much time with their heads buried in books, but their books were less salubrious in that they were sexy American magazines salvaged from the Yank's trash bins.

Despite my attention being elsewhere I was supposed to have been keeping an eye on Connie, making sure she kept away from the hot range and out of the larder.

'You stupid boy,' Auntie said, cuffing me around the ears to press home the point. 'Grandma kiss them better, there, there, darling. Did the nasty door trap your little piggies then?'

'I was looking after her,' I whined. 'I moved her twice to play with her toys but she moved back.'

I wished I could have said, 'ask her if you like' but knew that to be futile, a waste of breath and could expect no support. Auntie pushed me through the back door. 'Now go and do something useful, fetch that buggy from the gate and when you've dried it, fold it up and put it in the hallway.'

Walking slowly down the path and hoping to prolong my task as long as possible I entertained the vain hope that Auntie would be so busy consoling Connie that she would forget all about me. I stopped to watch a snail cross the broken path in front of me and began to reflect on our first meeting. She was a short fat lady and I remember seeing her waddle to the front door of the house as I was handed over by the billeting officer like the delivery of the day's newspapers or any other inanimate object. I hesitated at the gate but before I had any chance of making a bolt for it she seemed to read my thoughts and wrapped her flabby arms around me. On reflection I'm sure it was an over-the-top show of affection to impress the billeting officer who could then report another successful fostering. Being greeted by her was akin to that of an amoeba absorbing its prey. She opened the door and ushered me in. Thankfully there was no welcome party to scrutinise my arrival. My new billet lady was in her early fifties, a little over five feet tall with a round plump face and beady dark eyes which were close together under a high forehead. Her tightly raked back hair was tied into a short ponytail with a red ribbon and she had the appearance of someone who had just emerged from a swimming pool. She wore silver rimmed spectacles on the top of her head and was dressed in a black 'V' necked dress with a woollen shawl over her shoulders. Her more than ample bosoms were barely covered, they appeared 'low slung' and were only exceeded in girth by her waist which gave her a triangular appearance. Her legs were bare; she wore flat black canvas slippers and her general solid image was that of someone who could hold her own in a force nine gale.

I had particular cause to remember those glasses. She only used them for general purposes but had the habit of pushing them up over her head whenever she wanted to read small print. This she did during our many medical examinations, which sometimes she carried out more intimately than I thought necessary and much to our embarrassment. The practice seemed contrary to the obvious and I felt that her vision was greatly magnified without the spectacles which rendered the inspection that much more intimate. To this very day I have a 'thing' about people who wear spectacles in such a manner although now it's probably all a matter of looking "cool".'

By the time I reached the gate it was raining stair rods, I had no shoes and the chances of my making any better job of drying the buggy than I had in looking after Connie were pretty slim. Not wanting to risk another clout, I folded the buggy and withdrew into the privy. I sat on the throne with rag in hand pretending to perform my task, but quietly contemplated how soon it would be before I could leave the house all together, perhaps like Steven. He was the lad in the box room who had big ideas of saving enough money from his job in the paper shop to be able to live in a bed-sit of his own. The privy was not the most comfortable or sweet smelling of places to be and it was difficult to avoid the drips from the high level cistern. By pulling the string it was possible to empty the tank and stem the flow until it filled up again. In those days my DIY abilities were zero and I never thought of checking the ball cock or the overflow pipe. The view through the tiny window was little better than the one inside especially since our drab excuse of a back garden was just a mud patch with a broken concrete path leading to a broken back gate which leaned at a crazy angle. For the bigger boys this place was held in high esteem. It was somewhere where they could wedge the door shut and fantasise with their American magazines. Sometimes the high level cistern was useful for hiding things they didn't want Auntie to find. Nothing, not even the leaking cistern, the cob webs or the excrement fingered on the walls were a sufficient deterrent for their visits. It was the only private sanctuary which existed in the whole house and the one place which our aunties avoided as was evident from the fact that it could have benefited from a good soaking with disinfectant.

Connie's cries had stopped now, and Auntie was calling me in from the back door. She was no pushover, notwithstanding her sheer bulk and with her vast foster parent knowledge, seemed able to know what we were thinking. My time for completion of my task had long since run out when I heard her shout ring out from the back door so loudly that everybody in the back lane must have heard it.

'Come on Francis, stop hiding in the loo.'

I brought the buggy in, still dripping.

'It got wet bringing it in,' I said. 'I dried it once, honest.'

I could see she didn't believe me, but managed to scuttle down the hallway ducking as I did so to avoid that second swipe. This time the intended blow was more of an act of desperation than another cuff, she could see the elements were against her.

That day at five o'clock, like most days over the last four years, the ritual of preparing tea commenced. The menu never varied and our two aunties worked like clockwork, cutting a mountain of bread and spreading the margarine. Auntie did the slicing whilst sitting in front of the open range fire door, in a very unladylike fashion, warming her fanny with legs wide apart. It always amazed me how she never managed to cut off any of her ample body appendages as she pressed the loaf against her chest with her right hand and scythed away with the other. The slices were not always equal and sometimes died away to gossamer proportions at one edge, in fact I often felt she did it on purpose to generate interest at our mad hatter meal table.

Auntie Floe did the spreading from a dish warmed by the fire such that much of it was already liquid making it easy to spread. In this form there was the possibility of the margarine soaking through thereby covering both sides and I often thought it might have been quicker and easier to simply dip the bread, but Auntie used to say, 'Put plenty on and scrape it off again'. She did this very dexterously, making one dip of the fish knife cover four or five slices and any that was accidentally spilled onto her thumb was wiped on the next piece. That was followed by the annoying habit of licking her thumb and wiping it on her none too clean piny. It was a mass production, factory style operation and they worked like an efficient team being able to prepare some forty or so pieces in no time at all.

I remember overhearing their conversation one evening as I sat unnoticed on the stairs toward the end of our stay.

'What will we do when they've all gone home? In a way, I'm going to miss the little blighters,' Floe reminisced. 'Do you know Ma, it's nearly four and a half years since the first two came. Do you remember those two Dagenham girls?'

'Oh, yes, Lucy Meacock and Nicola something or other. Now what was her name, do you remember? Her parents were Welsh... Griffiths. That was it.'

Floe continued, 'I'm sure we did the right thing sending those two back. We shouldn't have allowed the billeting officer to pressurise us into taking them in the first place. The older one Lucy was a bit flighty and you would never have suspected she was only fifteen. I wonder what happened to them, I'd love to know but I wouldn't mind betting that she got herself pregnant before she was much older. Can you imagine the havoc they might have caused amongst this lot? What a girl, can you believe it? It seems just like yesterday. They came with the Robinson boys, Lance and Herbert. How time flies. When they've all gone, I think we'll do the house up a bit and do a bit of B & B. That'll be a piece of cake to what we have been doing, eh Ma?'

'I should say so,' said Auntie, 'although I think I might start putting on more weight not having to chase those brats up and down the stairs every five minutes. But we can't grumble, we've survived the war and we haven't done so badly. At least we've eaten OK and got a bob or two saved. It's a shame your grandma didn't last out a bit longer, I still miss her you know. Her bit in the bank will come in handy. She really wanted to be one hundred you know, still, it was a happy release that she didn't suffer or hang on too long. She's got a lovely view at St Michaels; she always said she fancied that spot by the yew tree at the top end.'

The business of preparing for tea went on. The bread and margarine was piled onto three plates, followed by three dishes of strawberry jam and another three plates of saffron cake cut in the same manner by the rubber tyre like figure at the fire. A collection of side plates and mugs, none of which matched were spread around the table. On the stove there was large double handled pot in which tea had been brewing for the last hour or so with result that the beverage had a familiar tangy taste we learned to expect. It was that or nothing. Often, a few new spoonfuls of tea leaves were added to the old ones which our aunties seemed to reluctant to throw out. That was one of those silly details that stick in the mind. It was something about tea leaves either being good or bad for the kitchen sink, but it was invariably blocked anyway. Only when I visited other houses, which was not very often, did I realised how different a mug of tea could be.

'We're a bit behind today, Floe, its twenty past five, you'd better get ready.'

Auntie Floe was the projectionist's assistant at the Pavilion cinema, a job which she enjoyed, not only because she saw all the films for free but also had a thing going with Alfie. With him she had one major understanding, no hanky panky during the first showing of any particular film. It was a request with which Alfie was all too pleased to comply. For him, it was a definite green light. Like Floe, Alfie had another job; he was an electrician and got on well with a number of other women in town. She never knew the full story of his playboy existence but for her it was a happy arrangement during difficult times, which were also influenced by the presence of the Yanks in town.

It was 1944, the war was still dragging on, but there was a sign of progress in that no longer was it being carried out above our heads, but now in far off Europe and the Americans had left to take part in the invasion of France. One day they were all there, the next, all gone, as if whisked away by some magic spell. Jeeps, chewing gum, cookies, all gone. They had been with us, virtually on our doorstep, having commandeered the local hotels for the last eighteen months or so. No-one could not have been aware of their presence or influence on the town, from their gum chewing drawling accent to their great sense of fun and gregarious living. This alone was far greater than that of our own forces and their leaving was something of an anticlimax both to the local girls and others who had joined them from outlying districts. Floe had not missed out either. As a part-time usherette and a good looking twenty two year old one at that, with legs to match, she soon attracted the attention of one particular ardent Yank. The friendship was not accepted too well by Alfie but he had no cause for complaint since he was already on thin ice with a few suspicious husbands in town.

During the war many a husband and wife were parted and there was a degree of 'when the cat was away, the mice will play.' Floe, her husband Richard and Alfie were no exceptions to the rule. Whilst Richard was at the local airbase, life for the two newlyweds was fine, at least during the weekends when he took every opportunity to come home. With a house full of evacuees, their privacy was limited, something the older boys were well aware of. In 1943 he was posted to another airbase, a move which was greeted with some delight by Alfie, but he still had to take turns with Wilbur.

Wilbur Dwight Capolla was a chef with an engineer combat battalion of the United States Army which took part in the liberation of Europe. He also liberated Floe and was a good friend of the evacuees, but to Alfie, he was a formidable adversary, too rich, too good looking, drove a jeep and could get nylons which the girls craved.

'There's only fifteen to tea tonight Ma,' said Floe. 'The Rowe brothers have been invited with Frank and Daniel to a tea party and cinema show by the Yanks at Mount Wise.'

Floe was aware of being discrete in referring obliquely to the Yanks knowing full well that her Wilbur was the chief instigator and organiser of the exercise. She had let it be known during one their pillow talk sessions that some evacuees had never been to a cinema in their lives. He was only too pleased to show his gratitude to Floe for services rendered and was able at the same time to earn brownie points with his superiors.

So it was that from time to time by way of special treat that the local platoon first lieutenant would invite a number of evacuees out for a cinema matinée followed by tea at their hotel. Foster parents were also invited, usually the younger curvy ones, as chaperones, the whole event being treated as an exercise in public relations. The kids were feted and treated as probably some of them had never experienced in their lives before even to the luxury of being picked up and brought back it what known as the American sports car, the Jeep.

'It does the Yanks good as well,' Floe said. 'It reminds of them of their own kids back in the States and they love to hear the patriotic and anti Hitler songs, especially those sung by the cockney kids.'

"Hitler has only got one ball,
Goring has two but very small,
Himmler is somewhat similar,
But poor Gobbels has no balls at all"

'Call the kids down from the attic on your way out Floe and pop the ration books in the butcher's letter box. See you in the morning. Bye, bye.'

Floe worked three evenings a week for main feature films and two afternoon matinées for cartoons. For these shows the cinema manager acted as projectionist while Floe took over the roll of usherette. Auntie knew that for the evening shows she could expect not to see her daughter again until breakfast time. She did not like late nights and usually by ten o' clock in the evening she was ready for her bed, tired out from carrying her heavy bulk on repeated journeys up and down two flights of stairs.

At meal times we were always hungry and didn't need a second reminder to be called for tea, but breakfast was a different matter altogether. I sometimes thought our neighbours set their clocks by our routines especially at breakfast time when the whole gang of us clattered down two flights of uncarpeted stairs. It was certainly no normal household and far too small for its residents but there was one redeeming factor in that it was situated in a seaside resort in Cornwall. Built in early 1900, the rooms were typically small and there seemed to be too many doors and dark corridors. My first meal time memory of it, early in 1941, was as a frightened seven year old being ushered through the ground floor passage into the kitchen to see eighteen silent white faces staring at me from a long wooden table. It was something of an Alice in Wonderland experience where my limited height was dwarfed by two things, the apparent height of the ceiling and the sheer bulk of my foster parent. Little did I ever imagine, a few weeks earlier, that I was destined to become one those white faced urchins seated around that table.

Everything was new to me. Being an only child the culture shock of having to share with so many others was devastating. On entering the kitchen for tea, we all had to show we had washed our hands. Rejections were sent back upstairs again which with regard to food on the table meant that our choice could be somewhat limited. Initially, all eyes were on me and I could see them summing me up, most having already decided in their own minds what sort of kid I was. I could almost sense them deciding if I would ever be a threat to any of them in any way. Auntie had kept them waiting for the arrival of their new inmate and now they were anxious to get started but her eagle eye was watching to make sure all hands were out of sight.

I sat at the end of the table with two other boys who were about my size; there was obviously a pecking order since the bigger boys were at the other end. Someone was given the job of roll call, a sort of introduction for my benefit, Eric, Roger, Mike, Frank, Lance, John, the list seemed endless and all a waste of time. The names kept coming but they went in one ear and out the other. I looked at each one as the name was announced and tried to match stare for stare but it only made me feel giddy. My face felt hot, my eyes filled with tears, panic set in and I wished the floor would swallow me up. The close scrutiny was unbearable, there was no escape and even the bench that I sat on seemed all the more solid and immovable.

The tea time ritual was a highly organised affair, things happened without any apparent signal. Suddenly all heads were bowed.

'For what we are about to receive,
May the Lord make us truly thankful?
Amen.'

As soon as Auntie had left the room there was a flurry of hands reaching out for the plates of bread and margarine, two pieces each. The big boys took the largest pieces, these being the thicker crusts and the smaller ones remained for those at my end. Frank and one of the Rowe brothers disagreed about their pieces and a squabble broke out with the result all four pieces fell to the floor. They then lost interest in who got what and delved into the remainder of the pile. The dishes of jam followed the same route down the table, after which the boys flopped a dollop of jam on each piece of bread and pressed the two together to make a sandwich. There were no knives on the table, which was probably a good precaution in view of the earlier event. I had never witnessed anything of this nature at a table before, having been brought up by a father who required far superior table manners. This was indeed some sort of mad hatter's tea party only in this case I was sure no-one would be falling asleep. Finally the rejected pieces of bread together with what was left of the jam arrived at my position by which time those at the other end had eaten theirs and were now viewing mine.

Had I been a fly on the wall or at any other time, I might have been amused with the spectacle, but being close to tears left no room for thoughts about anyone else except myself. There was a lesson to be learned but I was too wrapped up in my own situation feeling totally isolated to think about it. A wave of my hand was all that needed for the remaining pieces of bread complete with jam to disappear.

The mini doorsteps of saffron cake were next, as with the bread and jam, the same democratic distribution was adhered to. Again, the cake disappeared without trace. I could see that at least I was going to be very popular at meal times when two helpings of whatever were going to be available. I can't help comparing those meal times to normal family life with young children and an ever hungry cocker spaniel which acted as a vacuum cleaner when scraps of food fell from the table into its waiting jaws.

Mealtimes were a sort of challenge where the older boys established their superiority by making the younger ones aware which piece of bread or cake they deemed to be theirs and turning the plates so that a particular piece was opposite their place at the table. Prior discussions would take place to decide whether a particular piece at the bottom was bigger than say the third one from the top. Tea time might have been quite civilised if sliced bread had been available not to mention the time saved by Auntie in her tortuous cutting procedures.

CHAPTER 3

Floe liked her way of life, the freedom, the entertainment in all its forms including the relationships she had with the men in her life. She skipped about the house performing her household duties in an almost light hearted fashion when her bubble was at its height. She had every reason to be so with youth and good looks on her side and men virtually fawning at her feet. Life for Floe was at its peak. What is it comedians say about early married life? 'It's all down hill from here!' We kids benefited from her heyday when at times she would display something bordering on TLC by adding the odd extra titbit to the tea table without Auntie knowing. When the bubble burst, the 'downhill bit' began in earnest and the older boys noticed it first. Her demeanour changed which was soon followed by her choice of clothing and physical shape as the signs of an imminent birth became more and more obvious. Auntie always went to bed early as soon as we boys were safely cooped up in the attic. The norm for Floe to come home late changed too. Often she would arrive back before Auntie had gone to sleep, something which she soon picked up on even before Floe had made any announcement.

When Connie was born, she was like breath of fresh air, a distraction from the regimentation of being fostered. Even the youngest of us were potential baby sitters and vied to take her out in the pram sometimes for longer periods than intended. It was a reciprocal thing. As a resident of the same household I was never aware of her being there such as might have been the case in a normal house where perhaps twenty four hour attention wasn't readily available. My recollection of her, apart from when she trapped her fingers, was that of a happy child and I never heard her scream or cry for attention. But there was one occasion when our new found interest almost came to an abrupt end. A few of us were playing football at the 'Rec' while Connie was asleep in her pram which we parked at the top end of the slopping field away from our noise. Suddenly, to our horror, one of the boys noticed Connie wasn't there any more. Then another boy saw just the tips of two wheels which were still spinning, sticking out above the tall grass on the far touchline further down the pitch.

'Aw shit, Roger, I told you to make sure the brake was on,' accused Lance. 'Now we're in trouble, she could be anywhere.'

John added to our fears. 'I can't hear her crying either.'

We rushed over fearing the worst only to find Connie, oblivious of her lone journey, still asleep lying on a pile of grass cuttings. She looked as if she had been purposely laid there still wrapped in her shawl and covered by her blanket. Other than it being a bit muddy on the under side we were lucky that she was none the worse for wear. We did our best to clean her up and when questioned later by Auntie we nonchalantly blamed a passing motorist for having splashed her with muddy water, but it was a close call. Mike could never keep a secret. Often he would blurt out whatever was in his mind and it was only a sly kick on the ankle that prevented him. In hindsight perhaps he was being cleverer than we thought when if only Auntie had taken the trouble to look out the window she would have realised it hadn't been raining.

The secrets which we all shared, such as the pram incident and being chased by a Yank with his trousers around his ankles after we had disturbed his servicing of a local girl, helped to bond us all together. But in those early days my acceptance into the gang was yet to be established. My first meal was the beginning of my initiation.

Auntie waddled down the passage into the kitchen. 'Is everybody all right, have you boys been looking after Francis?'

'Oh yes Auntie,' they all replied in unison looking in my direction as if daring me to say otherwise.

I nodded and said nothing. There was no-one who would want to miss out on a few extras. I wondered if she noticed that my plate was still clean, but seeing the big plates empty began pouring out the mugs of tea which were passed around the table. Having been more than adequately stewed on the stove it still looked like tea but without milk or sugar I was not keen for a mug to be shoved in my direction. I found it strange that tea could taste so very different to that which I had been used to. There was another factor which may have affected it too in that the large smoky pot was the same colour both inside and out.

There was a rota system for washing up which was pinned to the back of the larder door and as I hated the chore I wondered how soon my name would appear on the list. Performing this duty at tea time was quick and easy, but at breakfast it was both messy and slimy with porridge residue. The porridge acted like glue and was probably the main contributor to the weekly problem of the blocked drain. My dread of eating it stemmed from the thought that perhaps the porridge had the same affect on our stomachs. Our next door neighbour Don was our odd job man and we often had to climb over him on our way to school as he busied himself in the culvert outside the back door.

I remember feeling more like an observer than a recipient at that first meal and got up to leave as soon as I could but Auntie caught me hovering around the bottom of the stairs. Lance and Frank were already half way up.

'Show Francis to his bed you two. He can go in the big bed. Auntie Floe has already made space and his clean clothes are in number eight.'

Little did I realise the significance of her 'in the big bed' directive. It sounded good that I was going to have a big bed but what did she mean about, 'made space and clean clothes'? I was already in clean clothes which were given to me earlier by the WVS lady at the evacuee marshalling office.

'OK Auntie,' said Lance as he beckoned me to follow.

They clattered up the first flight and then they entered what appeared to be a cupboard but which was actually the entrance to the attic via a winding staircase. At the top there were two rooms, one smaller than the other, both sparsely furnished with camp beds side by side in rows and an open fronted cupboard. We entered the larger room, neither of which benefited from the luxury of a door or any form of floor covering. The ceiling mirrored the profile of the roof on both sides with the exception of a small roof window high up at the back of the house. Low down by the side of the chimney breast there was a small door which afforded access to the roof space.

'That's your kip mate, sweet dreams.'

They both laughed as they plumped themselves down on two camp beds beneath the window, leaving me rooted to the spot and mortified to realise what Auntie had arranged for me. The bed was for the small boys just like me. I was to sleep with five others in the double bed and my pyjamas took the form of a floor length night shirt with short sleeves, no buttons and just a hole at the top. It was a large wooden affair with an open spring base covered by a flock mattress and the blankets were the hairy military type but there were no sheets. The pillows were a mishmash of cushions piled in a heap at one end. Without bothering to change I dejectedly threw myself down in my allocated corner space beneath the sloping roof and wishing the world would end, promptly fell asleep.

When I awoke, the light was on and somebody was shaking me. My bed was now fully occupied and rolled up bundles lay in the six camp beds. Then I heard that voice again. I looked over to see Lance waving at me and pointing toward the doorway.

'Go and have a pee, hurry up, the bucket's filling up.'

Was this a dream? I returned from the land of nod with a bang as I stumbled into the doorpost and became fully awake. Luckily I stopped just in time to avoid kicking the waiting bucket which was already filled close to the rim. I relieved myself as directed, being careful to avoid spillage and as my senses cleared became aware of the smell and noticed that someone before me had been less alert. There was a large wooden box behind the bucket which was splattered with urine. It was an RAF toolbox with an aircraft ensign, across the centre of which in blue lettering it read, 'R Manston 556249.' Other than to feel concerned about the contents of the box, I gave it no more thought and clambered back into bed, but before I had got very far in trying to avoid the other bodies, that voice rang out once more.

'Hey mate, you've got to change into the penguin suit and put your clothes in number eight. Auntie will come and check later when she goes to bed.'

Auntie 'coming to check' was something which the older boys looked forward to on her matinée days when she came home early and was at home all evening. Sometimes Floe's visit was a disappointment when she would be still wearing her slacks and apron, but then there were others when she was ready for bed wearing her shortie nightie. On these occasions the boys closest to the passage way experienced a real treat which sent them to sleep greatly relieved with a smile on their face. As time went on I learned that money used to change hands for the privilege of exchanging camp beds for one of three in prime positions.

I understood how the boys felt, especially the older ones, from my experience with Floe when first introduced to her in the sitting room. She was as different as chalk and cheese to her mother. I marvelled how one could be so fat and the other so slim. She was a young woman about twenty one years old and slightly taller than both Auntie and Grandma. Her dark eyes were set in a pale almost model face with high cheek bones and perhaps a larger than average size nose. Long dark hair flowed over her shoulders, which were broad like a swimmer's and she had big breasts. These produced the opposite effect to Auntie's to give the impression that she was top heavy. As she came forward to greet me her floral patterned cotton dress sagged open to expose more of them. She was not wearing a bra and I found myself blushing not knowing where to look as she completely filled my vision and then laughed when she saw my reaction. She was used to it and even at the ripe old age of seven I got the distinct impression that she was adept at flaunting her femininity to maximum effect in a teasing manner. If the truth be known she probably enjoyed teasing the older boys too who after all were not a great deal younger than herself, knowing full well that most were only pretending to be asleep.

As I changed into the nightshirt which was far too long I realised the accuracy of Lance's description with his 'penguin' reference. Sleep was now out of the question and I remained fully awake for the rest of that interminable night, listening to the noises emanating from my room mates. In my bed they were fidgeting, scratching and farting whilst elsewhere in the room some where having active dreams accompanied by shouts and indistinguishable mumblings. Feet were everywhere, three sets at each end. I entertained the idea of sleeping on the floor but there was very little free space available other than that on the landing. That too became unattractive when I remembered the smelly bucket.

Somehow, when it was too late, I must have dozed off but only to hear Auntie's voice echoing up the stairs. It was breakfast time and the grumblings in my stomach were telling me that perhaps I should have taken advantage of the offerings at tea time. But the aroma drifting up the stairs was not one to spur me into action unlike my room mates as they all tried to be the first into the one and only bathroom for the proverbial 'lick and promise'.

Once again I was last to enter the kitchen to find them all waiting, 'Oliver' fashion for their meal. As before, they were all eager to start, but the smell from the range caused my appetite to diminish very quickly.

The table was set with a bowl, plate and mug for each and now there were four more faces looking at me. I sat on the same bench as before feeling totally miserable and as if I had not been to bed at all. Not so many faces were looking my way now, some because they were still half asleep whilst others thankfully, had lost interest.

Auntie waddled into the kitchen and took the large cooking pot from the range, holding the two handles with kitchen towels. She put it on a wooden board in the centre of the table and proceeded to ladle out dollops of the contents with a wooden spoon, but she had to shake it repeatedly to achieve success. Working like a clockwork toy, methodically dipping and dolloping, she eventually filled all the bowls and pushed one in my direction. What was this disgusting lumpy mess resembling wall paper paste? It was porridge, Auntie's special glutinous concoction, the like of which I had never seen before.

Now that it had been standing all night on the range, it had formed a brown crust, giving no indication of what lay beneath. I could see the reason for the burnt smell. It had bubbled over and brown flakes were sticking to the bottom of the pot as well as the ring still smoking on the range. It had been made with water, sweetened with saccharin, burnt in the process and now I was expected to eat it. During the whole time of my foster days, I don't remember ever seeing the pot empty or hanging with the rest of the cooking utensils over the range. Invariably the porridge was burnt as a result of being topped up with more every day, stirred up with the old and the whole concoction left to mature on the stove over night. There was no lid so whatever visitors it had during the hours of darkness or what fell in was anybody's guess.

'For what we are about to receive' floated around the room once more. This time, my prayer was somewhat different and did not include, 'May the Lord make me truly thankful', but there was little chance that my amendment would be answered.

Again the flurry of activity soon followed the 'Amen'. Driven by hunger, I tried to make the utmost effort to follow the gang but the porridge was as disgusting as it appeared. I had never had saccharin and the fact that it was burnt sent my taste buds into panic. One spoonful was enough. No way could I possibly eat it despite my hunger or any promises of perhaps trying harder that I had made during the eternal night. Tears began to flow again as I watched the others tucking in with relish. There was a slight hesitation and a gesture of disgust on the part of one boy who found a beetle in his bowl. His companions on either side laughed and showed no sympathy. 'It's alright Peter, its well cooked.' In no time at all the bowls except mine were empty. Nobody wanted mine; had they had enough or did my tears dripping into mine help them decide? Nobody asked for more.

Breakfast didn't take long and soon the boys were running down the path to school, leaving me still at the table with my bowl of cold solid porridge that refused to go away. I suppose I should have been used to making the supreme effort and eating whatever was presented to me from the days when I lived at home. I remember my own father telling me not to waste good food and that if I didn't eat it then it would return tomorrow and the next day and so on until I cleared my plate. On that occasion it was semolina and when eventually I gave in I was promptly sick. I regarded that as something of a victory and 'one in the eye' for my dad. Auntie's reaction however was not quite so harsh but the result was just the same. She was not best pleased with me and on seeing that I had barely touched mine calmly flopped it back in the pot. She saw me look at her but didn't bat an eyelid. I was horrified that that same porridge, tears and all, would be reappearing again tomorrow morning.

After all the boys had gone to school the house seemed empty and in some odd way I was beginning to miss them already. They were comforting in some ways and just the opposite in others. I wished I could have gone with them, at least I would be out of the house and somewhat free. The feeling of being trapped was never ever far away during the whole of my evacuee days. I returned to my bed and lay staring at the ceiling until Floe came to tidy up. She took no notice of me and I heard her grumble about the brimming bucket. I almost made the suggestion that perhaps two buckets would have solved her problem of trying to avoid spills, but she was not in a talkative mood and I decided to say nothing.

'She's here Cicely,' Auntie shouted up the stairs.

Assuming I had fallen asleep, Floe shook me roughly by the shoulder. 'Wake up Francis the billeting officer has arrived to take you to school. Get your coat, it's not far but I expect the he will take you in his car and you'll see some of the other boys there too.'

There was a knock on the front door followed by a ladies voice.

'I am Ms Wendy Nicholson, Dowdales School, I will be taking Francis Tenby in today,' she said, 'apparently there's been a change of arrangements. The billeting officer has been called away and sends his apologies but he will call on Thursday with Francis's paperwork. I will look after him today and he might even join my class group. Is he ready?'

I was already on my way down, keen to leave.

'Oh, here he is, come on Francis darling; this lady is going to take you to school, say 'Good morning'.'

I was very much aware of the 'darling' bit which suddenly appeared in Auntie's vocabulary, since no vestige of any endearment or TLC had been forthcoming on her part to date. Although I had only been in the house for a short while I sensed that TLC was likely to be in short supply and that my foster parents were operating a business rather than a home. We had already been traumatised with the blitz, uprooted from our homes and a little would have made all the difference.

Wendy was very similar in build, age and stature to Auntie Floe, being in her early twenties, but with shoulder length blond hair which fell over my face as she greeted me with a welcome hug. She was nattily dressed in a tartan tunic and skirt and I liked her subtle choice of perfume. The greeting contrasted with that of Auntie's in which I remember being enveloped into odourless folds of soft tissue and nothing else. On arrival at the school we found the headmaster standing outside his office with arms folded across his chest looking serious.

Under his right arm he carried a short cane with brass ends which authenticated the name and title prominently displayed in yellow lettering over the door. 'Captain P.J.Tomkins, Headmaster'. At our first meeting, I managed to stifle a smile when I thought that perhaps his cane had been specially tailored to match his height. He was no more than five foot two; Miss Nicholson stood a good four inches taller. What he lacked in height was more than made up with his air of authority and military bearing. The top of his head was bald but he had bushy grey sideburns and a neat cropped moustache which turned up at the ends. He had a friendly suntanned face but when he turned his full attention on me, I felt that his blue piercing eyes could read my thoughts and in some ways he reminded me of my father. He too possessed that same look, one which told me as a mere seven year old that he would not be easily fooled.

'Ah, Ms Nicholson, I see you've got the new boy. I've been waiting to hear from some billeting fellow, but not had a pip out of him or his office.'

'I understand the billeting office to be short of staff,' Ms Nicholson explained, 'and a Mr. Freeman who currently deals with billets only is going to take on the extra duty of looking after schools. He will be responsible for liaison directly with headmasters in connection with new arrivals from now on. He has been unavoidably delayed and has phoned me to let you know that he tried on two occasions to contact you but you were engaged.'

'Ummmphh! Well he'd better improve his communication skills before I see him. I would have thought that phoning my office and to keep phoning until I became available would have been top of his priority list. As it is I've been waiting here like a spare part for the last half hour.'

As the headmaster voiced his veiled threat to some imaginary character further down the corridor he caught a wisp of Ms Nicholson's perfume. Like a drug it worked wonders on the Captain's demeanour causing the serious look to drain from his face and be replaced by smiles and something akin to positive drooling. She had his total attention as she explained the new arrangements and on her suggestion that I be assigned into her class, he immediately agreed.

My classroom was a crowded affair with boys roughly of my age, it being typical with all the usual paintings, pictures and information festooning the walls. The double desks were grouped together in pairs and I was invited to sit with two other boys on one of the few remaining empty seats at the front of the room. I nodded to my new classmates and Ms Nicholson introduced them as Dennis Turner and William Tribilcock. Dennis was a happy-go-lucky boy with an impish grin and noticeably better dressed than myself. As top boy he was a popular member of the class and seemed to be streets ahead of many of the others when it came to answering questions. William on the other hand was a tall gangly sort of boy with a speech impediment which made school life difficult for him.

I was pleased with my new teacher particularly because she was female. Experiences to date with male ones had not been very encouraging and 'fatty' Palmer, with cane up his sleeve, from my previous school fell into that category. Ms Nicholson, however, gave me the impression that she was very good at her job and soon put me at ease by showing her awareness of my vulnerability as a newcomer thrust into a class of strangers. No questions were directed my way. I was pleased with that too and in any case there would have been no answers. My mind was on food. I was starving and the smell of food cooking somewhere left little room for any other thoughts.

A bell rang to announce it was lunch time. I dared not think how little I had eaten in the last twenty four hours and needed no second invitation to follow the orderly queue, under ever watchful eye of the 'Captain' across the road and up around the corner to the dining room. I stuck close to my new friend Dennis who knew the ropes and soon found myself in another queue with a plate in each hand. Corn beef hash with suet dumplings followed by bread and butter pudding was soon gone. What he thought of my table manners or whether he took any notice of my eating the whole lot with a spoon was the least of my worries. Then and only then, did I take stock of my surroundings or new classmates.

The dining hall was a recent addition to the school and had been hurriedly constructed on a corner of the playground between the boys and girls sections. It was very much like the air raid shelters at home except on a much larger scale. The hall was divided on similar lines to the school in general with the boys and girls sections separate. Service worktops which ran the full width of the building divided the two halves. Preparation and cooking meals had been reorganised and was carried out at some central point elsewhere. They were then delivered by road to all the schools where only warming facilities were required.

Dennis, who had been joined by his friend Daryl, nudged my arm and was the first to speak.

'Did you enjoy that Francis? Since this new building has been built, the meals are much better than at the old hall. It was closed down because it was too small, too old and had mice and cockroach problems. The balloon went up when old Tomkins found one in his dinner. He went berserk, and got this place built in double quick time. There was a story that one of the dinner ladies did it on purpose but swore blind it was an accident.'

'Yeah, I'd like to have seen it,' Daryl joined in the amusement. 'It couldn't have happened to a nicer chap. Tell you what though Francis, if you had one on your plate today I'm sure you would have eaten it at the speed you went through your dinner.'

'You must have been hungry!' Dennis added, 'thought you'd be into mine if I happened to look out the window. Don't they feed you at your place?'

'I don't like the food and I haven't eaten since Tuesday. This morning it was burnt porridge and it made me feel sick.'

Daryl stared in disbelief. 'But today is Thursday, glad I'm not an evacuee.'

CHAPTER 4

Grandma, Auntie and Floe were having one of their quieter moments when all the gang in the attic were settled and Connie had gone to sleep. It was at such times they would switch on the alkaline battery radio to catch up on the War news and do the sewing and mending jobs. There was always a pile on the table by the sewing machine awaiting the attention by one of them. Make do and mend was the rule of day since foster child allowances were not sufficient to cover for new ones. When clothes were beyond repair, despite Grandma's recognised expertise especially with sock mending which she did with the aid of a cup and recycled wool from old jumpers, Auntie would go 'cap in hand' to the WVS warehouse in town. She would come home with boxes of assorted clothing, quite a large proportion of which had been supplied through the American war aid programme. I particularly remember the footwear and the occasion when all the boots were left ones but with a bit of wearing they could be moulded to make a pair.

Grandma would sit quietly sewing beneath the standard lamp alone to all intents and purposes with her memories of her eighty one years. Her long hair was silver grey and her hands bore the evidence of hard work from working as a barmaid in her husband's public house and raising a family during difficult times. At times when grandma had been operating the sewing machine or using the magnifying glass for a long time Auntie would interrupt her thoughts.

'You've done enough for tonight mama let's have a drink of port.'

'Alright luvy,' she would say, 'my arthritis is playing me up a bit. It must be the dampness getting to my old bones.'

Grandma was fond of the odd tipple and was a firm believer that her tot at bedtime would keep her going for many more years. Her bed-sit which was on the ground floor at the front of the house was so full of memorabilia there was little room for her bed. I only ever went into the room twice and on the first occasion I remember being frightened by the fox fur wrap which hung on the wardrobe door. The wrap was a complete fox fur from head to tail with its mouth open showing the incisors and the sparkling black eyes seemed to follow wherever I went in the room. She had a large collection of family photographs, some framed and hanging on the walls and others on every available table and sideboard surface. In pride of place by her bedside was the one of her husband in army uniform by the side which was a commemorative citation which he had earned during the First World War. Although we saw little of her all the boys appreciated her genuine understanding of our plight and felt she at least was their friend. There was one occasion when I had cause to accept that friendship and was thankful for it.

Of all the weekends when Richard, the owner of the toolbox, came home on leave, there were two particular ones which I remember more than the others. Things just seemed to happen and both have remained with me ever since. Richard was an RAF navigator at the local airbase which formed part of the South Western Coastal Command whose duty was known as semi non-aggressive. He navigated for a crew flying the updated 'Warwick' aircraft carrying out air-sea rescue missions and depth charge operations on enemy submarines. In one of his more affable moods when he joined us in the kitchen to warm himself by the range, he explained how important his job was compared with the rest of the crew.

'There are two people who are important in an aircraft, the pilot and the navigator. The pilot gets all the glory, all he has to do is fly the plane, but the navigator does all the work and keeps him on the correct course. There is always a lot of banter and rivalry between them but the rest of the crew is made up of what is known as 'gash' members who act as gunners or wireless operators.'

He showed us his collection of photographs of the various aircraft which hung on his bedroom wall. There were pictures of the Sterling, Halifax and the Lancaster but in pride of place on a chest of drawers was a scale model of a Warwick made entirely from matchsticks. He said it had taken him two years to build and would not allow anyone to touch it not even to dust underneath it. It was actually a converted Wellington, the plane used by Barnes Wallis in the bouncing bomb attack on the Rhur Dam in Germany.

We were all impressed with his military importance and our persona of him was further enhanced with him being well over six feet tall. To some of us, especially the smaller ones, with his bigger than average nose and deep set eyes, he was a frightening figure. His dark long hair was swept back with a centre parting which was firmly held in place with copious amounts of Brylcreme. On his limited forty eight hour furloughs he tried to spend as much time as possible with his wife of only fifteen months but with a full house such as ours, privacy was in short supply. The day to day demands of baby Connie coupled with those of the evacuees left precious little time for Richard and Floe to be together. Disturbance was inevitable. They took every opportunity to go out for walks like so many other service men we had seen, presumably for the same reason as a Yank we disturbed in the grass by the allotments. At tea one particular day, we had been warned that he would be at home at the weekend and that we should 'be seen and not heard' and 'watch out or else'.

Floe dressed up as usual in her short dress and high heels and waited in the sitting room for his arrival. Richard was aware of the older boys and happened to catch four of them peeping through the window when he unexpectedly arrived through the back gate. Pretending he didn't know what they were up to, he calmly went upstairs and brought their peep show to an abrupt end as he drowned them with a bucket of water from the window above. Auntie complained they would all need a change of dry clothes but Richard said they didn't need it after he made them run around the football ground several times to dry off. His leave periods were a dilemma leaving him only walks and the hours of darkness for prime time with Floe. The boys knew more about that than he would have liked and took great care to avoid another soaking.

We all heeded the warning until bedtime when and Richard and Floe were making the best of their reunion. Our bedroom was directly over theirs and the older boys used to come into our room, sometimes wake us up on purpose, so we wouldn't miss 'IT.' They were all prepared with an assortment of mugs and glasses which they had secreted out of the kitchen to use as listening devices on the wooden floor. Auntie used to complain that 'things' were missing from her cupboards and although she searched our rooms, never found any.

On this particular night the 'action' was unusually noisy as the bed rattled against the wall accompanied by shouts which could be clearly heard through the floor. Our entertainment came to an end when one of the boys jumped on the camp bed of another causing it to crash and flatten itself on the floor. For a few seconds, there was silence from the room below, followed by the sound of the attic door being wrenched open and heavy footsteps on the bare stairs.

We younger ones darted back under our blankets as four or five of our visitors made a dash for the doorway in a desperate race not to be caught. Robert bounded up the stairs, two at a time and switched on our light to find Frank blinking in amazement at his flattened bed. He went straight to him, the only one sitting up and daring to show his face. He received the full onslaught of Richard's annoyance. Later, when he was able to appreciate the funny side of the situation Frank informed the other boys that he thought he was being attacked by a gorilla. Wearing only his pyjama bottoms Richard, despite his lean appearance in his RAF uniform, was quite muscular and his arms and chest were covered with black hair.

'What's all this noise?' He dragged Frank by the back of his penguin shirt up to eye level. 'Who's running around up here, don't you know I'm trying to sleep?'

'I don't know Uncle, my bed's busted, that's all I know.'

'Well sleep on the floor then,' he said harshly. 'And be quiet about it or the next time I come up here it will be with my slipper. I don't want to hear any more, is that clear?'

All was deadly quiet in the other room, no-one daring to breathe. Richard switched off our light and paused outside the other doorway, then clumped down the stairs. A few minutes later when he was sure the 'coast was clear,' Herbert whispered to Lionel.

'You asleep mate?'

'You've got to be joking, I'm wide awake now. What do you want?'

'I didn't think I was going to be able to hold my breath any longer,' Herbert said, 'I nearly gave the game away when he stopped at our door.'

'Nor me neither,' whispered Lionel with head under his blankets trying to be quiet.

'My father tells me,' Herbert said laughingly, 'that too much humping and hawing like them two are doing and you go blind by the time you're thirty.'

With the vision of the boys crouching on all fours with cups to their ears straining to hear every sound, Lionel added to the prediction.

'In that case then Herbert, you'll go deaf by that time 'n all.'

Lionel's concocted maxim sent Hebert into a fit of laughter which he was only just able to stifle by burying his head in his pillow. Mike, who had been listening to their conversation, added his contribution causing all three to laugh together.

'Eh! What did you say? I can't hear you.'

'Shush! He'll hear us, go to sleep.'

The night Frank's bed was broken provided conversation for many a long and otherwise boring evening prior to falling asleep. I can only hazard a guess as to what proportion of our four years or so that we spent in that attic, but I for one, felt that I knew every knot and hole in every piece of wood and that I was on first name terms with all the spiders. Herbert and Lionel often fantasised about what they would do given half a chance with Floe and I'm sure the antics in the room below coloured their concept of marriage and possibly for many of the others too.

The second notable weekend was the one which I had particular cause to remember Floe's warning about, 'watch out or else' and to be grateful for Grandma's friendship. Bed wetting was always a problem. Often I could never be sure if I had done it or one of the others. Even though we were encouraged not to drink before going to bed, the bucket was always full long before we went to sleep. I repeatedly found myself in a wet bed. The realisation on waking was humiliating, undignified and I was often afraid to move from the warm spot in case I came into contact with my cold wet night shirt or that of somebody else.

At times when half asleep I could never be sure if I was relieving myself or not and then suddenly to discover that I was in full flow was annoying, but by then it was too late. Sometimes the noise itself would wake me up as I listened to the inevitable drip, drip, and drip again on to the floor as the mattress became saturated. It was a case of not wanting to say anything or even get up because then I would have to face the exposition and consequences. I used to hope against hope that my body heat together with that of the others would evaporate the offending liquid, but no such law of physics ever came to my aid.

There were times when the mattress had to be dried in some way but it was always heavy and cumbersome. Apart from the occasions when it was only lightly damp, it had to be lugged outside to be dried in the sun. This also provided us with the opportunity to beat the hell out of it with sticks to remove the dust and any uninvited guests. We treated this as a fun thing but I wonder what our more informed neighbours thought of the process. Winter times with less sunshine were a problem which was further magnified by the reluctance of the perpetrators to get out of bed in the cold attic. Being the last one to join the other five I provided them with a ready made excuse and was often made to feel guilty.

Two things cured me of the habit one being more pleasant than the other. I used to swear black and blue that it was always somebody else but on removal of the blankets the evidence was plain for all to see. In retrospect the frustration of our foster parents was understandable and serious measures were warranted. One night I knew I was guilty and Mike-the-squealer, as he was known, compounded my guilt by shouting down the stairs.

'Auntie, he's done it again, he's pissed the bed. Ugggh! My shirt's wet as well, I'm soaking.'

'And mine.' 'And mine,' shouted Roger and Eric together.

Mike set others shouting adding to the turmoil and continued to shout down the stairs.

'He's done a real one this time Auntie and it's dripping on the floor. We'll have to lug the mattress outside good 'n proper.'

Richard warned us that bed wetting simply had to stop or the culprit would be dropped into a bath of cold water if it happened again. There was none of the psychological line of approach that punishment would take the form of removal of some privilege. That would have been of no use to us, we didn't have any. What happened was no less than what I would have expected from my own father, although initially he would have tried another approach. He was a great one for extolling the virtues of tactics and elected himself to be an expert on such, relating it all to the game of chess. Whenever I did anything wrong or did not tell the truth he used to say he would find out by talking to me in my sleep. I knew then there was no point in covering up or lying any more. I believed him totally. Uncle Richard did not possess such powers and when he heard the commotion he immediately bellowed up the stairs.

'Right, Francis, you know what I said.'

Could I forget? Jumping out of bed I darted through hatch into the roof space behind the chimney stack, cobwebs and all. This was a place where we would hide when Auntie was on the warpath. There was no chance she could possibly squeeze through and Floe was terrified of spiders. It was the one place where we could stash anything knowing that it wouldn't be found like our collection of mugs, glasses and American magazines. But today was different. I knew Richard wouldn't be put off so easily and I was merely delaying the inevitable.

I heard him bound up the stairs and following the pointing fingers of my 'friends', he stopped at the hatch. Thinking I was safe I settled down amongst my friendly spiders.

'Where are you, you little squirt? Do I have to send somebody in to get you or are you coming out on your own?'

He sent John and Lance in to get me. This was all a game to them and couldn't wait to see the outcome, but to me it life or death.

The two ferrets hauled me out kicking and screaming into his outstretched hands and he carried me down the stairs under his arm like a bundle of washing. He headed straight for the bathroom where the bath of cold water was waiting for its victim. There was no escape. In I went nightshirt and all. No sooner had I touched bottom than I was out again in a flurry of foam and splashes which went everywhere, soaking Richard in the process. Slithering from his grasp, I managed to squeeze past him and out the door. I fell down the stairs in my desperate haste to escape, landing at the bottom where Grandma was standing, wondering what all the noise was about. Hiding behind her skirts I saw Richard at the top of the stairs, his face now dripping with water and his streamlined hairdo now not quite so slick.

'He had it coming to him; the little blighter's wet his bed again. He can't say I didn't warn him,' he said defensively.

'It's alright Richard, I'll look after him now,' she said taking my hand and going back into her room.

Sanctuary! She wrapped me in a large towel and sat me down in a chair. I felt like a mouse which had just escaped from the cat, my heart pounding but slowly beginning to normalise.

'Let's see if I can find you a sweet in my tin,' she said. 'So what's all this fuss about? What have you done? I can't believe it can be so bad as to upset Uncle Richard.'

'I've wet the bed again Grandma. He promised to put me in the cold bath, but I didn't believe he really would,' I said still shivering like a leaf from the shock. 'I hid in the roof space but the others gave me away—, scraped my leg and my arm—.'

'Oh! Dear, dear me, we can't have that. Let me see, I've got some ointment for your scrapes. I'll have a word with him in the morning, I'm sure it won't happen again,' she said as she gently applied the ointment and patting me on the head. 'How does that feel? You can stay here tonight and I'll make you a bed on the settee.'

With heavy curtains on the door and windows and full of old furniture, Grandma's room was quiet and peaceful, a sanctuary. There was strong aroma of camphor and her large double bed dominated the room leaving just enough space for a commode in the corner. Some of her old photographs were brown and faded compared to the more recent ones of Floe and Richard's wedding and Connie in her Christening gown. She saw my interest in the pictures and sat up in bed to tell me about some of them.

'I was born in Ireland and the big house with the horses and carriages outside was where I used to live. My parents were farmers and when the potato famine caused problems they lost all their money and eventually they brought me to England. I was about your age then and didn't fully understand why we had to leave.'

'Who are all those ladies in long dresses and big hats?'

'Oh, they were the suffragettes, I'm there somewhere but you would never recognise me. We ladies formed a club so we could vote and maybe become politicians. It was big thing in my day because women were not allowed to vote.'

'Were you a politician then, Grandma?'

'Oh! No dearie. I married my Albert; he was a publican before he had to join the army. That's him look,' she said picking up the photograph by her bed and wiping away some imaginary dust. 'Would you like to see his medals? I am very proud of my Albert, that's his citation.'

'What's a citation Grandma?'

'Albert won a special medal during the last war and this certificate describes how he did it. He was a machine gunner fighting in Picardy France and oddly enough he was killed at a place called Albert. I'll read it to you.'

'For distinguished gallantry and at the risk of his own life above and beyond the call of duty on 1ˢᵗ July 1916 lance corporal Albert Sanders inspired his unit by taking two volunteers with him on a dangerous mission to remove a stubborn battery of machine gun emplacements which were preventing the advancement of his company to link up with others who had been cut off. In the face of concentrated enemy fire the three progressed until his two volunteers were injured at which point Sanders continued a lone assault on the force of German troops. Although his company had sustained severe losses and in danger of running out of ammunition he used what little he had left to devastating effect. He charged the first position firing his revolvers with both hands and finally lobbed a grenade into the enemy dugout at close quarters. Whilst still under heavy fire and dodging between the trees Sanders eventually crawled to within ten yards of the adjacent machine gun position to kill the gunner with a single revolver shot. He then turned the captured machine gun to his flank causing two more positions to surrender without further loss of life. Five prisoners were taken and the battery eliminated. Commentating on his feat his commanding officer said Sanders was a one man army and that no commendation would be high enough to do justice to his act of bravery and ingenuity.'

She stood looking at the picture for a few moments. 'I think you should go to sleep now.'

I liked Grandma; she was protection and had gentle ways that reminded me of my mother. I was the escaping fugitive from the law upstairs and I felt safe in her room with the heavy curtains. We had only a short time to talk at any great length and I felt sure she had a wealth of tales to tell. She did start to tell me about her younger years and as if to make me feel better, said life was much stricter then. She said she came from a large family with four brothers and two sisters and that her father believed in children being seen and not heard. Right from a young age they all had duties to perform on the farm where they lived and respect for elders and other people's property was the rule of the day. There were pictures of her riding a horse and another of her whole family in swimwear on a beach. She laughed when I said they looked funny and were wearing too many things to be going swimming. I could have listened to Grandma all night, but why did it have to be under such circumstances? She must have known that at nearly eighty two she was nearing the end of her life and I've always remembered what she said to me before she tucked me up in my makeshift bed.

'Think of me when you can't see me.'

The next time I went into Grandma's room was about a year later when she was in her coffin, pale and cold with those smiling eyes closed for ever. She was the first dead person I ever saw. It had a profound affect on me. I was allowed to touch her hand to say 'Goodbye,' but this time there was no response, no sinewy grip and the feeling of her cold hand compounded the realisation that with her passing I had lost a friend.

The next morning after a good sleep and an early breakfast with Grandma I seemed to be enthused with the resolve to face up to my new surroundings and accept any challenges foster life threw at me. After the bath incident I was given a camp bed of my own to test my resolve not to do it again. I never did. The shock was more than just physical, it affected my sub conscious and although the treatment was severe, it worked and served as a warning to others.

When I met Lance and Herbert at school the next day they were both surprised to see me.

'Hey up! Can you see what I see Herb? Is it a ghost? You 'aint 'arf got a clean face, Francis. Did you enjoy your swim?' they teased, 'you forgot your swimming trunks 'an all. We were thinking about getting up a collection for your funeral when you didn't come back to bed last night. Thought you were a goner when Uncle shoved you into the bath and we didn't hear any more. Everybody made sure that they had a good pee before going back to sleep. What happened? Where did you go?'

'I bet Floe let him sleep in her bed,' Lance fantasised. You lucky little bugger. Cor!'

'No she didn't,' I protested, flushing crimson.

'Its true look, he's gone all red,' Herbert chipped in.

Memories of, 'going all red' as Herbert put it was something of a problem in my early years. On occasions when Auntie used to interrogate all of us after some household incident or when the police were involved I always looked guilty even though I was completely innocent. That was the case when money went missing from Auntie's purse until eventually the two Rowe brothers from London got careless with their spending and were caught red handed by the curious school headmaster who brought them home to face the music.

'For your information I spent the night in Grandma's room and I had a decent cooked breakfast with egg and bacon and I had butter on my toast.'

There was no reply as both wandered off muttering.

CHAPTER 5

Floe's evening attendances at the Pavilion Cinema were from Monday until Wednesday which left Thursday and Friday for her afternoon matinée shifts. The arrangement allowed her to spend as much time as possible with Richard when he came home on leave at the weekends. Her evening job was to assist Alfie in the projection room, a quite able young man who had managed to slip through the conscription net of the armed forces initially by declaring himself an invalid and in a job of national importance. He argued that his job at home was just as necessary as those at the Front and one of keeping up morale at home with propaganda films as well as providing entertainment for families. Richard had no time for him and made no secret of his thoughts to Floe that he regarded him as being no better than a conscientious objector.

Alfie took no notice of what other people said or thought. Still single and living with his mother in a fine house overlooking the harbour, he was not short of a bob or two and enjoyed life to the full. Secretly Richard was jealous of Alfie in that he appeared to be good at everything. His father had left him a fishing boat and he was a popular member of the fishing community especially when it came to socialising down at the harbour in the Moby Dick Tavern. His ability at sea earned him the position of coxswain of the local lifeboat and he was also popular with the Americans who paid him good money for fishing trips during which they provided all the fuel, food and drinks.

In his capacity as coxswain he was awarded a bronze medal for bravery in saving the lives of four evacuee boys from London who stole a yacht for a fishing trip. Only one of the boys had any knowledge of sailing and none of them wore a life jacket. When the weather suddenly changed from a sunny day into storm conditions the boys found themselves in trouble being swept further and further out to sea. The mast broke knocking one boy unconscious whilst two others were knocked into the sea by a free ranging boom. The fourth boy was not strong enough to pull the now dead weight boys back into the boat but managed to lash them together with rope to prevent them slipping away.

As luck would have it Alfie sitting in his front room with his father's telescope saw the perilous position the boys were in. He sounded the alarm and the lifeboat was launched. In the rough sea it was difficult to approach the yacht from either side with the boys strapped to one and the boom swinging from side to side on the other. Putting his own life in danger Alfie jumped into the sea with a life line to release the two boys in the water and then secured the boom. By this time the unconscious boy had recovered sufficiently and with Alfie's help all three were pulled into the lifeboat whilst the fourth was able to jump.

Newspaper reports of the incident acclaimed Alfie the hero of the day and it was further reported that one of the grateful parents made a sizeable donation toward lifeboat funds. Alfie played the whole situation down and declared the successful rescue mission the result of teamwork by his crew and all in a days work.

Floe described herself as a 'gofer' in that she fetched and carried the film reels from the lock up store at the back of the cinema in addition to attending his every need whist he was busy operating the projectors. In preparation for a show, she would mount two reels in each leaving the tails out for Alfie to do the tricky bit of feeding the film over and through the rollers. In the two years she had been working with him she was technically competent to operate the machines on her own. It was not uncommon when Alfie's attention was elsewhere for her to prompt him when the 'Q' spots appeared. These marks were the indicators for starting the next reel in motion in order to provide a smooth change over from one to the next. When not in the projection room Floe carried out her other function of usherette, assisted by another girl Moira, in which she was required to wear a natty tight fitting white trouser suit. Each girl carried a sales tray slung across the shoulders and wore a hat which was no more than a curved piece of white cardboard on an elastic band. The final touch to complete the uniform was a torch clipped into a breast pocket.

When Floe first met Alfie he operated the local milk round with a horse and cart, a job which he held for a number of years straight from school until he gave it up after receiving a kick from the horse. At first

Alfie felt like a fish out of water and when the manager of the cinema decided to give up his secondary role as projectionist Floe put Alfie's name forward. Auntie said she had recommended him in appreciation of his many dedicated years of service as a milkman working in all weathers but secretly she had reservations about his friendship with Floe. She was aware that Alfie used to spend an inordinate amount of time at their house early in the mornings before she got up. Alfie admitted to having no experience or knowledge of being a projectionist but with Floe's help managed to persuade the manager otherwise. He needed someone not only as a projectionist but also someone to act as a new broom in cinema control. With the influx of evacuees the manager and his sales girls were experiencing more and more incidents of cinema damage and general disruptive behaviour. He felt that the culprits were gaining the upper hand despite his threats to report them to their school or calling in the police. Standing at well over six foot compared to the manager's five foot two, the manager considered Alfie to be a suitable candidate.

In truth Alfie got the job because there were no other candidates since all able bodied men of his age had been conscripted into the Forces. The horse had in fact done him a favour on two counts. Firstly he received an appreciable rise in wages and secondly although the accident left him with a limp, he was able to use it in declaring himself unfit for National service. His limp did not prevent him from being a handyman about town and with his easy access to peoples' homes soon developed a reputation of being popular with the ladies. In his late twenties with dark bushy eyebrows and a fresh innocent looking face he could well have fulfilled many of the amorous rolls of the stars depicted in the films he displayed daily.

The cinema screen world was one in which he could escape from the real one and fantasise about actors such as John Wayne and Edward G Robinson. 'Stagecoach' the classic Western depicting John Wayne as the ultimate in rough-and-tumble heroism and youthful good looks was a particular favourite. Then there was Edward G Robinson's 'Little Caesar' the film in which the actor as a small-time hood and merciless killer rises to the top of the mob in the underworld. He enjoyed the apparent ability of the hero to be immortal and impervious to whatever came his way. In contrast to the blood and thunder films there were the musicals and romantic ones which were more appealing to Floe. The 'Wizard of Oz' in which Dorothy escapes into the magical world of 'Oz' to echo the constantly changing real world of relationships and how they were affected by home life and property during the nineteen thirties. Floe watched the film 'Stella Dallas' on all three of her evening shifts during the first week it was shown. It was an exercise in romanticism in which the leading actor chases fortunes as ardently as the women in his life. Away from the cinema screen both Alfie and Floe knew that real life wasn't like that although Floe did her best to have her cake and eat it. She had made that all important first decision with regard to the choice of a partner but when Richard was away she had needs like anyone else and Alfie was always ready.

Alfie had perfected his art of projectionist to the extent that he had plenty of time to turn his attention to Floe. Being cooped up in the tiny projection room provided Alfie with the advantage that there was precious little space for her to escape. Floe learned not to be there when amorous scenes where being shown in case Alfie was turned on and tried to copy them. Each film roll lasted for about thirty minutes and on at least one occasion Floe was saved by the 'Q' spot. He misjudged the timing and tugged Floe into his lap thinking more about some other spot on her rather than the film and in no time at all, various pieces of her uniform were elsewhere. He found she was a great tease and often said, 'No' when deep down he knew she meant, 'Yes.' She loved his attention but was careful not to allow him to go too far. On one of these occasions, he caused uproar in the audience by missing the 'Q' spot at a crucial point in the film which threw the cinema into darkness and allowed the film to run out.

'Alfie, Alfie,' she shouted in panic. 'We've missed it! The manager will be in here double quick.'

'OK, don't panic, I've got it all in hand,' he said, quickly flicking the switches with one hand and adjusting his clothing with the other.

Just as Floe warned, the manager did arrive but fortunately took longer than usual having been asleep at the time. When he eventually did arrive, the film had been restarted, the audience pacified and both were fully clothed and in control once more.

'The power plug to the second machine dropped out due to some vibration in the gearing,' Alfie lied to the Manager. 'I'll check it over in the morning,'

'OK, no harm done, these things happen,' he said laconically.

Alfie sat looking intently at the alleged faulty power plug to avoid seeing the smile on Floe's face until after he had left the room. Floe's recollection of the cause of the vibration was a far cry from that of Alfie's.

'You'll simply have to marry me,' he said jokingly, 'or it might happen again.'

There were times when the same thought of marriage crossed his mind in his other capacity of handyman and electrician. His mother was always telling him that as a single man, time was passing him by quicker than he realised and she hoped to see him settled before passing on. In the mornings he worked for anyone wanting his services but he only did the smaller jobs no one else wanted. Wendy was one of his customers who continued to use his services as an electrician following the death of her parents for whom he had worked for a number of years. He knew the cottage and electrical system well and it was convenient for Wendy to give him the back door key so that work could be carried out whilst she was at school. She knew he could be trusted to clean up after himself and that he could be relied upon to do a good job.

Her parents knew him well from his younger days when as a group leader with the boy scouts he would accompany them on 'Bob a Job' weeks and organise their outdoor pursuit activities. When Wendy was in her late teens, her mother used to use Alfie as a roll model for the kind of fine young man she hoped one day she might marry. He was popular with the scouts and parents trusted him to look after their boys especially when teaching them how to sail and during rock climbing and abseiling exercises. But that was a few years ago and since that time he had developed something of a Lothario reputation.

One fine Saturday morning when she asked him to call to show him what she wanted him to do the following week she took him completely by surprise by greeting him at the door wearing a long dressing gown.

'Would you like to come up stairs first, or would you like a cup of tea?'

Alfie who could hardly be described as having led a closeted life was quick to recognise the ambiguity of her greeting. His face beamed from ear to ear.

'I beg your pardon?' he said, despite having heard quite clearly.

'Oh Alfie, you are a lad,' she said on realising what she had said.

From that day Alfie felt that their relationship had entered a new phase, one which excited him along a similar path to that which he had with Floe, but unlike Floe, he had seen Wendy in her bathing costume when she sunbathed in the garden. As Alfie followed her up the stairs to the second bedroom where Wendy wanted an extra wall light fitted, he fantasised that perhaps today there would be no bathing costume beneath the gown. His thoughts caused him to stumble on the top step and to hold on to her for support, but the support was not there. He fell on the floor with the gown around his shoulders to reveal her youthful body wearing the bathing costume once more. Although his fantasy had been shattered he was relieved that he had been spared the total embarrassment of seeing her naked.

'Are you alright Alfie?' she said, not bothering to pick up the gown, 'I've been sunbathing in the garden.'

From his position on the top step he took a long lingering look at her from her bare feet and legs up over the curves, savouring every inch of her until finally, their eyes met.

'I am now,' he said with a broad smile, 'I'll tell you what, I can spare a couple of hours this morning. Would it be OK if I make a start on the wiring now, then I can finish the job next week when the plaster has dried?'

'Yes, that will be lovely I'll be in the garden if you need anything.'

Wendy carried the dressing gown over her arm as she proceeded down the stairs closely followed by Alfie on his way out to his van to collect his tools. His felt his pulse began to race as he watched the curves gyrate in unison with her gait until he lost sight of her as she went down the porch steps out into the garden. As he opened his van door the rush of hot air took his breath away. The affect of the morning sun on the roof made him begin to think twice whether it had been a good idea to start the wiring, knowing full well that he would have to work in the roof space. In the bedroom he found cutting the plasterwork in preparation to bury the wiring easier than expected and soon completed the installation of the wall light. Then he opened the ceiling hatch and poked his head through only to discover that the sun beating down on the roof tiles had raised the temperature to something in excess of one hundred degrees. There was nothing for it; his only hope of making the cable connection to the junction box was to strip down to his pants to be able to deal with the heat. He gritted his teeth, climbed onto the four-poster canopy and went for it. Although he worked quickly the handkerchief on his forehead to keep the sweat out of his eyes soon became saturated. It dripped off every part of his body. He doggedly persisted almost to the point of collapse. Then with one final effort he half swung, half fell through hatch on to the bed.

'Bloody Hell, that was hot. I must be mad,' he said to himself. 'Nobody in their right mind would have done that.'

He picked up a hand towel from the bathroom and went down to the porch for some cool air mopping his forehead, neck and upper body as he went. Standing with his back to the garden, he heard Wendy's slow hand clap and turned to see she was watching him. She rolled over on her stomach to cup her head in her hands.

'Your face is red and you look hot.'

'I can't tell you how dammed hot it is in that roof space. About fifteen minutes is all I could take. I very nearly passed out. What a turn up for the papers that would have been if you had to telephone the hospital to collect a half naked man from your bedroom!'

'Oh Alfie, don't be so dramatic, you've been watching too many films. Pour out two glasses of lemonade and come and sit by me to cool off. Don't bother with your overalls you're fine as you are.'

Alfie needed no second invitation. He joined Wendy in the garden with a glass in each hand noticing as he did so that she had removed the top straps of her bathing costume and peeled it down to her waist. She made no attempt to move as he slid her glass towards her. Alfie sat beside her and leaned back on his elbows with his legs outstretched as the sun came out strongly again from behind a cloud. He took a long swig of lemonade from his glass, almost emptying it in one go.

'This is the life, I could get used to this, roll on retirement.'

Wendy turned her head. 'You can't be all that much older than me and you've got a long way to go yet. Anyway, before you go can you do something for me? I can feel the sun quite warm on my back,' she said changing the subject, 'would you like to oil my back, I don't want to burn.'

'OK,' he replied in a composed voice, but inwardly he was anything but as he felt his heart miss a few beats. His work as an electrician had seen him in a vast variation of situations from risking his life high up on ladders and scaffolding, in danger of being trampled on in farm cow sheds and being forgotten in under floor spaces to working in luxurious carpeted mansions. Oiling a customer's back in a sunny garden was a new experience.

He dribbled a few drops of oil just below her shoulders and began to work with both hands in circular motions steadily down her back. Following the contours of her body he applied pressure to her muscles and tendons with firmness letting the movement come from within rather than from his wrists and elbows. She could hear him breathing in deeply as he moved over her body and out again as he applied gentle pressure massaging with the palms of his hands and exploring with his fingers and thumbs. He worked steadily with smoothness, rhythm and purpose.

'How's that?' he queried.

'Ummm lovely,' she murmured as she rolled her forehead slightly from side to side on her arms. 'You've got soft hands.'
'That's a result of years and years on the milk round, better than any hand cream. I've always tried to look after them.'

Alfie put a few more drops of oil on his hands and continued working his way down her back until he managed to slip one beneath the edge of her swimsuit. Wendy made no objection and shifted her body weight making it easier for him to continue. Feeling confident he undid the side buttons and peeled off the costume to expose her milky white cheeks. As he kneaded them in small circles with his thumbs and moulded with the pads of his fingers like dough ready for the oven he felt his pulse racing as well as definite urge in his loins. He could not believe his luck. Not in a million years when he left for work that morning did he expect the day would be like this. One thing he knew for sure; he had to exercise control, be cool, relax and take it slowly. He didn't want to break the spell; if he was relaxed she would be too and would feel it through his hands.

He moved down to her feet. Sitting on his haunches he bent her left leg upwards to expose the sole and ran his fingers expertly along the nerve endings. She felt various parts of her body respond as he moved his thumbs and fingers over each zone. Her eyes began to feel heavy and as she relaxed found it increasingly difficult to keep them open. Switching to the other foot Alfie continued with the therapy until he felt her body go limp as she relaxed into a deep sleep. It was the signal he had been waiting for. He slid one knee and then the other between her legs and gently eased them apart. There was no resistance. She was wide open and his for the taking. He explored her internal crevices with expert fingers. The time was right. He dropped his shorts, oiled himself and slid deep into her. She was smooth as velvet; he had reached his ultimate goal. He closed his eyes and had ridiculous thoughts about females which ate their partners after mating and decided that he was ready to die and die happy.

Gripping her hips with both hands he locked on to her and savoured every second of the pleasurable sensations which her body afforded as he increased the rate of his thrusts. He squeezed her cheeks tightly together pulling them into his groin as far as they would go. Wendy stirred. Something was different. She opened her eyes. 'Oh! My God,' she thought as she felt him probing deep inside her. Already her body had begun to respond out of control. It was too late to object. She moved in unison with his rhythm as the speed increased and the tingling sensations grew stronger. Alfie felt her back suddenly arch upward and freeze. He closed his eyes as his head began to spin. She groaned loudly as her body exploded and then collapsed motionless, completely spent. At the same moment he held his breath as he emptied into her with convulsive jerks. Short of breath and with a racing pulse he found himself panting to catch up. He buried his face into the small of her back and could hear her heart pounding too as he waited for his own to normalise. Finally, as she turned her head sideways he rested his cheek beside hers.

'Do you think we could get it together on a permanent basis sometime?' he whispered.

'I think you've done pretty well already. That was fantastic I can't believe how easily you did that. I wasn't expecting it.'

'Neither was I,' Alfie replied as he sat up and began to reflect. 'It wasn't supposed to happen. I feel guilty now for having taken advantage of you.'

'You took precautions, didn't you?'

'Of course.' The idea that she thought he went to work every day 'prepared for action' was something he found amusing.

'Well, there you are then, no harm done, think no more of it.'

CHAPTER 6

Auntie was in the kitchen making saffron cake when she called Floe to help with the greasing of the baking tins and to regulate the flow of air through the range. For all her apparent good eyesight at close range she never seemed able to adjust the flow properly. Floe, on the other hand, had a knack which Auntie suggested had something to do with her nickname. Monday afternoons, when all the washing was out of the way, was the day she made her cakes for the following week. With twenty plus mouths to feed they were cheap and easy to make, much like the porridge where a little went a long way. She found that when they were a week old the cakes were easier to cut and more filling to the boys. They were usually made with margarine, flour, milk, dried eggs, a small amount of powdered saffron and a few drops of yellow colouring, but that day they had an extra ingredient. She jumped when a gust of wind burst open the back door and when Floe came in she found Auntie on her hands and knees trying to salvage the as yet dry mixture from the floor.

'Can't afford to waste good food Cice, a little bit of dirt won't do the little beggars any harm and I'm sure they've had worse where some of them come from.'

'Probably,' Floe agreed. 'Here, let me do that, I can get down easier than you.'

'Just check there are no pieces of coal in there Floe, we don't want any dentist's bills,' she added as she shook the bowl. 'Oh, and by the way, Joe Freeman is coming around later. He sent a message with Miss Nicholson about his change of arrangements. He's bringing Francis's ration book, identity card and paperwork so we can sign the foster order,' she said, as she started kneading the yellow lumps of dough, one in each hand.

Floe stood up quickly and removed her apron. 'OK Ma, I'll change out of these dungarees and deal with him in the sitting room. You won't be signing anything with those hands.'

Auntie knew that Joe had a roving eye where her daughter was concerned and that Floe tended to flirt with him but she also suspected there was more to the relationship than just 'feeding Joe's ego' as Floe described it. She was prepared to turn a blind eye to some extent and let Floe 'deal with him' in her own way knowing that neither of them would dare try any hanky-panky close by in the sitting room. Floe was halfway up the stairs when Joe arrived.

'Hang on just a minute Joe, be there in a jiffy,' she called down the stairs.

Joe didn't mind waiting; he was always pleased to see Floe, however long it took. He was the deputy billeting officer, married to his second wife and father of eight children, four to each. In his thirties, he was a rather tubby man with quite a mop of mousey hair and sported a handlebar moustache; a throwback to his RAF days when he was invalided out for some medical problem. What ever it was, the problem did not deter his obsession for female company. He was a popular member of the town Council and wasted no opportunity to curry favour with his colleagues in order to further his visions of someday becoming Mayor. Ever alert, he was always ready to exploit any situation whether it was with male or female relationships, or matters involving personal financial gain. Whenever he called at the house he carried a small case supposedly containing his official papers, but there was a suspicion that it was always heavier when he left.

With nineteen ration books and a considerable income from the foster authorities, Auntie could obtain more food on a bulk basis than most. Joe was in a position to be well informed of Government planning and was willing to provide Floe with useful inside information in return for small favours. Floe regarded her flirting with him and the odd fumble as a harmless game, but the whole association was to the detriment of our diet. Whatever he took away with him was anybody's guess but our meals were always the same and we never ate anything other than porridge, saffron cake and sandwiches of either jam or fish paste. Fortunately our free meals at school which contained our rightful allocation of available rationing were our life saver. Our plates were always cleared and it taught us to appreciate the better meals which were not available at home. Joe's concept of rationing was that it didn't apply to him or the many mouths he had to feed.

'Hi there Joe, good to see you, I believe you've been on your travels again,' said Floe as she led him into the sitting room.

Joe was pleased with his reception especially on seeing Floe had dressed in her buttoned blouse, tight trousers and high heels. He followed her, patting her backside, as he did so.

'Stop it Joe, we've got business to do,' she said with a smile.

'So we have Floe, so we have,' he said as he dragged her onto his lap in the armchair immediately the door was closed.

'One day Ma will catch us,' said Floe, striving to swivel around in his lap to check that he had closed the door. 'She's busy making cake in the kitchen for now.'

The announcement was music to Joe's ears. With Floe's attention drawn more to the door than on Joe, the buttons on her blouse slipped open. Joe had been deprived of female company since Monday, a whole three days ago and now he was intent on making up for lost time. She felt his chubby roving hands in more places than she thought possible for someone with only two. She felt his hot breath on her neck and could hear his heart beating.

'I've really missed you Floe,' he said holding her more tightly as he switched the objective of his manoeuvres by slipping both hands through the side flaps of her trousers from behind. He held her flat belly with one hand as the other roamed lower down. She panicked when she realised that in her hurry to change she had forgotten her frilly bits. For Joe the discovery was a green light but for Floe it was time to call a halt. Struggling only spurred Joe on as his fervour gained in intensity.

Sooner than expected, Floe heard her mother clumping down the corridor. She flew off Joe's lap, opened the writing desk and secretly welcomed her mother's timely arrival. Making sure her back was toward the door, she hurriedly adjusted her clothing. Joe was more leisurely and opened his case, purposely dropping some of the papers on the floor as a distraction. Auntie opened the door without knocking to see Floe with her head buried in the writing desk and Joe on all fours gathering his papers together.

'Where did I put that lad's ration book? I'm sure it was here when I checked earlier.'

He searched amongst the pile of papers without looking up, pretending he hadn't heard Auntie enter the room. When his hand touched her slipper he jumped in feigned surprise.

'Whoops! Where did you come from?'

Joe had recovered his composure in double quick time to put on the act and Floe could see that he was a professional at recovering from such situations.

'Good morning Lou, we've almost finished here I think,' Joe said as he checked the now completed form from Floe and returned it to his case.

'I've made a cup of tea in the kitchen Joe, would you like to come through and have a piece of cake too?' Auntie said, satisfied that Joe's visit had been entirely business like.

'Oh, thank you very much Lou that would be nice. I've been too busy to stop for anything today, let's take five,' he said as he threw a relieved sideways glance at Floe.

If there was one thing Floe liked about Joe then it was his impish and boyish ways, something close to a Peter Pan syndrome, in fact on that basis he wouldn't have been far out of place amongst the boys upstairs. His cheerfulness was all the more surprising since the loss of his first wife who died tragically in childbirth less than five years earlier. 'Life was made for the living' was his mantra. He took up with his present wife within six months and added to his family two months later.

In the kitchen, Auntie made tea and gave Joe a thick slice of buttered saffron from one of the newer loaves in the larder.

'That's great; I didn't stop for breakfast this morning. This will keep me going—.' He stopped when he saw the pair of them smiling.

'What?' He queried after he'd taken his first mouthful.

'Oh nothing, just a private joke, but don't come for cake next week,' Floe suggested as she started to burst out laughing. Auntie joined in and finally when she saw Joe peering into his cake, decided to put him out of his agony by owning up to their antics. Joe continued with his cake and looked thoughtful as he sipped his tea.

'How would it be Lou,' he began, 'if I could co-opt our Floe here on the Billeting Council as a non voting member? With more and more evacuees arriving every day and the office being short staffed, I've put forward the notion that perhaps it would be a good idea to co-opt one or two foster carers in an advisory capacity to help with matters directly affecting evacuees. Furthermore it would be good for you to have an ear in the enemy camp as you might say. We have a particular problem with suitability of billets and carers which is where your end-of-line experience would be useful. At present we virtually have to park the kids wherever we can and sort out the problems later. It might only be for one meeting just a few hours a week and you would be paid for your services including expenses. And another thing, having one foot in the Council door, who knows where it might take you. What do you think Floe?'

Floe needed no more persuasion. 'Sounds like a career move. Why not?'

Auntie, Floe and Joe all viewed the possibilities in a different light. Auntie, with thoughts of Joe's reputation was sceptical but agreed anyway, swayed by his convincing argument. Floe saw it through rose coloured spectacles whilst Joe was elated at the possibility of seeing more of Floe at Council functions. When he referred to 'not knowing where it might take you' he had in mind the chance of taking Floe on an official visit to some other Council and possibly an overnight stay. He rubbed his chubby hands together when they both agreed.

'Why not indeed, let's bring it on,' Joe confirmed as he made his exit and made a bee line for the Council offices.

Worsening of the evacuee problem enabled Joe to put his plans for Floe's election to the Billeting Council sooner than he thought. Evacuation officials in Whitehall had been dithering over decisions involving the vulnerability of cities which were most likely to be subject to air raids. At first it was thought that Plymouth being a dockyard town would be left in tact to prove useful to the enemy in the event of an invasion. It was therefore given a low priority. The premise proved to be incorrect. The subsequent blitz prompted a hasty decision to evacuate two hundred children from Plymouth to Cornwall. Notification of the evacuation and a warning of more to follow shortly were received only days in advance. Additional evacuation staff had to be found at short notice. Floe was amongst a team of extra staff thrown into the deep end to help integrate the newcomers into an already overloaded community. Someone like Floe with a record of twenty plus evacuees who could show how it could achieved was the ideal person needed to persuade more people to volunteer.

Initially Floe found that demands on her time were greater than those outlined by Joe which resulted in loading Grandma and Auntie with extra work. From time to time as the situation eased somewhat, Floe would arrive home with parcels 'procured' from the Americans but the suspicion was that they were not as Joe declared, part of the American War Aid programme. Richard was not aware of any such aid and was more concerned about Floe not being at home on at least two of his precious weekend leave periods. He immediately jumped to the conclusion that Alfie was involved and only calmed down when Auntie explained recent events. She explained the career possibilities which had suddenly opened up for Floe and that eventually they could both benefit. Auntie was careful not to mention where Joe fitted into the equation.

As the initial flood of newcomers reduced so did the work load making it possible for the Council to reduce the workforce and expenditure. Joe made sure Floe's position was safe by pulling strings and exaggerating her input. He pointed out that she understood foster carers better than most and could liaise between them and the Council to reduce unnecessary paperwork. She could also reduce the need for 'imposed fostering'.

At council meetings Joe was careful not to show his interest in Floe more than any other female member. Floe integrated well and soon gained the confidence of members particularly those close to Joe. They spoke highly of his ability to organise and get things done, but outside his circle there were others who were scathing of his sometimes unorthodox methods. Floe did her best to ride the fence, to nod and smile in the right places and laugh at jokes just to make the teller feel good even though at times she didn't think they were funny at all. She found Joe's ability to get things done involved currying favour either on the basis of 'you scratch my back I'll scratch yours' or at the bar. He often used Floe to glean information she had picked up but there was one use he made of her which proved fatal for his council membership.

In the process Floe learned a great deal more about Joe than he was prepared to divulge. She was aware of his reputation with women but there was deeper and more ruthless side of him which he kept hidden, even from his wife. He badly wanted to become Mayor and actively cultivated his friendships with that sole purpose in mind.

When a property developer friend offered Joe the opportunity of having a school named after him, calling it the "Freeman Secondary" he saw it as a possible feather in his cap and a way of gaining popularity in the town. Plans had already been submitted to the planning authorities and were due for consideration by the committee. Anxious for progress, they arranged a private meeting between themselves and the Chief Planning Officer (CPO) to discuss the chances of the application being successful. The developer had speculated with a plot of land knowing that it would soar in value and let Joe know that he was prepared to pay 'dessous de table' kickbacks to him and the planning officer for council leverage. Joe fell in line with the plan and a few days before the meeting telephoned the planning office to arrange a venue away from council offices. When informed that the CPO was not available Joe duped Floe into delivering a package directly to his office bypassing the secretary. The package was labelled "For the personal attention of—." Unfortunately the secretary met Floe as she was leaving and being already suspicious that Joe had tried to meet the CPO elsewhere, immediately opened the package. It full of twenty pound notes. There was no message. She telephoned the police who arrived soon afterwards to arrest Joe, Floe and the developer. The arrest caused quite a stir, enough for one 'anti-Joe' colleague to declare, 'the shit has hit the fan this time'.

Local newspapers had a field day.

Councillors arrested on possible corruption charge.

Mr. Joseph Phillip Freeman, a well known town councillor of 25 Birkett Avenue together with Mrs. Cicely Florence Manston, a co-opted member in the evacuation department, of 12 Mulberry Road were taken into custody today following an attempt to bribe Mr. Andrew Roberts, Chief Planning Officer in connection with the planning application for the proposed new secondary school at Wilton Green. Also arrested was the builder and property developer Mr. Ronald Henry Jenkins of 'Utopia' Denton Court. All three have been charged and released on bail pending further investigations.

Auntie heard the news in a newsflash on the local radio station whilst the trio were still being interviewed at the police station. She panicked and horrified at the prospect of a possible prison sentence she rang Sergeant Thompson for more news but he was unable to supply any additional information. Our tea was late that day and as she was struggling through the tea preparations on her own, Floe returned home.

'They've released me,' she said as the pair embraced on the doorstep.

'I was worried sick about you Cice.'

'It's OK Ma, I've done nothing wrong; just been naive I suppose.'

'Well, I must admit, I've had my doubts about Joe. People talk you know.'

Two days later, a subsequent newspaper article made reference to Floe.

Council worker cleared of wrongdoing.

With reference to the article in Tuesday's edition of the Courier, it has been established that Mrs. Manston was an innocent party to the bribery case and has been cleared of all charges. She has accepted the apology from the Chief Inspector of Stanhope Constabulary who stated that the police were duty bound to make the arrest and question all possible suspects. Mrs. Manston has since resigned her position and has no designs on ever returning to public office.

The following week the Courier headlines were more alarming.

Shake-up at Council Offices.

The investigation into the bribery charge against Councillor Mr. Joseph Freeman has not been able to produce sufficient evidence to establish guilt beyond all reasonable doubt. Property developer Mr. Jenkins has denied any involvement and makes no claim to any sums of money allegedly made in his name. In a further statement he has said that as far as he was aware his application for planning permission was proceeding like any other and that he was hopeful of a satisfactory outcome to satisfy an urgent need for the proposed school.

Additional inquiries into Mr. Freeman's activities cast doubts on his integrity with regard to alleged illegal transactions conducted with the US Forces in the procurement of army supplies, but the camp commander would not be drawn into making any statement. Three other councillors were also implicated and all four have tendered their resignations. There was a somewhat happier conclusion to the debacle in that the Council has found themselves better off to the tune of five thousand pounds from the anonymous benefactor.

Auntie stopped short of telling Floe that she had been sailing too close to the wind with Joe but warned her not to be too friendly and trusting with men in future.

'People talk and in a town like this and it soon gets around without the help of people like Joe who after all was only looking after number one. He won't be coming around here anymore. I can tell you that Richard was not best pleased when you got the Council job and jumped to the conclusion that Alfie was involved with your extra time away from home. I purposely avoided mentioning Joe simply because he would have been an extra cause for concern. You are a very attractive young woman and it's only natural for men to swarm around you like bees to a honey pot. You've got responsibilities now so make sure Richard is number one in your life. I would hate you to become a statistic like so many other young wives whose men are away.'

'OK Ma, thanks for the pep talk. I'll try to keep work and pleasure separate and remind Alfie that my extended working hours are causing a problem at home.'

CHAPTER 7

Dowdales School was made up of a number of separate buildings some of which had been hurriedly constructed on a temporary basis and looked more like large sheds. They were basically timber with flat roofs unlike the more substantial steel dining hall which required more attention to detail and was built as a more permanent structure. The Captain's engineering knowledge and Army contacts had more to do with that than the less informed 'pen pushers' in the education offices. Extra accommodation was required to cope with the large influx of evacuees with result that the school was vastly over crowded and near breaking point. Despite the challenges, it was largely due to the Captain's tight ship policy and organisational ability that the school continued to operate successfully. In Wendy's class alone there were forty three boys which meant that the desks had to be pushed together to accommodate an extra thirteen places. All the other classes were similarly crowded making teaching very difficult. The boys came from all walks of life and although it was not officially recognised, discrimination was exercised between the locals, orphans and evacuees. I was well aware that being an evacuee I was at the bottom of the pile. Fortunately Wendy was one of the very few teachers who accepted us all as equal and where she recognised any spark of brightness or willingness to learn she did her best to encourage it.

Dennis and Daryl were both local kids and over our first lunch together they were surprised to hear my story of how I came to arrive at their school. As I talked, Wendy sitting on the next table overheard our conversation and made some notes on a small pad. Finally, she swivelled around in her chair to wag a finger at my two new friends.

'I couldn't help overhearing but I hope you two boys realise how lucky you are to live at home with your parents.'

'Yes Miss, we know, I've just told him that and he can come home and have tea at our house tonight,' said Daryl, looking genuinely sorry for me.

'I would leave it for a while Daryl,' Wendy said, 'but it's very kind of you to offer and I'm sure Francis will be able to visit you later. He came to school with me today and he doesn't know his way home yet. I promised his auntie that I would take him back.'

Wendy left the three of us to become further acquainted whilst she went to the school staff room where she had no difficulty in attracting the Captain's eye to let him know what she had learned from me. Whilst in the company of other staff members, the Captain exercised great restraint and was careful not to let his inner feelings toward her be common knowledge. He listened intently, nodding from time to time.

'Look my dear,' he said putting his hand tentatively on her arm, 'as you know this evacuation has given me many headaches and I am fully aware that settling these newcomers into our school leaves much to be desired. I must not be seen to favour any member of staff above another and I have to run a tight and disciplined ship. Anything else would result in failure. That has to be avoided at all costs. One of the causes why these children find themselves in such circumstances is that there is no vetting strategy for housing them and as such, the billeting department at the town hall can only do a half of a job. There is such a backlog of children waiting for foster homes that foster parents are now being ordered to take them. Believe you me there are some worse off than Francis. As a military man, I have to be objective, but I don't want you to think that I am not doing my very best to ensure that this situation improves for the better.'

'Well Captain, she said, 'I am gratified that you think that way and I for my part will assist you in any way I can.'

The Captain's mini speech was overheard by several other members of staff who clapped in agreement confirming that they too would assist the Captain wherever possible.

'Hear, hear,' Mr. Hoskins, the maths teacher added.

Mr. Patrick Hoskins was always first to applaud and complement the headmaster but all the other members of staff were well aware that his accolades were only skin deep. To be fair, his loyalty had been seriously tested when, despite being the most experienced member of staff, he was passed over with regard to the choice of assistant head. A few eyebrows were raised when the position was awarded to Miss Larkin on the personal recommendation of the Captain. There was a hint of prejudice in the air. It was obvious he didn't want his authority undermined in any way, especially by a strong character like Patrick, who apart from any other consideration, stood at least a foot taller.

The staff all knew their headmaster loved to be addressed as 'Captain' but many secretly thought that he was still pretending to be in the army. To some degree that was quite true and he himself preferred to carry his stick in true military fashion to maintain that connection. He regarded it as his badge of office. He was also able to exercise his tight ship policy with the local Home Guard where he had been selected as the most suitable candidate with World War 1 front line experience to defend the shores in our area. His qualification for the post was never in any doubt. As a single man looking for excitement he volunteered to join the Expeditionary Force which was defeated at the battle of Mons-Charleroi during early German skirmishes. He then saw action in the successful defence of Ypres in 1915 and witnessed terrible scenes of carnage in the battle of the Somme. It was after only two years in the army that his bravery and leadership finally earned him promotion to that of Captain in 1918 when the Allies entered Ostend during the liberation of the channel ports.

He organised the local platoon to build cliff top fortifications and to construct a number of look out positions. There was an occasion when yobbos broke into and destroyed one of them so that they could build camps of their own. He immediately blamed the evacuees but when he set a trap for the culprits and discovered they were local lads he was forced to tone down his temper and only deal with them to the satisfaction of their parents and the judiciary. In an effort to further establish his authority there were at least two occasions when he became physically involved with the boys.

The most notable occurred when one boy stepped out of line showing no respect for his authority. The Captain had his own way of dealing with such boys in the first instance by liberal use of the cane. Caning seemed to have little affect on one thick skinned boy with the result they became involved in a heated argument, but the Captain was determined not to give way despite being some six inches shorter.

When the Captain made as if to give him a good thick ear with the cane, the boy wrestled it from him and promptly threw it out the window. A hushed silence fell in the classroom as the Captain flushed crimson red and the boy fearing retaliation, squared up to defend himself.

'That's what I think about your bloody cane, you're not going to hit me with it.'

'Ho! Ho! Is that what you think you little toe rag? I must warn you that I am a black belt trained in unarmed combat and I've eaten bigger fellows than you for breakfast.'

Here the Captain teasingly adopted the classic karate poise.

'I don't care what colour your flipping belt is, you can't frighten me.'

The Captain looked more determined than ever to teach the boy a lesson and the rest of the class needed no convincing they were in for some fireworks.

'Is that so, sonny boy?'

'Yes it is! What you going to do about it?' The boy stuck out his chin taunting the Captain further.

At this point the Captain accepted the challenge.

'Alright my beauty, if you fancy your chances, let's go outside. There isn't enough room here because I'm going to give the hiding of your miserable life and spread you all over the playground.'

With this announcement the class erupted into a cheer with no fear of recrimination since it was obvious to all that as far as the Captain was concerned, they didn't exist any more.

The whole class scrambled over their desks toward the windows anxious to get the best vantage point. Other children passing by in the corridor broke ranks to witness the spectacle.

As soon as they were outside the boy stopped on a grassy bank, keen to strike the first blow. The Captain adopted his now familiar pose, then quick as a flash delivered a 'tsuki' to the boy's midriff followed by a 'mae-geri' to his legs, sending him sprawling. A groan rumbled from the biased audience as their champion was down without so much as throwing a punch.

'Cor! Looks as if 'Tomo' meant what he said then, Herby's going to be taken apart.'

Once down, the Captain fell on his victim, knocking the wind out of him and proceeded to apply a head lock. There was a lot of shouting and swearing from the boy with arms and legs flashing about in all directions. On the floor the boy's superior suppleness and agility came to his aid and was spurred on by encouragement from the classroom above. Pieces of clothing flew off and soon blood appeared on both faces. One passive boy in the classroom thought the fight had gone far enough.

'Christ! I think there're going to kill each other. I'm going to fetch Hoskers and tell him to get the police.'

'Nah! Na! Don't,' the whole class chorused.

'I don't think so,' said another boy, 'Hoskers will lap it up.'

'Let 'em get on with it, what a great show! Wouldn't have missed this for nothing,' another boy shouted.

'Hey up lads, they're coming in, I think they've had enough,' said another.

On their return, despite having visited the washroom on the way, both still showed signs of blood and The Captain's face was red in comparison to the boy's pale one. They returned to the classroom in silence. The confrontation was over. The boy returned to his seat whilst the Captain, complete with retrieved stick under his arm, returned to his desk to resume command as forcibly as ever but secretly struggled to regain his dignity.

After school that day, Herby was declared a national hero and parents coming to meet their children were amused to see him being carried head high out through the school gates.

'Old Tomo called a halt just as I was getting the better of him,' he boasted, knowing full well there was no winner.

The Captain's authority had taken a serious blow and Herby knew that he was a marked man. He didn't want to remain at the school for a moment longer than he had to and counted the days to the end of term.

Wendy loved to see men in uniform and when out walking with her spaniel dog, she often saw the Home Guard practicing their defence routines on the coastal headland near her home. It was her way of winding down after a day's turmoil at school. The day of the Captain's particular turmoil coincided with Home Guard target practice using live rounds. In the interests of safety, it was necessary for the senior member of the platoon to be present, but on that day the Captain soon found that the fight with the boy had taken more out of him than he dared to admit. He was in need off a less stressful activity and as soon as possible he dismissed his platoon, inviting them to join him at the local bar.

On her way home Wendy called at the bar to collect some bottles of ginger beer to take home and was surprised to find the Captain and a few of his men having a drink.

'Oh! This is a pleasant surprise to see you Ms Nicholson,' he said, 'Would you care to join us in one for the road?'

He had changed from his daily plus fours and tweed jacket which he usually wore at school and was now smartly dressed in his Captains uniform, complete with medals lanyard and whistle. She in turn was almost unrecognisable, wearing dungarees, sloppy jumper and short Wellington boots whilst her blonde tresses were now hidden under a woollen cap. No-one other than the Captain and his sergeant took much notice as she came in.

'Who's your lady friend then PJ?' the sergeant whispered as he moved his chair to allow Wendy to join the group.

The Captain's men were off duty and were allowed to be less formal than in the field, where he assumed total command and was adamant that sloppiness in any form could cost lives.

'Allow me to introduce one of my staff members, Ms Nicholson,' he said without elucidating her position any further.

The other men nodded and continued talking, whilst the Captain moved over to the bar.

'He must have got something I haven't,' the lance jack muttered to the others. 'She's a bit of alright, how does he do it?'

'He can turn on the flannel and knows all the moves but I can't say he's my favourite flavour of the week,' Patrick whispered, 'but he's my boss and I often wonder how different things would be if he was brought down a peg.'

'That would take some doing, there's not much of him now,' one of them commented.

The group burst out laughing, causing everyone to look in their direction.

Fearing that their conversation had been overheard, Patrick stood up to cover his embarrassment by pretending to visit the toilet. The Captain visibly bristled, but chose to ignore the group.

'What can I get you Ms Nicholson?' he said opening his money pouch and then closing it again as he approached the bar.

'Well actually, I came in to take some ginger beers home, so I'll have one of those if that's OK,' she said.

'Of course, no problem, in fact I'll get you a pack of six to take out, you can break into them.'

The Captain was very liberal with his Company's expenses and told the barman to put the bill on his chitty. The barman nodded, provided a wine glass and opened the first bottle ready for the Captain to return to the table.

Conversations around the table varied from the weather to the size of carrots to be exhibited at the garden club's local competition the following day. It was one of the Captain's rules that when off duty, discussions about the progress of the War were to be strictly avoided. He made sure that the popular slogan of the day, 'Walls have ears', was foremost in the minds of his men. Both Wendy and the Captain joined in the general conversation whenever they felt they could make a useful contribution but deep down they both knew what was really uppermost in their minds. Wendy finally emptied her glass and made a move to leave.

'I'll be off home now, thanks for the drink and the interesting chat. It's good to talk and listen to someone other than the children all day.'

The men got up politely and nodded whilst the Captain having finished his drink, made to open the door.

'I'll see you home Ms Nicholson,' he said, waving to his men as he followed her out the door.

'I don't want to drag you away from your men on my account Captain,' she said.

'Oh no it's OK we've just about finished, I was planning cut our games a bit short tonight, it's been a long eventful day,' he said as they walked toward her cottage.

It was the first time she had heard him describe his involvement with the Home Guard as being 'games' when secretly at school other male members of staff said the same behind his back. They regarded his reluctance to shed his army rank as Captain as vanity in order to be superior.

'Yes Captain,' she said, 'I did hear a rumour that you were physically involved with Herbert Matisley today but I could not believe it. You know how stories can be inflated as they pass from one to another.'

The Captain stopped abruptly and faced her head on.

'Look,' he said, 'when we are off duty and away from school, I wish you would call me PJ. I have the same arrangement with my men and it works well. If you don't mind, I would like to call you Wendy by the same token. I can't have you calling me Captain all the time or for me to call you Ms Nicholson, it's all so long winded.'

'Very well, PJ, I quite like it,' she said.

'And I can't say Wendy that I was proud of myself today, the rumour was quite true and I regret losing my cool but that weasel Matisley crossed the line and unfortunately, I followed suit. It was a bad day and I will make a full statement tomorrow in the staff room.'

She caught the tone of his voice, it was full of remorse. 'My God he is human after all,' she thought and as such, more in terms of being his equal than his subordinate.

They continued toward the cottage with a lighter step, both having felt they had broken down some imaginary defences. For the Captain they were defences he would loved to have broken down long ago but he knew that as head of the school, pecking orders had to be preserved. Wendy had been a member of his staff for eighteen months or more and the realisation that he knew nothing about her at all after she left school grew stronger each day. In his mind he thought that any red blooded man was not a man at all if he could ignore her good looks and female form. After some fifteen minutes, they stopped at the gate of an oldie-world cottage built during the early nineteen hundreds with a long garden laid mostly with lawn flanked on either side by flower beds and a gravelled entrance to the front door.

'This is delightful, Wendy. How long have you lived here?'

'I like it too PJ, it used to belong to my parents and I took every opportunity I could to come home during my college holidays. My father, who used to travel abroad a lot, bought it in preparation for his retirement and in the meanwhile I was good company for my mother.

Unfortunately, they've passed on now so I inherited it from them. I miss them a lot, but time is a great healer. Initially I thought I would not be able to live here on my own but I'm so attached to the house I don't think I could ever part with it. My two years at teachers training college helped me to get over the loss and then as you know I accepted the teaching post at Dowdales. I keep busy with the garden and I love the coast and countryside here. It's my retreat from school and I realise now how lucky I am that my parents saw fit to put me through college and prepare for my future.'

The Captain listened and realised how little he knew of any of the other members of his staff either and without going to any great detail he began to think that perhaps in future he might make it a policy to find out a little about each of them. If nothing else, it might be useful for him to understand and perhaps be more aware of what made his them tick. It dawned on him in a moment of self criticism that perhaps to date he had been too single-minded in his day to day operation of the school. If snippets of information about his staff came to light without probing, as in Wendy's case, so be it. Patrick Hoskins flashed into his mind; he would make a good starting point being someone he hadn't quite fathomed.

'Would you like to come in and let me reduce my debt by offering you one of your own ginger beers?' She enquired with a smile.

They both laughed aloud as the entered the front door, passed through the kitchen and into a small but cosy sitting room.

'Here we are PJ, take the weight of your feet, and make yourself comfortable while I get your beer.'

She went into the kitchen and returned with two glasses on top of the beers.

'You can open them, while I get out of these old togs and wellies,' she said as she went up the open plan staircase in the corner.

On her return, the beers were gassing invitingly in the glasses and PJ had already drunk half of his.

'I could get used to this,' he said, thinking of his own house where he had no-one to provide waitress service as Wendy had done.

'Without realising it Wendy,' he began, 'you've taught me something today. It just shows that even at my age there's still more to learn.'

'Goodness me PJ, what can it be? I wouldn't have thought it possible.'

'That's for me to know and you to find out,' he said tapping the side of his nose.

They chatted about the plight of the town's evacuees and the orphan home further out on the headland. He mentioned that he himself was an orphan and could empathise with the boys and that when he retired he intended to help integrate them from their confinement back into society. He told her something of his own life, how he had never married having been too involved with his military career and what plans he had for improving the school. Wendy spoke of her interest in playing the piano and that she had two girls, daughters of a friend, who made weekly visits to learn. Suddenly, she noticed PJ's eyes close as he fell asleep. Rather than wake him up, she began reading a book she had started earlier. It was Tom Brown's School Days, one of those classics which somehow she had not found time for before. There were a number of such books on her bookshelves given to her over the years and now finally she had made her mind up to read them. Looking over the top of her book, a chapter or so later, the Captain was still sleeping soundly, looking as if he would not be moving for many hours. Without disturbing him she gently laid a blanket over him. 'You're a funny old stick to be sure,' she murmured as she tucked in the edges and left the room.

He was an early riser. Réveillé was ingrained in his very being; to him breaking the habit would have been like losing half the day. A shaft of sunlight streamed across his face, waking him up. He stirred thinking someone was shining a torch in his face but then realised where he was; the unfinished beer still on the table.

'Oh my God,' he said to himself, 'What must she think of me?'

He was desperate to relieve himself and not wishing to clump around up stairs in an unfamiliar house he managed to find a suitable discrete patch of trees in the back garden. On his return to the kitchen he splashed his face with water, dried his hands and starting thinking about making a pot of tea and possibly some toast. He eventually found most of what he was looking for but the tea was a problem which almost caused him to give up. One glass jar labelled 'egg powder' saved the day. Looking at his watch he noticed that it was not yet quite seven and rather early to be returning the waitress services to Wendy. Armed with his tea and toast, he sat down at the table where there were a number of magazines and newspapers.

An hour later, he heard a timely movement in the bedroom above. He quickly made her a cup of tea, found a tray, went to her room and knocked smartly on the door.

'Room service madam,' he said with a broad grin as he pushed the door open with his foot.

Wendy was sitting up in an imposing and grand four-poster bed which was elaborately upholstered and rather too big for the room. Her blonde hair was draped over one shoulder whilst the other was bare except for the flimsy nightie strap. His pulse rate jumped into a higher gear causing him to take a deep breath before he could move forward.

'I can't believe that I crashed out in your armchair like that. When I woke up it was like being in a dream. What on earth must you think of me?'

'Don't think anymore about it PJ, your lapse has provided me with a waiter. I can't remember the last time I had tea in bed.' You had a bad day yesterday and needed a good sleep. You looked so peaceful I didn't have the nerve to wake you up and anyway it was quite a way for you to walk home at that time of night. The alternative was for me to give you a lift and I didn't want to go out again.'

'I've found my way around your kitchen. I can bring you some toast if...'

She cut him off in mid sentence.

'I don't eat breakfast as a rule, a cup of tea's fine.'

She made room on the bed and patted the spot for him to place the tray and in doing so he was immediately intoxicated by her fragrant perfume. Animal instincts began to take over his normally restrained feelings such that he had great difficulty in preventing himself from tearing back those silken sheets and taking advantage of her there and then. He felt his face get warm and his heart miss a few beats. Sensibly he moved back out of temptation.

'I'll leave you to your tea then Wendy; I'll be finishing mine in the kitchen until you are ready.'

He returned to the kitchen, desperately trying to normalise his heart rate as he went down the stairs and felt guilty about his improper thoughts. On Sunday, he thought absolution at Confessional would be his only salvation on penalty of numerous 'Hail Marys'. Half an hour later Wendy, wearing a full length pleated dress and loose fitting jacket, looking as stunning as ever, announced she was ready to leave for school.

'I'll give you a lift,' she said.

She drove a two seated Morris eight tourer which she could convert to a saloon model with the aid of a soft top canopy. Inviting as it was to be driven to school only inches away from this blonde beauty, sanity prevailed and he gracefully declined.

'It's only three miles,' he said, 'it's is a beautiful day and a good stiff walk into town will blow away the cobwebs. I need to set myself up for the day ahead. I want to address the Matisley case head on and take soundings amongst the staff. The boy is certainly a most objectionable character but I am afraid that my reaction will not be accepted by all. I may even have to consider my position as headmaster of the school.'

'I sincerely hope not PJ. If it's any consolation, I want you to know that you have my wholehearted backing on the matter and would hate to see someone like Matisley be the cause of your retirement.'

She drove away, fully confident that he would make the right decision as usual. Even his refusal of a lift into school was a good one when she entertained the thought that perhaps for all and sundry to see the two of them arriving at school together might set tongues wagging.

CHAPTER 8

There was a common phrase liberally used amongst the ranks of the UK armed forces, 'over here and over sexed' which highlighted their unwillingness to share female company. Other thorns in the UK forces side were that the Yanks seemed to have plenty of free time, their military service more laid back and they took full advantage of their greater affluence. In addition they buzzed around quite freely in their jeeps. Wilbur was no exception to the rule but to be fair he was as much available to any evacuee as he was to any girl who happened to be around. He was also well known and respected at our local Wesley church where he supported the Reverend Richards in providing entertainment with talks, slide shows and lessons on jeep motor mechanics. The Reverend made use of Wilbur when twelve of our crowd turned up one Sunday morning after quitting the Church of England further down the town over a matter of missing donations from the offertory plate. Following the incident where money went missing from her handbag Auntie questioned the whole lot of us starting with the Rowe brothers. Satisfied that we were telling the truth she delivered an ultimatum to the vicar that unless the accusation was dropped all 'her boys' would quit the choir en bloc. That Sunday the church congregation had to struggle along without one.

Wilbur and the Reverend got together and decided that with the number we were there was only one new identity which fitted. They nicknamed us The Twelve Apostles. We were a rough rag tag bunch of kids who didn't deserve the title and for most of us that was as close as we ever got to being religious. We liked Wilbur right from the start. One activity which always attracted a crowd was that of taking us to the beach for jeep driving lessons. I learned to drive one by the age of ten with the aid of special wooden blocks which he made to enable my short legs reach the pedals. But there was an incident at tea time one evening when our motoring education and association with Wilbur almost came to an end. As usual all the boys were seated around the table anxiously waiting to start. Floe was putting the last few pieces of cake on a large plate when she asked the boys what they had been doing that day. Mike was first to answer.

'We've been playing with Uncle Wilbur's willy on the beach Auntie,' he boasted.

'Yeah, and once we found out what to do, he let us all have a go,' Frank added.

A horrified and devastated Floe dropped the plate as she stared at Mike who had no conception of what thoughts were passing through her mind. She trusted Wilbur and asked herself the question 'Is this how he repays me? Has he used me to get to the boys?'

The jeep was a product of two American car companies, Willys-Overland and Ford Motor Corporation and the name 'jeep' was a derivation of the acronym GP for the General Purpose vehicle. Our Wilbur was keen to demonstrate the finer features of his 'Willy' as he called it, not thinking there would ever be a problem with language misinterpretation or we would repeat it to the uninitiated.

Auntie heard the plate smash as Floe screamed. 'Oh my God! No!'

Floe dragged Mike by his collar and frog marched him down the corridor where she met Auntie in the doorway on her way out to check if Floe was alright. Auntie rejoined Grandma in the sitting room followed by Floe as she barged in, shoved Mike into a chair and began an almost hysterical outburst.

'This is just too bad, I can't believe it, something will have to be done about this,' she blurted out. 'We'll have to report Wilbur to his commander. He will have to be moved on, court marshalled or whatever they do—!' She paused for breath. 'Go on Mike tell Auntie what you've just told me.'

'What on earth's the matter Cice? Sit down or you'll burst a blood vessel.'

'I washed my hands as best as I could Auntie,' Mike pleaded, holding them out in front of him for inspection. I managed to clean most off with sand and seaweed.

'Is that oil Mike?' she said.

'Yes Auntie I couldn't get it all off, I really tried, honest,' he said crossing his chest with the sign of a cross. 'We checked the oil level in the sump and changed a plug in Wilbur's jeep 'cos the engine was misfiring. We had a great time and I got up to forty miles an hour.'

'It's alright dearie, go back to your tea now,' said Grandma as she smiled and patted Mike on the head.

Grandma couldn't stop laughing and finally had to leave the room when she wet herself. Auntie giggled too, by which time Floe had managed to start breathing normally again. Grandma came back into the room.

'I've been reading about jeeps in the paper,' she explained. 'President Eisenhower says that with the jeep, the landing craft and the Dakota the Americans can win the war. It seems that with the help of your Wilbur they can educate our kids as well.'

Grandma and Auntie looked at Floe, sitting in a chair with her hand on her forehead. 'It was the way he came out with it,' she said. 'It was so sudden; my mind was elsewhere and I've smashed that big blue serving dish.'

'You're white as a sheet Floe, have a cup of tea,' Auntie suggested.

'Just shows how easy it is to jump to conclusions, eh Lou,' Grandma added as Floe returned to the kitchen. 'I like Wilbur, he's a nice young man and I know Reverend holds him in high esteem. When you were away visiting your friends last weekend, he delivered the sermon and spoke about the need for friendships and how the nations of the world can unite to defeat aggression. He will laugh his socks off when we tell him.'

Even Wendy got to hear of the story from one of the staff and from then on the familiar sight of the jeeps as they buzzed past her Morris were seen in a different light. On her way home from school one evening two of them tried to taunt her into a race on a straight piece of road. To general whoops and whistle calls she steadfastly refused to be drawn even though she knew her car had good acceleration and could give any jeep a run for its money. Her father had maintained it well and had improved its performance way above its meagre eight horse power, but the fifty horse power jeep even with the extra weight of four GI's would have been more than a match for any Morris, hotted up or not. Feeling a little flushed she stopped to open her gate when one of the jeeps returned.

'Hi there' the driver said, nonchalantly leaning out the open topped jeep. Hope we didn't upset you Mam, my pals are a little high spirited and I must apologise on their behalf. Allow me to introduce myself, I am Wilbur Dwight Capolla. At your service,' he said as he bowed and made a lavish sweep of his arm down to his waist.

With a broad smile he saluted in classic American style and made off down the road to rejoin his buddies. Wendy smiled, raised her hand in acknowledgement and continued to park her car without giving any further thought to the chance meeting. On the mat she found a brief note from her friend Ellie.

'The girls will not be coming this evening owing to feeling a 'little under the weather.' They are both feeling bilious having eaten something at school. Talk to you on Thursday.'

Ellie and Wendy were friends since their teacher training days and taught at the same school but Ellie had been away for a few days on a further training programme. Her husband, like so many others was away on active service in India and the Far East and she let Wendy know how much she missed him. 'Now that I'm back with my parents and until he comes home, it's like being single all over again.' Not having the responsibility of home and garden to look after, she looked for outside interests, which in a town full of Americans, was not difficult to find. She tried to be discrete in saying she spent time with Wendy and often used her as an alibi on occasions when she didn't return home to her parents. Wendy liked Ellie because of her 'joie de vivre' and had plenty of time to enjoy her company when the two girls were practicing on her piano.

Feeling she could make better use of her unexpected free time, Wendy spent the rest of the evening preparing for future lessons and catching up on marking test papers.

Back at school the following day, there was a buzz in the air with regard to the reported fight the day before. An announcement had been made at Assembly that there would be an immediate special meeting in the staff room and that classes would be delayed by fifteen minutes. The extra time was to be used to include a pep talk on the general theme of behaviour, body language and how to conduct ourselves in public. This was greeted with appropriate groans and cat calls from rank and file supporters of the Matisley crowd. No particular reference was made to the fight but there were further noises from members of staff in the Hoskins camp speculating that perhaps the Captain was proposing to resign.

'As many of you are aware,' he began, 'I was involved in physical confrontation with Herbert Matisley from class six and in order to clear the air I would like to apologise for the obvious disturbance and for any difficulties you may experience in the coming days. I hardly need to remind you of this boy's reputation and I will therefore be writing to the Authorities today explaining the situation and recommending that he be expelled forthwith. I invite any comments any of you care to make. Thank you.'

Much to the Captain's relief, the staff members clapped in agreement.

'I agree completely Captain,' Mr. Hoskins added, 'the boy's a bully, a thug and a rogue with only a few months remaining before he leaves. The chances of improving his education above the insignificant amount he has already achieved, I feel are very slim.'

General agreement broke out again with more clapping. There was also a hint of relief on some faces, especially when there was no talk of resignation.

Wendy experienced no such problems with her class. Any problems she did have were not connected to the Matisley case but from boys who were slow learners which necessitated the class being spilt into two streams. I joined Dennis and Daryl in the top stream and all three of us progressed well to the extent that we were always first, second, and third whenever any test results were announced. We competed against each other and soon found ourselves well above the standard of the others. Wendy was a born teacher and was always interested to encourage us and when later we took our grammar school entry examination, six months early, the three of us passed with flying colours. When the results were announced, however, the unnecessary discriminatory element reared its head once more to record that two local students and one evacuee had been successful. The odd thing about that pass result was that I never heard any more about it. At the time I didn't attach the degree of importance to it as perhaps I should have done and being on the list for repatriation to my home town I must have slipped through the net.

The policies of discrimination and segregation seemed to be ingrained into the very fabric of local Authority thinking and emanated right from the top. It was probably as a result of the sudden influx of too many evacuees from all walks of life and the fact that some people resented their arrival. Change can be difficult to except but sudden change even more so. A blatant example of the policy occurred when the register was called each morning. When a boy's name was called he had to answer and to state whether he was a local, an orphan or an evacuee. To conform in as small a way as possible with this requirement, Wendy merely suffixed each name on her register with an 'L', 'O' or 'E' making it unnecessary to answer in that manner. In so doing, although we did not realise it at the time, a little of our dignity was restored. Some people showed a lack of understanding and appreciation of the traumas we had suffered as a result of the blitz together with being torn away from our homes. We felt we were at the bottom of the pile and did not need any further reminder.

On Thursday that week, Ellie returned to school back from her further training course. In the staff room at lunch time she told Wendy that she'd had a fabulous time with some Americans who were carrying out manoeuvres and training on the nearby moors. With a number of other girls she had been invited to an evening dance at their camp.

'We had a great time, Wendy, you should try it. I've learnt how to jitterbug and jive, dances I've never tried before. Those Yanks never know when to stop. They were all over us and I didn't miss one dance. The chap I was with at the end was a bit cheeky, but I loved it. He said he would pick me up when they have their next dance on Saturday. It's going to be at the NAAFI club, you've simply got to come. Will you? Go on Wendy. Say you will. I guarantee you won't regret it.'

'I'll think about it Ellie. I can't remember the last time I went dancing; it must have been at college. Will the girls be coming tomorrow? We can have a chat then.'

Knowing Ellie could be very persistent Wendy began to get the feeling that her friend was not going to take 'no' for an answer. They were two unlike poles, introvert and extrovert which was probably why they got on so well. But it wasn't always like that. Wendy changed after separating from a fellow college boyfriend and it took a long time for her to get over the parting. Ellie was her best medicine and invariably they could be found together over tea breaks and lunches chatting and giggling about things which to others might not have seemed funny at all. Ellie had an impish grin which Wendy found infectious sometimes resulting in bouts of uncontrollable laughter for both of them. Her two girls were out of the same mould and at times Wendy found it difficult to make them concentrate on their music once one started to giggle.

'Yes the girls are feeling better. I'll bring them over as usual and I'll show you a few dance steps as well. I bet you'll enjoy it.'

When she arrived home that evening there was a large bunch of flowers and a pink envelope on her doorstep with a card attached which simply read, 'From the boys. Wilbur'. Feeling a little flushed she put the flowers in a vase and was just opening the envelope when there was a knock on the door. To her surprise, standing there looking clean and tidy as if he had made a special effort was Wilbur. Standing at least six feet tall, he had to lower his head to stand in the porch doorway. She guessed he was in his mid twenties. He was clean shaven with a military style close cropped haircut and wore shades like some traffic cop. As he pushed them onto his forehead with one finger to expose more of his face she thought he was better looking than she remembered from the brief meeting the day before.

'Hi Wendy,' he said, 'I've been waiting for you. Hope you like the flowers; they are from the four of us. Are they your size?' he said pointing at the envelope.

'I don't know,' she replied. 'What are they?'

'A couple of pairs of nylons you'll need for the dance on Saturday. I don't want to interrupt now but my buddies and I would like you to join us at the NAAFI club. We threw dice to decide which one of us would ask you, and I won. Can we pick you up at eight?'

He knows my name she thought, as she hesitated trying to find some way to refuse the almost total stranger. She convinced herself that he was a fine young chap so what harm could there be in going to a dance? It could be fun just like Ellie said, but what Ellie had forgotten to say was that having told her dancing partner all about her, the discovery of 'new talent' was all over the camp.

'Thank you for the flowers, they are lovely, but how do you know my name?' she asked.

'We go to dances as much as we can and my buddies make it their business to find out. We know all about you and now your one of us. Is it a date? Attractive girls like you are in short supply around these parts. I'd be proud to take you.'

'Well, maybe, I'll think about it.'

She made a move to close the door.

'OK! At least you haven't said 'No' then,' he shouted as he drove away.

The next day she caught up with Ellie in the school staff room before Assembly.

'I want a word with you,' she said trying to look serious.

'Why? What's the matter?' Ellie replied looking worried.

'You told your Yank about me and now a crowd of them want to take me to the NAAFI club on Saturday.'

'That's great,' Ellie said. 'You will have a fabulous time. I can give you some nylons to wear. Promise me you'll come.'

'Wilbur has already given me some.'

'Oh! You've met then and you know his name already, that's progress. He's rather dishy don't you think?'

In the evening Ellie and the girls arrived for their piano lessons and soon Wendy set the two girls working on a duet they were hoping to perform at a local music festival. In the meanwhile Ellie set up the gramophone player with a lively Count Base record.

'I'll show the basic steps of the jive first, I'll be the man,' Ellie said, removing her sweater. 'You will warm up quickly so take your cardigan off.'

After a short while both were perspiring and Wendy had acquired a pink glow.

'I do believe you've got it Wendy,' Ellie said, 'and when you're with a man it will be easier because he will push you around. I think you're a natural and better than me. There are other moves which only a man can show you, but you will pick them up soon enough.'

Ellie was careful not to elaborate on the 'other moves' such as the one where the man turns the girl upside-down and over his head, a move which always raises a cheer. She remembered that when it happened to her she almost fainted and had to hang on.

'Phew!' Wendy said, 'Let's have a drink. If I decide to come, what shall I wear?'

'Oh anything goes but don't forget you'll get hot in no time. With nylons you can wear cotton dresses.

The two girls came in from the music room.

'We've finish our piece, Wendy,' they said, not being entirely truthful. 'This looks fun can we join in, Mummy?'

'Well, it looks as if lessons are over for today,' said Ellie, more as a question to Wendy than a comment, 'we need two partners anyway. I'll put the record on again. Practice makes perfect they say.'

Ellie and the girls went home later than usual that evening and Wendy flopped exhaustedly on her sitting room settee to contemplate her new found activity. She had to admit that she began to look forward to seeing Wilbur on Saturday. Later on when she began to think more sensibly she almost talked herself out of the date by thinking that she was no better than Ellie's two excitable teenagers rather than a fully grown woman. Finally she had to admit the die had been cast and that Ellie would not allow her to wallow at home. She decided she had done too much of that lately and there had to be more to life than work every day. After all, as Ellie was keen to remind her that during their teacher training course only eighteen months earlier things were very different and she was regarded as something of a live wire. Now was her chance to rekindle those sparks and begin to enjoy herself once more. Ellie would be there too, so why not?

CHAPTER 9

Richard came home early one weekend with an extended leave period but he was disappointed to find Floe laid low with some illness she had picked up in the cinema. When Flo complained of muscular aches and pains as well as a sore throat, Auntie called the doctor who diagnosed influenza. He told her to stay in bed for four or five days and prescribed aspirin to relieve the pain. Richard's furlough was destined to be a waste of time and if only he'd known, he could have stayed back at the base where at least he had access to a games room and a bar. He found his choices to be somewhat limited and not wanting to disturb Floe or catch her influenza he took to sleeping on the sofa in the sewing room. Auntie suggested he might like to take over Floe's role for a day or two but not being a domestic type he declined the invitation. He felt like a fish out of water and soon became bored until Auntie finally suggested on the Saturday that he went out for a drink with some of his friends to the local pub. On his way he met up with his neighbour from number two, Sam McIntyre home on leave from his RAF posting to India.

'Well, what do you know? I was just thinking about popping around to take your lovely wife out for a drink,' he joked. 'Fancy meeting you again Russell,' he said using Richard's nickname. 'Where's Floe? Wouldn't she like a night out? Go back and fetch her, I'd like to see her.'

'She's a bit under the weather Sam; picked up some sort of bug from the cinema. I haven't been called that in years,' Richard added. 'Don't tell everybody, they'll want to know why.'

Sam was a piper and wore a traditional Scottish Highland No.2 uniform complete with Argyll jacket, tartan kilt with fur sporran and ghillie brogues. Around his waist he wore a belt with an elaborate buckle and a small dirk tucked into the top of his right sock. With his abundant head of red hair long side burns and suntanned face he could have passed for a much older man but in actual fact he was the same age as Richard. In contrast to Sam's suntanned hairy arms and legs Richard was white as a lily, clean shaven and wore a plain RAF uniform. To see them together they were chalk and cheese. They had been pals for quite a number of years going back to their school days and until joining the forces they were inseparable. Their friendship extended into their love life and even though Richard took over Sam's fiancé when he was posted to India, Sam volunteered to be Richard's best man at the wedding. There was no animosity since by the time of the posting Floe's relationship had cooled and she admitted that she couldn't see herself marrying Sam anyway. At first, Floe was not interested in Richard. She fancied someone with a bit more 'go' in him, possibly a character like Sam and even someone with a higher rank than private. Later when Richard became a sergeant and a navigator she changed her mind. The nickname originated from Richard's tenacity like a Jack Russell terrier not to give up on women at the first hurdle.

'Aren't you a bit overdressed for the pub Sam?'

'No, I'm proud of mine and I wouldn't wear yours, it's dull and boring. I'll bet you the first pint I get served before you.'

The challenge was a wasted one. For a Saturday night the local was as quiet as the grave with only two customers leaning on the bar staring absentmindedly into their beers, saying nothing. He tried to strike up a conversation but only succeeded in getting a nod from one and not even that from the other. On seeing Sam, the barman literally sprang into action with the hope that his night's takings would be quadrupled. Sam asked the all important question.

'Has the beer improved since I've been away—?' He took a large swig of his first drink and pulled a long face. He turned to Richard. 'Ah well, since we're here we may as well make a start on getting blotto, I feel I need a pick-me-up. This place has gone to pot since the last time I was here; I see they've even got rid of big Brenda. She could get the pub rocking with her antics on the bar especially when she performed her tap dancing routine. Let's down these two and find somewhere with a bit more life. There's a dance on at the NAAFI club, it gets a bit crowded with the Yanks, but the beer and cigs are cheap.'

By half past nine the Military Police were about to close the doors to prevent overcrowding, but Richard and Sam just made it in time. The live band was making quite a good job of a Glen Miller tune, 'In the Mood,' after what must have been something more hectic. There was a five deep crowd at the bar trying to get drinks and all the tables were full with men and girl dancers perspiring and looking flushed. Quite a number of chairs were creaking under the weight of men with girls on their laps and all the tables were festooned with drinks in various stages of consumption. From somewhere in the smoke filled haze of the near tropical atmosphere a voice was trying to announce the next dance above the noise of the hubbub at the bar.

'It's a jitterbug, all the Yanks will be up for this one, now's our chance for a drink Russell old chap,' Sam said as he forged his way to the less crowed bar. 'Four beers and two double drams Jimmy, thank you.'

His strong Scottish voice rang out, belying his mere five foot four stature and not for the first time the uniform magic worked and the barman immediately took his order. A table became free as the dancers made their way to the pocket sized dance floor in the middle of the room.

'This should keep us going for a wee while; a couple more of these and I reckon I could do that,' Sam said as he nodded toward the dance floor holding a drink in each hand. He half emptied his first beer and quickly followed it by upending the dram in one.

'I see you haven't lost the knack yet then Sam,' Richard said as he sipped at his beer in a more gentlemanly manner.

'Get it down you Sassenach, don't play with it,' Sam said with grin. 'The night is young.'

'OK Sam, I'll catch up soon enough.'

Richard was aware that Sam had not heard his reply. He was sizing up a girl of about his height at a nearby table wearing a tam-o'-shanter cap over short red hair. She was sitting on her own and Richard was surprised when she readily accepted Sam's invitation to join our table. It must be the magnetism of the kilt and the bare knees, but then on second thoughts he couldn't help wondering how two red heads would get on.

As the music stopped once more, the dance floor disgorged its inhabitants in the direction of the tables and a group of six, four GI's and two girls, joined Sam and Richard at their table. Two chairs were taken up with a GI and a girl in his lap whilst the other two GI's commandeered two more chairs from another table just as they were about to be taken up by two British Tommies.

'Not so fast mate, those are ours,' received no response from the GI's.

'Bloody Yanks!' one shouted. 'Not satisfied with pinching our women, they think they own the place as well. Put those flaming chairs back.'

All eyes turned in the direction of the two tables as the first Tommy drew himself up to his full height to reveal an inebriated heavy set man quite capable of handling himself in any confrontational situation. The GI's who were used to verbal abuse of that nature did their best to ignore him but only managed to enraged him further. A scuffle broke out sending the table, chairs, residents and drinks in all directions with the Tommy and a GI scrapping on the floor amongst it all. Sam jumped to his feet, ready to grab the culprit. The other Tommy, much shorter but equally drunk, waded in to his partners' aid with a futile swipe at Sam, missing by several feet only to receive a left hook bang on the jaw. Two more Tommies joined in with an attack on Sam. Richard joined the affray and tried to haul Sam to safety. Pandemonium broke out. One of the girls started screaming. Other dancers joined in, some to worsen the situation, whilst others tried to help separate the sprawling group. Whistles sounded as the Military Police barged in swinging their truncheons. No questions were asked as they directed blows indiscriminately in all directions to quell the riot in the shortest possible time.

It was all over in a matter of minutes leaving one of the girls and three men out cold on the floor. The girl and two of the men, one bleeding from somewhere, were loaded on to stretchers whilst the other man was quickly revived with a dousing of cold water from a fire bucket. The escapade came to an abrupt end as quickly as it had started and was followed by the crowd parting down the middle to make way for the stretcher bearers who were clapped and cheered as they made their exit.

Later that evening two policemen turned up at the house with news of Richard's hospitalisation. Floe was asleep having taken some medication and Auntie answered the door in her dressing gown.

'I was just going to bed. What is so urgent that it can't wait 'til morning?'

'Sorry to bother you so late madam but is this the address of RAF sergeant Richard Manston?'

'Yes it is. What has happened? Is he alright? I was expecting him home soon. He's my son-in-law.'

'Can we speak to his wife, Mrs. Cicely Manston?'

'I'm afraid you can't at the moment. She's not very well and asleep in bed. You can tell me. If it's bad news I certainly don't want to wake her.'

'Richard was involved in a stabbing incident at the—.'

'Oh! My God. No! Is he—?' Auntie interrupted.

'It's alright madam, he's had an operation at Morely General and he is out of danger. The surgeon found his identification and requested that you should know as soon as possible. You will be able to visit him in the morning.'

'Thank God for that. You did give me a fright. Richard's not one for fighting and brawls; he only went out for a drink at the local.'

Auntie found it difficult to sleep that night and only managed an hour or so of fitful dozes in the early hours. Around seven she heard Floe visiting the loo and asked if she would like a cup of tea with her pills.

'Now it's nothing to worry about,' she began as she put the tray on the bed, 'but your darling husband has managed somehow to get himself into hospital—.'

'No! Why? Who?' Floe looked terrified.

'Now, now Cice, I said it was nothing to worry about. He's not in danger and he has had an operation, I don't know what for. Anyway he's alright and you can visit him as soon as you're feeling better.'

With Floe confined to her bed, Auntie found it took longer than usual to prepare meals until she co-opted Steven into lending a hand. Being the oldest boy she thought the experience would be good for him, but first she had to make sure that he had clean hands. At first he was more of a hindrance than a help but he soon became as dexterous as Floe in buttering the slices of bread. The pair had just completed preparations for tea on the forth day when Floe suddenly appeared in the kitchen all dressed up ready to go out.

'I'm feeling better,' she said, 'I think I'll visit Richard in hospital and give him a surprise.'

'Oh, I am pleased you're up, I've missed you more than I would have thought possible, but thanks to Steven he has been a great help. If the truth be known I'm getting too old for this job Cice and I'm thinking that perhaps in future these boys should be doing something for themselves. Give my love to Richard. Tell him I'm sorry I haven't had the time to pay him a visit; I'm sure he will understand the relentless demands of all these boys.'

Back at the hospital Mr. Ryan briefed the nurse. 'The patient will be coming around soon nurse, let him know the situation and that his family has been informed. Page me if necessary, otherwise I will talk to him on my rounds in the morning.'

Richard slowly opened his eyes as the general anaesthetic wore off to see the blurred silhouette of a white coated nurse peering at him through the haze. He tried to move but pain shot through his body like a hundred hot pokers.

'Don't try to move young man, you are in hospital and just had an operation to save your life. It was a near thing, you are a lucky chap,' the nurse said as she gently prevented him from trying to get up.

'How did I get here? What's happened?' Richard said slowly.

'You were brought in with another chap and a young lady from a drunken brawl at the NAAFI club last night and you've had an emergency operation for a knife wound to your stomach. The knife missed vital organs by tenths of an inch and fortunately for you stopped just short of your vena cava, a large artery which carries blood from the lower half of your body. Mister Ryan, the surgeon, has patched you up and you should make a full recovery. You were in the operating theatre for three hours and at one time it was touch and go whether you would survive or not. You lost quite a bit of blood and needed a blood transfusion. He expects you to be up and about in no time.'

'Drunken brawl—young lady—NAAFI Club—,' the memory came flooding back and suddenly, he was wide awake. He remembered the fight. 'What happened to Sam? Who was the young lady? Does Cicely know?' He turned his head when he heard someone calling his name, but once again his body was wracked with pain.

'Hello Russell! What are you doing in hospital pretending to be ill? I was worried about you and asked the nurse to keep me informed the moment you came around. You're lucky the surgeon was on hand.'

It was Sam coming to check on Richard and make sure he was out of danger before watering down the story into a satisfactory report for Floe.

'That was not entirely a good idea of yours Sam to go to the club, but if it wasn't for that big guy, I might have enjoyed a dance or two. I have a feeling we'll be barred from now on. Our cards have been marked.'

'Very likely! By the way, I understand from the surgeon that when you were admitted you still had the knife in your stomach and it happened to be my dirk which I lost in the scuffle. Luckily no one removed it otherwise you would have lost a lot more blood than you did. It was lucky for me too because I was annoyed when I couldn't find it. You might be interested to know that it's not just any old knife but a ceremonial one with a ruby embedded in the bone handle which has a clan design. So you're half Scottish now you've been christened; consider yourself to be a McDougal. If it's any consolation you were right about being over the top with the uniform and if I hadn't worn it you might not have been stabbed. Anyway, Russell old chap you rest up. Don't worry about a thing.' I'll keep Floe up to date.'

True to his word, the morning after the police arrived, Auntie was surprised to see Sam on the doorstep, all spruced up and still in his Scottish regalia.

'Good to see you Lou, is Floe coming out to play?' He said with a smile. 'I've come to give you some news about Richard.'

'Why Sam, what do you know about it? We didn't know you were home.'

'I met him on the way to the pub and we spent the evening together. Sorry to hear Floe's not very well. Do you think I could see her?'

Auntie took Sam to Floe's room and knocked on the door. 'Are you decent Floe? You've got a visitor.'

Floe visibly perked up when she saw Sam. A spark of the love she had for him was rekindled when she saw how well he looked with his all over tan. She remembered the time when they used to joke together about his tan not being all over when he wasn't wearing his shorts. She accepted his fuzzy greeting kiss. Auntie sat on the bed while Sam strutted around the room recounting the whole NAFFI incident. He made Floe and Lou laugh as he made light of the whole affair but omitted to tell them how close Richard was to being a dead man. In turn, Floe brought Sam up to date with her news and introduced him to Connie, who was asleep at the time.

Sam spent the next few days acting as messenger boy between Richard and Floe and catching up with Richard's news since their last meeting at the wedding. Richard looked forward to Sam's visits to provide a distraction to his otherwise boring time in hospital. He was in a large ward with perhaps twenty beds all of which were occupied by patients with an array of conditions. Some were asleep whilst others who were awake were unable to speak through the masks and bandages covering their faces. A patient in the next bed was sitting up with no apparent visible injury.

'Sorry about the scuffle last night, it was partly my fault.'

Richard turned wincing once more as he faced the voice. He recognised the man instantly. It was the burly Tommy.

'That's honest of you, but I can't say you did me any favours. As far as I'm concerned it was entirely your bloody fault and all over a silly chair. If you had controlled your temper a bit more I wouldn't be in here having just avoided an appointment with the undertaker.'

'Yeah, I'm really sorry. The name's Tony. Nice to meet you,' he said, reaching out his hand to pat Richard's bed covers. 'I'm not too bad. Got a terrible headache, they say I've got concussion from one of the military police truncheons. I saw stars at the time and like you I woke up in here. Serves me right I suppose; got what was coming to me and I can only blame the beer. What a night eh?'

About a week later a nurse came in to say that Richard had a visitor. It must be Floe he thought. She's recovered. To his surprise it was one of the girls from the NAAFI club; the one who came in at the same time but he hardly recognised her. She was wearing a long blue dress nipped to a neat waist and a white jacket with brass buttons. The cut of her jib would have complemented any yachting marina.

'Hello, I believe your name is Richard isn't it? I came into hospital the same night as you from the riot at the NAAFI club. The nurse tells me you're recovering from what was potentially a serious knife wound. My injury was not so serious, only mild concussion from getting in the way of a misdirected truncheon. It was my first and last visit to the club. I was invited with my fiend Ellie by those four GI's. My name is Wendy,' she said putting her hand out to shake his.

'Well! I hardly recognise you. I wouldn't have thought you were the type of girl to visit a club like that. It was my first visit too. There were too many there and I think the MP's should have closed the doors earlier. I was with Sam the Scott. We only just got in so I suppose you could say we were unlucky. You look great. Have you fully recovered?'

'Yes thanks,' Wendy said, 'you look a bit pale though. Does it still hurt?'

'Only when I laugh,' Richard said, holding his side as he did so.

'I hope you didn't mind me seeing how you are, my friend and I were quite concerned that you were injured because of our group. I'll look in again later in the week if you like. It can be very boring in hospital as I discovered on my short visit.'

'It would like that, I'll look forward to seeing you,' he said as he held her warm hand with one and patted it with the other.

She smiled as she left the room with Richard watching her all the way to the door where she turned and they exchanged waves. Richard felt elated, even excited at the possibility of meeting her again, perhaps next time things might be different.

'Very nice,' Tony commented. 'I remember that one and thought at the time there would be a queue to dance with her.'

Richard had plenty of time to think whilst in hospital and even more so when he discovered from the surgeon, who had been checking on his medical records, that he was sterile. It was a bombshell from out of the blue; a psychological wound far worse than his physical one. That would heal but this was permanent. At the time Connie was born he had not questioned the validity of her birth, although he was suspicious and jealous of Alfie's association with Floe. In our attic we sometimes heard Floe and Richard having heated arguments especially when she came home from the cinema later than expected. Their short marriage seemed to be on a roller coaster journey; one minute the bedrails would be rattling and the next having an argument about Alfie. According to Richard, Alfie was someone who was quite fit and able, despite his faked medical certificate, to fight for his country. There was never any love lost between them.

It was while Richard was in hospital that the first seeds of marriage breakdown formed in his mind, something which Floe became acutely aware of when she was sufficiently recovered to pay him a visit. His reaction as she leaned over to kiss was purely perfunctory and devoid of warmth.

'What's the matter darling? Are you in pain?'

'As a matter of fact, I am, so you can cut out the 'Darling' bit,' he said quite angrily.

Floe stepped back quickly looking both astonished and horrified. What can have happened she thought; he was very endearing and considerate in her hour of need when they last met barely over a week ago?

'Well Floe, there's only one way I can say this. The surgeon had cause to check my medical history before my operation and has told me that Connie could not possibly be mine. Tell me the truth. Have you had sex with that cinema shithouse Randy Andie?'

'Randy Andie?' She looked puzzled.

'Your bloody cinema bloke.'

Floe was ready with an instant denial. 'His name's not Andie it's...'

'I don't give a shit to know what his bloody name is, all I know is he will have more than a limp if I get my hands on him and then he'll have real reason to shirk call up. The surgeon has assured me that I'm sterile and could not possibly have fathered a child. What have you got to say? Come on, out with it and don't lie any more. This is the last straw. We're finished. It's all over between us.'

Floe turned ashen white, all the colour drained from her face. She took a deep breath as if to speak but nothing came out. Tears streamed down her cheeks until finally she managed to utter a futile apology.

'I'm so, so sorry Darling,' she said as she fled from the room.

For both Richard and Floe, it was the worst day of their lives. In the space of a few short hours their world had come crashing down. How could either of them carry on? For Floe the solution was easier, she had a ready bed to go to and Alfie would be delighted, but for Richard there was just a void. Tony tried to console him by saying it was a common event and that casualties were not only at the Front, but Richard just wouldn't hear of it. He waved both arms as if to tell Tony to shut up.

Later we heard Floe come home, fly up the stairs to her room, slam the door and start crying bitterly. Auntie followed soon afterwards.

'What on earth's the matter Floe? What's happened? Is Richard alright?'

'He says it's all over between us and blames it all on Alfie.'

'Well my dear in a small town people talk and although I haven't mentioned it to you before I've heard rumours about Alfie and Gladys across the road has noticed Wilbur's jeep in the back lane as well. Then if that wasn't enough Joe Freeman's name has been mentioned; for a man in his position, I thought he was skating on thin ice. And another thing, I don't think you're coming home from work as late as you do has helped matters either. The way I see it my girl, like or not, you have a reputation, which for a married woman with a child makes it embarrassing for me when I'm out. I've seen the gossips nodding and whispering behind cupped hands. Don't forget we all suffer when something like this happens. So is it true then? Tell me the truth Cice,' Auntie demanded raising her voice so we could hear quite clearly through the floor. 'Have you and Alfie been carrying on?'

There was no answer from Floe. She continued crying.

'I take it that's a 'yes' then is it? I know Richard being away such a lot hasn't made things any easier for the pair of you, but all I can say is that you can't blame anybody but yourself. I had a feeling you were in for a fall.'

'Cor blimey, did you hear that,' Lionel whispered picking his glass up from the floor, Floe's been having it off with the milkman, how about that? Sounds as if it's all over,' wonder what Uncle Richard thinks of Floe now?'

They heard Auntie slam the door, clump down the stairs and apart from the odd noise from Floe's room time to time from, all became silent once more. For the next few days mealtimes were very quiet affairs. The boys watched Floe's every move hoping for some snippet of detail about the drama but none was forthcoming.

In the hospital, a nurse approached Richard's his bed.

'You haven't eaten your dinner Richard Manston 556249, you naughty boy! What's the matter with it? You asked for hash pie and peas too,' the nurse said, turning him over to see his face.

'It's my wife. Well she was! Not any more though,' he growled. Ignoring the pain he turned back over thinking more of the pain in his heart than the physical one. In an effort to shut the world out he buried his face in his pillow and closed his eyes.

The nurse could see Richard was beyond any words of comfort and left him to sleep his anger away but as a last crumb of comfort tried to tell him that perhaps a new day would bring new hope. But three more days dragged wearily and angrily away. It was no consolation to Richard to know that most of the other patients in the ward were trapped in the same time warp. Some were able to read or complete crossword puzzles but he was not in the mood for any of it. Tony was the only one able to get up and move around and although he tried talking to Richard it fell on deaf ears. Neither was he in any frame of mind for mundane chatter and when the weather suddenly turned stormy, he couldn't have cared less. The storm clouds had already broken over his world. He was full of self pity and searched in vain to think where he had gone wrong. I'm just another damned statistic he thought, a victim of the war, it happens all the time. At lunch on the forth day he was finally cajoled by the nurse into eating anything of substance and he felt better for it. In addition the irritation in the next bed was missing together with the sheets and pillows. Richard had recovered sufficiently to be able to sit up and was aimlessly looking out the window when he heard familiar voices calling him. He turned and saw Sam and Wendy standing together by his bed.

'Hello Richard,' Sam said reverting to Richard's correct name. 'We both met at reception. I believe you've met this young lady so I'll just say I'm glad to see you looking better and Hello and Goodbye. With her good looks I think she will have a better chance of cheering you up than me. We've heard your bad news. I'm so sorry old chap. I won't stay now. I'll look in again on my way back this evening.'

Richard was pleased to see Wendy.

'You are the best visitor I've seen all week,' he said. 'I'm pleased to see you. I've been through a bad patch.'

Wendy patted his hand.

'That's nice of you to say so,' she said. 'These things happen. Even my friend Ellie doesn't feel married anymore because her husband is so far away. It's so difficult when children are involved.'

Richard stared at her, saying nothing, she had unwittingly hit a raw nerve and he wondered how much she knew of his problem. Was it possible that Sam had regained Floe's confidence and she had blurted out the reason for the breakdown? If only he had known Wendy was referring to Ellie's children he might have been spared the embarrassment of explaining about Connie.

'What has Sam told you?'

'Well, it was the nurse actually. She said you've had a barney with your wife and she flew out in tears.'

'I'll tell you what Wendy, when I get out of here, do you think we could meet up for a drink? I could do with a shoulder to cry on.'

'I don't want you to think that I make a habit of picking up service men when they're low, but yes OK, that would be fine. My local is handy for me,' she said with a grin, 'I still feel guilty though and Ellie does too in fact she very nearly came in with me today. She sends her best wishes.'

'Your guilt is my gain,' Richard said, 'I'll find out how soon I can go home.'

Then he realised he didn't have a home to go to any more and two days later when he left the hospital he felt as if he was emerging from a dream but only to discover he was in nowhere land. There was no possibility of recuperating at home and he was tormented with his thoughts of Connie. She was his daughter and now she wasn't. His short marriage with Floe was a sham but he knew he had to push the experience to the back of his mind and move on. Like so many airmen life could be short and his next flight his last, there was no time for recriminations.

Wendy was sitting in the corner by the fire, facing the door with her ginger beer bubbling away. The pub was empty except for an elderly farmhand leaning on the bar. She was looking at the flickering flames in the fire when she heard the door open and Richard came in, smartly dressed in his RAF uniform showing no outward signs of his injury. She accepted his kiss her on her cheek without drawing away as if it was the most natural thing to do and she felt comfortable in his company. Although he had known her for only a short time he found he was attracted to her and hoped the she felt the same, but not through any self imposed guilt. He explained what had happened to his marriage with Floe without making any reference to Alfie. Even the mention of his name was painful. As the innocent party he explained that there was no way he could carry on living in the same house with Floe anymore. Whilst grandma and Lou would be on his side and full of sympathy the rift between himself and Floe would be irreparable. Wendy had no answers to his anguish over Connie. He was going to miss her excited greeting when he came home on leave.

'I will be going back to the base in a few days, so in the meanwhile I'll find a billet somewhere until I receive my recall. There are rumours that some crews are to be posted to another airbase where the numbers are down, so I'm a bit in limbo at the moment. But let's not be downhearted,' he said, 'I don't want to spoil your pretty face with any more of my problems.'

Wendy sat quietly for a while looking into the fire, deep in thought.

'Look,' she said suddenly turning to see his reaction, 'I've got a spare room you can use for a few days. Toby and I would be pleased to have your company and you would be doing me a favour.'

'Who is Toby?' He said, looking a little perplexed.

'Oh, he's my spaniel, he hates being cooped up during the day when I'm at school. You can do me a favour by taking him out on the downs, he knows the way so he won't be any trouble.'

'Well, thank you. I would be delighted Wendy, but we hardly know each other. Are you sure it would be no bother? I don't want to impose, although I think you know I'm hardly in a position to refuse. The air at home is likely to be somewhat acidic and the thought of sleeping on the settee with all those kids clumping about doesn't fill me with enthusiasm.'

The next day about teatime we heard heated discussions taking place in the sewing room and saw Richard packing his kit bag ready to leave.

We had seen him do so many times before, but this time Floe was crying and in some distress. She clung to his arm trying to hold him back whilst Auntie tried to block the door, but it was all in vain. He had said all he was going to say. His mind was made up. Roughly brushing them both aside and leaving without giving Floe his usual hugs and kisses, he stormed down the path, through the gate and was gone.

In Wendy's cottage he felt relieved. The door was closed on the past and now he was ready for a fresh start. As he lay in his short single bed with his feet sticking out the bottom he had time to reflect; to go over in his mind all past events and although it was too late, time to put the pieces of the puzzle together. He had had his suspicions, seen all the clues, but had chosen to ignore them and give Floe the benefit of doubt. And then there was Lou; she must have known and chose to keep quiet. As a last shot he wondered about the boys, perhaps he should have quizzed them, especially Steven and Lance; they were wily, street wise kids and didn't miss much. But he kept coming back to the same conclusion; he'd been a fool and should have done something about it before. The War had a lot to answer for.

He heard Wendy's bath water running down the drain and as everything became quiet in the next room he could smell the perfume as it drifted up passed his window filling his room and invading his senses. For what seemed hours he lay quietly staring at the ceiling and his mind played tricks with him as the shadows formed by the moonlight shining through the trees danced to and fro on the window. Finally he had the urge to get up. He stopped and tapped gently on Wendy's partially open door.

'Are you awake? Wendy,' he said, almost too afraid to ask.

'Yes I am,' she replied.

'I can't sleep; I've been staring at the ceiling for ages thinking about you.'

'Nether can I,' she said. 'I thought you'd never come.'

He went into her room and slid in quietly beside her. She was warm, receptive, and intoxicating. He leaned over and as he kissed her, he could hear her heart beating. She folded her arms around him and slowly as they held each other in a tight embrace, darkness deepened around them and they sank into another world.

CHAPTER 10

Back at school, following the Matisley incident, the Captain, with the confidence and endorsement of his staff behind him, threw himself with a renewed vigour into his polices for improving the school and education of all the children. His occasional chance meetings with Wendy were kept on a low key basis such that, although he found it difficult, he knew he couldn't be seen showing his feelings for her. One of his polices was to encourage outdoor activities by way of field nature studies, physical training and sport on the basis that a healthy active child would be more receptive to academic demands. The annual football match, staff versus the children, at the end of term was a particularly successful fixture which went some way toward mellowing the strictness of his tight ship policy. To even out the obvious difference in height between the two sides, the children were allowed fifteen players thereby giving as many children as possible the chance of a game. At half time they were also allowed a complete change of players as substitutes. It was odd that although the Captain advocated the need for sporting activities he did not practice what he preached. The older boys took great delight in running circles around him and for the major part of the match he rarely contributed much by way of teamwork or showing any incentive towards helping his side to score.

It was after one such match when the whole school was at a heightened level of excitement that the Captain followed Wendy into the store room on the pretext of looking for a football rules book. With very little room to manoeuvre between the packed shelves on either side, the captain found himself face to face with Wendy still wearing her shorts and lose fitting blouse. Once again her perfume invaded his senses driving all rhyme and reason out. The fresh air had invigorated him and heightened his energy levels to new heights such that his animal instincts took over. With staring eyes and flared nostrils he trapped her in the corner with her hands by her sides and kissed her passionately before she had chance to move out of danger. The ferocity of his attack took her completely by surprise. She felt his hot breath on her neck and could hear his heart pounding masked only by his thin T shirt. Exercise books, boxes of pencils and rulers rattled on the shelves above their heads. She felt that struggling against his superior strength would be futile and that trapped in the virtually sound proofed room it would be useless to cry out. Pinned against the bookshelves the Captain took full advantage of Wendy's body in an explosion of passion and desire which caused her to gasp and moan as she climaxed. Her natural involuntary cries were drowned by the shower of school material as it cascaded and rattled down from the shelves to the tiled floor. A trolley full of books scooted away and crashed into the door forcing it wide open.

Passing by at that very moment was Harry Snip from Four B. The door crashed open striking his left shoulder to send him sprawling against the opposite wall of the corridor. Whilst still on his hands and knees he turned to peer through dazed eyes at the reverberating door as it bounced against the trolley. He caught flashes of the normally tidy stock room now in total disorder. It was then that Harry got the shock of his life which rooted him to the spot. With his head still spinning he was surprised to see bodies thrashing about amongst the chaos as sunlight streamed into the room illuminating the pair. Arms and legs seemed all tangled up making it difficult for Harry to decide whose was whose.

'Close the door and don't move,' the Captain roared.

Wendy straightened her meagre attire and somehow managed to regain her composure but said nothing to the speechless Harry as she hurried off to the staff changing room. At the same time the Captain tugged on his shorts, climbed over the stock and forced the trolley back into the room. Without saying a word he locked the door, grabbed Harry by the collar and frog marched him in double quick time to his office.

Harry, still in shock and ashen white, was breathless from having been bustled into the headmaster's office. On the way he met his classroom pals whose chatter abruptly terminated as they stopped dead on the spot at the sight of the Captain and his victim in full flow. Without hesitating, almost as if he had not seen the boys, the Captain charged passed and slammed the office door behind Harry.

His pal Barry couldn't help breaking the silence. 'Wow! What's our Harry been up to now? He's never been in trouble before; he's too crafty for that.'

Like calling the kettle calling the pot black, two of the boys took a leaf out of Harry's book and crept up to the headmaster's door and hid below the glass panel to eavesdrop.

'Tell me what you saw, Snip,' the Captain demanded.

'Nothing Sir, honest I saw nothing, I was dizzy after the door hit me and the sun was in my eyes,' he lied.

Harry was a case hardened liar, even when caught by the police at the local allotments with his pockets full of vegetables he denied having stolen them saying that a gardener had given them to him. He got off scot-free. He knew full well that with the sun behind him he had seen everything including the Captain's bare white backside and parts of Ms Nicholson the likes of which he'd only seen before in the American magazines.

'Good,' the Captain said. 'I want you to remember that you saw nothing because If I hear anything to the contrary, you will be accused of lying and will be expelled from the school the same as Herbert Matisley. Do you understand me boy?'

'Yes, yes Sir, I do. I won't tell anybody Sir,' he whined.

The two boys looked disappointed when they sensed the interrogation was coming to an end.

'May I go now please Sir? I don't feel very well.'

'We'd better scoot before he comes out. Sounds as if he's seen something but he's giving nothing away.'

The Captain followed Harry from his office and immediately went to Wendy's classroom where he was relieved to see that she was teaching her class as normal. He knocked smartly on the door and poked his head around the corner.

'Ah, Ms Nicholson, may I see you in my office for a moment?'

In his office, the Captain adopted a serious pose.

'Wendy,' he began, 'I can only apologise for my appalling behaviour toward you and I beg your forgiveness. As you may be aware I have strong feelings for you but I have selfishly let those feelings get out of control and behaved in an unprofessional manner. I have therefore decided to think seriously about my continued position as headmaster of this school and will be addressing the staff tomorrow morning. You must do whatever you feel fit but I hope that my announcement will indicate the level of my remorse and act as a modicum of justice to you.'

'I cannot say that I would expect any less of you PJ, but I am sure that either one or the other of our continued positions in this school is untenable under the present circumstances. I will of course respect whatever decision you make.'

Wendy returned to her classroom with a certain amount of self recrimination on her mind and entertained the thought that perhaps she had encouraged the Captain where maybe she should have done just the opposite. She did not want to live with the blame for bringing a good headmaster down, despite his culpability in the store room.

In distinct contrast to Wendy's classroom, Mr. Hoskins was aware of an unusual atmosphere existing during his mathematics lesson which was heightened by the late arrival of Harry.

'Kind of you to join us Snip,' he sarcastically growled.

'I've been seeing the headmaster, Sir.'

Before Mr. Hoskins could make any more snide comments, Harry realised that perhaps 'seeing' was the wrong word to use. He quickly altered his excuse.

'I mean, I've been to the headmaster's office, Sir.'

'Don't waste any more time boy, get to your desk and be sharp.'

Barry and his pals were quick to notice Harry was not his usual smiling self and as he skulked passed Mr Hoskins, keeping his eyes on the floor, an audible murmur went around the room. Mr Hoskins rapped smartly on the top of his desk with his cane. Harry kept his head down, feverously trying to make his trembling fingers hold his pencil but failing in the process until finally it fell on the floor. He drew the attention of Mr. Hoskins once more.

'What's the matter, Snip?'

For all his strictness, Mr. Hoskins was not a man without compassion and on closer attention could see that Harry, still ashen white, was in a traumatised state. He was shaking like a leaf.

'Are you ill boy? Go to see Nurse Kelly. I'll check with her later, so don't skive off.'

Much relieved, Harry duly complied. 'I'm not feeling well nurse,' he began, 'Mr. Hoskins told me to see you.'

She sat Harry on the couch, felt his forehead, took his temperature and noted his pulse rate.

'Well Harry, I'm glad you came to see me, you certainly look out of sorts. Have you been running? Your pulse rate is very high. Do you feel sick or have a stomach ache? I think that perhaps you have been eating too many mixtures. I'll give you a note to take home. Make sure you give it to your parents and I hope to see you back at school next week fully recovered.'

'Yes Nurse, I will.'

Harry was pleased to agree to any number of symptoms from heart failure to pneumonia to ensure that he would be sent home. Getting away from school and putting as much distance as possible between himself and the headmaster was his main priority. He needed time away from the 'heat' and all the inevitable questions that he was sure his classmates would be dying to ask him. Any one of his imaginary illnesses could provide the basis of an alibi to throw the hounds off his tail. With time to think he changed his mind and concocted a story about having been caught by the headmaster as he relieved himself against the back wall of the school.

It was Friday, the last day of summer term and despite the foggy damp weather the Captain walked the three miles to school in an effort to clear his headache caused by lack of sleep. He had rehearsed his proposed announcement a million times throughout the ever-lasting night knowing that there was no alternative solution to his problem that his conscience would allow him to live with. His remorse was total. He hated himself and tried to think apart from one decision he had already made if there was any other way in which he could placate Wendy. There was one he decided but it was long term and one over which he felt he had no control. On the other hand perhaps he did.

'We have completed yet another successful term,' he began, 'although the end of term football match resulted in a crushing defeat for the staff at five nil. I am proud as Headmaster of this school to demonstrate to the pupils that winning or losing is of no consequence but what is important is to have taken part and to have played to the best of one's ability. For the last twenty years I also have endeavoured to do just that and now in my sixtieth year I have decided to hand the reins of this school over to a younger person who I hope will continue to take the school to new heights.'

The announcement took all the staff, with the exception of Wendy, by surprise. A few stared in disbelief. Mr. Hoskins positively beamed with the thought of seeing his name above the Headmaster's door whilst a few others murmured to each other. Close friends of Hoskins discretely gave him the thumbs up sign which he acknowledged but did so indicating an air of caution. Since missing out to Mrs. Larkin, he often had quiet discussions with friends concerning his chances. He was concerned however to learn from the jungle telegraph that there was a serious contender in a Mr. Whale, a younger deputy head from another school who was highly thought of by the local education authority. Wendy, by way of contrast, stared blankly at her colleagues desperately trying to hide the thoughts and emotions churning around in her mind. The Captain avoided making eye contact with her and chose to stare at some distant point at the back of the room.

'The fact that I have been most happy in my position for so long is to a large extent attributable to my staff past and present and I wish to extend my sincere thanks to you all. I must also pay tribute to everyone inside and outside the school who has contributed over the years for their loyalty and untiring efforts in all the work connected with this school. In latter years the evacuation programme has been particularly testing but in the face of great adversity, I am proud to announce that we have coped admirably and I thank you all for your part in doing so. I trust that my successor, whoever he or she maybe, will endeavour to continue our policies, traditions and principals which have been instrumental in making the school what it is today.'

At that point in his speech he paused for a poignant moment to glance sideways at Patrick Hoskins who steadfastly returned the look without saying a word.

'Make no mistake, being headmaster of a school such as ours is a serious post and one which carries with it a great deal of responsibility.

I would like to impress on my successor that at times the position can be both stressful and rewarding. Fortunately there are very few un-teachable Matisleys in this world and many others who are a joy to educate. In my retirement I would hope to meet some of them again and draw satisfaction from the knowledge that in my small way I had helped to show them the way forward to their chosen careers.'

'So now I look forward to my retirement to do some of the things which for so long I have not been able so to do. I hope to continue my Home Guard duties as long as they are required and to continue writing my memoirs of a long army career dating back to when I was a pale faced private. We are fortunate to live in a beautiful part of the country which I, like possibly many of you, have not found the time to fully appreciate. There are countless coastal walks, enhanced with fresh sea breezes and breath-taking views which I propose to explore. I will do so with pleasure in the knowledge, particularly on fine sunny days, that I don't have to join you, imprisoned within these walls. So now I take my leave of you all and wish you well for the future.'

Spontaneous clapping and cheering filled the staff room lead by the Captain's deputy, Mrs. Larkin who endeavoured to make an impromptu reply.

'I am sure that all members of the staff, including myself, take no pleasure in witnessing your release of the school reins. We are proud to have served the school under your leadership and realise that although time has moved on, there is a life for all of us waiting outside these walls. I have personally been aware that both your twentieth anniversary and dare I say, your diamond birthday, were fast approaching and I hope you will forgive me for pre-empting your retirement at this appropriate juncture. To this end, I have pleasure on behalf of the managers, staff, present and past scholars and friends to present you with a savings book containing fifty savings certificates as a token of our extreme appreciation of your service to the school.'

Energetic and spontaneous clapping broke out once again as each member of the staff lined up to shake his hand and wish him well. No-one, except the Captain, was aware that one particular handshake was not forthcoming and that as Wendy left the room she carried a deep secret.

In the Clarion Newspaper some three months later there was an announcement that a tragic accident had occurred during a Home Guard training exercise when Captain PJ Tomkins was shot and killed. It was followed by a long obituary outlining the Captain's dedicated and selfless services in World War 1, both to the school and the Home Guard. Wendy took particular note of the announcement which referred to the Captain's school record.

"Captain Tomkins was a highly respected pillar of our community whose morality and dedication to duty was an inspiration to staff and children alike. His sudden recent retirement after twenty years as headmaster was a major blow to the whole school and one which has set his successor a high bench mark to follow."

Wendy read the announcement several times in an effort to come to terms with the shock and thought how different it would have been if she had divulged her secret. The final statement was one which merely stated that as a single man he left no family.

The police investigation established that the Captain's body was discovered by a local person out walking his dog early one Thursday morning. He was accustomed to seeing the red warning flags on the approaches to the firing range when the Home Guard were practicing. His suspicions were raised when he noticed that they had been flying for several days especially when he knew from local notice boards that Friday was the usual practice day. When his Springer spaniel ran off over the downs and was missing for some time he blew his whistle for her return, but there was no sign of her. Later he tried again, this time he heard barking from the firing range. Normally his dog was very obedient which led him to make the reluctant decision to enter the danger zone knowing that something had compelled the dog to persist with its barking. At first, although the barking continued, the dog was nowhere to be seen. Eventually, the dog appeared from the trench behind the target boards, barking furiously. It was then that the man discovered the body of the Captain with a bullet hole plum centre in his forehead. He was slumped against the back of the trench, almost in a dozing position with his cap on his chest.

When the police were called, they set up an enquiry room at the local public house where the publican, well versed in everybody's business, had, in his mind, solved the tragedy at a stroke.

'Ask Patrick Hoskins a few questions. It's public knowledge that there was no love lost between him and the Captain.'

Later, when the publican quizzed the detective in charge, he was told that the Home Guard Unit had been very co-operative. It appeared that the Captain having retired from everyday school attendances was not missed until the following Friday, scheduled for grenade practice. His body had lain undiscovered for six days. Further investigation with the Home Guard platoon established the fact that on the previous Friday, blank cartridges were used, which posed the question of how the Captain could possibly have been shot. Describing the chain of events on that particular Friday, the sergeant said that the Captain left the dugout to check and reset the targets, but did not return. He had been seen talking to Miss Nicholson who was walking her dog outside the firing range. When the Captain did not return, male chauvinistic banter took place which led the platoon to assume that the Captain had other ideas of how to spend the evening. In his absence the sergeant followed normal procedure and took over supervision of the practice exercise still using blanks. On completion, the platoon then retired to the public house as per usual where the publican was quick to notice the non appearance of the Captain.

'Hey up Lads, where's your leader? Are you allowed out on your own tonight because he's too busy practicing his karate?'

'You could say that. He was seen earlier talking to Miss Nicholson so we won't be surprised if he comes in later with a smile on his face.'

Patrick's assumption was greeted with cheers, followed by, 'Get to work landlord. Eight pints please.'

After the Captain's retirement the whole ethos of the school changed with the arrival of the new headmaster, Mr. Whale. He was a slightly built unobtrusive man in his mid thirties whose stature bore no resemblance to his name. With no other redeeming characteristic to work on the children were quick to start looking for a nickname but they were thwarted by the new Head at his first school assembly when he stressed the point that his name was not 'Moby' but Mr. Whale and that if he heard anything to the contrary caning would be the rule of the day. Hoskins was the first staff member to start back room comments by suggesting that he had been passed over once more by an ex university green horn who thought he knew it all. Ellie and Wendy expressed their reservations about the 'new broom' and Ellie in particular began to miss the 'devil' she knew rather than the one she didn't. After only two weeks they admitted to each other that they were not enjoying teaching so much and began to look forward to going home at the end of each day.

It was one such day when a tired under-the-weather Wendy arrived home to find a strange letter on her doormat. She put it to one side thinking she would look at it later after the girl's piano lesson but an inquisitive Ellie was the first to notice that it was post marked 'Suffolk'.

'This is strange; who do you know in Ipswich?'

'I've no idea,' she replied as she slid a knife under the flap. 'It's a firm of solicitors!' Wendy exclaimed.

Wendy opened the letter, stood reading the first paragraph over and over several times before she dropped into a chair, as if in a faint, allowing the letter to fall on the floor.

Ellie picked it up.

'Would you believe it? The Captain has left his entire estate to you! What a lucky devil you are. I wonder why he did that, he must have fancied you!'

'I had no idea.' Wendy lied. 'I'm flabbergasted, really I am.'

'You are the sole beneficiary. You've got to telephone a Miss Harper to arrange a consultation with the Captain's solicitors. I'll do it for you, if you like. You don't look as if you're capable just now. Tell you what; I might even come along with you for moral support. What do you think?'

Wendy sat staring out the window unable to answer. She was back in the storeroom with PJ; the memory now as clear as it was in reality on that infamous day. She remembered his remorse and attempts in all manner of ways to make amends but she never realised that he felt so deeply as to make this final gesture.

'I think you need a stiff drink, Wendy. Here, drink this.'

Ellie placed the drink in Wendy's hand. She gulped it down in one swig, not even bothering to see what it was or stop looking out the window. Like an animal recovering from an anaesthetic, she shook her head to find Ellie staring at her.

'Shall I ring the number then?' Ellie repeated.

'What, oh yes,' she said absent-mindedly. 'Go on then.'

Miss Harper said that the executors were anxious to settle the estate as soon as possible and asked if it would be possible the very next day. Without asking Wendy, Ellie agreed immediately.

'There! All done and dusted. I'll drive because I know you won't be able to concentrate. I'll make sure you get there on time,' Ellie assured her.

'Thanks, Ellie, I would appreciate that.'

The next morning, Ellie duly arrived, all prepared for the journey with plenty of hot black coffee.

'I didn't sleep too much last night Ellie,' Wendy said as they set off. 'Thanks for taking me today I might have had an accident if I had gone on my own. Hours and hours ticked by slowly as I think I relived every moment of school life under PJ' from the day I first met him to the day he retired. The training site for the Home Guard wasn't all that far from home and the platoon always had a beer or two afterwards at the local pub. I particularly remember the day when I accidentally met them all there because it was the day of the reported fight he had with that boy Matisley.'

Wendy stopped short of telling Ellie the rest of the story of how PJ spent the night at her bungalow and she felt guilty for withholding the whole truth, but she was adamant that secrets, innocent or otherwise, had to remain hers and hers alone. Nobody must ever know, she told herself. A hot flush suddenly caused her to look out the window away from Ellie so that she wouldn't know just how close to the mark Ellie was with her next comment. It confirmed in her mind that her tight lip policy was more than warranted.

'I've never mentioned this to you before, Wendy, but everybody knew that PJ had a soft spot for you more so than the others. We all knew that he was a bit of a ladies man. Having said that, he was a very private person with what I regarded as a hard exterior which even his Home Guard platoon was unable to penetrate, so it's not surprising that nobody ever came up with any positive gossip. He exercised his tight ship policy to the extent that his home and school lives were strictly separate. The timing of his retirement was made to look appropriate but I was surprised like so many others how sudden it was. Mrs. Larkin suspected that he would retire after twenty five years rather than twenty but went ahead with the collection just in case. She then had to rush out during his speech to buy the savings certificates.'

'Let's put it this way, Ellie, I was aware of his keen interest in me, which only served to make me careful not to give him the slightest encouragement. I feel that if I did the flood gates would have opened, but as far as I was concerned, any relationship was completely out of the question based on our age differences alone.'

Wendy paused for a few moments, still resolutely looking out her window as images of the storeroom flooded through her mind yet again. 'Flood gates, flood gates' the words kept echoing in her head. They certainly did open irrespective of any encouragement she may or may not have given. She began to wish there was no will; that someone else more deserving should have benefited but quickly obliterated the thought with the fact that she was involved and had to face reality. The legacy was her payment for humiliation. Slowly she began to regain her composure once more and finally returned her interest to Ellie's driving and where they were going. There was a long gap where they were both alone with their thoughts until finally Wendy restarted the conversation almost as if she had just been speaking.

'Well, he certainly was a character, no doubt about it. His accident was a great shock to us all and I feel sorry for the platoon members who had to prove their innocence. The police asked questions about the guns in an effort to establish who used which but found it was entirely random. What a nightmare—! The police even questioned me after further information proffered by Patrick led them to believe I was the last person to see him alive. They upset me by asking me to re-enact the scene with a police officer immediately prior to the accident. In the end the coroner recorded an accidental death. For some reason the Captain returned to the target trench after we parted without the platoon knowing, possibly feeling it was safe to do so with the knowledge that only blanks were being used. Close examination of one particular rifle suggested a possible explanation of the tragedy. It showed signs of having been fired with a squid load which can happen when a bullet becomes lodged in the barrel. Whoever next loaded the rifle with a blank without checking the bore would have unknowingly dislodged the bullet.'

'That's terrible,' Ellie added. 'So nobody knew who actually fired the shot.'

'No, and I suppose we never will, although with all the rumours floating around with regard to Mr. Hoskins, he found it so unbearable that he moved away to another school. Gossip mongerers suggested that even if he didn't see the squid surely he would have felt the recoil. Hoskins was between a rock and a hard place. With the Captain out of the way, accepting the headship would have looked like proof of motive and if he left as he did he would have looked guilty anyway. I felt sorry for him.'

'Here we are,' Ellie said, interrupting Wendy's line of thought. 'The trip has been quicker than I thought. How time flies.'

In the solicitor's office Ellie settled down in the waiting room with a book she had brought with her fully prepared for a prolonged wait. She had only read a few pages when she was surprised to see Wendy appear in the office doorway, looking a little flushed and shaking the solicitor's hand.

'You were quick Wendy. Was everything OK?'

'All P.J's instructions to his bank and solicitor have been sorted out and I've got a large cheque. His will was complete in every minute detail almost as if he had planned his demise. The whole situation makes me feel quite uncomfortable.'

Returning to the car Ellie opened the passenger door. 'A nice fat cheque wouldn't make me feel uncomfortable as you put it, but I agree it's very baffling. We'll never know what was in his mind.'

CHAPTER 11

Eventually Floe, with a bit of encouragement from Auntie, went back to work in the cinema and seemed to recover very quickly from her trauma. They discussed the new situation, sometimes quite openly in front of us almost if we weren't there. She stressed to Floe that she had to face facts, move on and learn from her mistakes. Richard's wages stopped which meant savings had to be made but with the end of the evacuation in sight Auntie decided they could get by. The news of the marriage breakdown was a red-letter day for Alfie. He had discussions with his mother about the possibility of asking Floe to move in with them, something with which she was more than happy to agree. Floe, wanting to preserve some of her hard earned freedom decided to stay with Auntie, at least until the boys returned to their homes. Connie had to be considered too and having already lost one of her parents, moving in with Alfie, someone she hardly knew was not a good idea. Auntie knew that the strong bond which existed between herself and Connie was in jeopardy if Floe moved out. The day to day ritual carried on much the same as it did before but gradually becoming easier as our numbers reduced. There were four who were orphans with no home to go to. Lance and Herbert stuck together and joined the sea cadets whilst Steven was adopted by his uncle to work on the family farm. I was the last to leave by which time things had started to happen and I even enjoyed the last few months when I moved into the box room on my own.

At the end of the War Auntie and Floe set about putting their plans into action in earnest by renovating the whole house in preparation for a different type of client. They moved into Grandma's room which freed up their two rooms and the box room was converted into an additional bathroom. Dormer windows were fitted to the attic rooms, doors replaced and the floors including the stairs carpeted throughout. When the evacuees left, the town reverted to being a holiday resort once more and they had no difficulty in letting the rooms which they advertised as suitable for professional and business clients. The nineteen evacuees were replaced by just five tenants, but at a rent far in excess of the evacuee figure of ten shillings. Household income quadrupled and all went well until Auntie began to show signs of dementia. Only in her early sixties she quickly deteriorated until one cold night Floe found her wandering aimlessly in the back lane with no slippers and wearing only a nightgown. Flo decided to have Auntie sectioned and sent to an old folk's home in Bodmin where she eventually died. All the while, Alfie continued to woe Floe until his mother died and then they married and moved into his house.

Richard continued to visit Wendy for a few months after his divorce from Floe and he spent his weekend leave periods at her cottage. They even discussed living together on a permanent basis. Life for Wendy was idyllic with him but it was all too good to last. The bubble burst when he was posted to India where he joined his friend Sam. They never met up again, although at the start they wrote regularly to each other. Sam and Richard were back together again like two school boys and over a period of time the letters became less and less until they eventually stopped. When Richard's posting in India came to an end he was posted to an airbase in Wiltshire where he met and married his second wife Sarff. She knew that Richard had lived another life with Floe and being a very possessive type endeavoured to draw a positive line under his past.

The effect of the Americans being in town was just as noticeable when they left, as it was, when they arrived. It was quite an anticlimax. The hotels were dull and lifeless with no more jeeps buzzing around and local traders lost half their business overnight. Whilst they were there they injected an air of vitality and fun into the town which was appreciated not only by the evacuees but also by the local girls and those who joined them from other parts. As far as the oldest profession was concerned they were a source of all manner of foodstuffs, not available on our ration books, in addition to petrol and nylons. For Wendy, Floe and Ellie, all three in their time, were no lesser recipients of back door supplies for services rendered than any other women in town. For some who had lost their husbands and were evacuated with their children it was a case of necessity for survival.

For some GI's, I would hazard a guess that their primary action was not with the enemy but with any female in town. As kids we used to bump into them in all sorts of places, particularly the grassy banks between the football stand and the allotments. On the occasion when we disturbed one of them we saw the whole action just as it was getting 'hot'. The Yank was not best pleased, in fact he was so furious that he chased us across the field. With his trousers around his feet and his digits hanging free he had no chance of catching us. When he gave up the chase to return to his unfinished business, we rested to catch our breath. We dared not to think of what would have happened if he had caught anyone of us. Lionel was the first to make any observation.

'Did you see the size of his chopper then? Cor, what a Whopper Chopper! Biggest I've seen. Wait 'til I see Sydney, his is nothing.'

'Yeah!' Peter joined in, 'Whopper Chopper, he won't want to go boasting any more about his when we tell him.'

We all agreed on that point and laughed all the way home but it was with great difficulty that we were able to suppress our giggles at tea that night. Auntie became so curious to get a straight answer that she stopped making the tea at one point and only continued after some plausible fib from Lionel. Even the bigger boys were left in doubt. Education for the younger boys took a great leap forward that night and it was only when we were upstairs later all collected around the big bed that the full story was told. Sydney, for one, couldn't believe it and was convinced that we had made it all up. He even went to the loo to measure his and came back looking very dejected.

'Whopper Chopper' became a catch phrase amongst the smaller boys. If ever any of us were in low spirits it only needed to be whispered to set the whole gang laughing again. It was very much like that the day the GI's left, it was very sudden, one day they were there and the next they were gone. After Wendy and Ellie's experiences at the NAAFI club, when Wilbur's group was banned, the Americans began to organise functions in their own hotel billets where attendances could be more controlled. One such dance was arranged to take place at the local hotel where the 245th engineer combat battalion was billeted, for the very day of the embarkation. It didn't happen. News of the invasion of Europe filtered back to Floe that sadly on the first day when beach landings were attempted in Normandy, Wilbur and his companions where all killed.

All those who had known him were saddened by the news, none more so than the Reverend Richards, who delivered an obituary after his sermon one Sunday morning. He had received some personal effects from the US Military relating to his association with the church. One item was a photograph of a group of evacuees taken by Wilbur outside the church in 1943 which the Reverend mentioned in his obituary notes to the press.

At this point, Francis hesitated for a few moments, before taking the photograph from his wallet. He put it on the table and deliberately covered it with his hand.

'Torah!' he said as he showed us the photograph.

'This is one of my prised possessions. It's commonly said that a picture is worth a thousand words. Well, this one certainly is for me. I have very few photographs of my younger days and this one conjures up all kinds of memories which are indelibly printed in my mind.'

We looked at the photograph and tried to guess which of the seven little boys lined up against the church wall was Francis. After two attempts we gave up. Francis pointed to himself, second from the left, a tubby shiny faced little chap, wearing funny boots, short trousers and a tight jumper with holes in the elbows. His hands were clasped together on his stomach almost in an apologetic manner.

'I was only ten years old then and you can see from the body language the kind of subjugated life we lived, I was, as they say, 'afraid to say boo to a goose'. We were a rag-tag group, all different in every way not only in shape, size and age but also in character. The fact that we were all so different was probably a major factor in that we got on so well together; a sort of brotherhood. For many years I tried to make contact with them but only managed to find one, but that was only through a contact that happened to be in the same hospital at the time of his death. He died from cancer. I was pleased to hear that the lady said he was full of tales about his evacuee days, especially his 'whopper-chopper' one. I've had the picture blown up and framed now it hangs on my hallway wall at home.'

'A picture with a story,' I said. Molly nodded in agreement.

Francis returned the picture to his wallet. 'Only a couple of days before the embarkation when Auntie was away visiting a cousin, Floe invited Wilbur to a special tea at our house. It was special in that half the food on the table he brought with him including drinks Hershey bars and cookies. He introduced us to the game of craps, a typically American game in which people place bets on any outcome of the roll, or series of rolls of a pair of dice. Players can bet against each other in a game of street craps or against a bank in casino craps. The beauty of the game was that it could be played anywhere and after Wilbur's visit life in the attic was never the same especially on long summer evenings. Sometimes Auntie would take the light bulbs away to curtail our league table matches between the two rooms. We played with a bag of American coins, or lose change as he called it which he had collected from his pals for us to keep. As evacuees we had very little money and found that in the end we were more familiar with the American cent, nickel, dime, quarter and dollar than the English equivalent. We tended to use the terms on a day to day basis in shops where we were able to poke fun at say a sum like four and eleven pence halfpenny. Even Floe, who was going through a bad patch at the time, enjoyed herself taking over the roll of banker. She had a fit of giggling over some of the American sayings especially when Wilbur offered Roger some gum.

'Would you like some gum?' Actually meant, 'You've got bad breath.' Roger was not best pleased and could always be found chewing gum thereafter.

We all slept soundly that night after going to bed a lot later than Auntie would ever have allowed. We liked Wilbur and in the morning when Steven noticed that his jeep was still parked in the back lane he was quite complimentary as he drew it to Lance's attention.

'Good 'ol Wilbur, you lucky chap.'

'Yeah!' Lance agreed. 'He deserved whatever—don't let on to the others, somebody would be sure to blab.'

It was at about this time that I received news of my parent's death during an air raid in Bristol. We were all seated at the tea table as usual when our local police sergeant knocked on the door. Eric and Lance saw him coming up the path and they immediately jumped to the conclusion that one or another of us was in trouble.

'Hey up lads, who's in for it this time?' Lance shouted.

With so many boys in the house and the newspapers full of misdemeanours which occurred almost every day we were used to the police paying us regular visits. It was common practice for crimes to be blamed on the evacuees first when in more instances than not it was most likely to be an innocent looking local boy or girl. Right from the start when my particular tranche of evacuees arrived at the reception centre they managed to flood a bathroom, fuse all the lights and one girl fell out of a first floor window, luckily only to break an arm. No area was safe from crime. Raiding allotments, throwing cliff top seating into the sea and general pilfering from shops was common place. On this occasion my name came up in the conversation at the door.

'Oh, Francis, have you been a naughty boy then?' They all chorused and cheered.

'Francis, darling,' Auntie said, 'will you come into the sewing room with Sergeant Thompson for a few minutes?'

There was that word again, 'Darling,' it was all so put on.

'Bye, bye Darling,' the boys cooed.

In the sitting room the policeman had already spoken to Auntie.

'The sergeant has brought some sad news about your parents,' she said. 'They were visiting friends in Bristol when they were caught in an air raid and they have both been killed. We are so, so sorry Darling.'

I had not seen my parents since my evacuation some three years before and I felt unmoved and detached from them already. It was like as if the policeman was talking about somebody else. There were no tears, just sadness. Whatever Auntie or anyone else had to say made no difference; they were just words and completely meaningless.

'Can I go back to my tea now Auntie?' I said.

'Yes alright Francis, I will come and tell the boys for you if you like.'

The death of my parents at the age of ten saw me at the lowest point in my life. I was alone, but I've always remembered Auntie's very few words of consolation which contained any degree of heart felt sympathy.

'Little apples will grow again, when the sun comes out.'

I preferred to remember Grandma's words in connection with my loss.

'Think of me when you can't see me.'

A few of the other boys had already lost one or both parents and they were conditioned to almost expect and accept such events, especially those from London. As an orphan, I was allowed to stay with Auntie until the end of the war and then I was transferred to the orphanage at Fieldmoor House a few miles out of town. As Auntie had promised, at sixteen the sun began to shine for me and I found a job in Atkinson's grocer shop as a delivery boy. I was given a bicycle with a basket on the front. I loved being outside but on wet days I made sure that I could find something to do in the shop. Cycling, especially the hilly parts of town, kept me in good trim but with wages not being very good I always kept my ear to the ground on the lookout for a new job. When I answered an advertisement in the newspaper for a trainee in the head office of a local estate agent, Miles Booker & Sons, I eagerly applied and seemed to hit it off well with the manager right from the start. I remember the manager examining my almost blank application. I was keen to get the job, in fact any job which I thought had prospects and this one had the carrot of accommodation. When he smiled and said, 'This is good' I couldn't believe my ears. He explained he was looking for someone with a 'clean sheet' and no pre-set ideas, someone he could mould into the business. My lost grammar school pass was never an issue and as he further explained success didn't rely totally on qualifications but more on 'nowse' and common sense. Getting the job, firstly on a month's probation, solved two problems at a stroke. My wages doubled and I was allowed to move into the bed sit above the shop. It was the ideal situation in that I was never late for work and could always hold the fort until other members of staff finally arrived. At the end of my probationary term the manager liked the way I cleaned and painted the room. That was probably a reflection on my 'accommodation' in Auntie's house which spurred me on not to live in such conditions ever again. I worked for the firm until I became twenty three when I was offered the assistant manager's post in their Bristol office. When the manager of the head office retired, he encouraged me to apply for the post. The weight of his recommendation allowed me to step into his shoes which brought me full circle back to familiar surroundings.

CHAPTER 12

Aged forty three I had everything I ever wanted; a good position with the firm, a company car and a fine house with a coastal view. The business was doing well and properties in the area had become nationally well sought after. On one occasion when two of my sales girls were off sick with flu the agency was so busy that my assistant asked if I could to deal with two ladies who were looking for property in the area. They were both in their mid thirties, well dressed and good looking, in fact my first impression was that they were related. They said they were nurses at the Tootehill nursing home where they had live-in accommodation but they were hoping to get onto the property ladder and purchase a place of their own.

'Tell me what you are looking for,' I enquired. 'Will it be a house, bungalow or flat or do you just want to rent?'

'Oh no, we certainly don't want to rent, this is a long term thing. That would be waste of money. We would like a two bed room bungalow, with garden, garage and sea view.'

'Oh yes,' I said with a smile. 'Would you like a swimming pool as well? I think you want it all, like so many of my customers.'

There was no reply as their faces fell.

I immediately apologised. 'I'm sorry, I am being facetious. The good ones are very expensive, but there are a few needing a lot of renovation to bring them to acceptable standards. Would you be interested in that possibility?'

'We've been looking at prices in the area and we think that with a mortgage we could be thinking in terms of thirty thousand pounds.'

'You would not get what you're looking for with that kind of money unless you purchase one which needs a lot of work doing on it. Do you have someone who could do it, say a husband or family friend?'

'I'm afraid not,' the taller one said as the other giggled.

'Well,' I said, 'I think you should review your finances and think about less ambitious properties so that you can work your way up the property ladder. Have you thought about buying a flat or sharing with others? I know it can be disappointing but I'm sure that with dedication and hard work the two of you together could possibly do something. The thing is not to set your goals too high to start. Leave a contact number with the receptionist just in case anything comes along.'

They both left the agency with less spring in their step than when they came in. I felt sorry that I had dashed their ambition but I had seen so many before with similar inflated hopes.

About two weeks later, Joe Freeman a local councillor who I had met briefly at the golf club invited me to an evening meal at The Blowhole, a local restaurant. He was a man 'at the centre of things' as he called it and knowing that I was the recently appointed manager of Miles Booker & Sons, wanted to include me in his list of people to know.

Years ago there was a small café on the site but it had been developed beyond recognition and given a new name. I made the restaurant a favourite eating place and I often went there to host clients and staff members from our Bristol office. It was a very popular venue for locals and visitors alike with stunning coast line and sea views. Just further along the coast was an impressive attraction in the form of a blow hole which fired volumes of salt water and spray into the air as waves crashed against the rocks below. The full length conservatory at the back of the building which served as a second dining room was named The Rainbow Room on account of the times when the sun shone through the blowhole spray to form colourful rainbow archways which formed over the bay. Bookings for meals at such times were popular and diners regarded the event a final touch to guarantee the success of any function. The other attraction was the 'Poisson d'Farge' created by the chef, a Cockney through and through, who built up a reputation for his Dover sole speciality.

As usual, the restaurant was as busy as ever but Joe had booked our table some days earlier which was essential to avoid queues. He was also able to 'wave' his Councillor card to secure a good window position. Right from the start Joe was keen to let me know that he was a man with influence in the town and that he could 'make things happen'. I did a lot of listening and Joe did a lot of talking. He was quite interesting to begin with as he ran through the changes and improvements in the town over the previous twenty years. I got the impression that he claimed credit for a large proportion of them himself. He had done some 'homework' on me by checking my career over the period but was only able to make links with the Bristol office. I thought it best to leave it that way and said nothing. During a lull in our own conversation, when we were part way through our meal, I became aware of the increased chatter from a nearby table, where four women were seated. I recognised two of them from their visit to my estate agency. They smiled and gave a discreet wave which I acknowledged with a nod. Joe, who struck me as a man with more than a mild interest in the opposite sex for his age, noticed and swivelled rather obviously around in his chair to stare in their direction.

'Is there something going on there?' He whispered. 'They are a fine bunch of fillies, make no mistake. I can fill you in with all you need to know about them. Which one do you fancy?'

'Oh, nothing like that Joe, two of them just happened to be looking for property a few weeks ago and popped into the agency. I couldn't do anything for them and I think they left rather disillusioned.'

'I reckon I could do something for them,' he boasted.

I felt the wine was beginning to free Joe's tongue and tried to get him off the subject of women. There was a clash between two waiters both trying to enter the kitchen at the same time with empty dishes. A cheer from other kitchen staff was taken up by customers seated at the nearby tables, but Joe was undaunted and continued with his obsession.

'Isn't it time you hung up your boots on that playing field Joe, you must be getting on a bit. Are you sixty five yet?' I queried.

'I must admit the engine needs attention but the spirit is willing and when I was your age, things were different. There were women all over town waiting for my services, not to mention my two wives; in fact there was one particular little beauty—.'

I cut him off in full flow.

'Look,' I said. 'With all due respect this is not the type of conversation I'm too happy with, do you think we could change the tone?'

Joe, markedly surprised by my reaction, dropped his knife and fork with a clatter on his almost depleted plate and jumped up sharply.

'Well excuse me for nothing,' he said. 'Do you bat for the other side or something? You can pay the bloody bill yourself. Good bye!'

I remained seated with my mouth open, taken aback by his outburst as he promptly marched out, drawing the attention of the restaurant staff and other diners in addition to the four ladies. His parting shot was to throw his serviette in my direction. The chef came to my table.

'Is everything alright, Sir?'

'Yes, yes, fine thank you. My friend just remembered he had to be somewhere else. My complements to you chef, the fish was perfect.'

I looked across at the other table, where the women were trying to be discrete by paying more than an inordinate amount of attention to their plates. There was a temporary lull in their chatter like so many of the other diners as they shared my embarrassment. As soon as he had gone, conversations struck up once more accompanied by nods and gestures leaving me in no doubt that I seemed to be one of the few people who didn't know Joe. I looked across to the four ladies and made my apology.

'Sorry about that ladies, but I think I upset my friend.'

'I don't think you need worry too much about that in fact you've had a lucky escape. Anyway you're not the first one to upset him,' one of the older ladies informed me. 'He's on the local council and tried twice to be Mayor but failed due lack of committee support. I've known him since way back and believe you me he's not the kind of Mayor I'd like to see. How he keeps his seat on the Council at all is a mystery to me.'

I moved my chair closer.

'Allow me to introduce myself; I have recently been appointed manager at Miles Booker & Sons, the name's Francis— Francis Tenby. I only met Joe a few days ago at the golf club, he seemed anxious to include me on his list of people to know.'

'That sounds like Joe alright,' said one of the others disparagingly. 'I gather by the way he stormed out you won't be on his list anymore.'

'No I don't think so— and he's left me the bill. I can see I'll have to be choosier in future with the company I keep. I trust you ladies are a safer bet?'

'I think so,' they chorused, 'we're quite harmless.' The elder lady made the introductions. 'I believe you've met Jackie and Rose, I'm Amanda and this is Ellie. Jackie and Rose are psychiatric nurses at Tootehill House, Ellie was a school teacher, but has since married and I am on the District Council. That's how I know Joe. We don't often see eye to eye as you can imagine.'

'I merely objected to his coarse line of conversation in which he made some disparaging remarks about the four of you and told him to drop it. Because I didn't ogle all of you like he did, he accused me of 'batting for the other side' as he put it.'

All four giggled. 'Not that I think you need cheering up any more, but Joe has splashed out on these two bottles of wine without paying of course, so would you like to help me finish them off?'

We spent the rest of the evening chatting about their jobs and how things in town had changed over the last twenty years. Their conversation became more animated as the wine flowed and the evening wore on, but I was careful to steer away from drawing attention to myself. Being in a business in the public domain, I was well aware that careless talk could ruin even the most respected firm over night. Joe on the other hand was a person who thrived on it and used any titbit to build up his personal dossier of everyone else's business. I preferred to remain a private person with no particular leanings in any direction.

I became increasingly aware of Jackie, especially when she drew the conversation back to the property market and asked if anything had come up since last we met. She was very lively and full of enthusiasm despite the set back at the agency. I enquired if she and Rose had given any thought to my suggestion that they should revise their ambitions to something lower than their dream bungalow. I caught her eye once or twice when the others were talking and when I turned my full attention to her, expecting her to say something, she visibly flushed. Giving her an escape route I patted the back of her hand and made some comment about the wine but inwardly I had the feeling that we were going to meet up again soon.

For the next few days I found my mind wandering back to Jackie, her soft brown eyes and girlish looks seemed to be on every piece of paper on my desk until finally I felt I had to give her a call.

'Hello, Miles Booker, Estate Agency, here. Can I have a word with

Jackie please? I'm sorry I don't know the surname.'

'Oh, you mean Ms Clarkenwell, just a moment, I'll put you through.'

'Hello, Jackie speaking.'

I recognised the voice and suddenly felt weak at the knees like a sixteen year old and realised that I didn't know what I was going to say.'

'Hello Jackie, I 'mm just thought I would give you a call.' I said vaguely.'

'Yes?'

The ball was back in my court before I had had time to recover and felt sure she would notice my delay. Telling myself that I was a grown man forty plus, I pulled myself together and asked the sixty four thousand dollar question.

'I would like to meet you again sometime; do you think we could make a date and perhaps go for a bite to eat?'

'Yes, that would be lovely. How about Friday, I'm off at six.'

The reply was quick and I hesitated before answering.

'Is that OK?'

That's fine,' I said, let's meet beneath the clock tower at half seven.'

'I'll look forward to it. Bye.'

There was nothing more to be said. I felt elated that making a date with Jackie had not been as difficult as I expected. She had made it easy for me. Face to face I might have been tongue tied. I wasn't one to hide my life under a bushel; I been on a few dates in Bristol, none of which came to anything, but this one seemed different. But then I told myself 'aren't they all' and 'see how it goes'.

Friday seemed a long time in arriving and although previous lady friends had come and gone I was nervous about meeting Jackie. There was something different about her I couldn't quite fathom. We met and greeted each with a hug and a token peck on the cheek like any normal couple who had known each other for years. She looked stunning in her apple green trouser suit, matching high heels and light brown cravat type scarf. She had a shapely youthful figure which caused me to think about my own age and that perhaps I was too old for her.

'Let's begin with a coffee,' I suggested.

I took her hand and as we walked it felt good in mine and I gave it a little squeeze. She did the same.

'I was hoping you would ring Francis,' she said. 'My mind hasn't been on my work these last few days and my friends have wasted no opportunity in telling me so. In fact Rose asked me if you had anything to do with it and I flatly denied it saying I doubt if we would ever meet again.'

'I knew at the restaurant that we had to meet again,' I said. 'That twerp Joe Freeman did me a good favour without knowing it even though he left me the bill. I've regarded it as a good investment all week.'

'Well I've heard of some chat up lines over the years,' she replied but not that one.'

'You know what I mean,' I said defensively. It's meant to be a complement.'

'OK,' she replied. 'I was only pulling your leg like you did to us with the swimming pool.'

I gave her hand a squeeze and waited for her to carry on.

'Amanda is a useful person to know and she knows Joe from way back in the forties before I was born and at that time he was a billeting officer for the evacuation authority. She told me that he used visit my Grandma's house where he billeted some evacuees.'

'I know very little of him,' I said. 'That kafuffle at The Blowhole was entirely my fault really because I disagreed with his line of conversation. Perhaps if I had let him go on he might have hung himself. He was going to tell me about his conquests years ago but I cut him off and he didn't like it. Anyway, that's enough about Joe, what about you? Are you local? The receptionist at Tootehill said your name was Clarkenwell. I can't believe a pretty girl like you could possibly be single. You must have lots of boyfriends.'

'Like all girls, I've had boyfriends, but they haven't lasted. I can never tell with my job when an emergency might come along. Until three months ago my mother was one of the patients at Tootehill too so I tried to be there for her as much as possible which meant that sometimes I took other nurse's shifts.'

'Did your mother have psychiatric problems? How old was she.'

'She went into the home when she was just sixty which was quite early really,' Jackie said. 'Eighteen months later she died. The patients are all waiting to die you know and the nurses try to make life bearable but I think for Mum it was a happy release. Have you ever visited anybody in a home? It's very distressing to see them and the kind of world they barely exist in. My mother didn't know me in the end and fortunately she died in her sleep.'

'What about your dad? Is he still alive?'

'No, I am on my own now. My stepfather left me a bit of money and that's why I've been looking for a place to live away from work. All the staff could do with a break from time to time and being there twenty four seven can be quite depressing especially if you take it to heart.'

'I lost my parents when I was only eight, they were killed in an air raid on Bristol in forty four,' I added trying to be conciliatory. 'I tend to think of life as a continuation of circles and life goes on regardless until it's our turn. I'm not particularly religious but I once heard someone say, 'God only presents us with burdens He knows we can bear.'

'I lived with my grandmother and mother who ran a B & B until I was about nine and then one night my grandmother was found wandering in the dark, bare footed only wearing her nightgown. Mum and I were in bed when the police came to the house bringing grandma home with another lady who had recognised her whilst walking her dog. She was diagnosed with senile dementia and she had no idea who she was which resulted in her being sectioned and sent to a home in Bodmin. My mum and I visited her several times but I found it difficult to understand that she had no idea who we were. I loved my grandma and was sad when she died with no sign of recovery aged seventy three. That was four years ago.'

'Crumbs, you come from a fine family,' I said with a laugh. 'Sorry I don't mean to be rude, but have you considered having a check-up at the hospital lately?'

'I'm fine thank you,' Jackie said. 'I'm told that it doesn't naturally follow that I will be affected.'

'Did your Mum carry on with the B & B on her own after grandma left?'

'No, she sold the business and then my mother and I went to live with a chap she had known for years. She used to call him Clark after the actor Clark Gable but I never found out why because he looked nothing like him. When they married some time later he became my step dad, but I didn't like him very much. Just before I was eleven they sent me away to a private school, I think mainly to get me out the way because they travelled a lot. I didn't see much of them after that, only twice in fact during the five years I was at school. Reports of my progress were sent to them the whole time and I suppose they were good enough for them not to bother about visiting me. At times when the other girls had visitors I missed out. Then during the holidays when I remained at the school I felt like an orphan. My friends were very good to me and used to invite me to stay at their homes. I was sixteen when finally I went back to live with mum again, but it was only for six months whilst my application to join the RAF was being processed. By then I had grown up and things were very different between the three of us.'

'I suppose having finished your exams I can imagine you felt free and ready to enjoy yourself then?'

'Yes! Absolutely! My mother thought I was a wild thing and my step dad acted oddly toward me. Whenever I knew they were going to be out I used to invite friends into the house for parties but I had to be careful with the furniture and carpets in the lounge so we used to go into my bedroom. On one occasion when mum and Clark came back unexpectedly, there were two girls and two boys in my double bed having a romp for a film which one of the lads was supposed to be making. He was going to charge his friends to see it and was hoping to make a mint but I never heard from him again. The neighbours complained to mum later that two boys, who were practically naked, were seen as they ran out of the house across their gardens. After that my reputation went down the drain and the neighbours needed no convincing when she told them that I was out of control, a whore and a prostitute. None of it was true of course; I was just a sixteen year old having a good time but drew the line at having sex with any of the boys. That was one of the golden rules drummed into us at school that mistakes in that direction could affect our careers and indeed the rest of our lives. Clark seemed to draw the conclusion that I was sex mad nymph and at times I felt so unsafe with him, especially when he was drunk. Then I used to barricade my bedroom door with the wardrobe and the bed. On one occasion which he told my mother was an accident, he walked in on me while I was having a bath. I threw the metal water jug at him, cutting his head so badly he had to go to hospital to be stitched up.'

Jackie stopped talking while she drank the rest of her cold coffee and smiled.

'I bet you're wishing you hadn't invited me out Francis. I would quite understand if you walked out and didn't want to see me again.'

'On the contrary, Jackie, I'm quite fascinated to hear your story and I'm looking forward to hear what happened next.'

'My mother almost seemed to condone his interest in me and refused to believe anything I had to say which made me want to get away. I loved my dad but she tried to sour my relationship with him by saying that he was a rotter and a womaniser. After the divorce, my mother was given custody of me because dad, being in the forces, was not able to provide a stable home. There was a lot of acrimony between them and mum wouldn't even let me see him when he was home on leave. I think I was about ten when we were out shopping in the town one day and I saw my dad across the street. I tried to run over to him, but she grabbed and quickly dragged me into a shop so that he wouldn't see us.'

'Sorry to interrupt Jackie but I think this coffee shop closes at nine and it looks as if the waitresses are getting ready to close. I'm getting a bit peckish, how about you? Shall we go and have a bite somewhere?'

'And me,' Jackie said. I rather fancy that new Italian place that's just opened in Lowther Street. My friends recommended it when it first opened even though they had to queue. It was some sort of promotional do then but I don't know what it's like now. Would that be OK?'

'Great! I fancy some spaghetti bolognaise and some red wine.'

As we walked along the street, Jackie stopped outside a newspaper shop.

'I'll always associate this spot with my dad,' Jackie mused. 'This is the shop that my mother dragged me into so that dad wouldn't see us. She just wanted to cut him out of my life because of her failed marriage and I didn't think it was at all fair.'

The Italian restaurant was quiet with no queues. Peppi the proprietor said it was because of the local floodlit football match being played at the Dell and that the fans would pour in later after the match. It was a friendly bistro which had been recently started up by a couple of Italians who were on holiday and liked the town so much they decided to stay. Peppi was a football enthusiast who was in his element with the locals when it came to discussing the game. Photographs of his favourite players took up every spare inch of wall behind the bar. In contrast, pictures by local artists depicting the War years and the changes which had taken place in the town over the last fifty years were everywhere else. As we ate our meal Jackie pointed out particular ones she liked and even one with a photograph of her and some school friends taking part in the traditional Floral Dance as it made its way through the town. There was another from the war years which showed the GI's using a heavy armoured vehicle to move the town's lifeboat which had become jammed in the harbour entrance. I recognised it right away. It was a copy of a photograph taken by my former manager at Miles Booker which used to hang on his office wall.

After our meal, we took our bottle of wine and sat by the fire to watch the steam and flames rising from the logs which filled the room with a rich cedar aroma.

'This is the perfect setting to tell you the rest of my bedtime story,' Jackie said. 'Where were we?' .

'The newspaper shop,' I said.

'Oh yes. Just after my sixteenth birthday, a friend told me that I was of an age when legally I could make decisions for myself and not being happy with mum and Clark I complained to the police. I told them that the stories my mother had concocted were untrue and that I felt I was in danger. About two weeks later, my dad turned up at the house saying that the local authorities had been in touch and that I could live with him and his new wife, Sarff, at their home in Wiltshire. I jumped at the chance and my mother and Clark were both furious but I took no notice and left the same day.'

'Did your dad know about your plans for the RAF?' I queried.

'Yes he was quite pleased and said that he could pull a few strings to find out what progress had been made. About three weeks later I learned that my application had been successful and that I could join a women's military training school in Lancashire. In the short time that I was with dad I found Sarff to be jealous and hostile toward me. She wanted him all to herself and I often heard them arguing that as it was her house she hadn't been consulted about my coming. The RAF solved the problem and Sarff never even wished me good bye when I left. That was the last time that I saw my dad because about eighteen months later Sarff sent me a letter telling me that he was dead.'

'That must have been a shock,' I said. I suppose with your mother and Clark off your popularity list you must have felt as if you were on your own again.'

'The letter from Sarff was quite convincing and conclusive. She said that a Blenheim aircraft returning from a mission had tried to land in the fog at Driffield but was redirected to another airbase. The pilot, thinking he could land anyway, attempted to do so but overran the runway and in his effort to swing around for another attempt, crashed into woodlands killing all seven crew. Sarff then added that when the wreckage was salvaged a charred cigarette case belonging to dad was found and she posted it to me. That was eighteen years ago and until now I've always believed the story to be true.'

'Why now?' I asked excitedly seeing the look in her face change.

'I've been reading a book in which someone has catalogued all military crashes up and down the country including the death and injury to personnel and Sarff's reported crash isn't listed. Now I am carrying out my own investigation to see if I can find out what really happened. About ten days ago, I tried writing to Sarff but the letter was returned with 'Not at this address' written on it. When it arrived back a couple of days ago I could see that it had been steamed open so I'm very suspicious. I must have a word with Ellie, her husband was in the RAF and maybe able to help.'

'Crumbs, I bet you are!' I exclaimed.

'Anyway, after I completed my training in Lancashire I was posted to a camp in Lincolnshire where I was a Staff Nurse in an orthopaedic ward. I settled down there and shared a flat with another nurse who introduced me to a chap that I became engaged to but it all fell through when I found the two of them in bed together. I was so upset at the time that I thought I had to get away from it all and have a complete change. A posting came up in Cyprus which I jumped at and really enjoyed myself there until I had an accident with one of the patients. It was my own fault really because two nurses are supposed to be on hand when moving a patient but on this occasion the patient was only a little eight stone woman who I thought I could easily handle. Whilst helping her out of bed one morning to go to the bathroom she suddenly spun around, fell back on the bed and sent me sprawling backwards. There was a service trolley nearby which I crashed into and then I found myself on the floor, unable to move. In addition to some internal injury I damaged two lumbar vertebrae in my back which brought my job there to an end and then I became a patient there too for about six months.'

'That was a stroke of bad luck for you. Were you compensated for the injury?'

'No I wasn't because I had ignored the rules and afterward posters were pinned up in every ward to make sure that it didn't happen again.'

'From what I've seen of you so far Jackie you look quite normal on the outside. You must have fully recovered to be doing what you do now.'

'Oh yes I have,' she said with a smile. 'I was invalided out of the RAF and spent over a year hiking my way around Australia and New Zealand. It was one of those things I always wanted to do, a sort of reversal of what people do but they wait until they're retired to do it. After that I felt it was time I got a job again and met up with an old colleague who happened to be Rose, the nurse you've already met. She introduced me to Tootehill a private nursing home for convalescents and the aged. Then by pure coincidence my mother arrived there about four months later. When Clark died she seemed to fall to pieces and her doctor diagnosed her with kidney failure. She was barely sixty. After I left to live with dad we didn't keep in touch, not even with Christmas or birthday cards, so I had no idea that their drinking problem was serious. Of course I knew Clark drank too much from his drunken escapades with me but he didn't die with a drink related illness, he simply had a heart attack when he was swimming in the sea. He was missing for about a week and mum thought he had just gone off somewhere but then his body was washed up on Trelevan sands.'

'What an unusual family you were!' I said. 'You're beginning to worry me. Everybody you meet seems to end up dead.'

'Well, that's certainly true as far as Tootehill goes. I sometimes think there should be an inscription over the door making a reference to a one way journey. Anyway, don't let me keep you and I hope you don't go, but there's the door,' she said laughing.

'I find you too intriguing to go just yet Jackie. I think I'll hang on a while longer.'

'While mum was in Tootehill I suppose we had some sort of reunion and I relented toward her but for most of the time, perhaps it was partially due to the drugs, she didn't know me or what was going on around her. I often thought as I sat with her for hours on end, it would have been good to catch up with family history but she would only mumble and get things mixed up. Grandma gave me a few pictures but she didn't recognise any of those either, not even one of herself.'

'Yes I know what you mean,' I said. 'Some time ago, an old neighbour of mine in Bristol, a retired solicitor that I used to like talking to, was taken into a home where there were quite a number in a similar degenerative state. It was sole destroying to see them and I find it frightening that as sure as night follows day, many of us will end up the same way. You might be used to it but I found it un-nerving. I was afraid to turn my back on any of them just in case they tried to throw their arms around me in mistake for some visiting relative. Some just wandered around in a daze, while others lay in the beds, mouths open and teeth missing, no hair, drooling and staring with glazed sunken eyes into space. I felt guilty that I only visited him twice but I found I just didn't want to be there. All I can say is that to do the job as I presume you do must be as a result of some special calling. Personally, I would pin a gold star on each and every one of you.'

'Well, thanks very much,' Jackie said. 'But we don't do it for any badge, they're only bits of metal and wouldn't mean much to the girls. We like to think we're doing some good and making a small difference to the patients during their twilight days.'

'I'm older than you Jackie can I apply to have you look after me?'

'I'll get you an application form,' she said jokingly.

We had been comfortable by the fire, but now the bistro was

beginning to fill up with talkative football fans from the floodlit match who were disgruntled and animated about why their team lost. Peppi joked with them and offered to bring a dead beat Italian player to town who he suggested could do better. It got quite noisy as the beer flowed so I suggested we walk back to the clock tower where Jackie had arranged to meet Rose for a lift back to Tootehill. She was waiting in her little Austin Ruby car which she cranked into life as soon as she saw us coming.

'Hello Francis, don't snigger,' she said as she saw the smirk on my face.

'It keeps me fit, you know. I have to crank my baby into life each time because there's something wrong with the starter motor but somebody told me it was the gearing on the flywheel, so I don't know. Sorry to rush but I have to be in by half ten, it's my night shift.'

'I haven't driven one of these in years Rose, you must let have a go next time you're both off. I could have a look at that starter motor for you if you like. Can I give you a call Jackie? I'd like to hear the rest of your story.'

As Rose drove away I didn't have time to wish Jackie goodnight as I would have liked but suspected that our low key parting probably saved her from interrogation by Rose wishing to know every detail of our first date. Later the following week I realised that I hadn't made any arrangements with Jackie but before I had chance to phone, she called me at the office to say that she had been chatting to Ellie and something interesting had come up about her father. She suggested that the three of us meet in the Pig and Whistle on the Friday after six and I agreed.

CHAPTER 13

They were waiting for me. The pub was busy with early evening drinkers sitting at tables loaded with bottles and glasses, all drinking as if there was no tomorrow, but for some, as if they had waited all day for the bar to open. Jackie and Ellie were sitting near the door away from the main smoke haze created mainly by the smokers in addition to that of a mobile grill as it visited various tables.

I heard Ellie telling Jackie to wait. 'Be patient, I'll tell you the rest when Francis comes.'

'Hello, you two,' I said as I gave Jackie a discrete peck on the cheek. It didn't go un-noticed as Ellie slid a chair toward me.

'Ok, Ellie, now will you tell me? You've kept me on tender hooks long enough.'

'I was visiting a friend of mine in hospital,' she began, 'when I happened to mention to a nurse that you were curious about what had happened to your dad. I remembered that he had been treated for a stab wound after the riot at the NAAFI club and the nurse checked in the hospital records for the details. They showed that a Richard Manston 556249 was treated for a serious stab wound to the stomach and that excellent work by the surgeon, a Mr. Ryan, enabled him to make a full recovery. When I said you could find no record of your father's supposed crash I told her about the number.'

'I knew that he had a number like all service personnel,' Jackie commented. It was on his tool box with the RAF ensign, but I can't remember what it was.'

Bells started to ring in my head. The mere mention of a toolbox with an ensign and all the memories it held for me began to emerge. But then, I told myself, there must have been lots of toolboxes with RAF emblems. Surely, it must be a coincidence. I decided to ask more questions.

'Just a minute Jackie,' I said. 'I thought your name was Clarkenwell, if this RAF chap is your dad, why isn't your name Manston too?'

'When my mum married Clark, she took his name and at one time she thought of having an 'up market' hyphenated name but she changed her mind and I became a Clarkenwell too. She also started to call me Jackie because of the rift between herself and dad. Apparently he chose my original name which was Connie and she didn't like it.' All three of us went...'

'I don't believe it!' I interrupted and then took a full swig to empty my glass. 'It can't be true.'

'What can't be true?' Ellie queried.

'I need a stiff drink, anybody else want one?'

I went to the bar, leaving Jackie and Ellie staring at each other.

'What don't you believe?' Jackie said as I returned carrying three whiskies.

'I think you're going to need that Jackie. You're birthday is the 20th March isn't it? And you're Connie Manston.'

'Yes it is! How do you know?'

I leaned across the table and wrapped my arms around her. Ellie looked bemused as I gave Jackie a full blooded kiss on the lips and held on until she gasped for air. Ellie clapped and stamped her feet attracting everyone's attention in the bar.

'That's my apology for not looking after you when you were three years old and your Grandma gave me a clip around the ear for it. I was one of those evacuee kids in your Grandma's house during the War and you were not much older the last time I saw you. You were playing with the larder door and you trapped your fingers and Grandma blamed me. I bet some of your fingers are out of shape.'

'Yes!' Jackie said in amazement.

She was visibly shaking as she gave me her left hand. She showed a wide eyed Ellie her bent little finger which she said she had never been able to straighten properly.

'I remember that tool box too,' I said. 'It was in the attic behind the evacuees toilet bucket. There were eighteen of us mostly in camp beds but I shared a big double bed with five others and the bucket was supposed to keep us from pounding up and down the bare wooden stairs at night. It was always full and the toolbox used to get sprayed when either the bucket was full or some sleepy head missed the bucket all together. One of the bigger boys who slept in the box room below was always complaining because his ceiling was often wet with the leakages. On one occasion when the bucket was accidentally tipped over it all ran down the stairs and flooded through his ceiling and on to his bed.'

'Eighteen in the attic,' exclaimed Ellie. 'Six in a bed! Unbelievable!'

'Mum never talked about the evacuees, although I know from Ellie that at the time the town was overloaded with them,' Jackie said, now fully convinced that our past was connected.

'I used to teach the girls in Dowdales School,' Ellie explained. 'When the evacuees came, most of them being Londoners, the school had to be extended to house them all. Originally it was built for 125 boys and about the same number of girls but the numbers grew to half as many again with the result that even though other buildings in town were annexed, class numbers rose to fifty. Teaching was very difficult, desks had to be pushed together and to make matters worse some of the evacuees were trouble makers who didn't want to learn anyway.'

I listened to Ellie with interest as all the memories came flooding back. Although it was thirty five or so years ago, it seemed just like yesterday.

'You bring it all back to me Ellie,' I said, 'I remember the headmaster kept the boys and girls sections apart and there was a definite demarcation between them. My friend Dennis was once caught in the girls' play ground chasing a football from the boys' side after the whistle was blown. He was made to stand in front of the girls at assembly like some thief caught in the act and then later given six strokes of the cane by the headmaster.'

'Captain Tompkins was some character; he was very liberal with his cane and ran the school with a rod of iron. He had to really, with so many kids from all walks of life and some who had no idea of right from wrong or had any respect for property or possessions. At the time the crime rate shot up and it needed more people like the Captain to make any impression on the figures.'

'I was one of the 'goodie goodies' and never in trouble,' I assured Ellie. 'Ms Nicholson was my teacher and she looked after me and my two friends Dennis and Daryl. She was a good teacher and the three of us passed our eleven plus. I don't know what happened then. Do you remember her?'

'Indeed I do,' Ellie said. 'Wendy was my friend. 'You say Francis, you don't know what happened after you passed your eleven plus. Didn't you go to grammar school?'

'No I didn't, I was supposed to go back home but with no parents I went to Fieldmoor orphanage instead.'

'Well that's odd.' Ellie looked puzzled. 'Tell you what,' she continued, 'I'll look up some old school records and let you know. I'll enjoy trolling back through them, in fact it might set me going again on a book I've been thinking of writing about the history of educational achievements over the years.'

'Thanks very much, I would like to know and where Dennis and Daryl went.'

I explained how in the end it didn't matter anyway and turned the subject back to Wendy.

'We had some good times together and she taught my two girls on the piano. There was some talk about her having a fling with the Captain which was given some credence by the fact that he left his entire estate to her. She was a wealthy woman.'

'What do you mean? Was!' I exclaimed. 'She wouldn't be very old now. No more than about sixty I'd guess.'

'That's right. She died a few months ago and I was most upset. I was a bit older than her and had two children when we were teaching together. She was a newly qualified teacher at twenty three, single and a bit of a bobby dazzler. Her parents had left her well off and it was quite feasible for the Captain to take an interest in her, but he wasn't the only one. On the night when Jackie's dad went to hospital, Wendy and I dated a couple of American GI's and a group us went to a dance at the NAAFI club. I remember Richard being there with a Scotsman in a kilt and by chance we happened to be sitting at the same table. The club was crowded and a few British service men who were drunk caused a riot by accusing the GI's of stealing what they thought was their English girls. There was a lot of jealousy between the forces at the time because the GI's had everything but the British Tommy had to survive on what was known as the King's shilling.'

'This is the sort of thing I wish my mother could have talked about,' Jackie said. 'I feel as if a lot of water has passed under the bridge without me knowing, but I suppose being only a baby at the time she never thought to tell me. My early memories are of Grandma and mum running a guest house until I was nine or ten and then Grandma had some illness and went to a hospital in Bodmin. Later when mum sold the B & B she took me to see her. I remember that Grandma cried when mum said she was going to marry Clark and go to live with him taking me with her. I loved my Grandma and can't believe she had so many evacuees in the attic because what I remember of the two rooms was that they were lovely with dormer windows and a separate bathroom. We had one guest in each and they were there for as long as I can remember.'

'Well, I can assure you Jackie that my memories of the attic were not so pleasant but I would love to go back and see it now. I have a few ghosts to put to rest.'

'My husband was in the RAF and had a posting to the Far East during the War,' Ellie added. 'He says that now we have a service number for Richard that it shouldn't be too difficult to trace the name from the wartime personnel lists. We'll see what he comes up with, but it might take a little time because he knows from experience how long it can to get things moving with the MOD.'

'I would be very grateful Ellie,' Jackie said. 'I've been in the dark for so long now a few more weeks won't make any difference. Didn't I say Francis that Ellie was a walking newspaper? Well, now you know.'

'Some of the credit belongs to Amanda,' Ellie added. I think between us we could probably compile quite a comprehensive Who's Who magazine. I'd like to tell you more some other time, but for now I have to earn a few more crusts of bread. I'm so pleased that you two have been reunited after all this time.'

Ellie gave me a farewell wave and whispered something in Jackie's ear which she disguised with a friendly hug. Jackie flushed but I pretended not to notice.

'By the way,' I said, 'I didn't want to say too much while Ellie was here but a property you might like has come on the market. It's a bit above your price bracket but I'm sure I could arrange suitable terms with a mortgage company we use. I don't want to raise your hopes too much but perhaps you and Rose might like to review your finances and shake the piggy bank a bit more. This property will soon get snapped up so when do you think the pair of you would like an official viewing?'

'Oh that's great, we could arrange cover for an hour or so in the morning after our coffee break,' Jackie said excitedly. 'I'll have a word with Rose tonight even if I have to wake her up. She will be so pleased.'

'Steady on Jackie, you might not like the place, so keep an open mind. It's an older property, probably built in the twenties and needs a bit of work doing on it. The old chap who lived there was a bit of an invalid and has let the garden become overgrown but I would imagine it was quite something to see in its heyday.'

I could see that Jackie was excited at the possibility of being her own person in her own home and wanted to see the property right away but felt frustrated that the hours of darkness were against her. She finished her drink and suggested we have a walk through the park to dispel some her built up adrenalin and think more positively in the cool night air. Instinctively she took my arm and she felt comfortable by my side, step for step.

'Did you mind me kissing you like that in front of Ellie? I asked.

'Not at all Francis, our meeting like this has been just amazing like as if it was destined to happen. Ellie is a dear friend of mine, but I'm afraid that it will be all over Tootehill and probably the rest of town by tomorrow.'

'Will you be happy with that?'

'I'll get some ribbing from the girls at work, but I don't care. In the short time that we've known each other I find myself looking forward to seeing you again. You know so much about me and you've turned my world upside down.'

'I must admit that I feel the same. I see your face on every piece of paper in my office and on my ceiling at night.'

Jackie stopped walking and took me by surprise as she threw her arms around me, lifting both feet off the ground at the same time. I toppled over and we both fell onto a grass bank by the side of a park bench. As we lay on the ground kissing each other oblivious of the world around us, a passer by with her dog expressed her disgust.

'Can't you two wait 'til you get home? This place gets more like a rabbit warren every day, just like when the Yanks were here.'

We brushed each other down laughing at the same time.

'You could have a least sat on the seat first,' I joked.

'Good thing she didn't see our faces,' Jackie said. 'I could imagine your property sales taking a nose dive tomorrow.'

We arranged for a pick up after eleven in the morning and I left word with the office that I would be out for a couple of hours with clients viewing the bungalow and then possibly go to lunch. When I arrived at Tootehill, no one was waiting. I sat in the car listening to the radio when two nurses, one much younger than the other, dressed in white coats came down the driveway. The younger one tapped on my window whilst the other continued out the gate and disappeared around the corner.

'Hello, are you Mr. Tenby?' We've had a bit of an emergency this morning. If you like you are welcome to have a cup of coffee in our visitor's waiting room. I understand Jackie and Rose won't be long.'

'OK, that's fine. Hop in I give you a lift back.'

She looked admiringly at the car. 'Nice motor and so quiet too. My dad is teaching me to drive at the moment but his car rattles like a dust bin.'

I laughed. 'Well, you have to start somewhere. I won't tell you how many years it's taken for me to get this one. You are very young to be a nurse,' I observed.

'Yes, I'm eighteen; just started three days ago. I'm a trainee. My name's Sally.'

'You got me worried when I saw you and your colleague coming toward me two minutes ago. Someone once warned me when I'd lost my temper over something, that if I didn't 'watch it,' one day two people in white coats would come and take me away.'

She smiled. 'No need to worry there Mr. Tenby, we only take old people.'

'Anyway, nice to meet you Sally; this home is bigger than I expected.'

'I'm told it has grounds of about five acres but I haven't had time to look around myself yet. We have thirty two patients and they keep us all busy.'

The driveway was several hundred yards long, though manicured lawns flanked on either side with a variety of rhododendrons and trees. At some time or other I presumed that the large Georgian house which came into view as we rounded a curve in the driveway was a gentleman's country residence. It had been altered to suit its new occupants but very tastefully so as not to derogate from splendour of former days. Grandma's photograph of her fine house in Ireland flashed through my mind and I could just imagine the coach and four waiting for the master at the entrance. Sally hopped out just as Rose appeared in the doorway.

'Jackie's on her way. Sorry about the delay. I see you've met Sally so you know why.'

'Yes, bright little thing, I hope she fits in.'

'Well, she's got a long way to go. Matron sent her out for some fresh air after the poor girl fainted at the sight of blood. A patient fell cutting her leg but when Sally was asked to help pick the old dear up, she passed out as well. She's got to get used to that, we see plenty.'

Commenting on the building, I was just asking Rose to tell me something about its history when Jackie appeared looking flushed. 'Sit back and relax, I hope you've got plenty of money in your handbags?' I said as we drove off for our rendezvous with the bungalow.

'Lovely car,' Rose commented, 'more plush than my Ruby.'

'I'm sure this one can't go anywhere yours can't Rose, perhaps a little faster maybe.'

The engine was barely audible as the car moved effortlessly and smoothly to the outskirts of town where I took the coast road to Shipley Green, a small coastal hamlet with about a dozen or so older houses and bungalows, a public house and a sixteenth century church. We stopped at the gate of a quaint bungalow in a delightful situation overlooking the bay. The name on the unpainted wooden gate read 'Pic—dy,' the middle two letters were missing. Roses now out of control grew up and over the porch and the overgrown front lawn would have made an ideal home for any number of rabbits. The bungalow itself had been sturdily built, with rough-casting on three sides and the final end wall taken up mainly by a slate chimney stack down to ground level. The wooden windows were in a better condition than the gate but still needed a coat of paint. A pathway led to a back garden shed which was in a tumble down state and continued further on to a copse at the bottom. Edging stones and less overgrown areas indicated that at one time there was a vegetable garden on one side with lawns on the other.

'What's the name?' Rose asked.

'This is Picardy. What are your first impressions?' I asked. 'It's my experience that properties are either bought or rejected in the first five minutes of viewing. Some clients don't even bother to get out of the car and there are others who look with great interest only to turn away on seeing something like a broken window. They seem not to be able to sort out the really important features from the superficial.'

'It's cute and needs a lot of TLC,' Rose commented.

'The old chap that lived here was a bit of a romantic and named the house after his wife's favourite piece of music 'Roses of Picardy' and also in memory of his brother who was killed in the northern region of France with the same name during the first World War. When his wife died a couple of years ago, he was distraught with grief and lost interest in the house and gardens which were their pride and joy.'

'How sweet, he must have been a lovely chap and if we buy the place I would like to think that we could restore everything to its former glory in his memory. I love the name too. "Picardy", it has a ring to it.'

Jackie stopped talking for a moment. 'We've got to have this place Rose. I thought the name rang a bell. When my mother died she left me great granddad's World War1 medals and the citation that went with them. He died in Picardy too; perhaps the two soldiers might have known each other.

'That settles it. The coincidence is too big to ignore,' Rose added.

I could see both Rose and Jackie were in love with the bungalow straight away and carried on with the details in an effort to make sure they were well aware of the commitment they were proposing to take on.

'He died just recently and his executors acting on behalf of his one and only niece are anxious to settle his estate as soon as possible. An auction date has been set for the twentieth which gives you about two weeks to make your minds up. The guide price has been set at thirty five thousand pounds which I know is well above your present limit but there may be a possibility of a bargain. Valuation depends on condition and potential but what you must realise is that that figure is a guide only and could be higher or lower on the day. Several factors could have a bearing on the final sale price but the worst situation would be if two bidders really want it then the price could go way out of your reach.'

'I still think you're jumping the gun a bit Rose. Neither of has ever been to an auction,' Jackie began. 'Personally the whole idea of bidding perhaps thousands at a time, frightens me to death.'

'Well, you don't have to attend,' I ventured. 'You could employ the services of a solicitor to act for you. All he would need to know would be your price limit.'

'We will have to scrape the bottom of the barrel to do it, but we love it. There's a cosy feeling to the house even in its present state and I can feel a special kind of warmth in every room.'

'Will I take that as a 'Yes' then? Jackie.'

'Yes you may, definitely, we are both delighted.'

Rose and Jackie sat quietly in the back of the car, deep in thought, all the way back to Tootehill until I stopped at the entrance. Rose then broke the silence by saying that she intended to visit her parents in Truro as soon as possible to tell them the news. She thought there was even the possibility that they might help financially and perhaps she could enlist her brother to work on the garden. At the gate, she walked discretely on ahead leaving Jackie to say goodbye in her own passionate way.

Back in the office I wasted no time in contacting a mortgage company and discussed possible financial arrangements on my client's behalf based on the proposed guide price. Howson and Philps Partners, an estate agency in Liverpool which was handling the sale of Picardy on behalf of the niece who lived abroad had been given instructions for a quick sale. The agents cleverly arranged for the auction to be held in one of the meeting rooms of The Blowhole where they knew the attendance and possible interest would most likely be high. There was also the possibility that with a bit of Dutch courage from the bar prospective bidders might be less inhibited. Later on in the week, the two girls came into the agency.

'How did you get on with your parents? It's all up to you now Rose.'

'They were very helpful really, but we can only raise another two thousand or so between us,' she said looking a little disconsolate. 'They suggested, and we both agree, that we don't want to be involved with a mortgage. My dad is one of what you might call 'The old school' in that he doesn't believe in buying anything on the 'never-never'. The figures you gave us detailing the mortgage rates in addition to the indemnity policy over a period of twenty five years tend to make me agree with his 'never-never' policy. Just think we could both be in our sixties before we finish paying. That's a definite 'No-No.'

'It's such a shame that my mother drank away a small fortune,' Jackie added. 'Neighbours told me that doctors had advised both of them to cut down on their drinking long ago when I was still at school. The house being in a prime location overlooking the harbour was worth a lot of money but there was little left in the end. Fortunately, in one of his more sober states Clark was advised to open a trust fund in my favour for twenty thousand pounds payable on my twenty first, but when mum went into the nursing home I had to supplement her costs which ate into it. But I can't grumble really, Clark also paid for my private school education, so I must at least be grateful for that. Anyway it looks as if we'll have to call the whole thing off and wait 'til we've saved a bit more. We're both very sorry we've wasted your time.'

I sat stirring my coffee needlessly for a few moments while they looked out the window to watch leaves blowing along the street carrying their dreams with them.

'I don't know that you have.'

They both turned to see me smiling like a Cheshire cat, their faces full of hope but not daring to ask why.

'It's practically a done deal,' I said. 'I'll lend you the rest of the money as a sort of underwriter. I'd like to give you the chance to make something of Picardy as I'm sure the old couple would have liked. There would have to be one proviso though with any such arrangement because as you will appreciate, I could not be seen to be involved.'

Their faces lit up, almost in disbelief. Jackie sat with her mouth open.

'You're our knight in shining armour Francis,' Rose exclaimed. 'We will be forever in your debt. How could we ever repay you?'

'You'll both have to marry me!'

'I wish,' said Rose with a laugh, 'just say when.'

Jackie finally managed to close her mouth, stared at me for a moment and turned to hide her embarrassment by looking out the window. Rose anticipating Jackie's thoughts spoke for her.

'I think my house mate is pleased too.'

CHAPTER 14

The night shift was a difficult one at Tootehill. Rose went to bed after breakfast as usual but feeling dog tired, so tired in fact that she found sleeping difficult. A number of cases of food poisoning resulted in many of the patients being sick, for some not once but twice. Each one required a total clean up having soiled both their bedding and clothing. On top of that there were still those other patients who always required assistance every few hours to visit toilets. In desperation Rose had to physically restrain one particularly difficult man who had a habit of trying to escape during the hours of darkness. She had to call for help from another nurse and between them they managed to persuade the poor chap no-one was trying to kill him. In his demented mind he seemed able to call upon some extra strength in his effort to escape from the Japanese prisoner of war camp and now at Tootehill he was totally disorientated. It was not until five thirty in the morning that Rose and her colleagues were finally able to take a coffee break. Although potentially a dangerous situation, they were able to recall the man's highly animated antics and even be amused by them as he dodged and weaved his way around obstacles on his way to the exit.

'Hello…hello, can you see him Tobo?' he whispered. 'I know he's there. I can see his shadow on the wall. Quick, hide in here—he's coming.' And then, as the nurses grabbed him—. 'Ahhhhh—. The swines have got me—.Go—. Save yourself.'

When Rose managed to flop on to her bed too tired to change she had second thoughts about whether she should have allowed Agnes to top up her last mug of coffee. A tug of war was going on between the stimulant and her physical tiredness and the stimulant was winning. Thoughts of Picardy kept flooding through her mind such that in the end she decided sleep was impossible. She tried to think there must be some other way of raising the total purchase price without being dependant on anyone other than her colleague. In the past she had always heeded her parent's advice in financial matters and strived to follow her dad's particular mantra, "never-a-lender-or-borrower-be".

Suddenly she sat bolt upright in her bed.

'That's it. Matron! She's the answer to our prayers. Surely there must be slight deviations from dad's steadfast golden rules. I must wake Jackie,' she said out loud.

Without bothering with her dressing gown she went next door to Jackie's room and knocked three times.

'Are you asleep Jackie? It's me Rose.'

'No, as a matter of fact I'm not. I've been listening to you tossing and turning in your bed in there and I heard you talking to someone. What's the mater?'

'Yes I know, I've been too tired to sleep; must remember not to have coffee before going to bed. Listen—about Picardy—I expect you've been thinking about it too and that's half the reason why I can't sleep. Anyway, I've hit on an idea for raising the remainder of the cash we need.'

'But we don't need it now Rose, Francis has given us a clear path to be able to deal with the solicitor.'

'But you are forgetting the legal costs, commissions and whatever else might be involved. They all add up you know and could be the last straw. I tried to buy a flat once with two other students. The deal broke down at the last hurdle and we had to pull out losing our deposit in the process. It was money we could ill afford to lose and it taught me a lesson.'

'OK then, let's have your brilliant idea. What is that can't wait 'til morning?'

'What is it that we've got to trade? Jackie my girl.'

'Oh no, you can't mean—? You've really woken me up now. Tell me you wouldn't sink so low.'

'Get away with you, of coarse not. What do you think of this idea?' Rose said as she moved Jackie's feet to sit on the bottom of her bed. 'Let's make a proposal to Matron she won't be able to refuse.'

'Oh yes and what sort of proposal would that be then Rose? Say that we will work for nothing? Or shall we suggest she can't do without us and we think we're worth more? I can't imagine much else; you know she's a hard nut to crack.'

'What is it they are short of in this establishment? Well, I'll tell you.

Rooms and accommodation that's what! I propose that we offer our two rooms in exchange for a three month sub on each of our wages. These ground floor rooms are valuable. If we get our own place Matron will be able to shuffle things around and provide rooms for two more private patients. It's a win, win situation, I'm sure she would go for it. And another thing, if we were to be successful at the auction we would only be required to put down say a ten percent deposit, which would be no problem. Also Matron would need time to make arrangements and you know how long solicitors take to settle contracts, well by that time we would have the cash to settle outright. Francis told us that we might get a bargain on the day, so I think we should go for it.'

'Sounds plausible Rose, you seem to have got it all worked out but I've just thought of another advantage to the deal. We live in, right? Well we should expect a salary increase for moving out, don't you think?'

'Well done Jackie, now you're thinking along the right lines…must admit I hadn't thought of that.'

'So, are you saying we have both a Plan A and a Plan B?'

'Well, yes and no. I didn't mention this to Francis, but my dad pulled a long face when I told him about the possible underwriting and Francis himself touched on the subject when he said that he couldn't be seen to be compromising his position as estate agent.'

'You've got me worried now Rose. What will I say next time we meet?'

'Just leave it as it is for now. It's all 'ifs' and 'buts' at the moment and I have a gut feeling that all will be well and we won't need any Plan A. Let's think about it and I'll chat to Matron the first chance I get. The essential thing is that we both present a united front, two onto one as it were.'

'I am sorry Doctor but I can't make any commitments at this moment in time, but I wish I could help because I know what a great deal it would mean to Mr. Agiter to be near his wife. Let me assure you that if anything turns up I will let you know right away.'

Rose was passing the Matron's office later in the day and chanced to hear the all important part of her conversation. She stopped dead in her tracks and changed direction for Jackie's room.

'Talk about being in the right place at the right time Jackie, but you'll never guess what I've just overheard. Matron was speaking to someone on the telephone and turning a patient down,' Rose whispered. 'There must be a guardian angel somewhere answering our prayers.'

'Well I never, would you believe it? It's too good an opportunity to waste but I think we should leave it 'til after tea before we say anything. She might think we've been eavesdropping.'

'OK Jackie, you may have a point.'

After tea, Rose plucked up enough courage to knock on Matron's door only to find that she had gone out, but the next morning she was surprised to be beaten to the punch when she was summonsed to her office.

'Can I have a word with you in my office Ms. Robinson?'

'Certainly Matron, right away.' Rose dutifully complied, with all manner of thoughts racing through her mind searching for some mistake she might have made the night before. She took a seat in the matron's office knowing full well that her face might give her away.

'It's alright Rose, nothing to worry about,' she began. 'Merril has telephoned in for sick leave so I am rearranging your rota times as from tomorrow. I know it's your day off so I hope you've nothing planned.'

'Oh no, that's OK, I lead a boring uncomplicated life you know,' Rose said as she physically heaved a sigh of relief.

'I will post your new times on the notice board later today together with a few others. You seem to be unduly relieved Rose, was there something else?'

Again Rose felt that Matron was the master tactician ahead of her plans and perhaps she herself had been counter eavesdropped. It was time to test Plan B. Much to Rose's satisfaction Matron listened to her plan and seemed interested.

'I would like to see Ms Clarkenwell too if I may. I'll put out a call for her.'

Jackie arrived in the Matron's office feeling apprehensive but soon dispelled her fears when she saw Rose was smiling.

'Ah, Ms Clarkenwell, Rose has been outlining a proposal which I'm given to understand you are party to. Is that correct?'

'Yes, that's right Matron,' Jackie answered positively.

'Well, unless further complications arise I can safely say that I will seriously consider the matter. As you know available space is a priority consideration in this nursing home but I'm sure that you've already thought of that. Leave it with me for now, I've a lot to think about but will let you know as soon as possible.'

'Thank you Matron,' they both chorused as they both tried not to dance their way out.

'Pheeeew, at least she didn't say 'No,' Rose commented. 'What a relief.'

Four days later, I telephoned Jackie from Bristol where my successor in my old job had a problem with a property.

'Hello, Jackie love, you sound as if you've just woken up.' Sorry not to have been in touch and as I haven't heard from you either I imagine you've been busy like me.'

'Yes I have and yes I have. I was asleep, but it's good to hear your voice. Our rota times have been reshuffled and I am working 'twilights,' that's what we call nightshifts. It's been good in one respect that the weather has been foul so I haven't missed going out and bad in that sometimes when I wake up I have to think not only what time it is but also which day.' Eating meals at odd hours during the night is difficult to get used to and the rota has completely upset my metabolism. Thank goodness it's only for a week.'

'Oh, you poor darling, I was afraid for one moment that you were poorly. This call is just a quickie to say I miss you. I'll be back on Saturday to catch up with progress and call you as soon as I can.'

'That's fine, Friday is my last night shift and I'll be off 'til Monday and then back to normal. Love you; see you at the weekend.'

By the time we met in The Blowhole on Saturday evening, Jackie was feeling better but soon noticed that all was not well.

'Are you OK Francis?'

'No, not really, there's a bit of problem at the Bristol office, but I'll tell you about it later. What progress have you made with Picardy?'

'Clever old Rose has made a proposal to Matron,' Jackie began, 'and we think that we have a solution to our financial problem. She is going to let us know her answer shortly so if it works out we won't need your help. If it's OK with you, we don't want to appear to be looking a gift horse in the mouth but we feel we should at least try to be independent.'

'That's OK, actually I'm glad to hear it.'

'In the meanwhile we have contacted the agents to register our interest in the property and made a provisional arrangement with a solicitor outlining our present position,' Jackie explained. 'Now we're keeping our fingers crossed until Matron gets back to us. But enough about us, what has happened to you?'

'It's not me with the problem. A client at the Bristol office has made an official complaint claiming that the manager, a Mr. Brian Phelpps has deliberately impeded the progress of a property sale with a view to limiting the price in favour of a family member. It is a serious charge and if upheld in a court of law, could be damaging to company business generally. To make matters worse the local rag has got wind of the story, presumably from the client. How it will affect my branch remains to be seen, but one thing I am sure of is that the problem needs to be sorted and sorted fast. As far as I have been able to ascertain, there is no foundation to the allegation and I've doing my best to calm things down.'

'So what are you going to do now Francis?'

'Well it's out of my hands Jackie, the charge is being investigated as we speak and all I can do is to try to carry on as usual.'

A few days later whilst Rose and Jackie were on their coffee break in the staff room Matron called them into her office to announce her decision with regard to their proposition. On entering the office they found Matron sitting at her desk but not in her usual pose, head down, poring over piles of paperwork. Instead the desk was relatively clear and she was sitting back in her chair leaning against the wall. Her hands were clasped together resting on her chest and she was smiling directly at them with an air of satisfaction just as if she had completed a successful investment deal on the stock market.

'As you will both note,' she began, 'my desk is clearer than usual since I have pre-empted your acceptance of my decision with regard to your financial proposition. I have already started the ball rolling to relocate, hence the clear desk. I am prepared to make you an advance payment of two thousand pounds each on the proviso that you vacate your rooms by the end of the month. That figure takes into account the wage increase that I'm sure you will both be expecting as a result of the new arrangement. There is a pressing need for the accommodation reshuffle to be carried out with the precision of a military campaign so as to complete the work in the shortest time and with minimum disturbance to our patients. In arriving at my decision I have taken into account your co-operation with regard to the recent rota changes and the manner in which you carry out your duties during difficult times generally. I value your dedication to your work and express the wish that long may it continue. You will be pleased to learn that I accept your proposal and hope that in return you will accept the financial arrangement.'

The two nurses hesitated for a few moments whilst they exchanged glances of approval. 'Indeed we do Matron and we are most grateful,' Jackie replied.

'And I to you,' she confirmed. 'It's odd really, that only a few days ago, I must admit that a pressing need for accommodation arose which I saw no means of satisfying.'

Back in the staff room they attempted for the second time to refresh themselves with coffee and biscuits. This time they thought they deserved it more than ever.

Jackie whispered, 'for one moment I thought she was going to ask if we've been listening at her door. I found it so difficult to keep a dead-pan face when she mentioned her 'pressing need' and seemed to be searching our faces for an admission.'

'Me too, my heart missed a couple of beats. So, all-in-all my girl, I think we can say we've "done well". Give me five!' They clapped hands above their heads.

'I think you'll feel as I do,' Rose began, 'in the interests of progress we had to accept the offer even though we haven't made arrangements for alterative accommodation. And another thing, the deadline date is very tight but fortunately we still have time to give the solicitor the green light.'

'A ridiculous thought has just occurred to me Rose. I envisage the pair of us kipping down in Picardy on the floor in a couple of sleeping bags surrounded by a pile of other bags containing all our worldly possessions. Are you up for it?'

157

'Certainly, what matters is that we'll be under our own roof.'

On the day of the Picardy auction, Amanda and Ellie joined Rose and Jackie at the Blowhole for a mid day snack although the auction was not scheduled until two fifteen. As the auctioneers had hoped, both dining rooms were busy and Ellie drew the attention of the other three to the fact that there were quite a few dinners reading the prospectus for Picardy.

'These next few hours are going to kill me,' Jackie said as she tried to calm her nerves with another cup of black coffee.

'I think I'll have another too,' Rose added. 'I'm sure all will be fine. Anyway it's more or less out of our hands now and I can see our solicitor has just arrived. He's an insignificant looking chap but he assures me that what he lacks in size is more than made up for with his guile.'

'Oh yes I see him,' Ellie commented. 'Don't judge a book by its cover, eh?'

Inviting Amanda proved to be a godsend to Rose and Jackie. On the next table there were a group of women having a hen party, making a lot of noise and celebrating the imminent marriage of one of them for the third time.

'I know someone who can beat her record,' Amanda said.

She helped to pass the time as she told them about someone she had met the night before. Her ladies club had invited a guest speaker to talk about her experiences of having been married six times and was looking for number seven.

'Four of them died leaving her with quite a portfolio of property and a sizeable bank balance in the process. The other two were unable to keep up with her insatiable marital demands and divorced her on very generous settlement terms, happy to do so and be free. She now gives talks on her experiences to various ladies groups and associations. Marrying so many times was not a path she deliberately set out to follow but eventually it developed into a career. Her tips and suggestions are mainly directed at younger ladies. In that respect, the only regret she had was that of waiting until she was thirty five before she married the first time. She is very amusing and popular to the extent that she is in great demand despite the fat fees she charges. To my way of thinking she has the answer to the never ending struggle of equality between men and women and of course, a permanent career.'

The four women were still smiling when Ellie stopped Amanda.

'Did you see that?'

A quarrel had broken out between a foreign family and a waiter, the one who'd been serving them. He saw that as they were leaving one of the men accidentally dropped his wallet spilling notes on the floor. He collected them all together and was about to return them by tapping the man on the shoulder when the lady, presumably his wife, saw him with the wallet in his hand. She jumped to the wrong conclusion assuming that the waiter was a thief. She whispered something in his ear. The man's hand instinctively flew to his back pocket in confirmation. The waiter had no chance to explain before the man grabbed him by the collar uttering abuse at him as he did so, drawing the attention of everybody in the restaurant. Luckily, the waiter managed to slip away and quickly joined the cashier in his booth closing the door behind him. The waiter explained the situation to the cashier accompanied by the noise of the man thumping his fist on the counter and gabbling away in a foreign language.

'Steady on,' the cashier began. 'Say it in English please Sir, we don't understand a word you're saying. We know this is your wallet,' he said waving it in the air.

The man thrust out a fat hairy hand. 'Me, Give!' He demanded as he snatched the wallet away.

There were no 'Thanks' or any sign of appreciation as family left the booth, only their animated chatter which continued all the way to the exit. The waiter came out of the booth to receive a well deserved ovation.

'What a man! And they've stolen the salt and pepper grinder,' he added to the sound of more clapping and laughter.

The barman in an adjoining bar had to ring the bell several times to be heard above the noise. He announced 'last orders' prior to the start of the auction. Most people however had already slipped into the room un-noticed by the ladies and had taken up quite a number of seats leaving those at the front empty. Despite that, there were people who chose to stand at the sides of the room so that they could observe who was bidding from the body of the floor. When the four women entered the conversation level noticeably dropped and they became acutely aware that they were being watched. Rose and Jackie took comfort from the fact that they were not directly involved with the bidding process, but on the other hand they would not know if their solicitor was bidding or not. Would he be successful in making the final bid? That was the question. All they could do was to sit tight and watch.

CHAPTER 15

'Welcome ladies and gentlemen I am Nicholas Smythe of Lister & Co. auctioneers charged with the duty of conducting the sale of the property known as Picardy in the hamlet of Shipley Green.'

The auctioneer continued with his preamble endeavouring to present an attractive picture of Picardy as possible together with comments on its potential. He also made reference to the previous owners who had looked after it in bygone days but since that time the property had been neglected and it was the express wish of the niece that it should be reinstated to its former glory as a memorial to her aunt and uncle.

'There has been a not insignificant amount of interest shown in this property so can I open the bidding at forty thousand pounds then?'

Someone in the room let out a low whistle but no one answered his lead. Ellie nudged Rose and whispered, 'Crumbs, that's a high start. It's way above the top of your budget already. I hope for your sake nobody makes a move.'

'Is that a bid, Madam?' The auctioneer queried, looking in Ellie's direction as she ran her hand through the back of her hair.

Jackie's heart missed a beat, 'that's it, it's all over,' she thought. Rose followed the auctioneer's stare and nudged Ellie in the back. Ellie jumped. 'No, no sorry, I was just—.'

'Please pay attention madam, or you might suddenly find that you're the new owner.'

Laughter broke out in the room, breaking the air of trepidation.

The auctioneer continued. 'Shall we say thirty five thousand then?' But once again there was no response. Ellie stared at the floor not daring to move a muscle while Jackie and Rose kept their eyes glued on the auctioneer and his gavel.

'Shall we try thirty thousand?' Still no one moved a muscle. You could cut the air with a knife. 'Very well then, perhaps someone would like to make an opening bid for the sake of progress, we can't waste time on this the first property on the agenda. Time is money,' he added, looking a little irritated.

'Twenty thousand,' a small voice chipped in.

'Oh, come on ladies and gentlemen, let's be serious. This is a very desirable property and you all know that with renovation it will be worth two or three times that bid. Do you stand by your bid Madam?'

The lady smiled and nodded.

'Very well, I'll accept the bid at least it's a start.'

A murmur filled the room. The words, 'You might get a bargain' echoed through Jackie's mind as she exchanged looks with Rose. After the first so called bid, people seemed to suddenly come alive in contrast with the opening minutes and bids in steps of one thousand pounds steadily took the bid price to thirty one thousand. Jackie tightened her grip on Rose's arm when the bids slowed to a stop.

'I wonder if that's ours,' she whispered. 'We don't want it to go much further we have little leeway as it is.'

'I'll take five hundred,' the auctioneer continued.

Further increments took the price to thirty three thousand five hundred and then stopped all together.

'That must be it,' Ellie whispered. 'If it is, it's a bargain.'

The auctioneer looked disappointed as he looked around the room, almost pleading with his eyes as he stared at previous bidders daring them to continue. The audience watched as the gavel finally came to rest pointing at one particular bidder.

'The bid is with you sir,' he said, indicating someone who was standing just out of vision of the four women on the left hand side of the room. He waited for a long thirty seconds for someone else to trump the bid but no one took the bait.

He made a resigned gesture. 'Unfortunately, ladies and gentlemen we have not reached the reserve and therefore the auction is not conclusive until such time as I receive further bids. In the meanwhile there will be an interval of fifteen minutes until three o' clock when the auction of land at Morefields will commence,'

As the auctioneer sat down at his desk to review his paperwork the buzz of conversation began in earnest once more, this time partially due the confusion of people entering and leaving the room. Jackie and her friends waited near the doorway expecting to be contacted by their solicitor but no one came. Two men and a woman approached the desk. An animated discussion began in which a separate auction seemed to be taking place between the woman and one of the men until finally both moved away from the desk. It started up again a few moments later when another man came out of the toilet and approached the desk. This time the auctioneer could be clearly heard to ask one of the men whether he wanted to make a bid.

'No, I bloody well don't.'

'Ah! That's our solicitor,' Jackie observed, 'the solicitor is shaking his hand and he looks pleased with himself. I do believe he's done it'

'Oh my God,' Amanda exclaimed, 'and do you see who I see shouting his head off? That's Joe Freeman. Where did he come from? He must have been hiding like the weasel he is. I wonder what he's up to. Whatever it is, you can be sure he's up to no good.'

His voice could be clearly heard above all others as he shouted at the auctioneer and prodded the small man in the chest.

'This auction is a fix, we've been all been stitched up,' Joe challenged the auctioneer and then turned his attention to the solicitor. 'And I can prove it. You won't be smiling so much then.'

Joe Freeman marched triumphantly out of the room, but stopped to waggle his index finger at Jackie.

'Let's see whose laughing now, this is payback time,' he hissed.

Jackie was mystified and just stared at back Joe as he left the room muttering and waving his arms. He was joined by two other men and the trio ordered drinks at the bar. Joe stood defiantly viewing and enjoying his afternoon's devilry as confusion broke out, no one knowing what to expect next.

Amanda was the first to question Jackie. 'What was all that about? He seemed very sure of himself and must have something pretty solid on his mind to shout his mouth off like that. I'm sure he's up to something. I've known him for too many years not to know otherwise. Those other two with him at the bar are a couple of his cronies on the Council. They will be involved up to their scrawny necks in this too somewhere.'

'I've no idea at all Amanda. I'm completely in the dark. I expected to see Francis here this afternoon. Perhaps he has some answers.'

Amanda turned her attention to Rose. 'What about you Rose? You're very quiet. Do you know anything?'

'No, I'm afraid I don't. I am worried about the way things are going. To lose out now would be a great shame. All I know is that I've run out of time I should be making my way back to Tootehill.'

Rose said goodbye to her friends and was about to leave when she came face to face with me in the doorway.

'Jackie's been wondering where you were, something seems to have gone wrong with the auction. Sorry I can't stay but Jackie and the others are sitting over there in the window. They will tell you all about it.'

'Yes, I know already, that's why I've come over,' I said, 'your solicitor has phoned to put me in the picture. I'm going to have a word with him now.'

Jackie stood up to greet me and looked enquiringly at her solicitor who also came over.

'Did you like the opening bid, Ms. Clarkenwell?'

'It was very low and took me by surprise,' Jackie replied. 'But it was a woman who made the first bid. Did you know who she was?'

'No, she was just someone hoping to make a killing if no-one else wanted to bid. It can happen when a client just wants to sell at any price.'

The solicitor turned his attention to me. 'We've spoken on the phone but haven't met. My name is Horace Wilkins, employed by Howson & White, the company Ms. Clarkenwell engaged to bid on her behalf. Like the auctioneer said, it was a ridiculous opening bid, but it had to start somewhere and I think it set the mood for a final low bid.'

'Yes, I'm sure we're all pleased about that but I don't like what I'm hearing.' I replied.

Mr. Wilkins continued, 'some of you may have noticed that I was involved in the discussion with the auctioneer at the end and I'm sorry that I didn't make physical contact with you earlier Ms. Clarkenwell but it was important that as my client, you remained incommunicado. Unfortunately Mr. Freeman had ferreted that out already. I can now inform you that I successfully negotiated with the auctioneer to secure the property right on the reserve figure of thirty five thousand.'

Ellie and Amanda both congratulated Jackie by patting her on the back. 'Well done, you've now got a roof over your head,' Ellie said, 'and I'm pleased for you.'

'Hold on, not so fast,' Horace interrupted. There is a problem and Mr. Freeman has made a serious complaint stating that your estate agent is guilty of price rigging. He is backing it up quoting a similar case which has been reported in the press involving another branch of the same agency.'

Amanda puffed out her cheeks. 'So that's it! I hate to say I told you so, but I think you've just witnessed Joe being Joe and another sample of his maliciousness like he did at the Blowhole. He's been digging the dirt and by the smug look on his face he's chosen his moment well. I can't imagine he has any designs on Picardy for himself, but for some reason Jackie, he wants to stop you. He seems to be back with his old tricks. Somehow he's squirmed his way back on to the Council after a number of years in the wilderness. Voters seem to have short memories but there are some of us who know a dodgy egg when we see one.'

Right on cue, Joe saw that eyes were turned in his direction. He spilled half of his drink on the bar in his haste to join the group.

'Here we go,' 'Horace suggested, 'he's coming over to turn the screw.'

Joe swaggered over to the table triumphantly waving a small newspaper cutting.

Horace got up from the table. 'Who does he think he is?' Neville Chamberlain?'

'I think you're all beginning to see the picture,' he began as he flicked the cutting onto the table like an unwanted playing card. 'I've waited a long time for this moment. Read that if you will. The Office of Fair Trading was very interested and together with today's fiasco I'm sure they will carry out an investigation based on a suspicion of collusion having taken place to distort competition in favour of agency personnel. You missed a trick when we first met in the Blowhole,' he said turning in my direction. 'I think I can count on one hand the number of people I've been wrong about at first meeting and now you're one of them. I've been around a bit as you might say but when I tried to fill you in with information about certain people which might have been useful to you as an estate agent, you cut me dead.'

'And you left me with a restaurant bill for expensive wines which you ordered, not to mention the cost of the meal. You're kind of tittle-tattle is only fit for the gutter.'

'That's as maybe,' he went on. 'The jungle telegraph tells me that you and Ms Clarkenwell, nee Manston, are an item and it appears to me that according to the cutting, your company is suffering from an endemic disease which has broken out here too. I have lodged a complaint which when proven should see you looking for a job at the labour exchange.'

'What has my family name got to do with this?' Jackie said, jumping to her feet.

'Ah now, that's a good question, my dear Ms Connie Manston. I can see that I've touched a raw nerve and now I've got your full attention, just like I had with your mother to begin with years ago. I can see the likeness now as well.'

'When you were still in nappies, your mother and I were, as you might say, good friends. She was not shy of sharing her favours with all and sundry while your dad was busy with the RAF. She was very professional at it too and such a tease carrying on right under your Grandma's nose. I can give you a list if you like, but top of the list was the milkman. When I look back now the memory could well be the butt of some music hall joke involving the maid and the milkman. I eventually had to ditch her because she cost me my job, my reputation and my chances of becoming mayor of this town. The milkman with the imaginary limp which he adopted to avoid National Service became the projectionist at the Pavilion cinema and was someone you knew well. You will remember him as your stepfather, Alfie.'

By this time Jackie was close to tears. Amanda put her arm around her shoulders. 'He's digging deep in the barrel, but it will get him nowhere and we will make sure of that. My advice to you Joe is to give it up now while you've got the chance. Have you not heard the old maxim, "before you take revenge, dig two graves"?'

'Oh, very droll Councillor, but I haven't finished yet.'

'As billeting officer during the War there was a charge made against me for receiving rations destined for the evacuees, but no one was prepared to stick their head above the parapet. I think someone was jealous and wanted in on the act. Alfie was my prime suspect and the disclosure, probably divulged during some pillow talk, could only have come from one source, namely your mother. Unfortunately for me, shit sticks to a blanket. I lost my job, had a family of four to feed and got into debt, but I was fortunate enough to have some good friends to bail me out. It took quite a few years to regain my council seat and now I have a few scores to settle.'

'And you deserved it. Pity you didn't go to jail as well. You forget Joe, we go back a long way and I've got a good memory. You've forgotten the real reason why you lost your Council seat. You were charged with corruption in connection with the Wilton Green school proposal. The sad thing about it was you were able to squirm your way out because of lack of evidence, but we all knew and as you say, 'muck sticks.' So my advice to you Joe is drop this now, otherwise I predict that Francis won't be the only one on the dole. Think about it.'

'I have done and do you know what I'm going to do now? I'm going to have a pleasant round of golf with my pals and then go home to put my feet up. Don't leave town, I'll be in touch.'

Joe Freeman had had a good day. The rivalry which normally existed on the golf course between his pals and himself could now be forgotten. He felt enlightened and free of a burden he had carried for too many years. At last his chance to get even had dropped into his lap and he had already made up his mind that any words of wisdom from Amanda or anyone else wouldn't make a scrap of difference.

After Joe left, the atmosphere in the restaurant continued as before, full of chatter, laughter and movement as the waiters weaved expertly around the tables and chairs avoiding collisions with the swing doors of the kitchen. At Jackie's table there was silence as each one mulled over Joe's onslaught until Amanda finally broke into their thoughts.

'A penny for them, Francis.'

'You really wouldn't like to hear them with Joe upsetting Jackie as he did, but I can assure all of you he hasn't got a scrap of evidence.'

'That's quite true,' Horace added, 'and I am surprised that being a Councillor he has left himself wide open by making the accusation. He's made the biggest mistake of his life. He has assumed that Francis has bankrolled Jackie in some way and therefore compromised both himself and the company. I understand that no such arrangement has been made. The affair in Bristol combined with the auction of Picardy has triggered his grubby interest and he has swallowed the press release hook line and sinker. It seems clear to me that he has cottoned on to the possibility of killing two birds with one stone and the chance to get even with a few ghosts from the past. In his mind the opportunity has been too good to miss. I could imagine when he saw the first press report he couldn't believe his luck. It's going to be his undoing.'

'Well this has turned out to be quite an eventful day, to be sure,' I said to Horace. 'I need to spend a few hours back at the office to prepare for a branch office visit from Bristol tomorrow. In the meanwhile I would like you to arrange a meeting with the Office of Fair Trading, other interested parties and those representing our infamous Joe Freeman with the object killing off the charge. Damage limitation is important so make sure you remind the local rag that if they repeat the allegation they could be sued.'

Jackie edged forward in her chair. 'We don't have a lot of time either. We need to be out of our rooms at Tootehill soon and any delay with Picardy will leave Rose and me with a problem.'

Amanda tapped her fingers on the table. 'I've been thinking about that ever since you mentioned your dealings with Matron. My children have grown up and vacated the nest leaving me to rattle about in a house too big for me. How would you like to join me for as long as you like? I would welcome your company and you could come and go as you please according to your shift times. I would enjoy spending some time in my kitchen to try out some of my recipes on you. What do think?'

Jackie clapped her hand on top of Amanda's. 'That would be fantastic, but we wouldn't like to be any trouble.'

'We would expect to pay; we don't want to take advantage but it would be such a great help just now. Thank you very much.'

'I wouldn't hear of it. It will only be for a short while and I can afford it. Don't give it another thought,' she added as she left the restaurant.

After his pals left the golf club, Joe stayed chatting to the barman until the small hours at the nineteenth before going home. Somehow he managed to find his way and collapsed in a paralytic state on his single bed in the spare room without even taking his shoes off. His wife got up to check when she heard the thump but merely closed the door again leaving him to sleep it off. He awoke around six the next evening with his mouth feeling like a fur wrap as his dog bounded onto his bed carrying the evening paper in its mouth. He quickly scanned all twelve pages and called out to his wife.

'There's nothing there Mabel, not a word. What are they playing at?'

'You're awake then and about time too. You came home last night with a skinful. This room smells like a brewery. You've missed a Council meeting and your pal Herbert called but you were dead asleep. He says the meeting is the least of your worries because he has seen the paper too and contacted your reporter friend. There's talk of slander and possible libel which is why nothing has appeared in print. Your big mouth has bitten off something bigger than you can chew this time. What am I going to do with you Joe? You better get off your fat ass and do something about it and fast. And take a shower,' she shouted as she went down the stairs.

Joe couldn't help feeling his wife was right. He felt vulnerable, guilty and began to wish he had checked his sources more carefully. He tried to make several telephone calls but each one had been switched to message recording. Finally he shouted to Mabel that he was going out.

'I'm going to the club. The jungle telegraph is going to be my best bet to sort this out.'

At the club Joe ordered tonic waters instead of his usual pint and whisky chaser. He also did something else different. He did a lot of listening instead of talking. Being a Tuesday it was a quiet night with very few members which left him resigned to spend the evening leaning on the bar with only the barman for company. Luckily the barman had been on duty all day and had hovered up much of the gossip from the previous day's auction rooms.

He approached Joe making a few nonchalant sweeps of his cloth on the bar top. 'They say that a little knowledge is a dangerous thing but I know a little bit about the law. My university lad is full of it when he comes home. I hear you've got yourself into a spot of legal bother involving slander where you have made certain negative remarks about the estate agency Miles Booker & Sons. Unless you have irrefutable proof you could be drawn into an expensive lawsuit which would clear you out or even result in a jail sentence. You could try making a public apology as a form of damage limitation. Fortunately for you there was nothing in the paper today but not, I understand, for the lack of trying on your part. If it had the paper could have been sued in addition to all those who were complicit in the paper chain such as distributors and retailers. Even worse from a monetary damages viewpoint would have been for national newspapers to have got hold of the story. As far as I can see Joe, an out-of-court settlement looms on the horizon for you.'

A disconsolate Joe Freeman took all the barman's words on board and slowly made his way home only to be met by his wife at the gate.

'What now? What is it that's so important that it can't wait until I'm in the house? I've already had an ear wigging at the club.'

She pushed him in the back as he walked down the path. 'Well I fancy you're going to have a whole lot more in the morning, Miles Booker & Sons want you in their office at half eight sharp. You can toss and turn in the spare room again tonight while you work out your options. When are you going to learn that you've been sailing close to the wind? And don't think Herbert and the rest of your mob are going to be with you this time. You've dug this hole all on your own.'

'Alright woman, don't go on. Haven't I always tried to do what's right for you and the kids?'

During the course of the everlasting night Joe realised he would have to climb down, retract his accusations and accept humiliation. He had let his pent up anger fester over the years and now as much as he hated to admit it, Amanda's 'two graves' came back to haunt him. As to whether a plea of leniency would have any affect he had no way of knowing apart from which he knew deep down he didn't deserve any. There was nothing for it but to attend the meeting and hope for the best. He at least received some spark of sympathy from Mabel before he went out. She saw his dejected look and mellowed her anger as she gave him a perfunctory hug, stood back and straightened his tie.

'You had better fight your way out of your corner as if your life depended on it Joe Freeman and pray that the inquiry goes your way.'

Horace Wilkins opened the meeting and thanked Joe for coming. Joe decided to present his prepared statement before anyone else got the chance to turn the screw tighter by confirming the vulnerability of his situation. The meeting was short lived.

'Having given full consideration to the statements I have made to the Office of Fair Trading and the verbal public attack on both Miles Booker & Sons and Lister & Co auctioneers, I wish to withdraw those statements and confirm that they were completely unfounded. I intend to issue a formal statement to the press accordingly. In my defence I can only declare that they were made in a moment of anger and request that you exercise leniency with a view to avoiding any possible court procedures.'

'Thank you Mr. Freeman' Horace began, 'you have obviously come to your senses in the realisation that apart from the fact that court procedures can be expensive, a claim for damages against you could be crippling. As things are, damage to reputations has been limited and we expect your public statement to completely exonerate all parties concerned. To that end Mr. Francis Tenby would like to say a few words.'

Joe sank back into his chair as I turned my full attention on him. With his wretched look and lack of sleep he seemed to have been reduced to half his size which made me wonder how someone so small could cause so much havoc. The bumptious, loud mouth character from the Blowhole had evaporated with the night. I hesitated fully twenty seconds while he squirmed in his chair as I fixed him with a stare, wishing all the while that I had a powerful spotlight to shine in his face.

'To quote your words Joe I think your beginning to see the picture. Now I am not going to waste a lot more of every one's time on you because you don't deserve it. Both Jackie and I agree that the word 'revenge' has no place in our vocabulary. Equally, how you can harbour such malicious intentions going back over many years is beyond us. What happened then was of your doing and is of no interest to us. I expect you to make an apology to Connie since your past life has nothing to do with her directly. Prior to your arrival here today it was decided that the least said about this matter the quicker it would be settled. The agency does not wish to make any monetary gains from your demise and it has been suggested that together with your public statement you make a sizeable donation to a local charity. We suggest the sum of five thousand pounds would go some way toward the repair of your reputation. Think of it as if we are doing you a favour and consider yourself lucky. Have you any comment and do you accept?'

'Mabel won't be best pleased that we will have to dig into our pension pot to make that kind of donation. It's a bit steep, but I will have to remind her it could have been a lot worse. No doubt my seat on the Council will be reviewed so perhaps retirement and keeping a lower profile might be a good idea.'

'I'm sure we all couldn't agree more. Let that be an end to the matter.'

By nine that morning, it was all over. I telephoned Jackie right away and without any preamble blurted out the news she had been waiting to hear. 'Picardy is yours. The auctioneer will be chasing you and Rose for the deposit with the remainder on completion which should be in three to four weeks. Officially you will not be able to do anything until you receive the keys but I can't think it will do any harm to start clearing the gardens. Congratulations. Start packing.'

CHAPTER 16

Ellie was pleased for Jackie and Rose that the ordeal surrounding the purchase of Picardy was finally over. Amanda was more than happy that Joe Freeman's attempts to scupper the deal left him with egg on his face; something which was well overdue. She entertained the thought that perhaps this time his wife would put her foot down and make Joe honour his promises.

Ellie and Amanda discussed the idea of buying moving in presents and decided that attending the auction of Wendy's house contents due the following week would a good opportunity to do so.

'There are two reasons why I am interested,' Ellie explained to Jackie over the telephone, 'firstly, you will need bits and pieces of furniture before you move in so we've had a chat amongst your friends and decided to buy you something from each of us. Secondly, I knew the house very well and of all the nice things she had I would like the piano at least to stay in the family as you might say, just for old time's sake. My daughter is getting married in June and I thought it would be a good surprise present as she knows it so well.'

The auction was conducted by Lloyd Mackelroy & Sons, auctioneers under instructions from Dale Benton, solicitor, responsible for winding up the estate of the late Wendy Nicholson. When I collected Jackie and Rose on the day of the sale, I agreed to do so with more than a little interest and possibly to gain some further insight into the life of someone who had helped me personally. I felt connected and thought I owed her that much at least. Although I would rather have met up with her again in person, I was hopeful that by attending the sale it would suffice as a poor substitute. There was the possibility that I might even bid for some small memento but I was prepared to see how the auction panned out.

Ellie met us at the door saying that she had reserved seats for us in the front row and had registered her own and Jackie's interest in the sale with the auctioneer's clerk. She had been allocated two numbered sale cards which were of such dimensions that one had the feeling the faintest movement of which would have constituted a bid. Once again the women noted that there was a marked tendency for perspective buyers to collect at the back of the room, but this time they felt more at ease and were not concerned about who was bidding for what. In addition, there was no Joe and the sums of money involved were a great deal less than the thousands for Picardy. Ellie knew she wanted that piano. She felt a part of it and it simply had to stay in the family. Items of furniture and bric-a-brac were arranged around the edge of the room with the larger items, the piano amongst them, displayed behind the auctioneer's plinth.

The auctioneer was a man on a mission with no time to waste as he set off on a long list of items at a brisk rate. It was no place for the faint hearted. Thinking had to positive, clear and decisive. The auctioneer flew through the bric-a-brac and smaller items with nonchalance almost as if he didn't care whether the items were sold or not. He soon arrived at Ellie's piano. She wanted it at all costs. Her mind was made up and she was ready to flash her card tactically after the first three bids. It was a fine example of a listed 1937 Chappell grand piano with a sturdy German frame mounted in a polished mahogany case which was in excellent condition. She knew its history. She had to have it.

The bidding started off in lively fashion as the auctioneer accepted bids in quick succession, twenty pounds at a time, two twenty, two forty, two sixty. Then the bidding halted with a gentleman to our left holding the last bid. He was whispering to a man sitting next to him who wore dark spectacles and carried a white stick across his knees. The man had an academic appearance; balding on top, short white sideburns and pince-nez silver rimmed spectacles. She thought perhaps he was a trader in league with a piano tuner and they were hoping for a bargain.

'Come on now ladies and gentlemen, this is a fine piano in pristine condition. I'll take ten.'

Ellie discretely played her trump card.

'Thank you madam, two seventy.'

The gentleman bid again. 'Two eighty.' Ellie persisted. 'Two ninety.'

The auctioneer looked again at Ellie's rival bidder.

'Three hundred. Thank you sir.'

The vision of the look on her daughter's face when she learnt of her mother's wedding present spurred Ellie on.

'And ten. Thank you madam.'

'Three hundred and twenty, a new bidder at the back, thank you sir.'

One or two people murmured away to Ellie's right. The 'academic' looked disconsolate as he nudged his companion causing his stick to clatter to the floor.

Ellie refused to be distracted and discretely waved her card.

'Thank you madam. Three thirty, the bid is back at the front once more.'

The bidder at the back gave the auctioneer a "thumbs down sign" 'Are you done sir?'

'We have three thirty at the front then, I'll take five.'

A new bidder two rows behind Ellie waved her card.

'Thank you madam. We have three thirty five just here then, another new bidder. The auctioneer pointed his gavel at a well dressed elderly woman sitting with a young girl of about fourteen years old. The girl, unable to curtail her excitement clapped her hands and had to be restrained by the woman. The auctioneer fixed the pair with a stare. 'Pleeease—Madam.'

Ellie waved her card again, this time more positively, her face determined, cool as a cucumber.

'Thank you madam, three forty.'

There was a hushed silence in the room, everybody waiting for the next bid to come from the woman and child. The race was on. She hesitated and bid again.

'Thank you madam, three four five then.'

The room fell silent once more. Jackie grabbed my hand almost squeezing the blood out of my fingers. Ellie was defiant.

'I'm selling then at three four five, are you all done? Going for the first time, going for the second—.'

'Thank you madam, three fifty.' The woman waved her card again. Was she demonstrating to the girl never to give up or was she simply determined to win having made some rash promise? Perhaps it was the girl's birthday.

Low voices broke out in the room but soon fell silent once more. Jackie gripped my hand tighter, so much so that I had to register my pain by gently caressing the back of her hand. She smiled and eased off, her face quite pink with prolonged concentration. Ellie sat resolute, eyes fixed on the auctioneer, but outwardly still remaining cool.

The auctioneer was enjoying the ping pong nature of the auction. 'Thank you madam, still at the front then, we have three five five.'

The lady dropped her head and put her arm around the girl's shoulder. There were to be no more bids.

'I'm selling then at three five five, are you all done? Going for the first time, going for the second—.'

The auctioneer fixed the buyers with an icy stare.

'Sold! Thank you madam. Well done.'

The whole room erupted into frenzied chatter. I turned to congratulate Ellie, who was now showing the first signs of tension but also great relief.

'You're a cool customer, and that's a fact. Well done, I'm glad you stuck to your guns. I think some chap at the back has just left in a huff and the young girl, well, she left in tears.' Ellie felt sorry for the girl but for her there would be another piano somewhere else. This one was special; Ellie and the girls were related to it.

I turned my attention to Jackie.

'Can I have my hand back now?'

'Pheeew! That was exciting. I think I would faint to go through that again.'

Several more items came under the hammer, the auctioneer increasingly paying more attention to the larger items behind his rostrum where each was individually labelled with descriptive details. He arrived at the four-poster bed. My heart rate increased to a new level. He began to read from its card.

'Here we have a fine example of a King sized four-poster bed, circa 1850; a product of the former East India Company of Calcutta. A solid mahogany four-poster, the tester of which is composed of several panels in a carved frame, each panel individually carved with floral demi-lunes contained in thumb moulded lozenges enriched with punch work. The canopy rails carved with an interlinked lunette design; the design echoed in the projecting top rail of the head board above a protruding canopy and nine intricately carved panels. This piece is accentuated by style, romance and tradition. An heirloom this certainly would be, allowing future generations to enjoy its everlasting quality and beauty.'

'Who will start the bidding?'

The room fell silent as perspective bidders avoided the auctioneer's stare. The cat and mouse situation began all over again as they tried not to appear too keen.

'I will start the bidding at three fifty?'

'Thank you madam, three fifty it is then.' The auctioneer settled deeper into his chair pleased to be underway and that there was to be no protracted delay.

A lady three seats to our left bravely opened the bidding as she flashed her card displaying a hand encrusted with several gold rings and wearing a charm bracelet on her wrist. A flurry of bids followed from all around the room. There was a lot of interest in the quality item Lot 3682. The bids rose steadily in twenties until it finally began to slow at five ninety, still with the lady on our left. There was no doubt she was more than interested.

'The bid is with you madam,' the auctioneer's gavel stopped ranging around the room to point at the bejewelled woman once more like a magnet finally locating an opposite pole.

'I'll take ten. Thank you sir, I have six hundred pounds.' A new bidder joined the fray.

The lady to our left was persistent, but she was beaten by another bid. I felt the wind of a card directly behind our seats as it was hoisted aloft up by a new bidder.

'Thank you sir, six hundred and ten.'

The bids began to rise steadily again with the new incremental factor, six twenty, six thirty, six forty and on to seven twenty. The gold ring lady shook her head when the auctioneer fixed her with his stare, inviting another response. All eyes were fixed on the auctioneer as the gavel gyrated from left to right and back again around some imaginary ellipse.

'I'll need hardly to remind you ladies and gentlemen of the superb craftsmanship and quality of this item. It is indeed fit for a Queen.

'Do I have seven thirty?' The room was silent for a few breathless moments. 'If you like I will take five.'

'Thank you sir, I have seven two five to my right. Do I hear seven thirty?'

Again the breeze from behind ruffling my hair as it shot skyward.

'Thank you sir, seven thirty.'

The two bidders were locked in combat as the price rose to seven fifty. A pronounced sigh of desperation from behind accompanied the latest bid.

'The bid is with you sir on my right, do I have seven fifty five?'

The room was as silent as the grave, no-one fearing to breathe. The gavel began to hover over its target on the desk.

'If you are all done, I'm selling then at seven fifty, going for the first time, going for the second time—.'

My moment had arrived. Jackie's card lay idly on her lap. With the minimum of movement, I seized it and caught the eye of the auctioneer. He pounced like a cat that had been waiting for its prey.

'Thank you sir, I have a new bidder at seven five five.'

The first thing Jackie saw from the corner of her eye was that her card had mysteriously acquired a life of its own. Astonished and taken completely by surprise she turned to grip my hand once more, but seeing that my total concentration was with the auctioneer she quickly took her hand away. A buzz went around the room. The bidder on the right hesitated for a few moments for the buzz to subside.

'Thank you sir, seven sixty, do I have seven six five?'

Ellie shifted uneasily in her chair while Jackie stared at her feet too petrified to look elsewhere. I blinked at the auctioneer and nodded as I moved the card slightly.

'Thank you sir, do I hear seven seventy?'

The auctioneer scanned his audience. No-one dared move a muscle including the man on the right. You could hear a pin drop.

'Are you all done then, I'm selling at seven six five for the first time, for the second—.'

The auctioneer pausing for effect looked pleased with his mornings work.

'Sold at seven six five to the gentleman at the front. Thank you Sir. Well done.'

Spontaneous clapping echoed around the room. Ellie and Jackie both hugged me at the same time.

'Ellie, what did you think about that for a sale? I simply had to have that bed, it's magnificent. I particularly wanted something that was Wendy's, for the same reason that you bought the piano. I must admit that I had some small item in mind purely as a memento but when I saw that bed I decided my home was built for it.'

'It belonged to Wendy's parents,' Ellie confirmed. 'Her father spent a lot of time abroad and he brought it over to England from India as a present for her mother.'

I turned to Jackie, her pinkish complexion returning to normal.

'I had to smile to myself when you said you couldn't go through another sale without fainting if we were involved because I knew as soon as the auction began that I was interested. There can't be too many of those floating about.'

'I very nearly passed out, I couldn't look. It certainly is a grand bed, very elegant and the carvings are marvellous. It would be far too big for my small bungalow.'

'I have just the room for it. I'll be a king in my castle.'

I put my arm around her shoulders and whispered in her ear.

'Would you like to try it out sometime?'

The next two weeks seemed to fly by as I took time off from my usual haunts at the golf club, the beginner's lessons at the local swimming club and social invitations to various functions in town. Lloyd Mackelroy & Sons informed me that they would delay delivery of the four-poster for a maximum of two weeks at no extra charge for storage. In the meanwhile I concentrated on redecorating a large bedroom in preparation for the delivery, sometimes not stopping until well into the night. My former manager had given me first refusal on 'Four Pines' when he downsized into a smaller property more suitable for his invalid wife and to give himself more time to enjoy his passion, fly fishing. It was a large house, set in two acres of land, mostly given over to lawns but with a mixture of indigenous and tropical trees planted by professional landscape gardeners to display their beauty to maximum effect. The house had been designed by the manager with an adequate number of rooms suitable for his wife and five children together with maid's rooms in the attic. He used to say that he had a room for everything, two reception, two kitchens, seven bedrooms, a music room and a games room. As part of the sale he had left a grandfather clock, a full sized snooker table and a sit on lawn mower in addition to various items of furniture too large for his bungalow. Four Pines was an excellent house, well suited for entertaining but for the first six months or so I rattled around like a single pea in a pod. I tended to spend much of my spare time in the garden getting satisfaction from mowing the lawns in patterns like a bowling green.

It was the discovery of the four-poster which spurred me to concentrate more on the internal décor and to stamp my personal mark on the choice of fixtures and fittings. Various pieces of furniture took on a new look simply with a change of material coverings whilst others which had suffered at the hands of his five children needed more serious renovation to bring them back to life. The room I had chosen for the four-poster had a double bay southerly facing window overlooking the back garden which for the major part of the day was bathed in sunshine.

On the day of the delivery, I invited Ellie and Jackie to the house to make suggestions as to the best position for the bed in a particular room and to look around generally for any other ideas. I was well aware that living on my own as I had done for too many years was becoming something of a disadvantage in house which cried out for the feminine touch, a point which many of male friends were all too keen to point out. Ellie told me that where furniture was placed in a house was important; in fact she was a firm believer in Feng Shui and that she was convinced it worked. I picked Jackie up in the car, whilst Rory made arrangements to drop Ellie off at the house on his way home from shopping. Jackie had no idea about my house; it was something that I had purposely played down so that when she did eventually see it, the surprise would be that much greater.

'Oh my Lord, I had no idea you lived in a mansion! It must have cost a fortune. You could hide Picardy in one corner and not know it was there.'

'Well, there are advantages of being in the business you know. The property market has always been an interest of mine right back to the days when I left the orphanage. I knew then I wanted a place of my own and losing my parents gave me that added ambition to make sure it happened.

Starting as tea boy with Miles Booker was the best move I ever made.'

When we arrived at Four Pines, Ellie and Rory were standing by the drive entrance having an animated discussion.

'Are we in the right place?' Ellie called out. 'Rory says I must have got my directions mixed up as usual.'

'You certainly are, Ellie. Come in and wave your magic wand,' I said facetiously, knowing that she knew my views of Feng Shui. 'Why don't you bring Rory in with you? I'm sure he'll find the house interesting.'

As we drove up the drive, Jackie put her hand on my arm.

'It's absolutely fabulous. You've been a dark horse keeping this a secret. I had no idea.'

'Well, if we are going to be fiends, I didn't want something like this to influence you. Do you follow me? After all I know quite a bit about your circumstances and apart from other influences that's what has attracted me to you.'

'What other influences?' she said coyly.

'I'll let you know later.'

Rory was already walking down the garden when Ellie tapped on the car door window.

'Are you two love birds going to spend much longer staring into each others eyes? Rory's already half way down the garden sick with envy.'

As I took Jackie's hand, Ellie gave Rory a call and we all met up in the entrance hall. The polished pitch pine stairway stretched in an impressive arc away to our right up to the first floor and twin chandlers, which hung from the high ornate ceiling, illuminated the mosaic tile floor. Jackie stood with her mouth open again and she laughed when I gently closed it shut with my forefinger.

'You like?' I said.

Both Ellie and Rory were full of admiration as they went from room to room.

'It's going to take me more than six months to furnish the house as I would like it. As you can see, there are a lot of empty rooms and I hope to be able to buy quality rather than quantity just for the sake of filling the rooms. It's a big house and it will probably make me poor to maintain it but there are so many possibilities for future use.'

'The four-poster looks fantastic in the master bedroom Francis,' Ellie commented. 'It's in just the right position for Feng Shui and it would be spoilt by having too much clutter around it. A bed like that demands to stand on its own, but in Wendy's cottage it took up most of the room and half of its splendour was lost.'

'The piano would have fitted nicely in the drawing room and I would like to have bought that too but apart from the fact that I can't play anyway, I was pleased you managed to buy it.'

In the games room Rory was excited about the snooker table.

'I used to play quite a bit with the lads on our RAF base and challenge other stations on a league table basis. The table we played on was nowhere near half as good as this one,' he said as he rolled a couple of red balls up and down the table and bounced them off the cushions. 'Some of us could knock up quite a decent score with breaks of forty or more, but I haven't played for a while. I'd like to have a go at this one though. Do you play Francis?'

'Oh, all the time,' I lied and gave Ellie a wink. 'It would be good fun with a few beers to arrange a foursome with you and Ellie against Jackie and me.'

'I've never played,' both the girls chorused together.

'That will be half the fun, both sides with a handicap and as Rory is so hot I think I might need a little help from Ellie. Let's go to the lounge, does anybody fancy a drink?'

CHAPTER 17

On the way into the lounge Jackie asked Rory if he'd been able to make any progress with the MOD.

'Oh gosh, yes. I've been so blown away by the house; I've forgotten to tell you. I've got a file of papers in the car, I'll get them.'

In the lounge, the two girls had a sweet sherry whilst Rory saying he preferred a man's drink shared a bottle of beer with me.

'I wrote a letter,' he began, 'to the personnel management department at Innsworth Air base requesting information with regard to Richard Manston RAF 556249 and ten days later when there was no reply I decided to give them a call. A clerk informed me that the matter was pending and that I could expect a letter within the next few days. Finally, I received a reply and it seems the whole affair is a bit confusing.'

Intrigued, Jackie shifted uneasily in her chair while Rory began reading a letter from his file.

"Thank you for your letter dated 9th August asking for assistance to trace a fellow RAF colleague. It is always difficult to positively identify the right person with minimum information. Our only means of tracing service numbers is from an alphabetical index.

I found several entries for Richard Manston [with and without second Christian names] and the only one that could possibly match the criteria you supplied is the number shown above".

At that point, Rory broke off reading.

'There's a number quoted at the top of the letter supposedly belonging to Richard Manston which is 986271 but that isn't the number Ellie found in the hospital.'

'That's odd,' Ellie exclaimed, 'I wonder if the hospital got it wrong and the number belonged to somebody else in for treatment at the same time. With all the animosity between Forces and general accidents which happened all the time whilst on manoeuvres, service personnel were quite frequent visitors.'

Rory continued reading the letter.

"This former airman was born in Liverpool in 1917 and left the service in 1941. Unfortunately, though, there is no mention of any South Western posting. Or records are so brief that this may not be significant. I am not permitted to release this 1941 address to you but if you feel this man is the right one let me know and I will send your original letter (or any other you care to write) in the hope that if Richard Manston is no longer resident the current occupier may know of him. If this is not the man then regrettably I cannot assist you with so little information to go on".

'Well, I'm a bit disappointed,' Jackie chipped in, 'we seem to have hit a brick wall. Sarff is either lying or has genuinely moved on or the hospital record is wrong. The trouble is it was so long ago and sometimes I even ask myself do I really want to know or what I'm going to achieve anyway.'

'You can't give up yet Jackie,' Rory added. 'I think the affair is too mystifying not to pursue further and I think Ellie should have another word with her friend at the hospital. It's quite possible from what she says that a mistake could have been made. My curiosity has got the better of me and I will be only too pleased to get in touch with the Air Ministry again. They seem genuinely interested and so far I've found them very helpful. It just takes a long time for the wheels to start turning, but I'm sure we'll get there.'

'OK then,' Ellie said, 'I'll have another go. Why don't we meet again at our house on Friday? I should have something by then. Tell you what; I'll make up a bite to eat.'

Rory pulled a long face. 'You're welcome to our two up and two down, but don't expect any sweeping staircases and rolling lawns.'

'It's not the size of the house that matters Rory, it's the people in them. Jackie and I would be pleased to come.'

The next day Ellie asked her nursing friend if she would take a second peek at the records. She pointed out to Ellie that it might take a while to organise some sort of clandestine check since the records department were not to keen to divulge information about former patients. Ellie was pleased to discover that there had indeed been some sort of mix up with patient's details and that there were three service personnel in the hospital at roughly the same time, two of which had similar names.

On the Friday, when Jackie and I arrived, Ellie was putting the final touches to the dish she had prepared specially for the evening meal. It was a particular favourite for Rory who had a yen for Eastern foods as a result of his overseas posting during the War.

'I hope you like jumbo prawns,' she said over her shoulder from the stove. 'Rory give our visitors a drink, I can't leave here until the fish has been fried. Jackie, can I press you into service and ask you to pour this dipping sauce into the four small bowls.'

'Sorry Jackie,' Rory said, 'my wife thinks she's still at school, ordering the kids about, but she is a very good cook. This meal is my choice and I know you'll find it better than the sausage and mash I might have cooked. It's a Japanese dish known as tempura consisting of small pieces of fish or vegetables dipped in a light batter and fried in sesame oil until crisp and golden brown. Dipping sauce is made from Japanese rice wine, soy sauce and grated turnip. The side plate contains button mushrooms, spring onions, green peppers, aubergine, cauliflower florets, onions and bamboo shoots. The best bit is we eat with chop sticks which makes the meal not only amusing but also a social occasion.'

Rory and Ellie were experts with the chop sticks whilst Jackie and I had to be shown how to hold them. Using them was an even greater challenge with the result that the meal lasted for well over an hour.

'I think we should toast the chef for an excellent meal,' I said. Whatever you may think of your two up and two down Rory, Ellie's cooking has more than made up for any fancy house and sweeping staircase.'

'Coffee will be served in the drawing room Squire,' Ellie jokingly whispered in my ear.

The meal over and comfortably seated in the lounge, Jackie was anxious to learn what progress Ellie had made at the hospital.

'It was a bit awkward but a little cloak and dagger investigation has produced some new information. Apparently there were two other service personnel in the hospital at the same time as Richard. One of them, a Canadian, had a similar surname and by pure coincidence his Christian name was Richard too. His name was Murson and it was his service number we were given. Richard's correct number was 556249 and I've got his second Christian name as well. It was James.'

Jackie jumped to her feet.

'Yes it was,' she exclaimed. 'It must be Richard.'

'That's great,' Rory added. 'As the Air Ministry said in their letter, with the brief records they hold together with the little we know, any snippet of additional information could be crucial to solving the case. I'll send another letter with the new number and I think we should get an answer quite soon.'

'I'm getting quite excited now, thanks Ellie.' Jackie gave me a nod and stood up ready to leave.

Ellie motioned Jackie to sit down again. 'You can't go yet, I've made some progress with digging out school records for Francis. You did indeed pass your eleven plus exams and therefore qualified for a grammar school place. With your two pals, Dennis and Daryl, you were the only three from Dowdales School to pass that year. The education department here notified your home town authorities who in turn sent a letter addressed to your foster parents. There even is a copy in the files but I was not allowed to make another copy. The letter offered you a choice of two schools, Pridowe High and Sandside—.'

'Well, blow me down, I know them both well and I even gave a talk in Sandside some time ago about life in an orphanage. Against my better judgement, the headmaster Mr. Swinbourne pressed me on the choice of subject which I thought would send all the kids home crying. He explained that the talk was to be an exercise in teaching the kids to appreciate how much better off they were than those in homes. To brighten it up I made light of my experience, added a few jokes and the kids loved it.'

'As I said,' Ellie went on, 'when the authority received no reply they sent another but that received no reply either.'

'I think I can understand why Ellie,' I replied. 'At the time there was some turmoil going on in the house and I was moved out to two orphanages; the first one only for a few weeks and the second one until I was sixteen.'

'Your letters were not passed on and in the end your grammar school place was offered to someone else. Your two pals went to schools in Truro. If you were really interested I should think you could probably trace them from there through some Old Boys association.'

'Well, thanks Ellie for taking all the trouble and I would love to know how my two pals got on. In my mind I imagine that Dennis, who seemed to have everything on his side including brains and good looks, would probably have turned out to be an airline pilot or ski instructor. As for Daryl, well, they were like chalk and cheese, so I've no pre-conceived ideas at all. Anyway, if ever I apply for another job I'll add it to my CV under the heading of 'Lost grammar school pass'.'

We thanked our hosts for an enjoyable evening and feeling that at last Jackie was beginning to make progress in locating Richard we left in a spirited frame of mind.

Later the following week, Jackie telephoned me at the office.

'Rory's got a reply,' she said excitedly. 'We've arranged to meet at eleven in Toby's coffee bar next door to Amanda's office. Can you pop out for a while? Rory says I might need a shoulder to lean on.'

Rory and Jackie were already seated in Toby's with a third cup of black coffee waiting for me.

'Rory said I had to wait for you. He's been keeping me in suspense. I'm tingling all over.'

'I'd like to see that,' Rory said cheekily. 'I've received a reply. It's from somebody else at the same Air Ministry office. I'll read it to you.'

"Thank you for your letter dated 15th August with additional information re your long lost colleague. I have checked the records again and I am pleased to advise you that a Richard James Manston (556249) has been discharged from the Royal Air Force. I regret, however, that as our rules governing disclosure of information are very strict, I am not permitted to release his last known address. I would be prepared to redirect a prepaid letter if it is addressed as follows".

Rory looked up from the paper to see Jackie looking at him attentively, holding my hand so tightly that she was showing white knuckles.

'They give a forwarding address at the bottom of the page and then there's some hand written information. It reads—.'

"I do have a current RAF pensioner's address for Richard James Manston. If you want confirmation of your letter being redirected, send it to me in a covering envelope otherwise it will be sent on but you will not be advised when. Hope this is helpful".

Rory looked up again, this time with a smile.

'That sounds very positive to me. I would say that as he is still drawing a pension, or at least, one is still being drawn that your stepmother is either being paid illegally or she's been telling you porkies.'

'Well I'm damned,' Jackie exclaimed. 'What a woman! It wouldn't surprise me if she is guilty of both assumptions. I knew she was jealous of me and wanted Richard all to herself, but it seems she's been devious as well. She has let me believe all these years that he was dead. How could she be so cruel? For all she knows I might have married and he might have grandchildren and not know anything about them. She obviously wanted to draw a line under his past and pretend it never happened. I wonder if he is aware what she has done behind his back.'

'Unbelievable,' I said as Rory nodded his agreement. 'There could be a number of reasons why you've not been able to contact your dad but obviously she has blocked you out.'

'What do you think we should do now, Jackie? I don't think writing another letter to be forwarded to your dad would be any good,' Rory advised. 'In view of what happened to the previous letter, I can only imagine the same thing happening again.'

'I don't think you have any option now Jackie. We must go to Sarff and meet her head on.'

'Would you do that Francis? I can't expect you to traipse half way across the country to Wiltshire, although I might be a bit frightened to turn up out of the blue on my own. There's no telling what she might do.'

'Well, don't forget that I'm almost "family" too, so to speak and the thought of meeting Uncle Richard would quite something for me as well. I wonder if he remembers me, especially when I remind him of the evacuees. Consider it done,' I assured her. 'I would love to go with you, even if only to receive an apology when I tell him how much his actions affected me at the time.'

'I would sure like to be a fly on the wall when you meet,' added Rory. 'As for Jackie, I think I would take a cricket bat with me.'

'What can you tell me about your stepmother?' I'd like to have some idea before we meet face to face. I think I would recognise your dad after a few minutes but I'm sure he wouldn't have a clue about me after all this time. Have you got a list of things prepared in your mind as to what you are going to say to Sarff?'

Before Jackie had time to answer my first question I quickly followed it with a second.

'Or would you like me to say nothing until the air clears a bit?'

I had to admit that I was as anxious about meeting Jackie's parents as any new boy friend would be and needed to have all my thoughts and questions clear in my head before starting out. Renovations to Tootehill were being carried out for the next week which gave us a golden opportunity to take a few days off for an impromptu holiday. When I picked her up from Picardy I found that she had packed enough cases for both of us put together. Rose made no secret of the fact that she was quite envious and tried to give Jackie some whispered advice like an over protective hen, but it was only when I assured her that I would look after Jackie that she stopped teasing the poor girl.

'Well, she's quite rotund, or at least she was the last time I saw her.' Jackie started to paint the picture of her stepmother. 'With long black hair, a head band and pale skin I've always thought of her as a bit like a gypsy fortune teller. In fact she was the complete opposite of my mother and not the sort of person that I would expect to see my dad with at all. Apparently they knew each other before when Sarff was married to someone else at the RAF station. When she became divorced she acquired the house which provided a ready bolt hole for my dad. Leading up to my parent's divorce they both accused each other of all manner of affairs and relationships and I didn't like it because I loved my dad. They had terrible arguments, often she would throw things. Eventually, he'd had enough and left. I think she drove him out and when her attitude toward me changed as well that was the reason why I left too. Looking back on the day I went to live with dad I think he encouraged me to go with him partially because he knew how badly mum and Clark would take it. The inevitable dogfight ranged between them for ages and mum even tried to tell my dad that he was biting off something bigger than he could chew. She harped on about my wayward ways and that within a few days he would be glad to bring me back. But it was all in vain and in the end dad brushed all her arguments to one side. Also the authorities had advised him that it was in the interest of my personal safety.'

We set out for Sarff's house early next morning and progressed well until we were quite close. When she recognised the road Jackie sat bolt upright in her seat with both hands on the dashboard. I could sense her air of anticipation as she gave me instructions.

'It's further down the road, just after the petrol station on the left. You can't miss it there's a big yellow tree in the front garden.'

We were in a small housing estate which looked as if it had been built on the last piece of available brown land. Behind the houses there were commercial offices and an industrial site with tall chimneys. Jackie read the address from her notebook, 28 Stuart Road but we came to the end of the development without Jackie recognising the house.

'Well, that's odd, where's it gone? I'm sure this is the right place, I recognise those chimneys. Dad used to complain that at times the smoke affected his breathing. Turn around and go more slowly.'

With the 'missing house' now on her side Jackie was able to study the remainder more closely. Suddenly she called out.

'Stop here Francis, that's it, they've replaced the number and called it 'Wilton Edge.' I recognise the window in the gable end. That was my room. It looks a lot bigger than I remember, the garage at the side has gone and the garden has been made into a rockery. I wonder why they've got rid of the maple it was a beautiful tree with cream-edged coloured leaves, such a shame it was the brightest tree in the street. I'll see if they're in, and give you a wave if it's OK.'

Before I could stop her and tell her to slow down, she leapt out of the car, pushed open the gate and boldly knocked three times on the door. A dog barked and kept on barking until the door flew open. Jackie jumped back almost immediately when a dachshund ran out followed by two young children in full pursuit. A tall young lady then appeared in the doorway, profusely apologising on seeing Jackie's startled look.

'Oh, I am sorry; the children were looking through the letter box and saw you coming. Fritz will probably run all the way to the sports ground now. It's time for his walk anyway. What can I do for you?'

'I'm sorry to trouble you but I used to live here with my parents.

Obviously they don't anymore.'

'What was the name?'

'Manston'

'Gosh the Manstons, yes that's right, they did. They moved about three months ago. Look, I was just making a cup of tea. Would you and your husband—?'

'Oh, he's not my husband, he's—.'

'It doesn't matter; we're all worldly wise around here. Come in and have a cup of tea. Perhaps you would like to see how much my husband has changed and improved the house. It's amazing. When we moved in we couldn't agree on the ideas he had, they were all in his head and I thought he was going to wreck the place. How long ago were you here?'

'Thank you very much, we'd love to. I was in my teens then so I can just imagine how much it might have changed because my dad was a DIY enthusiast as well. I remember him saying there was a lot more he could do and there was potential for an extension. But what has happened to the beautiful tree in the front garden, the maple? We couldn't find the house because we were looking for it and you've given the house a name instead of a number.'

'Oh, we didn't do that,' she replied, 'the garden is more or less like it was when we moved in and we haven't got around to doing much to it yet.'

'I'm Vera Atkins and my husband Jack is in the shed at the moment. That noise you can hear is his new bench saw and he's like a kid with a new toy. I've threatened to put his bed in there because he's always making or mending something, but he will come in soon. He never says no to a cup of tea.'

Jackie followed Vera up the stairs which led off the kitchen.

'These are different; they used to lead off the hallway. I remember the hallway used to be much smaller; useless really because two people couldn't pass each other. Gosh! What an improvement with the bedrooms too. My room was a box room and not big enough to swing a cat around. It's amazing what someone with an eye for these things can do.'

Vera led the way down the stairs to the sitting room and no sooner had she poured the tea when Jack's hyper-sensitive nose brought him out of the shed.

'You've done a great job with the house Mr Atkins,' Jackie commented. 'It seems much bigger; quite different to what I remember, but I was only a slip of a girl then.'

Vera patted Jack's behind. 'Your trousers are dusty Jack, sit on a towel.'

He dutifully obeyed, limping to collect one from the kitchen as he did so.

'Accident at the base six years ago,' he said, 'smashed my leg in four places when a block and tackle broke whilst carrying an engine. Two of us got hurt; the other chap was worse than me and used to live in this house.'

Jackie's face contorted in sympathetic pain. What did he mean? 'Worse'. Vera noticed too and recognised her anxiety.

'Oh, Jack, you've jumped the gun. This lady is Richard's daughter. I've invited them in to help explain about the Manstons. She used to live here and has lost touch with her parents.'

'She's not my mother,' Jackie explained, 'she's my stepmother and is responsible for my losing touch because she told me years ago that my dad had been killed in an air crash.'

'Well would you believe it Jack? I've always thought that wicked stepmothers were only the figment of imagination in some fairy tale but now we've met a real one. That's terrible, how could she say that? Actually, I'm not entirely surprised because Jack and I have often queried how a nice chap like Richard could have married Sarff. And I'll tell you another thing. I've always been interested in the meaning of names and when Jack wanted to call our Stephen 'Damian' I told him it was a name for someone who exercised control over others, a sort of evil spirit. Sarff is just as bad. It's a Welsh name meaning 'snake.' From what I know of her together with what you're telling us, I think she lives up to her name. We've never been able to think of them as a loving couple.'

'Like us,' Jack added, patting Vera's leg.

'Jack and Richard used to work together at the airbase until the accident and he's known Sarff for many years from when she used to work there too. I'm Jack's second wife; his first one Doris was accidentally killed in a road accident three years ago. I've always lived in the area and there's never been any shortage of gossip where Sarff was concerned.'

'You can say that again Vera!' Jack continued, 'there was quite a shindig when Sarff left her husband to marry Richard. There was even a court martial for a fight at the base involving all three of them. We all thought her husband was unfairly dismissed the service. It seems that Richard has had more ups and downs in his life than most and until recently it looked pretty bleak what with not being a well man, being confined to a wheelchair with back injury and married to Sarff. And as if that wasn't bad enough, he has been diagnosed to be suffering from asbestosis which has developed into lung cancer and mesothelioma. There are a few others in the area who have similar concerns. That was about nine months ago and since then I know he had been thinking about moving somewhere healthier.'

Jackie looked distressed as she cupped her face in her hands. 'I had no idea dad was so ill, Sarff has kept it all a secret.'

'We're both sorry to be the bearer of such bad news and what a shock it must be but actually although it sounds bad I should think it will buck him up no end when he sees you. Jack used to take him to a RAF club once a week to have a natter with old workmates and then your dad could be his old cheerful self once again for a few hours. You must tell him we both miss him.'

Vera stopped to refill our cups on seeing Jack slide his mug nearer the teapot.

'Jack could empty the pot on his own, and I don't know where he puts it.'

'Six or so months ago,' she went on, 'Richard had an amazing surprise to learn that some lady friend from years back nominated him as a beneficiary in her will. She's left him a rich man. Life doesn't seem to be fair and we would be pleased for him if it wasn't for Sarff being virtually in charge of his affairs. They are such a different couple. Sarff is materialistic and Richard is just the opposite, in fact he told us he would willingly swap the windfall to be healthy again. When the news arrived, Sarff made sure of Richard's claim, the very same day, by hiring a taxi all the way to Warminster even though Jack had offered to take them a few days later. Putting that aside, Jack and I have a lot to be thankful for because Richard managed to arrange a quick sale of this house to us at a knock down price. Apparently, Sarff inherited a bungalow in Bangor from an aunt some time ago which until now has been looked after by her sister. So that's where they've gone. Sarff said it was for Richard's health but the truth is she wanted to be near her Welsh relatives. I believe there's a crowd of them so we don't expect to see him again. Jack was upset that he didn't even have a chance to say goodbye, perhaps with a drink at the pub to wish him well. The sale of the house was a clinical affair, just a quick legal arrangement based on a note from Richard to his friend Jack.'

Jackie listened quietly without saying a word. Secretly she aware of the implications of Richard's condition and that as Jack had already mentioned his future looked bleak. Sarff had by far and away exceeded Jackie's worst fears that she was fully committed to separating Richard from his former world and or any relatives for one greedy purpose. Whilst she was keen to draw a line under Richard's past she was not above scheming to cash in on the proceeds. If Richard was confined to a wheelchair and in poor health surely her next move would be to obtain a court order to look after his affairs. Experiences at Tootehill led her to have fears that she might have other plans too, perhaps confinement in a home or even sectioning. She had to be stopped, but how? Jack suggested a starting point.

'Discovering that your dad is actually still alive must be quite a shock. I suggest a good night's sleep is what you need now young lady. Start afresh tomorrow and then maybe after a decent breakfast your problem might not be so great. Try the Bluebell Inn Francis, they serve good grub and the rooms are all en suite. I know the manager, tell him I sent you.'

We thanked Jack and Vera for their hospitality and booked into the Bluebell a matter of minutes later. The young man in reception assumed we were a couple.

'A double is it sir? Back or park view?'

194

'No thanks, two singles please, park view.'

His roving eye practically undressed Jackie as she stood waiting patiently in the foyer and then he gave me a quizzical look as if to let me know I was missing a golden opportunity.

'He thought we were married,' I said as we made our way to our rooms.

'Yes, I know. It would have been easy to pretend we were, but thanks anyway. It's been a long day and I'm going to take Jack's advice and try to sleep on what we've learnt. I felt more confident about meeting Sarff before speaking to Jack and Vera but now she seems to have changed into someone quite different, someone who will swat anyone who gets in her way like a fly. I'm so glad you've come with me.'

CHAPTER 18

We ordered two full English breakfasts but Jackie was too apprehensive to make much of an impression on hers. I enjoyed mine and cleared most of hers as well. Having pigged out on my breakfast, I turned down the offer of a packed lunch but I persuaded Jackie to at least take something with her thermos of coffee. Jackie was anxious to be on our way and we set off for Bangor in search of the Sarff family stronghold where we envisaged Richard to be a captive.

If only we could find him on his own it would be ideal but with Sarff's past actions in mind we were well aware that it was just wishful thinking. Jackie's imagination ran wild as she told me that in her sleep she saw Sarff with a shot gun peering through a stockade surrounding the house ready to repel all invaders. All her friends were there too thrashing the air with their clubs and knives and then she said she woke up in panic when the face materialised into that of Rose. Looking at her watch it was still only half four in the morning, but eventually she said she fell asleep again and then she dreamt about crowds of people and roads full of traffic.

'That's hardly surprising,' I told her. 'We've been seeing them since yesterday and you're not used to wandering too far away from Tootehill.'

Our first port of call in Bangor was to squeeze ourselves into a telephone kiosk where we searched the listings for Sarff's family name of Donkin. We had to start somewhere. Our problem was that Sarff would now be a Manston, a name not in the listings. By moving to Wales without letting anyone know the forwarding address, Sarff had covered her tracks once more. To a private investigator finding her probably wouldn't have been a problem given time, but time was something we did have too much of. With our limited knowledge of the area it was gong to be a matter of luck; a needle in a haystack. Jackie thumbed her way through the pages of a dog eared directory until she came to the 'DON's' and cried out.

'Would you believe it? Three pages of the 'D's' have been torn out!'

'Surely that must be a coincidence Jackie.' I stared in disbelief. 'I can't believe she's deliberately gone around the area tearing out pages. That's got to be one step too far. If she has it tells us something—.'

Jackie closed the book. 'And what's that Sherlock?' She said with a grin.

'Perhaps we're closer than she would like us to be.'

'Quick then, lets find another kiosk, I smell blood.'

We both left the kiosk laughing much to the amusement of a gentleman who had been waiting patiently but couldn't help overhearing our conversation. He followed us with his eyes as he watched us get back into the car and smartly drive away. What thoughts of skulduggery he thought we were up to was anybodies guess.

We drove on several miles before we found another telephone box or even someone who knew where there was one. The directory was fairly new, complete with all its pages. We thought the family name would not be an easy one to find in a directory where we expected every other name to be a 'Jones' or a 'Griffiths,' but to our surprise we found seven 'Donkins' of which only three were listed for Bangor. At the first address there were two elderly ladies but at the second we struck gold without even getting out the car. We followed their directions to the next address but must have taken a wrong turn somewhere and found ourselves on the outskirts of town in the direction of Bethesda. The houses were beginning to thin out as more and more fields began to appear until eventually we came to the conclusion we had lost our way. I stopped the car. Jackie poured two cups of coffee while I checked our map again. A lady pushing a wheelchair passed by, in fact she was so close I could have touched her.

'Oh my God, it's them Francis!' She spluttered over her coffee. 'It's them and poor old dad is trussed up like a parcel. It's a good thing that we weren't facing the other way, she might have recognised me and our element of surprise would have been lost.'

'I didn't hear a sound they just seemed to float by,' I said. 'I wasn't looking in my mirror and I didn't see Richard's face but from this angle he could be anybody. All I saw was a bundle with a trilby on top in a wheelchair.'

'There's no doubt about it Francis, I'd recognise her gait any day by the way she flicks her left foot. She damaged her ankle when she was a child by getting her foot jammed in a street drain which one of her sisters had lifted. She's lost weight too by the look of it.'

'Well, they've gone into that dormer bungalow next to the one with the privet hedge and the trees behind it so I suggest you have a bite to eat with our coffee while we've got the chance. Somehow I don't think she's going to get out the best crockery and chocolate biscuits when she sees you.'

The bungalow was an older one, probably built in the twenties, with no outstanding features. There was little evidence from the outside that any work had been done on it for a number of years and various shrubs in the garden were growing out of control. Weeds were growing through the path and the scrappy bit of lawn needed cutting. Faded curtains were drawn in the dormer window giving the impression that that part of the house was permanently out of use. It was just the sort of house where one might to find an older person or a recluse. It was my experience that such people seem to like to hide behind high hedges or the old favourite, the yew tree. The property was well on its way to being 'detached and secluded,' a common phrase which estate agents, myself included, often use.

'I'm too much on edge to eat now Francis. This is it. I've got to strike whilst the iron is hot.'

'Calm down, you've waited all this time so another five minutes won't make any difference and I don't think they're going to run away now. Hold on for a while to give them time to take their coats off and sort themselves out. The sight of you turning up on their doorstep is going to be quite a shock as it is and I imagine that as she hasn't heard from you for some time, she will be thinking she's seen you off.'

Ten minutes ticked anxiously by as Jackie sipped at her coffee and made a brave attempt to eat a sandwich, all the while strumming with her fingers on the dashboard with her free hand. Her apprehension was beginning to affect me too until I finally closed the sandwich container and agreed that the time was right, if only to stop the non musical fingers. I had no idea what I was going to say, perhaps it would be wise to say nothing until Jackie and Richard had become fully reunited. I had the feeling that that could be quite some time in the future. My reunion was unimportant compared to that of Jackie's and then I contrived the idea that maybe my knowledge of past times might be a useful card to keep up my sleeve.

We parked the car where it was and made our approach on foot, not wishing to draw attention to ourselves by arriving in my Humber Sceptre. As we got closer we became aware of a large flock of rooks jostling for position in a tree just beyond the back garden. More and more birds were joining them, cawing and kaahing in an animated fashion as if to tell the others to move further along the branches. 'Caw! Caw! Move along, I can't see'; they seemed to be waiting for something and all looking in one direction toward the garden and bungalow. Could it be they knew of our mission and were expecting fireworks or was it simply that they were eyeing up the remnants of lunch? Jackie stopped walking and tightened her grip on my arm.

'Look at that Francis, isn't that eerie and what does it remind you of?'

'Ho! Ho! Yes. Well it has to be 'The Birds' Alfred Hitchcock's film adaptation of the Daphne Du Maurier story,' I replied. 'I would say that if ever there was an omen or harbinger of impending disaster then that's got to be it.'

Jackie stared back wide eyed. 'You think so?'

'No come on, they're only birds roosting. It's what they do and I'm only joking, let's get this over.'

I held Jackie's arm as we sauntered up the path to the front door, purposely holding her back so that if any eyes were peering through curtains at the sound of the gate, they would not be aware that we were any other than a normal couple, possibly looking for directions. Jackie walked up the ramp and rang the doorbell. Sarff opened the door still wearing her coat.

'Yes, what can I do for you? Oh! Hello Melissa, fancy seeing you again.'

Jackie looked puzzled, surprised by Sarff's quite civil reception.

'Hello Sarff, I'm not Melissa, I'm Jackie. You can't have forgotten.'

Sarff let out a cry. 'Oh my God, is that you Jackie? I don't believe it. Where have you come from? How did you—?'

A voice from the lounge cut across her cries.

'Who is it Sarff? Open the door. Let me see.'

The wheelchair crashed against the lounge door causing it to swing outwards sharply and swing back again as it rebounded on the back wheels. The huddled bundle still complete with trilby trundled up behind Sarff as she stood in the doorway open mouthed and speechless. I drew some consolation from the fact that on first appearances, I did not recognise the shrivelled little old man with a rug across his knees. I thought this can't be Uncle Richard; my Uncle Richard was well over six foot tall, its got to be somebody else and felt sure that there was no chance of my being recognised either.

'Hello Dad, it's me Connie' she called out over the shoulder of the now transfixed Sarff who was still holding and half leaning on the door handle.

The man's eyes opened a little wider, almost fearing to open any wider in case his ears were playing tricks. Then he heard it again as Jackie repeated herself.

'It's me Connie, your daughter.'

Despite being an invalid, I thought for one moment that he was going to stand up as he rested both hands on the arm rests and tried to push forward.

'Get out of the way woman, let me see. Don't stand there gawping.'

There was nothing wrong with Richard's sight or his memory where Jackie was concerned. His body may have been in poor health but his was mind was active and clear as a bell. He roughly pushed his way in front of Sarff with open arms to welcome his long lost daughter. Jackie sank to her knees as they both embraced.

'Connie, Connie, Connie I'm so sorry,' he sobbed into his daughter's shoulder.

'I never thought I would ever see you again, Dad. I thought you were dead but something happened just by chance and I've managed to trace you though the MOD who told me you were still drawing your pension.'

'When you stopped letting me know how you were getting on I wrote several letters to your military camp, but never received any reply.'

'Well so did I Dad. I even tried to get the MOD to give me your address but they refused to budge on the grounds of confidentiality.'

Jackie, still on her knees, turned to ask Sarff a question. 'Have you any idea what happened to—?'

Sarff's worst nightmare was unfolding right before her very eyes. This can't be. She stared at Jackie, her eyes full of hate. She opened her mouth as if to speak but merely gasped and without saying a word, rushed down the corridor and up the stairs. A door slammed.

'You must excuse Sarff, she's obviously in shock.'

'I bet she is, Dad. We've got a lot of catching up to do.'

Richard guided his wheelchair through the double swing doors into the open style lounge-kitchen-diner each of which were separated by partial glass screens. All the lights were on to dispel the gloom cast by the bushes in the front garden and the heat from the gas fire was beginning to warm the lounge portion.

'We've been out for quite a while visiting one of her sisters, that's why it's a bit cold,' he said pointing to his hat. This used to be three rooms but I've had it altered so that I don't have to struggle with doors. Come in to the lounge, Connie, we've only just come home so there's fresh coffee by the fire. Bring your man too.'

'My man, as you call him is Francis. We're just good friends and he's been good enough to take time off to help me find you. We've had a bit of a struggle what with one thing and another but we had a stroke of luck when you passed by our parked car about ten minutes ago. You were so close I could have touched you. Did you see the car?'

Richard put out his hand to shake mine. He was shaking, totally overcome with shock. 'I can't thank you enough young man and I'm glad you didn't give up. You've made me a very happy man and I'll always be in your debt.'

'I'm only the taxi man; Jackie's done all the work.'

Jackie poured three cups of coffee. Richard asked for his to be black and strong with two sugars. He drank his coffee and then another before he calmed down and I noticed his hands weren't shaking any more. Jackie moved a chair to sit beside him and both held hands.

'I'm really surprised and pleased to see you, Connie. After all that's happened since I last saw you, I more or less resigned myself to thinking you were a part of the past, gone for ever. When you stopped sending me letters and Christmas cards, Sarff convinced me that perhaps you had hitched up with some lad or other and were too busy to write home. I was very much aware that Sarff didn't take to you but that was partially my fault. They say that when you marry someone you marry bag and baggage and accept all their faults, good and bad. In the early days, I felt she did that and we were blissfully happy, but that was when we both worked at the airbase and we socialised quite a lot with a good crowd of mates. I'm a great believer in biorhythms and then life seemed to sail along on a high for a couple of years or so, but inevitably, everything fell apart. I think there was an element of familiarity breeding contempt which resulted in Sarff's then husband and me having a fight. It all happened at a camp dance when her husband was naturally jealous of my attention to Sarff on account of me being foot lose, single and fancy free. There was a court marshal because of the pandemonium which broke out and the damage to MOD property. The net outcome of it all was that her husband, who was known to have a bit of a temper, was dismissed from the service. We all sympathised with him, but despite the efforts of the gang, the ruling was upheld and he took it badly. Shortly afterwards Sarff divorced her husband which left us free to get it together.'

'I must tell you Dad,' Jackie continued, 'we paid a visit to your old house in Stuart Road and met the Atkins family. Jack and Vera were very kind and they helped us to find you here. They were very concerned about you and they were quite open about the fact that they wouldn't be sending any Christmas cards to Sarff. Jack sends you his best wishes and was sorry not to have been able to say goodbye over a pint or two.'

The telephone began to ring but before Richard could answer, it stopped.

'Oh, it's alright, Sarff will have got it in the bedroom. If it's her relations she's talking to, she will be on the phone for ages. They are quite a big family and close nit which is the reason why we've come to live here. I would like to have stayed in Stuart Road and I'm going to miss people like Jack and Vera, but now I'm confined to this blessed wheelchair any social life is down the pan.'

Sarff's muffled voice could be heard as it got more and more agitated. We could hear footsteps, which with her gammy ankle, sounded like the tick of a badly levelled clock, as she paced the room above.

'She's going at it twenty to the dozen this time. I can hear some Welsh bits; she does that when she doesn't want me to know something. Turning up out of the blue like you have has really upset her. I can't imagine why.'

Jackie immediately latched onto his words.

'Oh, I can Dad,' she said with conviction, 'and I don't think you're going to like it, but I'll tell you later. Tell us about your accident, it's such a shock to see you like this.'

'Well, it was all a bit odd really but we were never able to prove anything. I sometimes wonder if Sarff has a deep secret as far as her ex was concerned. We've talked about it of course, but she flatly denies knowing anything. I think looking back at it all now that perhaps she regretted granting him the divorce on the grounds of her adultery with me. She knew that the case was false but still agreed with it. When he was dismissed the service he took it badly, so bad if fact that it was rumoured he had vowed to get his own back. He thought we should both have got the chop. The accident happened about three months later when the normal crane operator was off on sick leave with appendicitis. His place was taken by another chap who was very friendly with Sarff's ex and the story goes that the night before they were both seen in a pub and that money was supposed to have changed hands for an 'accident' to happen. During the court case the judge ruled the evidence as not admissible. From the inquiry into the accident it was established that the evidence pointed to a genuine mishap due to grease on an engine and therefore it would have been very easy for a load to slip. The unfortunate thing was that although there were four men involved in the working party, Jack as well as myself were caught which was another point in favour of the defence that no particular person was targeted.'

'I suppose you could say that you were very unlucky.'

'Yes I suppose so, but life has its ups and downs and although being confined to a wheelchair is no joke, not long ago I had a stroke of good fortune which has gone some way to even things up. On one of my weekend leave periods during my service days I came home to find your mother laid low with influenza which left me at a bit of a lose end. Also on leave at the time was my mate Sam who was a bit of a live wire and he conveniently arranged for an evening of wine women and song to cheer me up. We went to a NAAFI club dance and met some very nice girls but they were already fixed up with American GI's. The long and short of it was that the recognised animosity which existed between the Tommies and the GI's boiled over into a fight and I got in the way of knife intended for somebody else. I was in the wrong place at the wrong time.'

'Yes, I know that bit,' Jackie interrupted. 'That's more or less where my curiosity about you began. Not long after I joined the RAF, Sarff wrote me a letter saying that you had been killed in an air crash. I've got it with me and you must read it. I think you'll find as I did that it's very convincing.'

Richard read the letter, quickly scanning his premature obituary, before raising his voice in a wild outburst. He thrashed the arm of his wheelchair several times with the rolled up letter.

'The bitch, if only I could get out of this wheelchair, I'd swing for her. For a long time she has wanted to pretend my former life never existed, but this was a cruel thing to do. I can't believe it. I knew there was something, but this—.'

'And that's not all of it,' Jackie added. 'I've even brought the charred cigarette case which she said was recovered from the crash site. She must have planned and schemed for a long time right from the beginning to cut me out of your life.'

'So that's where it went. I looked for ages for that. It was a prize that I won at an RAF base for boxing and there used to an inscribed shield on the back. I would never have believed that anyone could be so devious. They say you never really get to know people deep down and this convinces me that after all these years, Sarff is no exception.'

He stared wildly into the fire for a few moments and then spoke to me directly for the second time by asking me to get him a stiff drink from the drinks cabinet. Up to that moment I was careful not to interrupt their conversation, in fact I sat slightly to one side just in case trolling back through his memories might cause him to scrutinise me more closely. But his focus was totally on Sarff and this was Jackie's day and not mine. There was a creak from a door followed by another from the carpeted stairs. Richard was too distracted to notice but Jackie flashed her wide eyes in my direction, raising an index finger to her ear. We had not noticed that the telephone conversation had finished and all went quiet once more as Jackie carried on talking, now with the knowledge that she was sure Sarff was listening.

'I've lived with that knowledge for so long and believed it until recently when I happened to be reading a book some chap has written in which he lists all the military air crashes up and down the country. Your crash not being there set me thinking. A friend who saw a report in newspaper archives detailing your incident at the NAAFI club and another teacher who was there at the time made enquiries at the local hospital. Much to their surprise, despite first being sidetracked by a man with a similar name to ours, they found your medical report and RAF number service. After that we checked your number with MOD records and found that you were still drawing a pension. A letter I addressed to you at number 28 was returned, *"Not at this address"* but I was suspicious about it having been steamed open and resealed.'

'If that's the case then it's all becoming clear now what has happened to our mail in both directions,' Richard suggested. 'Sarff has intercepted it and with me not being able to get to a letter box she probably burned them. Not only that, she is always first to check the mail in the morning and then leaves me to open the bills. It seems she made a fatal error in sending your letter back. No doubt she read every word and recognised the danger of being found out. If she had burnt that one too, you might not be here today.'

Richard stopped to gaze into the fire for a few moments. We waited until he had had time to sort out the turmoil and revelations that were flooding his mind before he turned his attention back to Jackie.

'What was the name of the teacher who was there at the time?' He asked, knowing full well the answer.

'Wendy Nicholson,' Jackie replied. 'Her involvement was in the newspaper report too and she had to answer some awkward questions from the headmaster of her school together with some officials from the Education Authority. They asserted that she had jeopardised the reputation of the school. She was a very popular teacher and well thought of by the rest of the school staff who voiced their criticism of the assertion on the grounds that she just happened to be in the wrong place at the wrong time. When she died prematurely, she was mourned by a large congregation at the local church where her friend Ellie read a very moving obituary. It was not long ago that Francis and I attended the auction of her property and winding up of her estate which took quite a bit of time since she had no family.'

Whist Jackie was speaking, Richard leaned forward in his wheelchair, listening intently to every word. Finally he was able to let Jackie know his stroke of good fortune.

'It was Wendy who included me in her will,' he said.

Jackie sat motionless as her bottom jaw dropped open.

'Did she really Dad? Why did she do that? Did you know each other then?'

'We became friends whilst I was in hospital. She felt guilty about the NAAFI affair saying that if her group had not taken over our table, the stabbing might not have happened. She visited me quite a few times and afterwards we dated and became lovers; we even thought about living together, but a posting to India put a stop to all that. We wrote a few letters to each other for a while, but sadly it all came to nothing. I can't remember how many years ago that was now, in fact I never gave Wendy another thought that is not until six months ago when I received the solicitors note. She's left me quite a packet and I feel quite embarrassed really, but if I had the chance I'd trade the whole lot to get rid of this blessed wheelchair.'

'So you've proved the point that money doesn't necessarily make you happy then,' Jackie added philosophically. 'When the Atkins said you had moved to Bangor I was surprised because if I remember correctly you were not keen on the Welsh. It had something to do with one of your commanding officers being Welsh and for some reason he had taken a dislike to you and as a result, if any dirty job came up at camp, it always seemed to come your way.'

'Yes that's right. I remember 'Café-Taffy' as we used to call him because he used to leave the lads square bashing while he sloped off to the canteen where he could watch us from the window. He enjoyed all the more when it rained.'

'So now here you are in Wales.' Jackie added.

'Yes, I afraid so but it was mainly Sarff's idea. I went along with it to some degree because it was supposed to be for my health. I need quite a bit of attention and I know I am a burden, but she says that with her large family here they will be able to help out from time to time to give her a rest. But that's not quite the way it has been of late because there seems to be a shortage of family help when I need it and as often as not I have to wait until Sarff returns home. Fortunately I do have neighbours who will help out when I get desperate but I try not to bother them too much. I can understand now why in the end she didn't have too many friends in Stuart Road. There were plenty of my friends there who were quite willing to lend a hand but they didn't like the idea of Sarff bossing them around.'

Sarff had heard enough. The lounge door burst open, hitting the back of Richard's wheelchair as it did so. Her face was streaked with anger and immediately directed the full onslaught of her personal nightmare at Jackie.

'Why couldn't you have let sleeping dogs lie? We were quite happy without you turning up. Now it's my turn to upset you. When I sent you that letter back to you, it was all for your own good. You should have left it there; made a clean break.'

Jackie stood up and moved closer to Sarff.

'What do you mean, 'made a clean break'?'

'If you've come here chasing his money, you're out of luck. He's not your real father, you know,' Sarff hissed aggressively.

'You are a nasty vindictive woman. How dare you say such a thing? Of coarse he's my dad and he always will be.'

Jackie flashed her eyes at Richard to find him shifting uneasily in his chair barely able to return the look of assurance that she was asking for.

'There you see, he can't answer. Who's lying now?'

Sarff sat down in an armchair with an air of supremacy, with her arms folded across her chest. She had dealt one of her trump cards and glared at Jackie as if daring her to go one better. For the first time, she turned her attention to me, jumping out of her chair as she did so to poke me in the chest and deal another sneering attack hoping to rule me out of the equation once and for all.

'I bet you didn't know that did you Francis? What do you think about your wife now?'

'We are just good friends,' I explained.

'Well, perhaps you might give some thought to your friendship and ask yourself what sort of family you could be getting involved with. You'd better believe me my friend because you are about to open a whole Pandora's box of truths which if you're sensible should send you scurrying out that door. My advice to you is to cut lose while you're ahead.'

I moved closer to Jackie and rested a hand on her arm.

'I'll be the judge of that thank you and I don't need any advice from you, in fact from what I hear you'd better get used to the idea of seeing a lot of me. I'm staying put, so you can say whatever you like, it will make no difference.'

Jackie rubbed the back of my hand and turned to give me a peck on the cheek. Richard tapped the arm of his chair. 'Hear, hear!' He said as he cleared his throat and took on a more serious look to address Jackie.

'I am sorry to say that for once Sarff is telling the truth. Let me explain—.'

'This should be good,' Sarff butted in. 'I can't wait to hear how you get out of this one. Like I've told Jackie, I've protected you all these years from your dubious past and you should have drawn a positive line in the sand when you married me. If I remember correctly, things were different then and I provided a roof over your head when you needed one.'

'But I have my birth certificate, with you and mum as parents,' Jackie interrupted.

'Yes, that's quite true. We brought you up as our own quite normally during your younger years, but it was when I went to hospital with the knife wound that my doctor told me that I was sterile. As a result, your mum and I had an argument right there in the hospital which soon led to the divorce. You were quite young and living with your grandma and we decided not to tell you until later. Well, 'later' never seemed to come and the fact that I was not your biological parent has been a problem ever since. In fact, it has been more than that; you might say it has been a source of blackmail which has long hung over me until now.'

'Too dammed right it has and all of your own making,' Sarff butted in. 'So now it's all out in the open, your real father was Alfie, the randy milkman-come-projectionist.' Her eyes opened wide as she flashed another of her trump cards at Jackie.

'Alfie,' Jackie exclaimed. 'How do you know that?'

'Aha! Now there's a good question. There's a lot I know that even your so called father doesn't know because I got to hear of it when I attended the reading of his mistress's will. While he was in the solicitor's office I met another family, a woman with three children. The woman asked me lots of questions wanting to know who I was and in return she told me Wendy Nicholson was her mother. And do you know what? Surprise, surprise, your infamous Alfie was her father too and like you he was not named on the birth certificate either. She said she was born in a convent and never met her mother or father and didn't know anything about the affair until recently when she learned of the will. As a professional teacher, Wendy didn't want to be saddled with a child so she paid for her keep at the convent until she was sixteen. Apparently she'd been able to hide her pregnancy from her fellow colleagues and Alfie never knew. She said that when she came of age she had been allowed to leave the convent on the basis that she was too much of a free spirit and live wire to be considered nun material. She admitted that the assessment was quite correct since for the last twenty years or so she had wandered from pillar to post, or man to man, to use her own words, trying to support her children in any way she could. You have a half sister with three children of her own and like mother like daughter she has never married. Her name is Melissa Nicholson and she was overjoyed to be a beneficiary. She lived in a single mother establishment in London at the time but I imagine that has all changed now. The world gets more like a rabbit warren every day. What a joke.'

Knowing that the mere mention of Alfie would upset Richard, Sarff spun his wheelchair around to peer directly into his face in an attempt to prompt a response. She was taken by surprise as he quickly spun the chair back again to roll over her foot in the process. She cried out in pain but there was no apology. He ignored her and angrily pushed her away as he moved to the other side of the room. He was annoyed that she could be so blunt with Jackie and felt that it was his place to reveal the truth and not hers. She was dealing her trump cards with maximum malice in the hope that Jackie might see her stepfather in his true colours, but the revelation had quite the opposite affect. Feeling that Richard was being taunted and stressed unduly, she put her arm around his shoulder.

'I don't care,' she continued, 'as far as I'm concerned, you brought me up and loved me as your own. I admire you for that even though for a long time Mum didn't tell you the truth. Actually, it settles a lot of doubts about the time that I spent in Alfie's house and why he acted so oddly with me. I remember the time when Mum took me out shopping for my school uniform and I saw you in Main Street on the other side of the road. She dragged me into a shop doorway so that you wouldn't see me and when I tried to get free she pushed me into the shop and held the door shut from the outside. The shopkeeper thought we were most odd. At times when I chanced to catch the pair of them arguing, they would clam up as soon as I appeared. I assumed it was about my private school costs and later when he died he left me some money, which I now realise was really a guilt payment. When I questioned Mum about it saying that as he was only my stepfather and I didn't expect anything, she still didn't say anything. Perhaps she thought it would be best if I never knew and accepted my birth certificate on its face value. It was also her way of covering up her infidelity, a secret which she took to the grave. She never had the backbone to tell me in the hospital even though there was some sort of reunion in the end. As you know Dad, living there was beginning to be difficult and possibly even dangerous which is why I contacted the local authorities. As my legal guardian I was pleased when you took me away and I understand now why they were both so upset.'

'I afraid there was a lot of things your Mother didn't tell you. Your Mum dated my best friend Sam before me and when the friendship began to pale I moved in and although we got married, Sam still remained my friend. In fact, he was the best man at our wedding. He always held a torch for her and took a keen interest in all she did. It was not until your Mum and I split that Sam was able to confide in me about her antics and break his bond of silence without seeming petty or needing to score points. She was a nymphomaniac and Sam knew about Alfie long before I did, although I did have my suspicions when she used to come home from the cinema long after shows had finished. My leave from the RAF base was limited, so what she did for most weekends was a secret between her and your grandmother. Having a house full of evacuees provided her with an excuse, often saying that they were too busy for anything but work. Sam received his information about her exploits from his sister Moira who worked with her in the cinema. Your mum used to confide in Moira who was older and wiser but being the person she was, never acted on any advice. In fact, she had affairs with at least two others at the same time as Alfie. There was an American GI and closer to home, the billeting officer, Joe Freeman. Your grandmother was aware of both, but either because she wanted to preserve the marriage or didn't want to upset the running of the house, she kept quiet.'

Richard paused to empty his glass. He looked drained and relieved at the same time. 'As far as I'm concerned, now that the secret is out, it makes no difference. I brought you up as my daughter and accepted you as such and I can see no reason to change now. It is equally obvious to me that you have accepted me as your dad, despite all the complications and without knowing anything about my present circumstances you have gone to a great deal of trouble to find me. I love you for that alone.'

Putting her arms around Richard's shoulders, Jackie kissed him on the side of his cheek.

'How touching! Where's my camera?' Sarff was sarcastic to see Richard and Jackie together. 'I haven't finished yet,' she continued. 'Do you want to know why I called you Melissa when you arrived? Well you're the spitting image of your half sister, two peas in a pod if ever there was. Pity Alfie's not around to see the evidence of his passion.'

There was that name again, Richard saw red.

'Get out of my sight,' he shouted as he threw his empty cup and saucer at her only to miss and hit the wall causing them to shatter in a thousand pieces.

Realising that she had dealt all her ace cards to no avail Sarff sprang out of her chair and flounced out the room cursing in Welsh as she went.

'She will be on that phone again for ages now, you mark my words. She usually rings her sister Charlotte for advice and Dutch courage.

She's the brains of the family and she can wind Sarff up like a toy doll.'

A few moments later, there was a ting of the phone as it engaged which Richard acknowledged by pointing his right index finger to the ceiling like some imaginary gun.

'I think we've got time for a cuppa and perhaps something to eat before the next episode. She will be back, have no doubt. See if you can find your way around the kitchen Connie.'

Richard used Connie's name quite freely. I wondered as he turned his wheelchair to face me directly whether he would be so in tune as to remember me. There appeared to be no outward signs. Indeed, I convinced myself, why should there be, I was only a small child and perhaps there were too many other faces in that house for him to remember. I felt that the way in which we had both changed made it very unlikely that we would recognise each other purely on a physical basis alone. Perhaps the bath incident took place in a moment of anger which was soon forgotten on his part. For me, the memory was so strong that I imagined there to be a water mark on my forehead making it blatantly obvious. Despite my uneasiness, all was well and I decided not to resurrect the memory. He had had quite enough distress for one day and I decided not to add to it.

Jackie busied herself in the kitchen for some time opening and closing various cupboard doors before she emerged carrying a tray set up for afternoon tea.

'I've managed to find a few things but still can't find the milk jug so I've had to bring the whole bottle. I've brought an extra setting for Sarff, perhaps a cup of tea will calm her down.'

'That's very considerate of you Connie but I don't think judging by the bumping around that we've heard from upstairs that she will be in any mood for socialising. I think she'd rather slit her throat than sit with us now and although I think I know her pretty well, I can't imagine the torment she will be going through having been caught out. There's no telling what she will do next, with or without Charlotte's backing.'

Just as Jackie was pouring the tea, the lounge door flew open again right back against its hinges causing her to jump and spill the tea into the tray. Sarff stood full-square in the doorway with her arms folded across her chest, fully re-energised and once more back in attack mode.

'Oh, this is very cosy, thank you very much. Seeing as how you are being so well looked after my dear Richard by your so called daughter perhaps she would like to take over and look after a few of your other needs too. I wish you the best of luck my girl and you will find out soon enough what I've had to cope with all these years. You will think twice when you've got to get up at three, five and seven at night. I'm going to have a well earned night out and I'm taking the car. I might even take a holiday and be back when I'm good and ready. Don't wait up. Goodbye.'

Richard laughed as she left the room, he even looked happy for the first time since we had arrived. 'She won't go far, there's too great a magnet here,' he said as he tapped the pouch on the inside of his wheelchair. We both looked in his direction but for the moment he left the pair of us to speculate what secrets it held.

With that she stormed out leaving the lounge door swinging on its hinges and the front door wide open. She tortured the car into top gear even before she reached the bend in the road barely fifty yards away and accelerated to leave a plume of smoke in her wake. Neighbours in a nearby garden looked up to comment on the apparent haste. A lady on the pavement clipping her garden hedge from the outside, barely five feet away from the speeding vehicle, lost her hat and dropped her shears as she wheeled around to check the driver.

'That was Sarff,' she said to husband who was on his hands and knees weeding on the other side. 'She was sure in one hell of a hurry, I wonder if something has happened to Richard. Go and check Gethyn, he may have had some sort of accident with his wheelchair.'

Gethyn, who was an agile ferret of a man in his sixties with a boyish build jumped up and took a short cut into his neighbour's garden by squeezing through a gap in the fence. Seeing the front door wide open and no apparent signs of life he popped his head into the hallway.

'Hello Richard, are you OK? Do you need any help?'

Jackie met him as he approached the lounge.

'Oh, hello, I didn't know Richard had visitors. When we saw the car fly off we thought there might have been a problem.'

Richard appeared behind Jackie.

'I think you could call it that Gethyn, but the problem is all to do with Sarff. As you can see I'm fine, in fact I'm feeling better than I have done for years. This is my daughter Connie. We have just been reunited after losing touch for neigh on twenty years. Bring Gwyneth over later and we'll have a drink to celebrate.'

'Right ho boyo, that's great. She will be relieved. She was quite concerned about you when she saw the car shoot off like that. The way she was driving we were convinced you were on the floor or something. Glad to see you're OK though, but I've got reservations about how much rubber there will be on your tyres when she comes back. See you later then.'

CHAPTER 19

True to his word, Gethyn returned with Gwyneth early in the evening sooner than expected. At the time I was talking to Richard confident in the knowledge that he had no recollection of our last meeting some thirty five years ago. Connie was in the kitchen clearing up after preparing an evening meal.

'You didn't waste any time getting back then Gethyn.'

Richard's non complementary jibe at Gethyn passed over his head un-noticed. Whilst his neighbour was good hearted and always willing to help he was somewhat naive and took directives too literally. He was putty in his wife's hands; the ever ready model of a dutiful husband programmed to her demands like a remote controlled robot. Richard moved his wheelchair away from the sofa to make room for his guests to sit down. His wife Gwyneth was a large woman who reminded me of another big woman I once knew; the size that I might have expected her to be if she had carried on stuffing herself for the last thirty plus years. She waddled passed the wheelchair and sat down with a bit of a flump.

'Well, you know me, any excuse for a free beer,' he said as he sat upright on the sofa with his hand outstretched to be served by some unseen waiter.

Gwyneth's ample bulk being about four times that of her husband caused Gethyn to bounce back into an almost standing position as she sat beside him.

'Where are your manners, Gethyn? Put your hand down and wait to be asked. What will Connie and—.' She stopped talking to look in my direction.

'Francis' I said, 'Francis Tenby. Jackie and I are just good friends.'

Gwyneth looked puzzled. 'I thought Richard called her Connie.'

'Well yes and that is her real name, but it's a long story.'

'Will you be waiter Francis?' Richard said before Gwyneth could ask any awkward questions with Connie still in the kitchen.

Connie reached the drinks cabinet ahead of me as I struggled to get up from the rather low armchair. 'It's OK Francis, I can do it.'

'So why have you two not been in touch for so long then Connie?' Gwyneth persisted with her questioning.

Richard sensed that Gwyneth wanted an answer to the star question right from the outset. 'There's a one word answer to that, 'S-A-R-F-F,' he said spelling out the name.

Richard then began to relate the whole story to his neighbours and got as far as the alleged air crash when he saw Sarff arrive back by car. She was accompanied by her two sisters, Mavis and Charlotte and brother in law, Griff. He thought she had either written the car off or now she was returning with reinforcements to continue where she left off. Led by Sarff, all four hustled up the path, pushed open the front door and burst into the lounge without knocking. Gethyn who was next to the door, jumped up more by surprise than anything else, used the moment to greet Griff, his working colleague from the paper shop.

Not to be outdone by Sarff, Richard greeted her sarcastically.

'That was a short night out. Did you have a nice time? I was hoping to arrange a holiday myself and not to be here when you came back.'

Sarff took a step toward Richard but thought better of being goaded into retaliating physically. Instead she merely muttered something under breath in Welsh which caused the trio to clap.

Griff tried to diffuse the situation with his, 'hi-di-hi there Griff old pal, nice to see you. Have you come to celebrate too?' They gave each other a hug.

'I'll give you celebrate. We'll see about that,' Sarff retorted. 'We've come to put you all straight on a few things and before you get any big ideas Connie, I've no need to remind you who your real father is, but for the benefit of our guests, Connie's father is 'A N Other' as you might say. So I don't think that's a good reason to break open the Champaign.'

Gwyneth audibly whistled. Gethyn couldn't help himself as he addressed Richard. 'I thought you said—.' He hesitated, 'that's a funny name, never met that one before.'

'Sorry,' she apologised to Richard. 'Stupid man,' she whispered in her husband's ear.

Gethyn registered his disapproval. 'Oh dearie, dearie me. Oh! I get it now, she's not—.' He stopped when Gwyneth slapped his leg quite sharply. 'Sometimes you can be so dumb, it's unbelievable.'

'You may well whistle Gwyneth, but you don't know the half of it.' Sarff continued, 'this is my house left to me by my aunt which means to say I can tip you all out whenever it suits, and that includes you Richard, my darling husband.'

Gethyn and Gwyneth, taken by surprise at Sarff's vociferous manner sat up straight as they placed their half empty glasses back on the coffee table as if they had been joined at the shoulder. This was a side of Sarff which they hadn't seen before. They looked at each other almost as if they were both thinking the same thing. 'This is going to be one hell of a reunion celebration.'

Richard glared at Sarff. 'That's fine by me. Just say when, I can't wait to leave, you dried up old bitch. And I'll tell you something else, as I lay awake for hours last night so many things that have bothered me for years have suddenly become clear. I've started putting two and two together and I don't know why I didn't do so a long time ago. As for those Law of Attorney papers you were angling for me to sign,' he said tapping the pouch on his wheelchair, 'well you can forget them because they've gone up the chimney in smoke. I don't need them now and I'm sure Connie will look after me if I ask.'

Connie was close to tears. 'Of course I will Dad. We won't ever be separated again.'

'That's very touching, but I don't think you know the whole story and what you will be letting yourself in for. Your so called father looks no bother all trussed up neatly in his chair, but has he told you of his other problems, asbestosis and incontinence. Try dealing with that my girl,' she shouted as she poked Connie in the chest.

Gwyneth and Gethyn felt uncomfortable as they witnessed the human tennis match. They sensed the situation was beginning to develop into a physical confrontation as I jumped up to shield Connie from further abuse. Sarff backed away between her two sisters as she realised that perhaps her anger had got ahead of her. She suspected she was in danger of retaliation. Gethyn made an attempt to act as a peace maker by appealing to his friend Griff to use his influence with Sarff. Charlotte sprang into action in defence of Sarff and pushed Gethyn back on the sofa.

'Keep your nose out of our affairs, you little twit. What's it got to do with you anyway?'

'Who are you calling a little twit?' Gwyneth jumped up with surprising agility as she approached the three sisters in defence of her husband. A scuffle broke out between Gwyneth and Charlotte whilst Mavis with her small frame bounced off Gwyneth's superior bulk like a tennis ball off a brick wall. She crashed into the table scattering bottles, glasses and drinks in all directions over the carpet.

'I think we should go now Gwyneth,' said Gethyn as he rejoined the affray by pushing his meagre frame between the two women and finally managed to usher his wife out the door.

Richard followed in his wheel chair, knocking Sarff's handbag off the door handle as he passed.

'I'm sorry about all this. You can see what she's like,' he called out after them as they quickly made their escape toward the garden gate.

Connie did the best she could to put the table back and clear away the debris. Mavis made no attempt to help but merely chipped in her two penny worth.

'Well, that's got rid of two of them, now for the others.' Mavis was a small woman with a big mouth, the type of person to talk big in company of her own clan but when separated would probably not be able to say 'Boo' to a goose.

Sarff ignored her and continued her attack on Connie. 'I'd give you a week my girl looking after him and you'd come begging me to take him back. It's a twenty four seven job getting up all hours, changing bed sheets every five minutes, wiping his backside, cleaning the sick and the shit off the carpet and doing a hundred and one other menial jobs. You do-gooders are all the same. Wait 'til you—.'

'Save your breath,' Connie interrupted, 'there's nothing you can tell me that I haven't dealt with before. For your information I am a trained nurse employed in a nursing home for the aged and infirm. I've been doing all those things for years so you can forget your week's trial.'

Sarff sensed that another one of her of her ace cards had been trumped. She shifted uneasily in her chair as she threw a look in her sisters' direction inviting them to back her up. Charlotte took the hint.

'Let's face it, we all know why you've turned up now, it's all about the money. Admit it. I've seen it happen before and it's the classic example of the children ignoring their parents for years and years only to turn up when they're on their last legs. I've worked in hospitals too and I know what happens to patients suffering from asbestosis. They develop lung cancer and die within three years.'

'Thanks for that Charlotte, just to remind you that I am still here,' Richard said as he beat his chest with both hands. 'You put things in such a subtle way, straight from the hilt.'

'I knew nothing about Dad's condition or his finances,' Jackie retorted. 'I'll remind you that it was your sister who kept me in the dark and cut me out of his life, so tell me how I was supposed to know? It seems to me to be a case of the kettle calling the pot black and if anyone has designs on Dad's money it's you and your family. It's so obvious and useless for you to pretend you have Richard's best interests at heart when I can see just the opposite. You are like spiders in a web, waiting to pounce. I don't think I've caught you out a moment too soon.'

Charlotte stopped dead in her tracks. Jackie suspected that perhaps Sarff had not told her sisters the full story until recently and the seeds of doubt were beginning to sprout in their camp. Finally Griff had heard enough. The vocal tennis match was over and deep down in his mind he had to admit that Jackie had proved her point. He searched for a reason to leave.

'I can't stay here any more I've got to be up early in the morning to meet the paper delivery van and organise the boys with their bags. Let's go you two,' he said to Charlotte and Mavis, 'Sarff can come too if she likes.'

Sarff stood up reluctantly. 'Don't be thinking I've finished with you yet Richard,' she said as she dug a finger into his shoulder, 'I've only just begun.'

Richard moved the lounge curtain to watch as the four of them flounced down the path as quickly as they came and took off in Griff's car with Sarff gesticulating and glaring back at him from the back seat. Thoughts of how she had changed from the RAF days when their social life was at its peak flooded back into his mind. He had to admit that even then she showed signs of deception but he was too blind with the excitement of the chase to recognise them. She was equally complicit in furthering the relationship and finding in Richard that spark which was sadly lacking from her tired marriage. What the hell, he was single and fancy free, could he be blamed for taking his chances? The marriage vows he had made not once but twice came back to haunt him. His conscience told him what a fool he'd been. Both the women in his life had made them too but now he realised that they had been lightly made.

"From this day forward, for better, for worse, for richer, for poorer, in sickness and in health, to love and to cherish until death do us part".'

They were strong words indeed but it was a declaration which he thought he meant at the time. All those years ago it was a level playing field but now someone had moved the goalposts. Something had to be done. Connie had come back into his life. When married to her mother he was either too young or his horizons too limited to be concerned about far off decisions like making a will. With Sarff it was different, apart from the fact that they had both been around the block and learned a few things, there were other considerations such as property, pensions and money. And now there was a golden egg, the inheritance. It suddenly struck him that in his existing will Sarff was his sole beneficiary.

'I'll have to change that,' he quietly murmured, still looking out the window.

'Change what Dad? Surely you're not thinking of altering the garden?'

'Not quite,' he said. 'As far as I'm concerned I don't give a damn what happens to it, I'm going to be off out of here as quick as I can.'

Then he turned to look away from the garden with a smile on his face. 'Well perhaps I do care. Do you know something Francis? Connie has given me a good idea. How would you like to dig a big hole and I'll shove Sarff in it? On second thoughts, perhaps not but I'll ask you to do something else for me if you will. Will you be staying tonight?'

'Of course, we'd be delighted.' We've both got a few days off and I would like to help in any way I can.'

'Would you ferry me into town tomorrow? If not I can ask Gethyn.'

'No problem,' I said as he turned back toward the window, 'it will be my pleasure. Connie's time is limited but I can take as many days as I need so long as I keep in touch with the office.'

The following day we took Richard into Bangor for an appointment with a Mr. P. J. Morgan of Lewis, Steel and Simpson, Solicitors. His secretary came to the door to meet us and we were ushered with some difficulty through the passageway into a lift only big enough for two people and a wheelchair. Jackie said she would take the next trip. On the third floor the secretary stopped the lift opposite Mr. Morgan's office and I waited for Connie to arrive.

'Mr. Morgan is ready for you so I'll take you straight in Mr. Manston.' She knocked, opened the door and started to wheel Richard in.

'It's OK, I can take it from here,' he said as he propelled himself forward, anxious to get on.

Jackie arrived and the secretary asked if we would like to wait in the visitor's room further down the corridor.

'If you like you can make yourselves a hot drink from the machine,' she said, 'I'm sure they won't be long. I'll call you on the intercom when Mr. Morgan is ready.'

It was rather gloomy room with straight backed school type chairs arranged around three sides and a small table in the middle littered with out of date papers and magazines. The walls were bare and the only vestige of life in the room came from the bubbles rising in the coffee machine. I took a look at the brown liquid and wondered how long the coffee had been stewing to produce the so called beverage which looked as if it would make a good substitute varnish for a garden fence. I declined to partake.

In contrast, Mr. Morgan's office was bright and cheerful with pictures on the walls, but Richard had no time for them. He was a man on a mission with only one thing in mind. He proffered a brief 'Good morning' and came straight to the point, 'I need to revise my will there's been a change of circumstances.'

Mr. Morgan sat with his elbows on his desk and his hands clasped together as if getting ready to pray. His desk was clear except for his telephone, intercom and a writing pad which had doodles penned into one corner. He was a large man with the build of a Buddha wearing spectacles which were too small for his face. He wore a white jacket, waistcoat and a 'V'-necked shirt which exposed his hairy chest but his head was as bald as a coot. His chair backed on to a large window which flooded the room with light and provided a panoramic view over the town. Up close to the window he also had a bird's eye view of the busy main street below. It was surprisingly quiet with the street noises either being absorbed by the Victorian buildings or blown away over the two story ones opposite.

'OK a codicil, we can do that easily enough. Copies of your existing will have been forwarded from our other office in Wiltshire by my colleague Mr. Tattersall who wishes to be remembered to you. Your new document will supersede any other wills you have made and will become legal as soon as it is witnessed by non beneficiaries. Have you got someone with you who can fulfil that role?'

Down in the street below, Mavis Charlotte and Sarff were out shopping for a new jacket which Sarff was intending to buy as a present for Mavis on her sixtieth birthday. Whilst in town they were also going to make sure that all their arrangements with Anne's Pantry restaurant were in order. It was to be a joint birthday celebration for Mavis and a reunion party with old school pals of all three. The reunion was the first one to be organised since leaving their college some thirty five years earlier. Planning had proved difficult owing to the fact that the women had dispersed far and wide with some living abroad. The organisers considered it to be something of a success to have located twenty eight former students all of whom had agreed to attend.

They chatted excitedly as they discussed the shops they had already visited. So far they had not been able to find anything which Mavis really liked but in the last shop there was a 'maybe'. She complained that designers didn't seem to cater for what she described as 'normal women' but more so for models who were as thin as a rake and half as tall again as herself. Sarff and Charlotte were not unduly perturbed, treating the exercise as a social occasion and one for retail therapy. Although they were already kitted out for the 'do' they still tried on clothes if only to act as models for Mavis. Eventually Mavis saw just the jacket she wanted in a shop window. As they were about to enter three of their friends with two other young women were leaving carrying parcels. One tapped Mavis on the shoulder.

'Hello birthday girl, they've got some nice things on sale today, latest fashion just in,' she said as she gave Mavis a hug. 'I've had a job stopping my daughter Jennifer buying the whole shop.'

'I hope they are not 'latest fashion' High Street prices,' Sarff queried, 'but I think I'm out of touch with them and the ones I've seen so far have been exorbitant. I'm going to think twice the next time I decide to clear out my wardrobe. Frilly little things made of nothing command ridiculous prices. I think its all man generated.'

Jennifer the youngest of the group pricked up her ears. 'Well it's the price you pay to keep your man interested.'

Mavis led the laughter. 'You talk as if you know all the answers, how old are you anyway?'

'Old enough to know what men like,' Jennifer cheekily replied.

Charlotte joined in the banter. 'You young things grow up so fast; sometimes I think too fast. With my Griff I don't think he ever knew and it's bit late now to start looking. Do you know, I don't think he'd notice if I started making tea in the noddy.'

They all laughed until one of women spoke to Sarff.

'We were looking out the window just two minutes ago and we saw your Richard having problems getting through the doorway of the offices across the street. He had two people with him. He's such a tolerant man and must have the patience of a saint. I don't know how he lives with that wheelchair and I've never heard him complain. It makes me think how lucky we are to be able bodied and can pop in and out of shops without bothering with ramps and such. Did you bring him into town with you?'

Sarff wasn't listening as she wheeled around to stare across the street.

'That's 'L L S' the solicitors isn't it? I wonder what he wants in there and if it's got something to do with yesterday, I'd love to be a fly on the wall,' Charlotte said being nosey.

One of the women quizzed Charlotte. 'Why, what happened yesterday?'

There was no answer as Sarff let out a string of bad language in both Welsh and English causing a few nearby shoppers to stop and stare in her direction. She rampaged on for quite a few minutes oblivious of her friends or that everyone within twenty yards could hear her. The worst side of Sarff was on display once more only this time she had a public audience.

'That will be Connie and that damned bloke of hers sticking his nose in. I'll put a stop to their little game, there's a thing or two that solicitor should know. I don't care what they say, it's the money they're after and you can't tell me otherwise. But they're not going to get it. It will be over my dead body first.'

She was familiar with the office and knew Mr. Morgan from a previous visit when she enquired about the necessary paper work for taking over Richard's affairs. The future of the Donkin family was at stake. Sarff's fire had been successfully stoked by Charlotte who came up with the idea of getting Richard to sign the Law of Attorney papers. She felt the situation was beginning to spin out of her control and all because of Connie. By burning the papers she convinced herself that Richard was merely delaying the inevitable. She looked up at Mr. Morgan's office window and could visualise Richard with pen in hand, signing her life away. It would take more than a mere Charlotte stop things now and she was the woman to do it. Blind rage told her that she had to do something drastic, leave no stone unturned in her effort to stop Richard in his tracks. She didn't care how many 'Hail Marys' it would cost her on Sunday, she would lie if she had to.

'I haven't slaved and looked after him all these years for nothing. That bastard of a girl is not going to do me out of what is rightfully mine. I've served my time. I'll tell him that Richard is in no fit state of mind to make major decisions. That he is in the early stage of dementia and that he forgets things and tries to wander off in the night in his pyjamas. I'll say steps have taken for him to be sectioned. And another thing, Connie is not a blood relative.'

Mavis and Charlotte waited for Sarff to finish her tyrannical rampage. The rest of the group stared; the laughter and smiles of only a few moments ago completely erased from their faces. They were in no doubt that Richard's visit to the solicitors could mean only one thing and that Sarff had decided to act to prevent that at all costs.

'We'll come with you, three voices will be more convincing than one and we'll back you up with anything you say.'

The offer fell on deaf ears.

Mavis held Sarff's arm as she waited at the kerbside to prevent her dashing across the busy street. The traffic was nose to tail on both sides and every one of them seemed to be in a hurry. At times the larger vehicles had to exercise extreme care not to hit pedestrians who were too close to the gutter. It was now an established fact that the street was no longer fit for purpose in its present form. With the increase of both volume and size of vehicles the highways authority had recently been contemplating ways and means to ease the situation.

Sarff stopped her outburst long enough for one of the women to bid farewell. 'We will see you later; it is at eight isn't it?' Another one chipped in, 'we're so looking forward to the do and meeting old pals again. Hope you've got your speech ready Mavis?'

'Yes I have and I'm scared to death,' she shouted back as she turned to wave. In that instant Mavis felt Sarff slip from her grip as she dashed across the street with eyes focused only on the office entrance. The traffic lights switched from red to green unleashing the accelerating vehicles like a pack of greyhounds out of a starting gate. Immediately there was a squeal of brakes followed by a series of thumps and the sickening sound of shearing metal as vehicles concertinaed into each other. The side flap of a tipper lorry burst open spilling a load of fine limestone aggregate across the pavement sweeping all before it. Shoppers were engulfed and driven back. Shopping bags and bodies all became part of the flood which crashed against the shop window and streamed well inside the entrance. Timber and building blocks mixed up with vegetables and paint skidded along the street. One heavy wooden purlin shot through a tailor's shop window decapitating the models and a concrete one flattened the 'No right turn' sign. Smoke began to drift skyward from the back of a car with a crushed boot. The diver kicked his door open just in time to see the vehicle explode in flames as he fell over some obstruction in the road. Two ashen faced ladies on the other side fainted as others pointed in disbelief at the underside of the leading vehicle which had skewed across the road to end up on the pavement facing the wrong way. Screams continued long after vehicle engine noises subsided as one by one the drivers gained access to their ignition switches. A cloud of dust and smoke mushroomed upward causing a shadow to float across office windows above. Sarff was nowhere to be seen.

CHAPTER 20

The muffled noise echoed up to the roof tops and the window rattled slightly as the cloud blocked out the sun, causing a shadow to float across the back wall of Mr. Morgan's office. He swivelled in his chair to catch sight of the end of the plume as it spiralled skyward and dispersed over the buildings on the other side of the street. In the waiting room Jackie was reading and heard nothing. She looked up and smiled as the magazine on my lap slipped to the floor. I had fallen asleep having missed out the night before on Richard's sofa which was comfortable enough apart from the gap between the two halves. A satisfying sleep is difficult to achieve by going at it in a half hearted way and not sinking into folds of sheets and a duvet. The thought of sleeping upstairs was out of the question when I remembered the faded curtains in the dormer window and using Sarff's room would have given me nightmares with the possibility that she might come back in the dead of night.

Richard's answer to Mr. Morgan's question fell on deaf ears as he peered down into the street below. He opened the window and leaned out to get a better view of the street and both pavements.

'There's been a multiple accident and it looks a bad one,' he informed Richard. 'Perhaps now they will introduce a one way system. Minor accidents happen all the time but I've not seen one quite as bad as this. Its chaos down there; I can see at least a dozen or so vehicles involved. I wouldn't mind betting that a number of people have been hurt this time. The road is too narrow for present day traffic and for some time I've advocated in favour of a pedestrian precinct but no one has paid any attention. Perhaps the authorities will do something at last instead of a lot of yakkety-yak. It's a great shame somebody has to get hurt before anything happens.'

'Accidents happen all the time Mr. Morgan, that's why I'm in a wheelchair,' Richard commented almost despairingly. 'Now, can we get on please?'

'Oh, I'm sorry Mr. Manston, yes of course. Now, where were we?

Ah! Yes, non-beneficiary witness. Is someone with you who could fulfil that role?'

Convinced that he now had Mr. Morgan's complete attention, Richard continued. 'I want my will revised in favour of my daughter, Connie Cicely Manston. She is to be my sole beneficiary and I have brought a Mr. Francis Tenby with me as a witness. He's an estate agent and a family friend.'

'Excellent! But I hope you realise Mr. Manston that your wife Sarff will have a legal claim too under her marital rights.'

'Yes Of course but I am relying on you to make sure she receives as little as possible. As far as I'm concerned she has forfeited any rights she may have had and deserves nothing.'

'One other thing Mr. Manston, according to our records your last will and testament makes no reference to your daughter.'

Richard smiled, 'and there was a very good reason for that. When it was drafted I had lost touch with her and my second wife Sarff made sure that that was the way it would remain. Behind my back she was in contact with her however and wrote to announce my premature death in a fake air accident. I will never forgive her for that. Sarff also knew that Connie had changed her name to Jackie Clarkenwell, adopting the surname of her mother and step father. At that time Jackie was ignorant of the fact that her step father was in fact her father. Her mother and so called stepfather colluded to keep her in the dark for their own selfish reasons.'

Mr. Morgan scribbled some notes on his pad and relayed them to his secretary on the intercom. 'And when you've done that, will you and Mr. Tenby join me in my office? I need both of you to witness Mr. Manston's amended will.'

'Did you hear all that noise, Mr. Tenby? There's been a terrific pile up in the street,' the secretary said as she escorted me into the solicitor's office. 'It looks bad; I expect there will be a number of casualties. You may have to leave through our back yard because I can't open the front door.'

'Not a thing,' I replied, 'I tried reading a magazine but dozed off only to wake up as it slipped off my lap. There was something going on at the back when we first came in, but after that, nothing.'

'Oh yes, there are some excavations going on in the courtyard, we've had problems with our drains; thought you might have noticed the smell when you arrived.'

In the solicitor's room, Mr. Morgan quickly checked the new documents and set about their completion.

'My secretary can act as a witness, so if you will Mr Manston, sign there, there and there and Trish will do the same. Very good, that's it all done and dusted. Is there anything else I can do for you?'

We rejoined Connie in the waiting room. 'You were quick,' she observed.

'Well there was not a great deal to it really; more like an amendment than anything, just easy money for the solicitor.'

'Perhaps he will spend some of it in that dreary waiting room then,' Connie suggested.

The secretary pulled a long face. 'My salary might be a better place for it.'

She escorted us back to the lift and rechecked the door to the pavement. It opened a foot or so but no more. We couldn't see anything but the noise hit us suddenly like a train passing through a station.

'It's no good, we'll have to go the back way,' she suggested as I wheeled the Richard's chair backward down the narrow corridor.

As she opened that door, again there was lot of noise only this time it was more to do with the contractors digging up the yard. A pile of rubble blocked our exit. The foreman waved both arms.

'Go the other way, you can't get out here.'

'We've got to get out here, this gentleman has to go to hospital right away,' she lied.

The foreman relented. 'OK! But you might get a bit muddy,' he warned as he directed the bulldozer driver to give us a lift in his bucket.

'There's always a first time for everything,' Jackie joked as she steadied herself against the bucket arm.

As I held on to Richard's chair, I wondered how anyone would be able to escape from such a building in the event of something like a fire. With narrow corridors on three levels and no fire escape, the last thing anyone would welcome would be blocked exits. The driver lifted his unusual load high over the rubble and yard door to deposit the bucket with surprising skill to achieve a gentle landing. Richard joined in as we clapped the driver. He waved and bowed.

The side entrance led on to the pavement where there was complete chaos as police and ambulance sirens wailed. People were milling about trying to help; others were sitting on the pavement in a dishevelled state whilst a breakdown lorry was preparing to remove a blue van from the pavement. On the opposite side of the street a small mechanical shovel which had managed to squeeze along the pavement was busy reloading the limestone chippings back on to the tipper lorry. One of the ambulances was already leaving the scene with two of its wheels on the pavement and blue lights flashing. Two public spirited shop keepers had taken a big risk in dowsing the car fire with their own fire extinguishers. A policeman noticed the wheelchair and thinking we were involved in the accident asked if we needed an ambulance.

'No thanks,' I told him, 'we've just been attending to some business and we are leaving. We can't stay here,' I said to Connie, 'with your dad's wheelchair we would only get in the way, let's find a way out and get your dad home. Whatever has happened here we will get to know soon enough. The radio and papers will be full of it.'

On the other side of the road Mavis was busy brushing dust off her sister's coat where she had fallen on the pavement. She was bowled over by a large empty cardboard box which had fallen off a rubbish van. Other people were doing similar things as they picked themselves up and collected their bags and parcels. Shop keepers and shoppers alike were crowded into doorways just simply looking, unable to believe what they were seeing. Charlotte and Mavis were too preoccupied to notice the trio leaving the solicitor's office.

'Have you seen Sarff yet?' Charlotte asked Mavis. 'Did you see where the others went? What a mess! I've never seen anything like it—! It will be a miracle if nobody's been killed.'

'No I haven't. I was holding her arm just before the accident but she managed to dash off as we were speaking to those others. I bet she's in the solicitor's office right this moment giving Richard a good ear wigging. She obviously couldn't wait for us.'

'Let's check,' Charlotte suggested, 'that's where she will be for sure.'

The pair picked their way through the gaps in the queue of misshapen vehicles, over headlight and windscreen glass, a lorry bumper, a smashed box of cabbages, spilled paint and general building materials. A lone policeman tried to send them back but eventually gave up when he saw other people trying to do just the same in other gaps. They heard his frantic call on his radio as he requested backup; he had little chance of exercising any degree of control on his own. Sliding over the bonnet of a car the pair managed to land on the pavement a few yards away from the office door but they couldn't get any nearer. Access to the office was blocked by debris piled up against it and a piece of wire had miraculously wound itself around the door knocker. The secretary was leaning out the first floor window above their heads.

'Hello, is Mrs Manston still upstairs?' Charlotte queried as she tried to brush the dust off her coat once more.

'No, sorry, we've only seen Mr. Manston. Are you sure you've got the correct day? Does she have an appointment? I can go and check if you like.'

Mavis stared wide eyed at Charlotte and gripped her hand. 'I'm really worried now; the stupid woman. Why didn't she wait? We'd better check with the police if she's been taken off in one of those ambulances.'

Back at Richard's house, quite a number of neighbours were in their front gardens chatting to each other after being informed by the postman. Gwyneth and Gethyn spoke to the trio through the garden hedge as Connie wheeled her father down the path.

'Have you heard about the accident in town? The postman said he had a narrow squeak and saw the pile up in his rear view mirror. He said he was delivering mail further down the street and you know how he exaggerates things sometimes but he swears it's one God-Almighty-of-an-accident—; bodies all over the place.'

'Yes Gethyn, we were there,' I informed him. 'We won't stop to talk now. We want to get Richard settled and Connie has been upset by it all. I suggest we wait until we hear the full story.'

Having sorted out the will Richard was feeling much brighter and suggested that we had tea in the summer house. The weather had perked up too and the sun was beginning to shine through the fast disappearing clouds of early morning. 'We can listen to the radio there and hear all about the accident.'

It was well on into the afternoon before any official news began to filter out between programmes; initially as short announcements containing little detail. Eventually at five thirty a major report was made.

"The town centre witnessed a serious road traffic accident involving some fourteen vehicles at eleven twenty this morning. It has been reported that eleven people have been taken to Hayfields General Hospital, four of whom are in a critical condition; five others are less serious with head and body injuries whilst the remainder have been treated and discharged. The cause of the accident has yet to be determined. Further details will be announced as soon as they become available."

'Those poor people,' Connie said as she began to fold up the table and deck chairs, 'to think that they went out this morning to do whatever in town only to end up in hospital. I think we were lucky not to have been caught up in it ourselves, it could only have happened a few minutes after went to see the solicitor. We never heard a thing in that back room.'

'No not a thing. I felt something but paid no attention to it as I was half asleep at the time.'

'Mr. Morgan's office was directly above it,' Richard began. 'I heard something like a door closing but then I saw a cloud of smoke drift across the window. Mr. Morgan looked down into the street and told me what had happened. He said the street at that point is a sort of black spot and the accident was the worst he had ever seen.'

Meanwhile, on the other side of town, Mavis and Charlotte gave up looking for their sister after they quizzed a policeman who was unable to give them any information on missing persons. He suggested that perhaps she had gone shopping elsewhere and they would probably find her back at home. Eventually they made their way home just in time to answer the telephone. It was Anabelle, the organiser of the reunion dinner party.

'It's cancelled' she blurted out, 'I'm afraid our reunion is out of the question and the restaurant has confirmed that no bookings can be accepted for the foreseeable future. Janice Wilmot and Samantha Stevens were both injured in the accident and are in hospital. Janice was lucky;

only sustained superficial injuries and is being kept in for observation but I'm afraid Samantha is more serious.'

Trying to hold back the tears, Charlotte answered the call. 'We think Sarff is missing too and may be in hospital but when we rang the police they couldn't tell us anything. They suggested ringing a special accident number at the hospital which we did several times but the number was permanently engaged. We are going in to check for ourselves, will we see you there?'

At the hospital the sisters found a queue of people trying to read a list of accident victims even before the porter had chance to pin it up on the door. Charlotte pushed in with Mavis close behind. They scanned down the list and their hopes rose when they couldn't see Sarff's name but they were short lived as Mavis read a note in smaller print at the bottom of the page.

"Two victims admitted as yet unidentified".

With hearts in their mouths and hoping against hope, they joined another crowd of people as it engulfed the enquiry office. Three administrators were trying to answer telephones and speak to people at the same time. One was attempting to multi task with a phone in each hand as well as conversing with an impatient visitor. Volunteer telephone operators had been drafted in to help but their inexperience was proving to be more of a hindrance than a help. An argument was going on between one volunteer and a lady who had been misdirected to the wrong ward. There was a suggestion that over anxious callers were being sent in the wrong direction on purpose to give them a 'chance to cool down.'

Mavis caught the ear of another as soon as she mentioned, 'unidentified'. She came out and led the pair to a small waiting room where she told them that someone would come to see them shortly. A nurse who joined them a few minutes later verified that two ladies were unidentified and asked for a full description. Both sisters helped to compile a picture of Sarff and what she was wearing from which the nurse was able to confirm that such a lady had indeed been admitted but she carried no identification.

Saddened by the news, the two sisters bombarded the nurse with a string of anxious questions hoping for answers.

'Is she conscious? Can we see her? How bad is she? Will she be OK? Is she in the operating theatre? How long—?'

'Please! The nurse interrupted to stem their flow of questions. 'I can't tell you very much at the moment other than your sister is being operated on as we speak, so I will ask you to be patient. Wait here and I'll see you again as soon as possible.'

Mavis sat down whilst Charlotte unable to rest paced the room. She stopped when Anabelle came in to join them. She cupped her face in her hands.

'What a nightmare! I can't believe this is happening. They couldn't identify Samantha at first but then someone found her handbag. The office has told me that she's sustained a serious leg injury and lost a lot of blood but the emergency services were able to get her here in time. What about Sarff, do you know anything yet?'

Mavis enticed Charlotte to sit down while Anabelle ran through her story. She said she had managed to escape into a shop doorway as a rider-less motor bike scythed its way along the pavement and careered into Janice and Samantha.

'Janice received a head wound and a few scratches but Samantha found herself trapped beneath the machine. Her leg was spurting blood and it took four of us to remove the bike as gingerly as possible. A man who seemed to know what to do took off his tie and made a tourniquet with a piece of wood. I reckon he saved her life and I managed to get his phone number but he was reluctant to give it to me.'

An hour and a half later the nurse returned accompanied by a surgeon still wearing his white gown and his face mask hanging around his neck.

'This is Mr. Hepplethwaite the surgeon who has been operating on your sister.'

'I'm sorry to have to tell you that your sister passed away on the operating table about fifteen minutes ago. We did everything we could to save her but serious internal injuries rendered that impossible to achieve. We are really sorry for your loss. If you wish you can go and see her in a few minutes.'

The two sisters let out an agonised howl of pain. Mavis was first to recover sufficiently to vent her thoughts while Charlotte sat with her head in her hands mumbling to herself.

'Oh my God poor Sarff, what a way to die. We will have to tell Richard. He will be shattered. In his condition this could be the end of him.'

'Will you tell him Mavis? I don't think I could bring myself to be the bearer of such tragic news. I know they didn't part the best of friends last night but even so—.'

'Oh, I was only making a suggestion,' Mavis interrupted, 'I was hoping you would do it. I know I am not on his 'Best Wishes' list. The best thing would be to let the hospital know she was married and for them to notify the police. We will tell them that her husband is an invalid in poor health and we are worried about what would happen if we tell him. We could ask them to do it. They will have all the details and are used to dealing with such situations with specially trained officers who can be more tactful than we might be.'

The nurse came back. 'You can see your sister now.'

'I'm not going to like this one bit,' Mavis said as she held on to Charlotte. Dead people and chapels of rest are not my scene.'

In the ward Sarff looked as if she was asleep. There was no obvious sign of injury, even her hair had been brushed and there was not a mark on her face. Charlotte held her hand and gently kissed her on the forehead. 'Until we meet again,' she whispered. Mavis collapsed into a chair distraught and completely overcome with emotion. She was unable to bring herself to say 'Goodbye' to her sister and had to be assisted out of the ward in a wheelchair.

Meanwhile, back at home I had just finished stacking the garden furniture while Jackie was preparing to wheel Richard back inside the house. The doorbell rang which was immediately followed by three sharp taps on the glass panel.

'Can you get that Francis?'

I opened the door to find two police officers waiting, a police sergeant accompanied by a woman police constable who was holding a ladies handbag wrapped up in a plastic bag.

'Mr. Robert Manston?'

'No, I'm Francis Tenby, just visiting.'

'Can we speak to Mr. Manston please?' the police constable enquired.

'Yes, he's in the lounge, please come in.'

Richard could see from the bay window that his visitors were police officers. He felt his heart miss a few beats as he asked himself the question, 'What has Sarff got in store for me now?'

'This is daughter Connie,' I informed them.

The woman police officer took the handbag from the plastic bag and gave it to Richard. He noticed it had a tear on one side and the strap was detached at one end.

'Do you recognise this bag Sir?'

'Yes I do' Richard replied. 'It belongs to my wife Sarff but it looks a bit battered, what has happened to it?'

'We are very sorry to inform you Sir that your wife was caught up in the major RTA which occurred earlier today in Bognor town centre. She was admitted to Hayfields General at eleven forty but due to the multiple injuries which she sustained the surgeons were unable to save her life and…'

Connie let out a gasp of horror as Richard shifted uneasily in his chair to stare at the ceiling.

'I knew she would do something but not this.'

'She was pronounced dead at three twenty eight this afternoon.' The constable continued, 'she was not carrying any form of identification but her two sisters, a Ms. Mavis Donkin and a Mrs. Charlotte Fallowfield were able to supply information which led to her being identified. They also made a formal visual identification of the body.'

'I so sorry,' I said as I tried to rest a consoling hand on Richard's shoulder but he shrugged it off without saying a word as he wheeled his chair to the end of the room to be alone with his thoughts. We sat quietly with the police officers for a few moments which seemed endless until Richard finally snapped out of his private world to return to his place in the window.

'Well that's that, c'en est fait,' he said reverting to one of the phrases from his limited foreign list; 'it's all over; the end of the line.'

The police constable took out his note book.

'According to the details of the accident which we have so far been able to ascertain, the van driver who ran into your wife stated that although he took evasive action he had no chance of avoiding her. Skid marks on the road which terminated on the pavement corroborated his statement.'

'Another witness, a Ms. Samantha Stevens who was also injured made a statement from her hospital bedside that she had informed your wife immediately prior to the accident, as she was about to leave a shop, that she had seen yourself and two others entering the offices of Lewis Steel & Simpson. Apparently your wife became agitated and dashed out on to the pavement with her two sisters and the last she saw of her was that she was preparing to cross the road. Ms Stevens also stated that she did not witness the actual accident because she and her companion were immediately caught up in the aftermath. It would appear that for some reason your wife did not exercise due care in crossing the road in her anxiety to catch up with you. It is therefore our conclusion that your wife was primarily the cause of the accident and therefore solely responsible.'

The constable looked up from his notebook, still holding his pencil.

'Is there anything you think I should add Mr. Manston?'

Richard looked calmer after his initial reaction.

'Only to add as possibly a final piece to your jigsaw that we had an argument in this very room last night from which I think she had assumed that I was about to change my will in favour of my daughter. It is a long story but I would be prepared to make a statement of explanation which I'm sure my solicitor, Mr. Morgan would support. In case you are surprised at my apparent lack of emotion I can't say that after twenty years of marriage that we were in love any more. She was responsible for my losing touch with my daughter for the major part of that time and that she committed a crime for which even now I am unwilling to forgive.'

'Well Sir we were advised of your medical condition and our brief was to exercise extreme care in our duty of announcing the death of your wife but it would appear from your marital state of affairs that you have made our job that much easier. We understand that your two sisters in law shared your wife's anxiety with regard to your visit to the solicitors and they were reluctant as members of your family to be the harbingers of bad news. Finally, are we to assume that your daughter will be caring for you in the immediate future?'

'That's correct officer,' Connie confirmed, 'apart from my father's immediate needs there will be funeral arrangements to be made.'

As the police officers made their exit they were observed by the ever watchful Gethyn who had to be restrained by his more tactful wife from checking on Richard once more.

'We'll know soon enough what the police visit was for.'

Gethyn was about to move away from the window when he noticed Connie closing the lounge window curtains.

'Oh my God,' he said crossing himself as he turned to face Gwyneth, 'I've just seen Connie closing the curtains I wonder if one of the family was involved in the accident?'

Likewise Connie for her part just caught a glimpse of Gethyn as he turned away from his window.

'I think your decision Dad to close the curtains so early has been seen by Gethyn as clearly as if we had signalled by semaphore. Would you like me to confirm it? I think we can do without his questions.'

'Yes, OK then. Say whatever,' Richard replied resignedly. 'By telling him we will have no need to tell anyone else. Everyone in the district will know in no time.'

Richard sat staring at the pattern on the curtains without saying a word as he waited for Connie to return. I walked into the kitchen for no reason other than to remain silent as well since I felt there was nothing I could say that would be in any way helpful. I took two glasses and poured a stiff drink into each, downed the first one myself and placed the other beside him without saying a word. Connie took much longer than expected but by the time she did return I noticed his glass was empty. He turned away from the window to announce that he had made some decisions.

'We need to talk,' he began as we settled on the sofa to listen. 'This is certainly a situation I never ever envisaged and yet I'm almost sorry —,' he paused to take a deep breath, 'even relieved that this has happened and yet whatever feelings I've had, God knows she never deserved to die.'

Connie got up and rested her head on Richard's shoulder. 'Its OK Dad we know. There's no need to explain.'

'I've come to a decision because I can't expect you to look after me indefinitely. You've both got jobs to go to. I'm going to arrange two things to start with, firstly arrange for Sarff's cremation and secondly arrange for accommodation at a nursing home I know not far from here which has a good reputation. It's expensive but you get what you pay for as they say and I will receive first class attention twenty four seven which is exactly what I need. It will only be for a short while during which time I will be able to invite Jack and Vera to visit me with the sole purpose of finding another home, possibly with a live-in carer, back in Wiltshire where all my friends are. I know I have to be realistic and face the fact, as Charlotte so bluntly put it, that 'I'm on my last legs' and my time is limited.'

'Oh Dad,' Connie groaned, 'we've lost so much time.'

'And another thing,' he went on, 'this was Sarff's house and I don't want any more to do with it or even live in Wales any more. I'm like a fish out of water here. Just to show that I don't bear any animosity toward any of her relations and that I'm not a schemer like she was I'm going to let Charlotte and Griff move back in. They used to look after the house for Sarff and I think a good deal of Charlotte's ill feeling toward me personally has arisen from the fact that she was not best pleased when we moved in. But that was Sarff's decision, not mine and after all it was her house to do as she pleased with. I know the whole family had ideas of doing something together when I kick the bucket. Charlotte and Griff in particular, had plans for my legacy and persuaded Sarff to think about buying another property which the Donkin clan had fancied for years. It was a large sea front house on the outskirts of Bangor overlooking the Menai Strait which they knew would be coming on the market within the next year. They wanted to ear mark the property early so that the current owners wouldn't be involved with expensive advertising and agency fees. The intention was to provide jobs for them all by modernising and then operating a bed and breakfast business. I can see now that the first stage of the scheme was to get me to Wales. Sarff had a big problem with convincing me to live in Wales at all and I must admit that I had reservations about being absorbed into the Donkin family. Practically ever since I received news of the will, Sarff seemed to spend more and more time on the phone talking to the family from Wiltshire. She used to revert to speaking Welsh when she thought that perhaps I was listening. I felt that I was being swallowed up by an octopus, wheelchair and all. I could have moved out I suppose, but didn't give it much thought and anyway she would have moved heaven and earth to stop me. Believe you me, in the short time you've been here you've only seen a little of what she was capable of but having lost you Connie I was alone and vulnerable. Somebody once told me about a certain group of people they were having problems with, 'put them all in a bag, shake them up and I don't know who would get out first.' That's exactly how I see the Donkin clan. My idea is as I say, let Charlotte be in charge for now but to bequeath the property to the family as a whole and let them fight it out.'

'That's very generous of you dad, a gift with a sting in the tail. I like it. What do you think?' she said as she glanced in my direction.

'Sarff has taught your dad to be Machiavellian too. He will need watching in the future that's for sure.'

After the climax of Sarff's demise events moved quickly. The whole of her family turned up for the cremation and Connie arranged a week's bereavement leave whilst I returned to my office on the understanding that I would return to pick her up when Richard was settled. She felt slightly guilty about calling her time off 'bereavement' when in fact she did not share the Donkin's degree of remorse. Richard didn't want to attend the funeral with all its pomp and pageantry and dug his heels in saying she didn't deserve it. He had reservations about cremations but changed his mind when he thought of the smoke created by her process belonged with those of the Law of Attorney papers. Connie managed to persuade Richard to attend the ceremony by telling him it truly was a celebration but not necessarily of her life and certainly not a time for tears. Richard thought about Connie's choice of the word 'celebration' and came around to agreeing with it. He thought perhaps he could go even one better and copy the Chinese way with fire crackers and a ceremonial boat launching in the sea. There was something symbolic in the visualisation of her funeral pyre as it floated passed the dream B. & B. on its way out to sea.

In contrast Charlotte had her own ideas and put forward a special request for the ashes saying that she intended for them to be sprinkled over the garden and that she wanted a memorial plaque to mark the spot. When she asked Richard for his thoughts he agreed but secretly thought that the idea was somewhat morbid and for Sarff to be 'still there,' albeit in spirit form, was an even greater reason for him to live elsewhere. At the wake after the church service he announced his intention of not wanting to benefit in any shape or form from Sarff's premature departure and that Charlotte and Griff could move back in. They were both pleasantly taken by surprise but the question of ownership left them looking rather mystified. Richard enjoyed the moment and could almost imagine various family members sharpening their knives and making early plans in the event of this or that happening. As it was, various neighbours expressed the view that they were lucky to retain the bungalow at all, but losing out on their ambitions was something they found hard to swallow.

Accommodation at Farmleigh Nursing Home became available within a matter of days after Richard and Connie visited the establishment. Connie let it be known to the matron about her role at Tootehill and discussed at length Richard's needs and care. She was impressed with the general level of care and whilst she took the opportunity express her thoughts on where improvements could be made she was tactful enough to praise others which she thought could be implemented at Tootehill. It was important for Richard to have made the choice for himself and she felt confident that he would be looked after as she would have wished.

CHAPTER 21

Connie spent the next few days in the visitors' quarters of Farmleigh whilst Richard settled in. She was able to take him out to enjoy the gardens and make a start on getting to know him again free from the encumbrances of Sarff and family. Once inside the gated entrance of the Home, which was formally a gentleman's residence, built on a thirty acre estate, Richard began to modify his feelings about living in Wales. A small river fed a lake frequented by all manner of water fowl whose numbers varied through the seasons with migratory birds. He soon became acquainted with the half dozen or so gardeners and handymen who were more than happy to lean on their tools to chat. He told Connie that his idea of buying a home elsewhere with live-in care was not such a good one after all and that he would be quite happy to spend the rest of his days at Farmleigh. He had no need to go chasing his friends in Wiltshire; they could come to him.

Later when Connie was sure that Richard had everything he wanted and that Bognor was nothing but a bad dream she telephoned to say she was ready to return to Tootehill. Rose had been in touch and wanted me to let Connie know that she was looking forward to seeing her so that shift working could return to normal. When I arrived at Farmleigh Richard was waiting to go out into the garden and asked to see me on my own while Connie finished packing. Contrary to my opinion of what I thought was her excessive amount of luggage when we set out I had cause to compliment her planning for the unknown.

Richard looked a different man, refreshed and even some of the tortuous lines in his face had gone. I followed as a nurse wheeled his chair into the garden and stopped by a bench seat facing the lake. She tucked his shawl around his shoulders and told me to let her know when he was ready to return.

'I can't believe how much has happened during this last week or so,' he began, 'it seems much longer since you brought Connie back into my life. I must admit that before you came I was resigned to ending my days with Sarff and near the point of giving up to the inevitable. My life was not my own anymore. In a manner of speaking, the accident has forced me to make decisions which I should have made long ago and I owe you my most sincere thanks in helping me to do that. Of coarse none of us could have predicted the chain of events but in the final analysis, I think you would agree that whatever private thoughts I have, they are best unsaid. Let it suffice to say that I am relieved it's all over and ready to move on.'

'Farmleigh is fine place to be and I've decided that I don't want to be anywhere else. Everything I need is here and no doubt this is the sort of place that Sarff would have been pleased to leave me. I would have been out of her hair while she counted the days for me to kick the inevitable bucket. It would have fitted in nicely with her plan or rather Charlotte's plan to get me out of the way. As things were her future looked much brighter than mine. She was a wiry old bird and I thought she might have hung on for another twenty years at least. It just goes to show none of us know what's around the corner or in her case on the other side of the road. I've had a lot of time to think while I've been here and now I want to have a serious talk to you.'

'I've been wandering if we would find a suitable occasion to do just that,' I said, 'and feel guilty of not having done so already.'

He turned away from the lake to look directly at me. 'You and Connie—,' he paused for my reaction, 'I've been asking her about you, about how you came to meet and so on—.'

I felt the hairs on the back of my neck quiver as I guessed what he was going to say next. It was the first time since our meeting a week ago that he had spoken to me at any length on a one to one basis.

'You've forgotten me, haven't you?'

'Me, forgotten you!' I exclaimed as I realised he had turned the tables on me. 'No, just the opposite in fact I was sure it was you who had forgotten me and I purposely let it stay that way because I thought you had enough on your plate what with being reunited with Connie and every thing else which has happened.'

'You've changed a lot,' he said, 'you were only a kid but it was the name which popped into my head last night as I was trying to sleep that brought it all back to me. All those kids, I must say I don't know how Lou and Cicely managed. Wasn't there about twenty or so of you? I

243

remember that attic with you all crammed in like rabbits in a hole. And then there were my leave periods. Coming home, if I dare call it that, was a bit of a nightmare with not much privacy. Those were the days weren't they?'

'Yes, it was a long time ago, but the memory is still as vivid to me now as it was then. You taught me a lesson which I haven't forgotten nor ever will.'

'I've have had pangs of regret ever since, Francis old chap. I am sorry and must admit that the cold water bath treatment was rather severe.'

'Thanks for that, I never expected an apology after all these years. In some ways I can look back and laugh about it. 'Water under the bridge' or in this case 'down the plughole.'

'About you and Connie,' he went on, 'what an amazing chance meeting, I can hardly believe it. It seems that you are partially responsible for bringing Connie and me together again and I can't thank you enough. She thinks the world of you and what I've seen of you two together I would imagine that you feel the same way about her. All I can say is should you two get it together then you have my wholehearted approval.'

'We will see,' I said guardedly.

'Now there's something else I wanted settle before you buzz off. Connie has told me about Picardy and I would like to do something about it without her knowing just yet. She has said very little about how she intends to manage financially and has purposely avoided the issue. That's where you can help me.'

'I'll do what I can. Her job at Tootehill is not the most highly paid in the world and she is sharing the costs with Rose a colleague of hers at work. Rose has arranged a loan from her parents and in addition they've struck a deal with the matron for a sub on their wages which together with their limited amount of savings just about gets them over the line. They had a few tense moments at the auction as bids approached the final one they were prepared to make. The sale did not reach the reserve but their solicitor managed to secure the property later for thirty five thousand pounds. Initially I offered to help but in my role of agent for the property I have to be careful to avoid a conflict of interest. After all, we've made no secret of the fact that Connie and I are more than just friends. A rather unsavoury character from the past has already attempted to scupper the sale by voicing an objection on that very basis. Fortunately he had no evidence to substantiate his claim because Connie and Rose had already turned down my offer saying that they wanted to be independent and free from outside help.'

Richard listened quietly without looking in my direction. 'I thought so. It sounds a very convoluted way of raising the cash. They are obviously very enthusiastic about Picardy to have gone to so much trouble.'

'Yes, it's an old bungalow which needs a lot of work to restore it back to its former glory but has great potential and they have a very good circle of friends who can't wait to help.'

'With what you've told me it makes me doubly aware that Connie has not asked me for a bean even though she could use some so I'm going to cover the total cost. I would like her to enjoy it now while I'm still alive and I want you to give her a cheque but not until later when you think the time is right.'

'She will be over the moon with that and I'll wait until the completion date when the remainder of the purchase price will be payable. It's a great shame you won't see her reaction when she receives the cheque but I imagine she will be telephoning you within seconds.'

'The pleasure will be all mine to think that at last I will be undoing some of the pain which Sarff inflicted. I'm feeling a bit tired now so I think you two should buzz off quick, I hate goodbyes. Send a nurse out and tell Connie I've gone to sleep. Best of luck and keep in touch, I would like to know how you get on.'

I found a nurse and a short while later met Connie with her cases in the hallway on her way out to say goodbye. We could see the nurse reading a book and sitting next to him. He was asleep with his head on his chest. I told her that he had fallen asleep while we were talking and when I quizzed the nurse about it she said that had to be expected with the new drugs he'd been given.

'And guess what? We've had a long chat and he has remembered all about me from the evacuee days. He surprised me by saying that I was the one who had forgotten instead of the other way around. Anyway, the nurse has said not to disturb him. Shall we go?'

Alterations at Tootehill had gone on a pace whilst Connie was away and Amanda did all she could to make her temporary move as uncomplicated as possible. Rose had moved in and removal men were installing the remaining small items of personal furniture in Connie's room which Amanda decorated with small posies of flowers. She was keen to catch up with Connie's news and took the opportunity to spend some time in her kitchen preparing her favourite recipes for a moving in dinner party. Although photographs of the accident had appeared in newspapers no details of the cause had yet been released. Connie's 'near thing' was sure to be a topic of interest. With more time to study the photographs in detail the realisation of how close to disaster we were was highlighted. Photographs had been taken from every angle including one showing a derrick lifting the van which knocked Sarff down and another of the actual doorway where we would have been.

After the meal, Connie surprised every one by announcing it was time for the speeches. She offered me the first chance but I declined saying that I hadn't contemplated making any. Rory led the cheers and everybody clapped when he followed with, 'Thank god for that.'

'OK then, I will,' Connie began as she scanned the faces around the table. 'I would like to make an announcement. Firstly I would like to thank Amanda for this impromptu dinner party and for doing so much to help Rose and me whilst we're homeless. Secondly, I am indebted to all of you working as a team investigating my dad's case and to Francis for being so patient and helpful during the whole Bangor experience. Many missing pieces of my family history have come to light to help me complete the puzzle. Thirdly, I have to announce that I'm no longer 'Jackie'. My name is 'Connie', Connie Manston, the one my dad chose when I was christened. Other than that,' she said with a smile, 'I am the same person as I was over a week ago.'

'Well, well, hello Connie, goodbye Jackie, pleased to meet you.' Rory joked as he reached across the table to shake her hand and give her a peck on the cheek.

'And I couldn't agree more,' I said as I walked around the table to give her a hug from behind.

'You're not quite the same person as you were a week ago—.'

'Oi, Oi! What's been going on while you two have been away then?' Ellie queried.

'Oh, nothing the likes of that,' Connie visibly blushed.

'Did I hear, more's the pity?' Rory whispered to Rose.

'Your dad gave me something for you,' I continued, 'and he told me not to let you have it right away but I could do so when I thought the time was right. I had it in my mind to give it to you later but while we have our friends here I think this is as good a time as any.'

I gave Connie the envelope which she eagerly tore open.

'It's a cheque,' she said staring at Rose, 'and it's for thirty five thousand pounds.'

'Woweeee,' Rory exclaimed. 'Have you got any more of those Francis?'

'Oh my God, Connie, that's fantastic,' Rose took the cheque out of Connie's hand. I can't believe it.'

'You're dad said it was to cover the cost of Picardy so you don't have to borrow from Rose's parents or take a sub from your wages. He also said you were to write to him when you need any more. You are a rich girl now. I think a toast to your good fortune is in order.'

Connie slipped back into her chair. 'My legs are shaking. I'll have to sit down. Pour me a double somebody.'

Rory looked around the table for empty glasses as he recharged his own. 'Are we all ready? To think this has all happened because of the discovery of an RAF service number, unbelievable. Just think a few digits this way or that and nobody would ever have been any the wiser. Sarff would have got away with it. Justice has been served and it just goes to show that crime for her didn't pay. Whether or not her demise was divine retribution is something I wouldn't know any thing about.'

After the dinner party, Connie asked Rose to stay for while to have a chat about Picardy.

'What would you say Rose to my buying Picardy outright as my dad has suggested and you pay me some nominal rent? In that way your parents won't have to scrape the bottom of the barrel and we will be independent of Matron's sub and we both keep our savings. I imagine Matron will be pleased too for being let off her side of the deal. It's a win, win, and win all the way.'

'Absolutely, indeed it is, but I think we should let the deal with Matron remain; after all she is a winner too. We've no need to explain our change of plans and would be silly to turn down the extra ready cash. I think the technical term is 'contingency money' and I know from past experience you can never have enough.'

'Ok Rose, I agree.'

'I still can't get my head around the way things have turned out,' Rose added. 'It's a great shame that Sarff died but just considering the accident itself she was entirely to blame. I feel sorry for the other people who were hurt as well, fortunately none fatal.'

'Not many tears were shed at the cremation in fact I had a hard time persuading dad to go at all. In the end he agreed just to be seen to be 'doing the right thing' as he put it. There was a lot of acrimony between him and the family and I know he surprised them all by saying he had no wish to benefit from Sarff's death. Charlotte seemed to be the driving force behind Sarff and dad knew she in particular had an eye on the money to the extent that she advised Sarff to get dad to sign Law of Attorney papers. After Sarff had shown her hand he caught on and spiked their guns by burning them. Dad finally silenced Charlotte by letting her and her husband Griff back in the house and donated the property to the family as whole. It seems we caught up with them not a moment too soon. Every day I thank my lucky stars; it's like a fairy tale complete with a wicked witch.'

Connie had barely settled back into working routine at Tootehill when I telephoned to say that the completion papers were ready for signing and the outstanding moneys due. Now that Connie was in a position to be able to purchase Picardy outright the completion was a simple affair.

Rose and Jackie wasted no time in arranging a girls' day out at the house with Amanda and Ellie to celebrate their purchase. Since making the announcement at Tootehill offers came flooding in from colleagues willing to help with the restoration. When they arrived, work was already well under way with a large bonfire burning at the bottom of the garden. The transformation soon became evident after a few short hours with the whole the team working together. Ellie poured the wine

'Dare I enquire about Connie?'

'Indeed you may,' he said with a smile. 'Here she is, right on cue.'

We turned in our seats as a sprightly lady in her mid to late sixties with greying hair and similar healthy completion to Francis came into the cafeteria. She began to apologise.

'I'm sorry I'm late love, but I stayed and had tea; Herb brought home enough Chinese chow-mein to feed an army. You know what his appetite is like. I thought you might have gone home but when I passed and your car wasn't there I decided to check if you were still here. Have you eaten?'

'Allow me to introduce my wife Connie,' Francis began and smiled when he saw the surprised look on our faces.'

Connie looked puzzled. 'What's going on? Have I missed something?'

'Oh Connie, we're so sorry but we thought you were dead. Francis has been entertaining us over a delightful evening meal and telling us all about his younger days and Manston Pines. When he didn't mention any more about you after your retirement and the fact that he's working here we assumed he was on his own.'

Noises coming from the cafeteria kitchen together with the fact that we were the only three remaining customers led Francis to make the first move. Molly and I had been totally engaged with his story and not noticed other customers leaving or the waitresses giving the tables their final anti germ spray treatment for the day. We received the message loud and clear; there was no need for any "sorry we're closing now".'

'Tell you what Matt, why don't we all retire to our place for a cup of coffee?'

We followed their two cars down the canal tow path to the small collection of dormer bungalows sprinkled along the seafront overlooking the bay. They parked in the driveway of one which had been built on an elevated piece of land at the end of the road.

'We've spared no expense with this house,' Francis explained; 'you name it, we've got it and we're very happy here. We reckon the panoramic views from the picture windows of the whole bay from one end to the other are enough to die for.'

Connie soon prepared coffee and suggested we all retire to the lounge where Francis moved a low table and chairs into the bay window. She was anxious to know how we came to meet her Francis.

'We were both evacuees,' I explained, 'and we've been comparing notes how we've chanced to bump into each other today. We're really sorry we had you dead and buried but Francis—.'

'Yes, I'm sorry too, but I haven't finished my story. While I'm keeping myself busy at the supermarket just three days a week, Connie does voluntary work fetching and carrying elderly folk to from local hospitals. She enjoys meeting the type of people she's used to and can do as much or as little as she pleases. But there's one more piece to complete my jig-saw. Connie has been visiting Melissa, her half sister and her husband Herbert who now live in Cornwall. After she received her share of Wendy's estate she sorted herself out and has since married. Connie was curious about Melissa and eventually they made contact with each other through an agency. That was about eighteen months ago and since then they've been like two peas in a pod and never seem to stop talking, much like any sisters. Melissa never met either of her parents and it was only as a result of the discovery that Connie's stepfather was still alive that she was able to answer Melissa's many questions.'

'Yes we are very much alike in many ways,' Connie continued, 'the odd thing is that Melissa's children have grown up and now she and her husband Herbert are much like us with a nice bungalow, retired and with no worries. The routes we have taken or rather those destined for us to follow have been so different. Melissa's path has been a lot bumpier than mine and we are both happy to think that she has earned her happiness. The price I paid for mine was just a matter of a bent little finger.'

GORDON FINN is an electrical engineer, now retired and enjoying life but not without some concern to note that the years appear to be passing in two's. He found this reality was emphasised more clearly during a recent conversation he had with an elderly gentleman of ninety two who said that the days were passing so quickly it was like having breakfast every five minutes. At his present age he is beginning to agree.

Gordon Finn writes purely for pleasure with the added satisfaction that by doing so, he keeps his grey cells ticking over. In his secondary school days he remembers that writing an essay of one hundred lines or so was a major feat which he found difficult. Now, usually late at night, he finds his pen has a will of its own and ideas materialise from the ether without any preconception.

'Yesterday's Porridge' is his first novel, the inspiration of which originates from his real life experiences of being an evacuee during WW2. In 1941 he was uprooted from home to be dumped into a foster care home with many other similar aged children who came from war torn cities up and down the country ravaged by the Luftwaffe. The novel charts the fictional lives of the people associated with that home.